CRESTMONT

Holly Weiss

Crestmont
©2010 Holly Weiss

Edited by Star Publish LLC
Cover Design by Catherine D. Brown

ISBN: 978-1-935188-10-0

Library of Congress Control Number: 2010925275

All scripture quotations, unless otherwise indicated are taken
from the King James Bible.
Psalm 68:4,6, marked TLB, taken from The Holy Bible, New
Living Translation. Tyndale House Publishers, copyright, 2002.

A Star Publish LLC Publication
www.starpublishllc.com
Published in 2010
Printed in the United States of America

In memory of my parents,
N. John and Dorothy L. Weiss
Who nurtured my other voice — singing.

Acknowledgements

I am deeply indebted to Fred and Elna Mulford, owners of The Crestmont Inn, for their enthusiasm, generosity and willingness to share personal anecdotes as innkeepers as well as their knowledge of the hotel's history. Bush and Barbara James graciously gave me permission to research their publications about the original Crestmont, replete with floor plans, menus, contracts, family history and other fascinating details. These sources are listed in the bibliography for the reader's interest. My husband, Ernest L. Whitehouse, gave me patient, tireless support and wrote the poetry of the Paper Bag Poet. I thank T.C. McMullen and Janet Elaine Smith of Star Publish LLC for their expertise and patience. Catherine D. Brown's brilliant cover design brought a depth to the book words could not express. My cousin, Nancy, and friend, Jean, read every word of the manuscript, giving me encouragement and feedback. Tina, Deb, Sarah, Mary, Sally, Roberta, Laurie, Janet, Laurel, Joyce, Ralph, Bruce, Alice, Ann, Jane, my book group, my voice students and others, encouraged, prayed and contributed in their own unique ways.

I could not have completed *Crestmont* without the help of the Eagles Mere Bookstore, the Eagles Mere Museum, and the people who shared their stories about Eagles Mere and the Crestmont; Cooie Klotz, who gave me her pink applesauce recipe, Louise Reighard, whose grandfather owned the Lakeside Hotel, Bonnie Adams, Charlie Gardner, Paula Holcombe, Fred Holmes, Edwina Vauclain and Kay Wilson. You know how you fit into the puzzle that became *Crestmont*, and your help was invaluable.

Lastly, I am indebted to the visionary people of Eagles Mere, past and present, who have endeavored to preserve the heritage of a special town, the purity of the lake and the wholesome spirit of life in a unique place.

A Star Publish Book

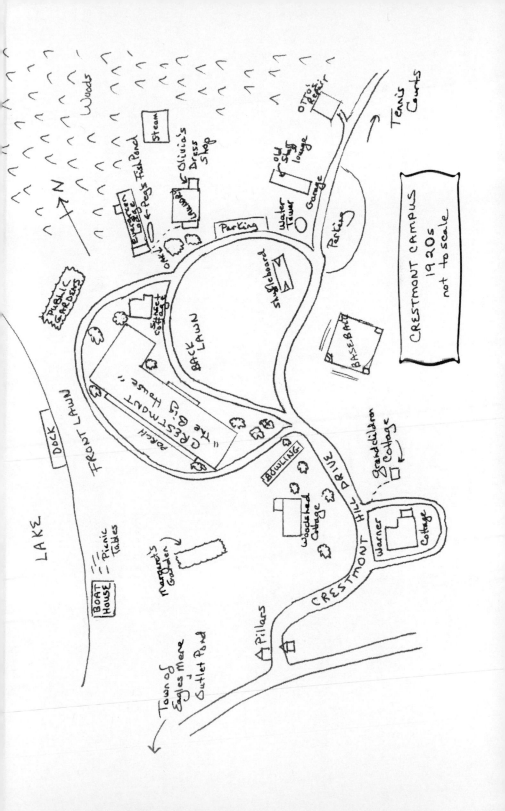

Author's Note

I was inspired to write this novel when my husband, Ernie, and I stayed overnight at The Crestmont Inn in November, 2006. The restful atmosphere of the inn, the graciousness of innkeepers Fred and Elna Mulford, and the beauty of the surrounding area captivated me. More importantly for this work, the rich history of the inn struck me. We stayed in The Evergreen Lodge, which was converted into its current form from staff quarters built in 1926. Small staff rooms that housed two or three waitresses in the 1920s through the 1970s were cut through to create the large and luxurious suite where we stayed. Original transoms over the doors and antiques from the inn's early years perked my interest about how these staffers lived and worked. I have attempted to remain faithful to the spirit of the Crestmont in my imaginings of their stories.

William and Mary Warner, William and Margaret Woods and Peg Woods Dickerson are actual people who, at various times, administered the original Crestmont Inn. Eleanor Woods was the younger of the two Woods daughters. Sid Fox served as faithful steward from 1901-1947. All of their names and dates are real. Their characterizations and that of opera singer Rosa Ponselle are wholly the author's creation and in no way are intended to represent their real lives. Warren Sloan was my maternal grandfather. He invented the automatic pinsetter with his partner, Joe Clark, and later sold the patent to AMF Bowling. The other Crestmont staff, guests, and residents of Eagles Mere are entirely fictional.

In an attempt to steep myself in the historical knowledge necessary to lend the novel authenticity, I made numerous visits to Eagles Mere and The Crestmont Inn during the writing of this book. I interviewed not only the Mulfords, current owners, but also former employees of the inn. Shopkeepers and residents of the town shared stories with me. Thanks to all who fueled my enthusiasm to research a place about which they are impassioned.

Writing fiction affords the author the flexibility to modify events to suit the story. Although I endeavored to maintain the spirit of Eagles Mere, I found it necessary to make some revisions in its physical and historical detail. I expanded the size of the lake to give shore front to The Crestmont Inn's property. The reader may note certain liberties taken in historical dates, such as the inception of the tennis tournaments. I hope others who love Eagles Mere will be forgiving of any modifications necessary to make the narrative plausible and enjoyable.

The Crestmont Inn, a unique historic country inn, is a hidden treasure in the northern foothills of the Appalachians. It is nestled in the mountaintop town that seems timeless, Eagles Mere, Pennsylvania, which is listed in the National Register of Historic Places. Beautifully appointed rooms, sumptuous dining, gracious innkeepers and attention to detail are some of the many reasons to visit the inn. Set on the highest point in the picturesque Victorian village, the inn is surrounded by state parks, breathtaking vistas, and one of nature's wonders, pristine Eagles Mere Lake.

There have been many attempts to explain how the mountaintop lake came to be. I gave a new twist to an old Indian legend. I hope a spirit of healing is reflected in my retelling of the story.

Bush and Barbara James, former employees of The Crestmont Inn, reflect on Eagles Mere. "To really understand Eagles Mere is to know...that indeed the stars do shine a little brighter here, the lake is purer, the air fresher, the wild flowers more abundant, the people friendlier; and life moves inexorably slower so that what little time we are permitted can be more fully spent in escaping to our private island on the mountain."

"It is not by idle chance that I have come here."
—Latin proverb

⚜

"Sing praises to the Lord...oh, rejoice in his presence.
He gives families to the lonely..."
—Psalm 68:4, 6 TLB

Prologue
Eagles Mere, Pennsylvania

"I will arise and go now, for always night and day
I hear lake water lapping with low sounds by the shore...
I hear it in the deep heart's core."
—William Butler Yeats

THE EAGLE RESTED ON THE HEMLOCK, QUIET BUT INTENT. HIS DARK brown plumage blended with the branches, his yellow hooked bill the only hint of his presence. He watched for the coming of spring and for the enemy of the deer. His keen eyesight, coupled with his ability to swivel his head, enabled him to see the Haudenosaunee moving across the land from the north. Spreading his majestic wings, he soared high, willing the approaching Native Americans to feel his disapproval and change direction. He did not fear for his own safety, for he knew the Haudenosaunee revered him, but he sensed impending danger for his friends, the scarce white deer.

The Haudenosaunee, also called the People of the Long House, ignored his entreaty and continued their approach. When they reached his mountain, he called to warn the deer. They clambered for safety up a small hemlock-covered hill that rose above the valley, sacred in its peacefulness, home of the swallows and bluebirds.

Ever mindful of his family's hunger, the eagle sought the mice and squirrels that breakfasted upon the succulent Juneberry bush. He swooped down, grabbed his prey with his talons, and soared over the valley to his nest. The basin he crossed was cut into a mountain, with springs of water rising from its floor. Rhododendron, mountain laurel, hemlock and white pine gave eagles nesting places for their families and shelter from the wind.

Stormy Torrent, chief of the Haudenosaunee, gazed respectfully at the soaring eagle and felt its presence a good omen for his people's hunting. Annually, after the Maple Festival in the spring, he led his people south from the lakes shaped like fingers to find new planting grounds for the corn, beans and squash that sustained them. Some of his people still wore the cornhusk foot coverings from last harvest. He needed to find deer for venison and leather for tunics, leggings and moccasins. A mountain rose before him. Thrusting his spear upward, he began to climb. Obediently, his people followed. He anticipated the aroma of venison smoking and the dancing and singing of the women and children for the joy of sustenance. His newly captured Susquehannock slave, Laurel Eyes, would keep him warm at night.

Laurel Eyes, frightened and angry, labored behind him with her packs. Her tribe, the Susquehannock or the People of the Muddy River, had refused to join the Five Nation League and were thus hated by the Haudenosaunee. Capturing her was a conquest bestowing great honor on Stormy Torrent. The Haudenosaunee women equally shared respect, leadership and the carrying burden with the men in the tribe. Laurel Eyes, however, struggled not only with her own pack but also his, her strength fueled by hatred. He had wrenched her away from her life. Now she longed for her life to be over.

Stormy Torrent surveyed the valley, a chasm cut into the earth with curious wellsprings dotting its bedrock. He knew the rumor that the Susquehannock had chosen this as the sacred departure place for their dead and he could feel the eerie presence of the enemy spirits. Momentarily afraid, he knew he must demonstrate courage by descending into the chasm to desecrate his enemy's burial grounds. Laurel Eyes would accompany him and he would break her. She was his now, all ties to her Susquehannock tribe severed.

With a high-pitched cry to summon the attention of his people, he grabbed Laurel Eyes and pushed her toward rock steps that led below. Not wanting to dishonor her people's remains, she stubbornly planted her feet in refusal. He dragged her, wailing, into the depths. His people watched. Only the echoes of her screams cut the silence that followed.

The Haudenosaunee waited, fearful of the Great Spirit's punishment for their arrogant leader's desecration of the sacred spot. The wind soughed through the hemlocks, counting the minutes that passed. A squirrel, ignorant of the tension, scolded his mate. A final anguished scream echoed from below. Then silence. Stormy Torrent, his face contorted, returned alone.

"The one known as Laurel Eyes is no more. Her spirit has joined her people, our enemy. I confess to you, my children, that I have committed a wrongdoing. Had I not forced her into disgrace, she would not have died of sorrow in the chasm. We camp here tonight. The deer have punished us with their absence, so there is no meat. Tomorrow we move south."

The night passed long for the people. Eventually, they slept. The Great Spirit looked down upon them, weeping for the foolishness of Stormy Torrent. His eyes welled with tears of sad forgiveness, flowing into the basin. The eagle awoke, and his hot tears joined with those of the Great Spirit. All tears mingled together, producing a soft, cleansing rain. The rain grew stronger, filling the lake. All night the tears washed away the evil that had been done.

At dawn, the Haudenosaunee awoke. Amazed, they watched while the sun cleared the mist from a crystal, tranquil lake where the chasm had been. Afraid to allow them to drink, Stormy Torrent bade them pack quickly. He led them south, never to forget what had happened in this magical place.

The deer, reassured of their safety by the eagle, carefully descended the little hill. Before them lapped peaceful, sweet water, which in meeting their tongues dissolved their fear along with their thirst.

"Name the water 'Spirit Tears,'" called the eagle. But the Great Spirit wanted instead to honor the inhabitants of the woods that surrounded it.

"Let the cherished white deer whose lives were spared name the lake," declared the Great Spirit.

Humbled by the honor, the deer cried in unison, "The eagle saved us with his warning and joined your tears for Stormy Torrent. Let the lake be called 'Eagles Tears, Eagles Lake, Eagles Mere.'"

And the Great Spirit smiled because the lake was named for the forgiveness that filled it.

Eagles Mere, Pennsylvania
1899

"A MAN OF YOUR STATION NOT STAYING AT THE LAKESIDE?" THE CLIENT mocked after William Warner concluded their disastrous meeting. Warner could not in good conscience offer the loan requested, no matter how intriguing the venture. He turned the petition down flat, citing the collateral offered as insufficient. Warner was a whiz at handling money, but twenty years in the banking business had soured him. He took pride in the reputation of his Germantown bank, but the drudgery of the same clients, the same negotiations, the same city, bored him. Tired of merely being competent, he longed for a challenge.

He took a spin around the tiny mountaintop town to wind down after the meeting. Accessible by a cog rail line and enfolding a pristine lake, Eagles Mere seemed the perfect place for summer patrons. The Monroe Boarding House he had chosen for his visit lay about a block and a half away from the prestigious Lakeside Hotel, which towered over the main road amidst numerous sizable cottages. Wishing he had treated himself to a more luxurious accommodation, he sighed at his propensity for frugality and mounted the boarding house steps for a nap.

Mrs. Poole, the owner, was sweeping the hallway when he entered. Sidestepping a pile of dust, dog hair, and other unrecognizable waste, he said, "Your ceiling needs repair, madam."

"That's what they all say," she said through a toothless grin. "Home for a nap, I see."

Later he awoke, wrinkling his nose at the smell of musty sheets and stale tobacco smoke. William Warner rolled off the bed, dodging a piece of peeling paint that drifted down from the ceiling. He cracked the window, letting a blast of March air freshen the dingy room. Combing the tangles out of his long, black beard, he stared out the window, noticing a small hill on the opposite side of the lake, littered with stripped hemlocks and rotting branches. His charcoal eyes stared at the devastation, then dropped to take in the late afternoon sun shimmering on the lake. He consulted his pocket watch: 4:40 p.m.

He recalled Mrs. Poole mentioning a cyclone that had come through in 1892.

A man of vision could do something with that hill.

Calculations tossed around in his head. "Foolish money frittering," his wife, Mary, would whine. Foolish? Pish-posh. Not merely a monetary investment, his plan would provide respite away from the city for those like himself who were pummeled by the stress of everyday life. He bolstered himself against the competition with the other hotels in town, but assured himself that what he envisioned was unique.

Warner's adventurous cousin, Henry, had money and connections. Surely he would know a reputable architect and would even want to invest in the venture himself. Warner excitedly grabbed his journal and sat on the edge of the bed. Tearing a sheet from the journal, he made some quick computations. He added the sizable amount he had saved through the years without Mary's knowledge to what he calculated a mortgage on his Germantown home would produce.

"I'm planning a grand Victorian inn," he wrote his cousin, "where families can enjoy countless amenities along with swimming, boating, horseback riding and other summer activities."

Warner's handwriting grew large and jagged as he described the transformation of the cyclone-devastated hill into a summer resort. "Are you interested in investing?" Forcing himself to breathe, Warner signed and folded the letter.

Jumping up, he rushed to the window and studied the hill. Mother Nature had cleared it for him, saving labor and money. The residue of the fallen trees would have to be eliminated and then carpenters could begin work. He clambered down the stairs and hit the floor hard, waving the letter in Mrs. Poole's face.

"Do you provide stationery? I need an envelope."

"Envelopes are sold at the general store."

"Please tell me when the mail is posted here."

"10 a.m. Come sit down. Sup's on." She spooned out some slimy looking stew into a chipped bowl and slammed a plate of biscuits on the table in front of him.

Disappointed in the meager fare, he asked, "How does one obtain a bath in this establishment?"

Playfully tucking a greasy strand of wiry hair back into her bun, she sat down opposite him, laced her wrinkled fingers together, and watched him eat. "Well, for a quarter I can fill the tub off the kitchen with hot water. Of course, a dip in our nice pure lake is free." Smirking, she raised a clouded blue eye in a dare. "It's fed by underground springs, don't you know, and there is a legend that it once was an Indian burial ground. Course, in March it's a little chilly, even for a real man."

Disgusted by the insinuation, he flipped her a quarter and dismissed her by finishing his meal with his nose buried in his stew.

The bath unclenched his muscles. Smiling as he lay in bed later, he anticipated his daughter's reaction when he returned home and shared his ideas. Margaret would be excited, he felt certain, and would want to participate in the planning.

Warner was again the only guest the next morning at the breakfast table. Mrs. Poole hurriedly set out cornbread, molasses and milk, and then wiped her hands on her oily apron. She plunked down a bowl slightly out of his reach and put a tin mug of steaming coffee to his left. Rearranging the breakfast fare in a proper manner, he broke the cornbread into the bowl, spooned molasses over it and added milk. Eating quickly, he returned to his room, impatient to be about his business. Warner checked himself in the mirror, straightened his tie, and frowned as he picked a piece of cornbread out of his beard. He set his ledger neatly inside his suitcase and checked out. What a lesson Mrs. Poole had taught him. He intended to anticipate the needs of his guests and treat them with deference, not as toys with which to be dallied.

Smiling confidently, he left the post office shortly after ten and strode east on Eagles Mere Avenue toward the knoll. Masses of yellow crocuses opened their mouths to drink in the morning sun. The paste of stale cornbread still on his teeth, he recalled the yeasty aromas from the bakery where he usually stopped for a pastry on his way to work. Breakfast at his inn would offer several choices of fresh summer fruit, eggs, cereal, biscuits, toast, preserves, waffles, pancakes, bacon, ham and homemade pastries.

A little outlet pond greeted him at the base of the hill and he excitedly began his climb. Mountain laurel and bird song encouraged him along the way. At the summit, ideas flooded his brain more numerous than the felled branches around him. Impressive view of twelve counties over a pristine lake. Writing desks with embossed hotel stationery. Distinctive cupola. Courteous waitresses in starched uniforms serving gourmet food on fine china. Bathrooms with hot and cold running water and bathtubs en suite, as they say in Europe. Flower gardens. Elegant common rooms with glittering electric chandeliers. Stately pillars marking the entrance to a grand winding drive. Call bells for bellhop service. Grandfather clock gracing the main lounge. Quality concerts by gifted musicians. Canoeing, swimming and water games on a spring fed lake. Gracious hosting to needy guests. He needed an impressive name for the inn and a massive roll top desk from which to properly administer it.

A stunning view of the lake took his breath away as he reached the top of the mount. Standing motionless at the center of his new universe, he mentally transformed Cyclone Hill into The Crestmont Inn. Amidst the devastation surrounding him, William Warner planted his feet 2200 feet above sea level and knew he stood on opportunity.

The Crestmont Inn
1910 – 1911

"You have to correct this," thundered William Warner, stomping his foot. "You've got a dance listed on this bulletin board for tonight. We always have a hymn sing in the West Lounge on Sunday night."

"It's Tuesday, Dad," William Woods patiently reminded his father-in-law. "You and Margaret always gather flowers on Tuesday. You helped her arrange fresh floral bouquets just this afternoon."

"No, I am quite certain that was yesterday. I distinctly remember adding some of my famous roses to the vase in the main lounge to impress the guests checking in on Saturday."

Woods bit his tongue. "Let's find Margaret and ask her." He bustled in to his wife's office. "Margaret," he said through gritted teeth, "You are the only one who can control him. I am trying to get the bulletin board set up for the weekend activities and he insists it's Sunday again. Do something with him so I can get some work done, please."

Margaret Woods battled more frequent bouts of disquietude over the disturbing fluctuations in her father's behavior. When William Warner, builder and owner of the Crestmont Inn, began his decline, she was the first to notice and the last to admit that he could not continue in his leadership role. It only made sense that her talented, capable husband, William Woods, should take over.

She met her father in the hall, affectionately curled her arm through his and led him into her private office. "Daddy, you know how overwhelming July can be with us sending out last minute August confirmations. Would you help me? I know you've memorized all the names of the guests and the weeks they stay with us." She loved spending time with him and didn't mind balancing keeping him occupied with completing her own work.

Sitting him down in a chair opposite her desk, Margaret wound the Crestmont stationery boasting "View of Twelve Counties" around the paper spindle of her Remington typewriter and typed "July 10, 1910." Pressing the carriage return several times she said, "All right, Daddy, tell me to whom I should be sending confirmations."

Her father, comfortable with this routine, combed his fingernails through his black beard and recited, "The Hedgemore's. They are always late in requesting a reservation and complain when they are offered rooms on the third sleeping floor. Then there would be Mrs. Emit Darling and Mr. and Mrs. Harold Rodgers. Very gracious people, the Rodgers. They have been coming to the Crestmont for years, and write me a thank you note after each visit."

Margaret's fingers flew over the keys while she mentally kept a clear distinction between the names tumbling out of her father's mouth and the people to whom she actually needed to send confirmations. In many cases, despite her father's mental deterioration, he was correct. Guests often returned the same time year after year. It was the newer people whose names William Warner could not remember.

Months passed and all Margaret wanted to do was to sit at his bedside. Her father's decline over the winter had been slow, but steady. The doctor's diagnosis of a weak heart that would stop beating in a few weeks was difficult to accept, but the real heartbreak was watching his brilliant mind slowly ebb into oblivion.

William Woods, Margaret's husband, had been acting administrator of the inn for several months due to her father's illness. At the moment he was downstairs in his new office, working at the substantial desk her mother felt he needed, planning a June convention hosted by the Crestmont.

Margaret, however, craved her father's presence. Even in his senseless state, somehow she would let him know he was not alone. All of a sudden, his eyes fluttered open as he dug his yellow fingernails into the sheets.

"I'm here, Daddy." She brushed the hair off his forehead with her fingers, yearning to hear his calm voice again.

He appeared to be completely lucid. "Moppet," he said, using his pet name for her, "I have so many things to tell you and so little time." Raising himself a bit in the bed, he regarded her with an unexpected intensity that bore both an opening of hope in her soul and a wound in her heart. "You've always shared my Crestmont dream. Please continue it after I am gone. Always offer quality. The key is to give the guests what they need, even when they aren't aware what that is. You have always been so strong. I know you can do this."

He laced his fingers across his chest and prayed, "Thank you, God, for my inn. It has blessed and sustained me."

Resentment seethed in Margaret. It was inconceivable for her to anticipate running the inn while her father lay before her dying. When she lifted her head, his eyes were closed, the moment of clarity gone. Why had she looked away? Suddenly, she heard an odd hissing sound.

"What is it, Daddy?" She rose and put her ear close to his mouth, and he haltingly managed to say something that sounded like "forty." She searched his face. His eyes momentarily locked on hers, then lost focus and retreated into the tangled mass that used to be his sharp mind. Margaret knew he was gone. She rose, put her ear to his chest and heard nothing.

Paralyzed, she sat with him a long time. Her mind moved from benumbing pain to tearful memories of his proud, animated face and dramatic gestures when he had first ushered them into the grand lobby. In one year's time he had planned the inn and had brought in two hundred carpenters to build it. He passionately nurtured it for the next eleven.

Margaret, a woman in her twenties, wanted to climb back up into her father's lap and feel his long arms cradle her. She wanted to relive the days when, as an adolescent, he had shared with her his idea of building the Crestmont. Finally, without knowing how much time had passed, she willed herself to go downstairs to tell her mother and William.

"At least he died a good death," the doctor said, after examining her father's body.

"A good death?" Margaret cried incredulously.

The doctor moved his glasses back up onto his nose as he closed his bag. "When the patient doesn't have to suffer, we sometimes refer to it as a good death."

The comment pained her. She had suffered, watching the father she loved replaced by a person who didn't even recognize her. All because of an untreatable dementia.

How many tears are there in a person?

Margaret found a rare moment of solitary reflection two weeks after the funeral. Tears came, flowing beyond control, especially when she walked into the library where her mother had moved her father's desk. Wiping her eyes with her handkerchief, she took two slow breaths to compose herself. Praying silently for strength, she reverently ran her hand along the back of the chair he had so capably occupied for ten years. She sat down and pulled it in toward the desk. Untying the laces of her shoes to let her feet breathe, she realized that the big feet she had always hated were an unwelcome gift from her father. She visualized him on the telephone, rocking back in his chair, one big foot slung over the other knee, demanding more hot water from the steam room. Her fingertips lovingly explored the empty nooks and crannies where her father had systematically kept his orderly paperwork.

The desk from which William Warner's heartbeat had breathed life into the Crestmont Inn was relegated to the library. Margaret resented that something so private was available for anyone to intrusively open drawers or sit and write a letter, but that was what her father would have wanted. He venerated any way he could share himself with his guests. To honor that, she had a plaque made and mounted on the top of his desk:

William Warner
1853-1911
Creator of the Crestmont Dream

"Foolish sentimentality," her mother said when Margaret showed it to her. Mary Warner, who had resented how the Crestmont had taken them away from her family in Germantown during the summers, now seemed eager to assist in running it with William Woods.

Warner had systematically taught his daughter every aspect of managing the summer resort precisely because he could see that his wife was dispassionate about it. Margaret found it difficult to respect her mother, who had chastised her father so frequently in life and seemed so easily to have gotten over his death. The one solace Margaret could find in her own grief was that she had been loving and supportive to her father when he was alive.

"If only you were here, Daddy," she whispered as she lay her head down on her hands on the desk. She was horrified at herself for resenting his last request. The enormity of what he had asked engulfed her. She understood that it was her responsibility as his daughter and protégé to ensure that the quality of the Crestmont continued, but she now felt none of the strength he claimed she had. Visions of putting her own needs aside in order to fill those of the guests revolted her.

The 1911 summer season would begin in three weeks. Although June 15th was the official opening, some guests arrived early and stayed in the rooms with fireplaces to keep off the late spring chill. Correspondence confirming arrival dates for the waitress and housekeeping staff was complete. While Margaret finalized menu preparation for the fine table for which the Crestmont was noted, William and her mother planned guest activities and ordered supplies.

Craving solitude, Margaret donned the crocheted white sweater that hung on the back of her office door. Instead of going past her husband's office to exit via the main lobby, she turned left and inspected the lounge across from the dining room. Gold and white patterned wallpaper above the chair rail peeled from the corners at the ceiling. She would have to bring this to William's attention. She knew she could not push too much at one time, because he could get persnickety if he felt he had not had an idea first. Leaving the big house through the back door, she noticed some rips in the yellow awnings her father had put up.

Descending the Crestmont hill for the Laurel Path that wound around Eagles Mere Lake, she entered a narrow clearing where huge pink blossoms, set against the small evergreen leaves of mountain laurel, towered over her. Clusters of flowers washed in pastel peach, pink, and creamy yellow sprang out from the larger leaves of the lower-lying rhododendron, whose tangled masses of branches curled up from the ground like snakes. Margaret loved walking the entire path around the lake, so close to the water you could hear it lapping, yet separated from it by dense undergrowth. Today, however, she continued straight out to one of the Crestmont docks to gaze at the lake and the little footbridge that separated it from the outlet pond on the south end.

Her father had constructed wooden benches here so that one could sit and enjoy the breezes making swirls of gold, green and blue in the pristine lake waters. Tears came when she realized her father had seen and attended to every aspect of the inn.

It would not be that way with William. She loved her husband for his magical way with people and his vision, but his organizational skills were weak. Margaret knew she would have to tend to the practicalities upon which a business was built, and find ways to motivate William to solve problems he didn't initially see himself. The prospects of running a business and caring for her baby, Peg, were daunting.

A verse she loved from Isaiah 41 came to her: "For I the Lord thy God will hold thy right hand, saying unto thee, Fear not; I will help thee." She considered the Edgemere Hotel across the lake. Knowing it had survived through several generations brought her hope. Perhaps it was not her father that was the strength of the Crestmont, but rather the example he had set. Margaret prayed she could find some healing by accepting the responsibility to follow in his footsteps.

Bethlehem, Pennsylvania
1925

GRACE DIDN'T WANT TO BE, HADN'T ASKED TO BE, BUT WAS DRAWN TO him. George was not especially handsome, but there was magnetism in his quiet kindnesses. She knew he loved her sister, Lily.

Lily and Mother deliberated over the guest list, heads bent over papers dimly lit by the kerosene lamp on the dining room table. George left the room, wearied by the bustle of wedding plans. He found Grace in the pantry, opening a tin of cookies for the tea that would sustain them through the guest choosing. She and George had exchanged longing looks before, but this felt different. Shifting, she searched for escape. His eyes clouded and he seemed unusually shy and confused.

"Grace, I want you to know I love Lily," he breathed quietly, "but this thing I feel for you, I can't..." Then he gently cradled her face with his hands and kissed her lightly on the lips. Stunned, she forgot to push the desire for more away. Too late, anyway. When she opened her eyes, he had vanished.

Her mind traveled miles, trying to decide what to do. The wedding was to be in May. Grace decided she would stand up as maid of honor for her younger sister, and then leave. Diminishing Lily's happiness by explaining served no purpose except self-expiation, so she would simply remove the temptation of herself from George's life.

He had been the only one to whom Grace could talk about her dreams. He would listen patiently and encourage her, commenting on how beautifully she sounded when she sang in church.

She wanted to sing, to be famous, to make something of herself on the stage. Her parents, ashamed of what they called her "flightiness," usually lectured her when she mentioned these aspirations. She was weary of the grillings about why she wasn't yet married, why she hadn't gone on to college and what was she going to do with her life. She was twenty-two, and no interesting beaus had presented themselves. Her mother often chided, "Why must you be so independent, Grace? Just let a young man know you need and admire him, then maybe you wouldn't be alone."

She set the cookies on the dining room table. Lily pushed her blonde hair back off her face and studied Grace curiously. "Have some tea. Join Mummy and me," she invited.

"You and Mother seem to have it under control. I'm quite behind in folding Mrs. Wright's laundry. I'd better go." Before Lily could protest, she swiftly escaped to her room.

Sitting at her desk, Grace studied the February frost hanging on the window. She had already saved money by doing laundry for some of the elderly members of the Moravian Church they attended. She always gave ten percent to the church and half of the remainder to her father. The rest she hoarded. She estimated that in three months she could buy a train ticket out of Bethlehem after Lily's wedding, and have a little money to tide her over. Then she would get a real job and earn enough to get to a big city. Feeling better now that she had a plan, she moved the kerosene lamp from her desk to the nightstand. Plumping her pillows, she settled back and picked up *Song of the Lark*.

She remembered Mrs. Herbst, the reverend's wife, speak softly in her ear on Christmas Eve, "Here's a book I know you'll enjoy."

Grace loved the story of how a small time girl had worked her way to New York City and eventually became a famous opera singer. Knowing she didn't have the talent for opera, Grace reasoned that maybe there was a place for her in vaudeville. It never occurred to her that the only place she had ever sung was in church. A dream, after all, needn't be fueled by particulars, only by desire. She had read that Buffalo, New York, one of the frontrunners in producing electricity because of the energy available from Niagara Falls, had two huge theatres open year round. Reassuring herself that Buffalo would be less daunting than New York City, she determined to go there and do "big time" on the stage. Closing off visions of her father's dark, disapproving face; she set the book aside and drifted off. She slept fitfully.

She awoke to an oak branch tapping on her window, complaining of the cold. Grace loved Sundays. Encouraged by the plan that was brewing in her head, she dressed carefully for church. Usually Rev. Herbst gave a very good sermon, but it was the hymns that drew her to the little Moravian church. Even when she didn't have a solo, she loved the singing.

A family dinner followed church. George sat next to Lily, smiling broadly. Father was his usual taciturn self at the head of the table. The aroma of her mother's specialty, chicken bathed in velvety lemon sauce, touched Grace's nostrils, but she ate without pleasure. She sat aloof, withered by her mother's griping that she had not yet learned how to cook.

"Mrs. Antes, that was the finest meal I have had since last Sunday at your table," George announced, with a forced cheerfulness. "Lily and I will do the dishes."

Hoping Mother and Father would take their Sunday afternoon nap, Grace excused herself to her favorite brown chair in the parlor. She buried her head in the classified section of the *Philadelphia Inquirer* to hide from any intrusion into her privacy. She didn't care much for the news, but it was interesting to read what jobs were available. An ad caught her eye.

Crestmont Inn of Eagles Mere, Pennsylvania
Seeks summer employees.
Work in a beautiful lakeside mountaintop inn with
Fair wages and working conditions.
Female - Waitresses, Housemaids
Male - Lawn boys
Chefs (Trained Negroes only need apply).

Underneath was an address with instructions for requesting an interview.

"A beautiful lakeside mountaintop inn" sounded like a dream, but she had no idea where Eagles Mere was. Could she work there for the summer and earn enough money to go on the road? Grace copied the address and stole upstairs to write the application letter. After correcting and recopying it three times she signed it and stuffed it in her handbag, intending to post it on Monday. She must offer to pick up the mail for a while, she reminded herself, so that no one else from the family could intercept the reply.

Grace could hardly believe her eyes when, ten days later, she opened a response on official Crestmont Inn letterhead.

Dear Miss Antes,

We regret to inform you that we cannot put you on our waitress staff because of your lack of experience. We would, however, be happy to interview you for the cleaning staff of the inn. Please present yourself to our office no later than Tuesday, June 15th for an interview. If you require transportation, our car (labeled clearly The Crestmont Inn) provides a shuttle service from the Wilkes-Barre train station every Tuesday and Thursday beginning June 1st. You may meet the car at the east entrance of the station

between 11 a.m. and noon. Please reply to inform us of
the day of your arrival.

Yours truly,
Mr. William Woods, President

She formulated a plan and quickly wrote back, confirming her interview on June 7th, a week before the deadline. She would stay for Lily and George's wedding in May, and then make preparations to leave. The three months before the wedding would drag by and she dreaded the wait. Avoiding George was one thing, but pretending nothing was awry around Lily would be next to impossible.

❧

Had three months really passed so quickly? Mother was busy in the kitchen, humming the wedding march as the guests mingled in the parlor. The wedding had been beautiful and George was careful never once to glance Grace's way.

Lily hugged her before she left for her honeymoon and said, "I love you, Grace. You'll be the first to hear all about it when we get back."

"I love you too, Lily." Under her breath she said, "Don't judge me too harshly." Lily shot her a quizzical glance before George swept her away into his Model T Ford with a "Just Married" sign above the spare tire on the back.

❧

Grace quickly finished ironing Mrs. Wright's blouses and flew down the stairs and out the door to deliver them. After pocketing her dollar, she calculated that she had $20 saved and hurried to the Bethlehem Public Library.

"I need a map of the part of the state that shows places near Wilkes-Barre, please." The librarian pushed a huge atlas across the counter.

Grace was ready to ask for a magnifying glass when she finally found it. Eagles Mere was about sixty miles northwest of Wilkes-Barre. If the Crestmont Inn's car left the train station at noon, she might arrive in Eagles Mere before 4 p.m. She hoped that wasn't too late for an interview, because she didn't have the money to stay overnight anywhere. She checked the train schedule from Allentown to Wilkes-Barre and found an early morning train. The problem was getting to Allentown before eight in the morning. Returning to the counter, she asked for an Allentown telephone book. Finding just what she wanted, she went to the public phone booth, dropped in her coins, and dialed the number.

"Allentown Young Woman's Christian Association. May I help you?"

"How much is it to stay one night, please?"

"Fifty cents for supper and a cot in the dormitory. Biscuits and coffee are available for breakfast."

"I'd like to make a reservation, ma'am."

"It's not necessary. We always have extra cots. Please check in by four."

"Thank you." Grace knew that Rev. Herbst went to Allentown on Tuesdays for a clergy meeting. Perhaps he would drive her to Allentown and she could take the Wednesday train to Wilkes-Barre. Cheered now that she had a plan, Grace perked up.

After church two weeks later, she pulled Rev. Herbst aside. He agreed to give Grace a ride to Allentown for a shopping trip, but frowned when she asked him not to tell her parents. Explaining that she also had a few things to pawn the family no longer needed, she figured she could take a sack with her things in it without him becoming suspicious.

Composing the letter to give him after they got to Allentown was difficult, but she was sure that after Rev. Herbst read it, he would understand what she was really doing without feeling responsible for participating in it.

Dear Rev. Herbst,

I want you to know that I won't be in front of the library at 3 p.m. as I promised you this morning. I'm going to leave home and find my own way in the world. Don't worry about me, since I have a definite plan and a place to go. You know from our conversations about some of the problems I have at home. I know that you'll respect my privacy and won't try to stop me. Please tell my parents I'll write when I get settled. They would never let me go if they knew about this, so I had to do it this way. I hope you will forgive me. You and Mrs. Herbst have always been so kind to me. I wish God's blessings on you both.

Sincerely,
Grace Antes

On Tuesday, Grace hopped out of his car. She ran around to the driver's side to say thank you and hand him the letter, then dashed off without looking back. That was the last time she would use the name "Grace." From now on she would be "Gracie," setting out to find her place in the world.

She flew down the street, blinking back tears because she had lied to someone she cared for and respected. She would miss the Herbsts and the warmth and love she felt at church. And the hymns—oh, how she would miss the hymns.

Fanning her face with her straw hat worked off some nervous energy, but did nothing to stop the trickle of perspiration trailing down her chest under the double layer of underclothing she had squeezed inside her blouse and skirt early that morning. Her sack held her Bible, the *Song of the Lark*, a nightgown, the bathrobe she fondly called her pink shrug, more underclothing, an extra blouse, sweater, writing pad, toiletries, and a small lunch. Not only was the sack cumbersome, but worse, she was sure it would also attract attention.

As she turned down Broad Street, she saw a sign, "Second Hand Shoppe, Goods Bought and Sold." She stepped inside and breathed a sigh of relief when she spied a small red suitcase with tan leather trim. The tag said $2.00. Gracie bought the suitcase, some pencils, a brush and comb. A bright yellow jewelry box with a poem drew her in:

It's the song ye sing
And the smiles ye wear
That's a makin' the sun
Shine everywhere.
—James Whitecomb Riley

The poem was perfect. It would greet her every morning and remind her of her mission. She didn't own any jewelry except her watch, the choker around her neck and her fake drop pearl earrings, but she had to have it.

A new life demands a significant marker, right?

After bargaining with the sour-faced man behind the counter, Gracie got it for a reduced price, and then asked the man for directions to the library and the YWCA. He sighed, narrowed his bushy eyebrows, and wrote down the directions for her.

As she was leaving, a beat up alarm clock in the window caught her eye. The idea of reporting for work promptly was new to her. If she was going to have a job, she wanted to be sure to awaken in time. She slipped back in the store, gave the man her sweetest smile and asked to see it. Made in 1915, it was nickel plated with Roman numerals on the face. Dents covered the sides, but for a quarter, maybe it would do. Firmly making the shopkeeper wind it up and check the alarm, she handed him the money and left.

Allentown loomed over her five-foot-three-inch frame more than Bethlehem ever had. The buildings were imposing and the city itself more crowded. People obviously knew exactly where they were going. She walked by a diner and smelled pot roast. Her stomach churned. Then she passed a beauty parlor with a sign in the window "Bobs, 35 cents. Tuesday only." Grant's

Hardware offered a special on shovels. Juggling the suitcase and her pack made her feel conspicuous and uneasy.

She turned right on Court Street and found the Municipal Building. The big clock outside chimed eleven times. Needing to take stock, Gracie went inside. Relieved to find the ladies' washroom empty, she quickly repacked her belongings into the red suitcase.

Returning to the building plaza, she settled down next to one of the two huge stone lions out front for security, pulled out her sandwich and munched on it while she watched the people go by. The women here were very stylish with skirts and hair shorter than Gracie's mother allowed. Feeling dowdy, she did a mental inventory of her money, afraid to take it out of her purse. She had spent $3.25 at the second hand store. She had only $12 left and she knew her ticket would be about half that.

She craved a fresh image for her new life. Should she do it? She tucked that decision away for a few minutes.

An hour later, unruly blonde curls lay on the floor. Gracie peered at her new image from the beauty shop chair. Green eyes, wider and more open to receive the world, gazed back at her. A fashionable bob cut just below her ears, not straight or crimped but bouncy, framed her face.

"It's the best I could do for the price. Crimping is another 15 cents," apologized the salon girl as she dusted stray hairs off the back of Gracie's neck with a big powder brush.

Gracie leaned into the mirror and tipped her head from one side to the other watching her hair bounce. She flashed a delighted smile. "It's perfect."

She felt younger and definitely more self-assured.

En route to Eagles Mere
1925

PEOPLE BUZZED AROUND THE ALLENTOWN TRAIN STATION THE NEXT
day, stopping only to check departure times or to collect their
children and suitcases. Gracie bought her ticket, hurriedly
counting the rest of the money in her purse. Selecting a magazine
called *Time* from the newsstand next to the ticket counter, she
leafed through it, lingering over an article about President
Coolidge.

"Watch it, Missy," growled a man pushing a huge steamer
trunk on a dolly. She jumped out of the way and hastily handed
the vendor the money for the magazine and a Milky Way candy
bar. Thinking she might feel less overwhelmed outside the station,
she checked the board for the departing platform for the Wilkes-
Barre train and dodged her way out of the terminal.

On the platform, people were crammed into each available
seat, but quickly rose to board when the train to Philadelphia was
announced. Gracie sat down alone, set her red suitcase between
her legs, and wolfed down the candy bar. She glanced distractedly
at the cover of the magazine, realizing she hated the news and

politics, but instructed herself to read it on the train to Wilkes-Barre so she could be better informed.

Ducking her head nervously when people filtered in to catch the next train, Gracie spied a book someone had abandoned called *Sister Carrie*. Quickly, she snatched if off the bench and browsed through it. The main character was a girl who wanted to go to Chicago and be a famous actress. Excited now that she had a friend with a similar goal to keep her company; she put it in her suitcase just as the conductor called "All aboard!" Nervously climbing the steep steps onto the train, she settled into a brown leather seat and opened the *Time* magazine. She tried to read, but remorse gnawed at her concentration like a woodpecker hammering her skull.

"Ne-e-xt stop, Wilkes Ba-a-are." Clutching her red suitcase, Gracie stepped off the train with an unsettling combination of anticipation and fear. After consulting a man in a maroon uniform with a name tag on his breast pocket, she found the east entrance of the train station where she was to meet the Crestmont car. The clock on the wall said 10:45. Sitting on a bench in the sun, she nervously paged through her magazine while she waited.

A huge black Buick Touring Car pulled up to the curb with "The Crestmont Inn" painted on the side in yellow letters. A spindly man in his mid-twenties climbed out. He was impeccably dressed in gray and black pinstriped trousers and a gray jacket. Gracie guessed the yellow of his tie had been chosen to match the lettering on the car. He was so skinny that she giggled, imagining herself pushing him over with one finger. He had a very prominent Adam's apple, a broad forehead and a face that narrowed into a pointy chin.

Waving to someone behind her on the tracks, he shouted, "Dorothy, still keeping those students of yours in line?" His wide smile made Gracie relax a bit.

Shyly, she stepped forward. "Hello, my name is Gracie Antes. Is this the shuttle to the Crestmont Inn?"

"You must be the new girl." He stuck out a bony hand. "I'm

PT, driver, bowling alley attendant and gofer for Mr. Woods, Crestmont's owner. Hop in."

"Well, I don't know. I mean, my interview is this afternoon. Will we make it on time?"

"Yup." Feeling like she had been given an order, Gracie slid into the middle seat of the car.

The generously proportioned middle-aged woman he had called Dorothy ran from the platform to the car, straw hat flopping, struggling with a suitcase and hatbox. She threw her free arm around PT and kissed him loudly on the cheek. "Oh, my word, if it isn't PT. Isn't it a long time between summers?" He stashed her suitcase in the trunk along with Gracie's, and Dorothy slid into the passenger seat in the front.

A sickeningly sweet odor of roses filled the car. Gracie discretely wound her window down a few inches to let in some air.

"I nearly missed my trolley to the station. Dear me, I am just neither here nor there without my car. I need to pick it up next week, PT, so I'll be shuttling back here with you. Hello, there, dear," she said, extending a hand back to Gracie. "I'm Dorothy, one of the antique waitresses."

"Pleased to meet you, ma'am. I'm Gracie Antes."

"Oh, please don't ma'am me. My students do it all year and it makes me feel old. I need my Crestmont summers to liven up these forty-five-year-old bones. Call me Dorothy. Whew, it certainly is hot enough. Oh look, there's Isaiah and Olivia. Yoohoo!" She beckoned to them from the car window. "All aboard the Crestmont shuttle."

A burly man with skin like coal and big apple cheeks protectively ushered a dainty woman with copper skin into the car. The woman's elegance and quiet nature made Gracie like her immediately.

"Guess that's it for this run," PT said, starting the engine.

After they introduced themselves, Isaiah pounded Gracie on the back and said, "One big happy family, right, Olivia?" He drew the palm of his wife's tiny hand to his lips and kissed it. Sniffing suspiciously, he wrinkled his nose. "Lord Almighty, Dorothy, I hate that roses stink stuff you wear. Don't you bring that smell into my kitchen, hear?"

"It's imported Ashes of Roses eau de cologne, Isaiah," she corrected him. "It was Lawrence's favorite, bless my dear husband's soul, and as long as Sears carries it, I will continue to wear it. And as far as your kitchen goes, there are so many aromas floating about no one will notice a little perfume. Besides, Mrs. Swett loves it and says so each summer when she hands me a fine tip."

"I don't know how you can be so hotsy-totsy to those old biddies in the dining room. They act like they run the place instead of Mr. Woods. You are crazy to take those tables near the lakeside windows, Dorothy. Why, you have to deal with all three of them at once, plus two husbands. Who's that one always feeling like she's sick—Mrs. Pennyswoon?"

"Mrs. Pennington, Isaiah. Be kind, now," Olivia said softly, with a slight accent Gracie couldn't identify.

"First of all, Isaiah," Dorothy instructed, "if you ever stepped out of your kitchen you would see that the west window tables afford a commanding view of the lake and are therefore reserved for our, shall we say, more faithful, well-to-do guests. Secondly, Mrs. Woods has graciously assigned them to me because she feels I have the maturity and skills to mitigate some of their outlandish behavior."

"Hey, PT," Isaiah chuckled, "translate, please."

"Dorothy is good at keeping the Rude Regals in line, so Mrs. Woods gives her the tables where she gets really great tips."

"Thanks, pal," said Isaiah.

"Oh, my word, I simply am beside myself when I hear people call them the Rude Regals. They are people with problems, just like you and me. Mrs. Pennington's ailments are an indication that she needs some attention. Miss Woodford simply feels she is of a higher station than anyone else. If I can show some special attention or give deference to make someone happy, then I will do it. Besides, I find it a challenge to use my people skills on a higher level with the adults at the Crestmont than with my elementary students."

The more everyone else talked, the more Gracie knew it would take some doing to feel like she fit in. Her stomach grumbled, and she wished she had bought more than a candy bar for lunch. The clouds she watched from her window glided like wavy streamers in the sky. As they motored toward the Crestmont, her eyes got heavy. Realizing that she would need a lot more energy before the day was over; she turned her head toward the window and tried to sleep. "Dear God," she prayed, "Please make this be all right. If I was wrong to do it, then turn it for good."

After a long drive, PT slowed the car when they passed through stone pillars on either side of the Crestmont driveway. They ascended a steep hill to an immense three-story brown building with yellow awnings. PT parked the car. Gracie stood nervously by while the others grabbed their luggage and dashed off in a flash, saying, "See you soon!"

"Come on, I'll show you to Mr. Woods' office," PT said, lifting Gracie's suitcase out of the trunk. Gracie took in the immensity of the porch as they walked up the center steps. Once they were inside the striking lobby area, PT pointed to a huge grandfather clock. "That's my favorite. Name's Old Tim," he explained. "Mrs. Woods' father had it shipped from England when he built the place."

Gracie's heart started to flutter. Oh, honestly, what had she gotten herself into? She tried not to trip over her own feet.

PT knocked on an office door, flicked his eyes toward it and said, "They're swell people. Good luck."

"Come in!" called a high-pitched, authoritative male voice.

The Crestmont Inn
Summer 1925

I

SHE STEPPED INTO THE OFFICE. A SHORT MAN WITH BLOND HAIR PARTED
in the middle sprang nimbly to his feet and shook Gracie's hand.
"I am Mr. William Woods, and this is my wife, Margaret. We are
the owners of the Crestmont Inn." He sat down as quickly as he
had risen, adjusted his tie, and aligned his cufflinks perfectly.
Mrs. Woods, with dark hair and large brown eyes, stood calmly
next to his desk. Her serenity was a comforting contrast to Mr.
Woods' energy.

"Mrs. Woods, we have before us a Miss Grace Antes, applying
for a housemaid position.

"It's An-tees, sir," Gracie blushed, afraid of Mr. Woods'
reaction to the correction. "And, if you please, I like to be called
Gracie."

"Antes. That's a German name, is it not?"

"Yes sir. It's Moravian, sir."

"I know of the Moravians. Persecuted religious order from
Bohemia. After a great spiritual renewal in the eighteenth century,

they emigrated to this country as missionaries. Many settled here in Pennsylvania. I am sure I have sung some of the music they composed."

"William." Margaret Woods guided her eyes over to Gracie.

"Ah, yes. Gracie. Where are you from?"

She lowered her eyes, intent on taking advantage of the musical connection, and blurted out, "My great-great grandfather was John Antes. He made musical instruments and composed music when he was a missionary in Egypt. He was tortured there by the locals, then he came back to this country and his music has been sung in Moravian churches all over ever since the 18th century. Oh...I'm from Bethlehem, sir."

"And how did you hear about the Crestmont Inn, young lady?"

"I saw an ad in the *Philadelphia Inquirer*, sir."

"Have you ever worked in an inn or hotel before?"

"No, sir."

"Have you been employed as a housekeeper before?"

"No, but I know what clean should be and I am a fast learner. At home I took in laundry for some of the older folks at church and made some money that way."

"What brings you all the way over here to Eagles Mere?"

She nervously studied the floor under his immense desk. Buffalo, the stage, singing, finding a new life in the big city—all flew through her mind. Diagnosing these as inappropriate responses, Gracie replied, "The ad brought me here, sir, and now that I am here, I know I will like it." She lifted her head with a hopeful smile.

William Woods rocked back and forth, heel to toe, studying her. Winking at his wife, he said, "There are three kinds of people at The Crestmont Inn, Gracie. Tell me who they might be."

"Why, there's you, Mr. Woods, and Mrs. Woods of course, then people like myself hoping to be staff...then there's the staff." Counting as she talked, she realized she hadn't gotten to the most important people. "Mr. Woods, I'd say there are the guests, you and Mrs. Woods, and the staff."

"Who are the bosses at The Crestmont Inn?" he probed.

Suspecting this was the key question, Gracie broke out of her habit of saying what she knew Mother and Father wanted to hear, and spoke her mind. "I think actually, sir, the guests would be the bosses, in that you want to make them as happy as possible while they are here." A flash of pride for her newfound clarity of thought coursed through her.

He clicked the roof of his mouth with his tongue, shot a glance at his wife and asked, "Mrs. Woods, do you suppose we have found a new housemaid here in Miss Gracie An-tes?"

"I do, dear." Mr. Woods smiled warmly. Gracie straightened her shoulders.

"Well then, Gracie, your salary will be $15.00 per month, with an extra $15.00 in September if you complete the season, which ends on Labor Day. The rest of your salary will come from tips and you will receive free room and board here at the hotel. Please accompany my wife, who will explain your duties and answer any further questions."

"You have come at a good time," explained Mrs. Woods, leading her down the hall away from the main lobby where Gracie had entered with PT. "We are not yet at the height of the season, so you will have a chance to ease into the July rush." Gracie paused, gawking at two immense portraits on the wall. "That is my mother," Mrs. Woods said. "And this one," she touched the frame, "is my father. He envisioned and built the Crestmont twenty-five years ago." When Mrs. Woods smiled, her dark brown eyes drooped down at the corners. She hesitated, then patted her chignon of shiny brown hair and pointed out three ladies' parlors on the left. A painting of a young girl dressed in yellow satin, holding a baby in a lace christening gown flowing with pink ribbons, was mounted on the wall across the hall. "These are my children, Peg and Eleanor."

"Such beautiful little girls," Gracie said, admiring the painting.

"Oh," Mrs. Woods laughed. "The painting is several years old. Peg is fifteen now and Eleanor nine. I am sure the girls will make themselves known to you. They love it when a new staffer comes in. Come along, then, Gracie. I will show you the staff dining room and Room 109 where you will live this summer."

The hall ended at what Mrs. Woods called the West Parlor directly opposite French doors that led into the dining room fitted with perfectly aligned white linen covered tables. Gracie gasped at the huge glass windows on the left of the room. "Ah, you haven't seen the lake yet, have you? It is what makes Eagles Mere special." Mrs. Woods beckoned her to the window. "Come here." Gracie's breath caught when she saw the striking view of water twinkling in the afternoon sun.

"Well, now that you have met my family, let me show you what you will be doing this summer. You are our only new housemaid so far." They passed through swinging doors into an immense kitchen, filled with aromas of pork, rosemary, and apples. Isaiah was leaning over a steaming huge pot, pumping a potato masher up and down.

"Evenin', Mrs. Woods."

"Hello, Isaiah. I'd like you to meet Gracie, our new housemaid."

"Yes, ma'am, we met on the drive from Wilkes-Barre. Hey there, Gracie."

"I am sure Gracie is tired from all her traveling. Will you have someone send a dinner tray up to 109 for her?"

"Sure thing, Mrs. Woods."

Gracie's stomach grumbled as they passed through the fragrant kitchen past a small door into a tiny dining room. "This is the staff dining room. Breakfast is at 6:15 in the morning so we can begin serving the guests at 7:30. Staff lunch and dinner are after the main dining room empties. We expect a quiet and respectful attitude from our staff, and a diligence to anticipate the needs of our guests. Mr. Woods and I strive for fairness with our staff, but we also demand your best effort. If you have any questions, my office is readily accessible. Come now, it is five o'clock and I must hostess dinner at six. You shall need to sign your contract and then we must fit you for a uniform and give you some linens."

Mrs. Woods carried Gracie's uniform on a hanger up the back staircase next to the dining room. Gracie followed with linens in one hand and her red suitcase in the other. Indicating small glass burners about eye level when they reached the second sleeping floor, Mrs. Woods said, "These glow night lamps are lit by the night watchman before sundown and stay on all night." She opened a door at the end of the hall, revealing another section with five rooms on each side and two bathrooms. "Female staff sleeps in the back west wing of the hotel or what we fondly call the big house. Here you are. Room 109. Your dinner will be up shortly. Surely you wouldn't mind a quiet evening in your room after all your excitement today. You will take the rest of your meals in the staff dining room. Goodnight, Gracie. Welcome to the Crestmont family."

"Oh, thank you, Mrs. Woods. You have been so kind."

"Oh, honestly, Gracie, what have you gotten yourself into?" she hammered herself after she was safely ensconced in her room and had devoured the pork dinner delivered by a round-faced waitress named Mae. She carefully reviewed her notes of Mrs. Woods' directions. Gracie understood how to clean the rooms, but would not know until tomorrow exactly where they were. Being the newest housemaid on staff, she knew she would get the worst assignment.

Her room was tiny, but clean and adequate. The window next to the small bed was covered with a simple lace curtain. In addition, there was a wardrobe, a dresser and a nightstand with a kerosene lamp. Gracie breathed a sigh of relief to know that she could comfortably read before retiring. Dusting off her red suitcase before laying it on the bed, she began unpacking. Her Bible and *Sister Carrie* went on the nightstand. She hung her everyday skirt, two blouses, and the crisp new size eight green uniform with its removable white collar and white apron in the wardrobe, along with her pink shrug. Mrs. Woods had measured her, stating kindly but firmly that Crestmont girls couldn't order uniforms from the Sears catalogue because the hemlines were too high. Washing the detachable collar by hand would help her keep the uniform neat and clean until Olivia had finished sewing the second one. Gracie was relieved to learn that the inn provided the uniforms as long as they were turned back in at the end of the summer season.

Analyzing what she had not yet unpacked, she mulled over the two dresser drawers and decided to put clothes in one, paper in the other. She placed her nightgown, sweater and underclothing in the top drawer and into the second, her writing tablets, pencils, magazine and copy of *Song of the Lark*.

Lovingly lifting the yellow jewelry box out of her suitcase, Gracie set it on the newly starched dresser scarf, mouthing the words of the poem. She fluffed her new bobbed curls in the mirror and felt more cheerful. Opening the window, she leaned out and drew in the scent of the pine trees. Yeasty, cinnamon smells from the kitchen met her nose. Isaiah must be making rolls for tomorrow's breakfast. Glad to have met some people during the drive, she decided she liked Isaiah immediately and wished she had been able to get to know his wife, Olivia, the dressmaker.

She emptied her purse onto the bed. Carefully unfolding the bills she had stashed in her coin purse, she counted. Six dollars. When she added to that the salary spelled out in the contract she had just signed, her shoulders rounded with worry. She needed really good tips to afford a decent dress and travel expenses to Buffalo.

Her sister's face kept appearing in her mind. She tried to erase it, only to see Rev. Herbst, hat in hand, explaining to her family the circumstances of her disappearance. The old feelings burned in Gracie's throat. She couldn't help her attraction to George, and she couldn't stop being jealous of Lily for having him. At the same time, she felt sorry for Lily, the innocent one, who had no idea of the complexity of the situation. What recourse did Gracie have but to leave? She told herself she should write so Lily wouldn't wonder why her sister had vanished for no good reason.

Instead, Gracie pulled around her a protective wall and put off writing the letter for another day. She needed to feel good about herself. Here at the Crestmont, she felt hopeful that might happen.

Pulling a writing tablet out of the dresser she figured she should write down things to work on to better herself. She listed "Clothes, Singing, and Vocabulary" and left spaces to fill in details later. After much consideration, she added, "Save money" and "Read."

Books always brought her solace, so she dove into *Sister Carrie*. She couldn't get past the first page without writing down words she didn't know. Tearing a small piece of paper off her tablet, she wrote "waif," and "susceptible." Maybe she could work up her courage to make a perusal of the Crestmont library and sneak a peek at a dictionary sometime after her shift.

Gracie padded down the hall, wanting to wash up before bed. When she opened the bathroom door, she bumped into the waitress who had brought up her dinner. They smiled at each other and the girl left. A needling voice from behind a screen gave Gracie an uneasy welcome.

"Yep, first week check in with the Rude Regals has to be the best entertainment of the summer. Don't ya agree, girlie? Did ya see Mrs. Pennington wipin' her eyes while her poor husband's draggin' her through the main lobby? She wants the whole world to know she's miserable. It was the spider bite last summer, right? And sunstroke the one before? This summer she'll probably claim some jellyfish bit her, like she was swimmin' in the sea or somethin'. Don't know how her husband takes all that mopin' and moanin'. And those other two.... All I can remember is Sweaty and Miss Drama. Never actually get their names till I hear Mrs. Woods greet 'em. They have to be three of the....Whew, it's gettin' hot in this bath! Slammin' Jack, am I glad Mrs. W didn't give me their rooms, although I hear the tips are great, them havin' all that money and all. Do ya know who has 'em this summer?"

Gracie, unsure of who this girl was talking to or about, washed up quietly. Behind the screen, water sucked noisily down the tub drain. Out stepped a naked, compact woman, maybe eighteen or so. She lovingly toweled her curly red hair, while water dripped from her freckled body. The shiny gold bracelet around her right ankle caught Gracie's eye.

Tipping her foot out to display it, the redhead giggled. "Like it, huh? It's the bee's knees all right."

A pool of water around the girl's feet began snaking toward Gracie.

"You must be the new one. I heard you were older. Listen, girlie, don't think just because you're new Mrs. We'll cut you any slack," she carped. "She expects perfection from all of us; it's just that those of us who are experienced know how to deliver. This is my third summer, ya know. I started when I was sixteen."

There was a split second to slip in "My name's Gracie."

"Bessie."

Later on, two loud raps startled her out of her reading. Padding tentatively to open the door, Gracie was greeted with a towel in her face. After she took it, she got a better look at the curly red bob and thin nose. Pouty lips snapped, "It's called a communal bath, which means ya leave there what was there when ya went in, and take with ya what wasn't. That means this towel of yours goes with ya when ya go. Got it?"

"Oh, sorry." A hot flush crept up Gracie's neck at the angry outburst.

"See ya on the floor." And with that, Bessie was gone.

The girl's abrupt exit stirred feelings in Gracie she couldn't identify. Hopes of making new friends dwindled as she climbed into bed, carefully set her new alarm clock and tried to sleep. The last two days ran over and over in her head. She had walked out of Lily's life as quickly as Bessie had stamped down the hall. How must Lily feel? Turning that over in her mind, she decided she couldn't settle it for herself right now. She had a new job and she needed to focus on not making any mistakes with that.

ളെ

The next morning, Gracie awoke to the smell of bacon drifting up from the kitchen. She stuck her head out and realized her view was the parking lot, but no matter, the morning sky was gloriously clear. She was halfway done dressing when her new alarm clock clanged. Shutting it off, she dressed and hastened down to meet Mrs. Woods who explained that, as the newest housemaid, Gracie would be cleaning Rooms 62 through 73 and the four bathrooms in the west wing of the second sleeping floor.

"Gracie, these rooms are around the corner from your staff rooms. They are occupied by servants of the more well-to-do guests."

Feeling more centered now that she understood her duties, Gracie stepped into the staff lounge for breakfast. There were two long tables, one completely filled with younger people laughing and chatting, totally oblivious to her. She timidly went to the buffet and poured herself coffee, then filled her plate with scrambled eggs and a cinnamon bun. At the other table, Bessie was stuffing bacon into her mouth, jabbering to three men. Gracie recognized Dorothy, the lady from the car, but she was deep in conversation with a stern-looking woman in her forties. There was no sign of PT. The only empty seat was next to Isaiah, the chef, but he was bobbing his head emphatically while he talked to Olivia and another dark-skinned man at the end of the table. Gracie didn't want to bother them, so she sat down and ate alone.

A handsome man with pomaded black hair and a moustache yelled from the buffet. "What happened to that last cinnamon bun, Isaiah? It's been driving my smeller bonkers."

Gracie assumed she should apologize for taking it, but before she could work up her courage, Isaiah piped up, "Only one for each staffer, Otto. The main dining room gets the rest. I don't care if you are a crackerjack mechanic; you still only get one of my fabulous cinnamon buns."

She got a whiff of Ashes of Roses as she stuffed the last of her cinnamon bun into her mouth. She craned her head around to see Dorothy standing behind her.

"Good morning. Have you gotten yourself all together and ready for your first day?" Gracie nodded, trying to think of something nice to say when Dorothy patted her shoulder and said, "Well, I'm off to fill fifty cream pitchers."

People seemed to take that as a signal to get up. They carried their dishes to a wooden cart on wheels, scraped their plates clean into a trash can, and deposited their silverware into a big bowl of water. Gracie did the same and bumped into Bessie.

"No, don't dump it all into one. Food scraps go in this can and napkins in that one. Hey, name's Gracie, right? A little advice, girlie, make sure ya finish your stayin' guest's rooms before ten."

"Yes, Mrs. Woods explained how the cleaning schedule is different for guests who are staying and those checking out," Gracie said, trying to be civil to the freckle-faced spitfire. "But people don't check out until Saturday, right?"

Bessie rolled her eyes as if to say "What an idiot," stuffed Tutti Frutti gum into her mouth, and turned on her heel.

II

Zeke breezed around the driveway on Saturday, blue and white streamers flying from the handlebars of his bike. With one deft move he hopped off and stashed the bike under the back of the hotel porch. Smoothing his unruly black hair, he brushed off his maroon bellhop jacket. "Afternoon, Mrs. Woods. Here in lickety split time for 3 p.m. check in."

"Zeke, it appears that black cat followed you to work again. I don't want to see it inside. Mr. Woods finds it upsetting. Do you hear my words?"

"Yes, ma'am," he said, with a deferential nod. As soon as she was gone, he picked up Shadow, giving the cat a scratch between the ears and a gentle nudge. "Off with you, then. See you in the lounge." Shadow yawned, and set out down the lawn.

Gracie opened a window to shake out her feather duster. A young man with a head full of curly black locks grinned up at her.

"Hey there kiddo, Zeke's the name, bellhop's my game. Betcha you're new. Know where the staff hangs out?" She shook her head as dust balls floated down toward him.

He wagged his thumb. "Above the garage, behind the big house, after dinner. We jazz it up good on Saturday nights." Waving goodbye, he dashed into the big house with a straight back and an important air.

Well that was it. She would have to go if they were playing jazz. Maybe she could sing something.

Singing helped pass the time while Gracie cleaned, but she hated scouring the shared baths. Solvo, the toilet bowl cleaner that boasted eradicating all stains, stung her eyes until they watered. No matter. All the house maids probably had to put up with that. She flowed from singing hymns to some popular songs to keep herself company. Working alone was a relief because she didn't have to worry about coming up with something interesting to say. By the fourth day she found the cleaning fairly easy. The servants were probably so tired of doing for their bosses, Gracie assumed they kept their own quarters neat just for their own sanity. She eagerly checked the tip envelope in each room but was disappointed to find only five nickels when she dipped into her apron pocket at the end of the shift.

Peeling off her uniform and slipping into her comfy pink shrug, she dove into her book. "Taciturn, acquiesced." More words to motivate her to find the Crestmont library, which she had heard was well stocked with good literature. The more she read, the more she realized that Carrie had never intended to become an actress, but had gone to Chicago to improve her station in life by allowing men to take care of her. She had subsequently merely fallen into the acting profession. Gracie could see that Carrie was no role model for her.

Her own desire to be self-sufficient meant that she had not only to prove herself at work, but also needed to make friends.

Her "you should" button beeped repeatedly the more she thought about Zeke's offer to stop by the staff lounge. Nervousness clung to her like chains.

Oh, honestly, just go. You don't have to stay.

She munched on the apple she had taken from lunch and argued with herself that she could postpone her decision until after she was dressed. Considering the invitation was one thing. Actually going over to the staff lounge was quite a different matter.

She pulled the skirt and blouse out of her wardrobe and laid them on her bed, contemplating them. Finally, she tore off the pink shrug and dressed. Scrutinizing herself in the mirror, she lifted her right eyebrow and asked herself why she paid good money for a new bob she wasn't willing to show off. She tucked some blonde curls behind her right ear, liked that effect better, and headed down the back stairs. As she crossed the parking lot, she squinted back toward her room, wondering why she had never bothered to see where it was from the outside of the Crestmont.

"Staff Lounge" was burned into a wooden sign mounted next to an outside staircase on the wooded side of the garage. Gracie could see that this space gave the staff more privacy than if it was on the big house side of the structure. She relaxed a bit when she heard "Has Anybody Seen My Girl?" A tune she knew! She climbed the stairs.

Once inside, she was pleasantly surprised to see PT at the piano. He hadn't mentioned that he played. Zeke tipped his index finger in her direction in greeting, but he was the only one who seemed to notice her. An odd assortment of old boxes presumably used for chairs surrounded two tables for playing games. Dorothy sat alone at one, fiddling with the barrette at the nape of her neck as she frowned over a crossword puzzle. Electric fixtures on the walls brightened the room. Gracie wondered why the garage building had electricity when the upper floor rooms in the big house did not.

Bessie sat on a faded couch, her arms folded tightly across her chest and her ankles crossed on the scratched coffee table. Her left foot wagged crossly, the ankle bracelet catching the light from a dilapidated table lamp. Her lips were skewed in an angry pout and her cheeks were so brightly rouged that Gracie hardly recognized her.

Bessie squealed when a stocky boy with a wide chest and short legs sauntered into the room. "Jimmy boy!" She flew at him. "Where the Sam Hill have ya been? Ya left me up here all alone. Made me bait for some cad to play with, like PT here."

PT reddened, closed his eyes and dug his bony fingers deeper into the keys, immersing himself in ragtime.

"Well I'll be jiggered, Bessie," Jimmy said. "Mr. W made me mow the whole lakeside hill. I just scrubbed up a bit after for my best girl."

"Aw, sweetie, was it horrible?" He reeled when she jumped on him, winding her legs around his waist.

Shadow, the cat, appeared out of nowhere and pounced on top of the piano. Nestling down to enjoy the vibrations, it contentedly licked its paws. Dorothy slammed down her pencil and moved over to the piano.

"PT, I am just beside myself with this Scott Joplin nonsense. Why not play something we can sing?" He grinned and plunked out "That's My Baby."

Zeke fished around in his pockets and asked, "Otto, did you pinch my harmonica again?"

The cinnamon bun man from breakfast laughed. "You couldn't keep that harmonica in your pocket if it were wired shut, Zeke."

Gracie sang along, but felt out of place amongst them.

On Monday, she finally worked up the courage to find the library. Certain it was late enough that the guests would be in their rooms, Gracie grabbed her vocabulary word papers. She tiptoed down the back staircase, awash with murky shadows from the glow lamps, to the main floor. Glittering chandeliers lit the hallway as she passed the West Parlor and the smaller ladies' parlors. She hesitated a moment to admire the portraits Mrs. Woods had shown her on her first day. After she passed the Woods' offices, the hallway opened into the hotel's main lobby. Gracie stopped at the entrance, taking it all in. She had passed through this striking room with PT a week ago and hadn't noticed the open, magnificent space.

Huge windows were adorned with cream-colored cornices from which hung matching draperies held back with green tassels. The wallpaper was the color of budding spring leaves alternating with a thick glossy cream stripe. Small wooden tables, hugged by groups of wicker chairs cushioned in a floral pattern, were scattered about. In the center of the room was a magnificently carved chestnut table with a marble top, holding a stunning fresh flower arrangement. To the left, an impressive wooden staircase led up to the landing of the first sleeping floor. Double doors on her right led outside to the front lawn. The whole effect seemed to bring the outdoors in. A stone fireplace stood across the room from her. Old Tim ticked away guarding the east hall that led to the library.

Light from the immense lobby chandelier filtered into the library as Gracie passed through a large archway. Comfortable leather armchairs were grouped at the entrance with end tables and lamps that had been turned off. Shelves and shelves of books lined the walls and windows reached almost to the ceiling. A floor lamp with a lemon-colored shade patterned with amber leaves dimly lit the room. Thinking she was alone, Gracie jumped when she heard a squeak from one of the leather chairs.

Mrs. Woods peeked around the wing of the chair, startled. "Oh, Gracie, dear, it seems we both are up late. What brings you down here at ten-thirty at night? The night watchman will be around soon to turn out the lights."

"I need a dictionary, ma'am."

"Whatever for, Gracie?"

"I read my books before I go to bed. When I find words I don't know, I write them down so I can look up their definitions. I want to improve my vocabulary."

"What are you reading now?"

"*Sister Carrie*," Gracie announced proudly.

"Oh, that poor dear. As I recall, she went to Chicago to better herself and then wound up a lonely, selfish person."

"Oh, I don't know," breathed Gracie. "I haven't gotten that far yet."

"Well, I won't spoil it for you. I will tell you that running from home to be a famous actress wasn't exactly what Carrie expected. I'm impressed with your interest in reading. Please feel free to borrow anything you want from our library here. Just write your name on the card and put it in the lending box over on the desk. We also keep *Barron's* and *Time* magazines, although the guests tend to take them to their rooms and we lose track of them.

"I see your new uniform fits well. Olivia is a master seamstress. When you need the other one washed, you can visit the laundry house down the rear lawn just west of the garage."

Rising with effort she said, "Well, Mr. Woods will be waiting up for me. Sometimes I like to sit here and enjoy the quiet at night after the guests have retired." She ran a finger along the bookshelf behind her and pulled out a heavy book. "Here's the dictionary. You can sit here at my father's old desk to look up your words, if you like." Mrs. Woods lovingly placed her hand on an immense cherry roll top desk filled with cubbyholes and tiny drawers.

"Goodnight, Mrs. Woods. And, oh honestly, thank you for the offer to use the books."

"You're welcome, dear. It's nice to know we have someone on our staff so diligent about learning." With a tired smile, she started to leave the room, and then turned back. "Gracie, if you don't mind me asking, is your family pleased that you are with us this summer?"

"Yes, ma'am," Gracie stammered, ashamed at the bold-faced lie.

"Good. Tomorrow it will be just a week since you came. I hope we have made you feel at home." Checking her watch pin, she said, "I'd better get back to the Woodshed. Many tasks make for much fatigue. Goodnight."

"Goodnight, Mrs. Woods."

"Woodshed," that's what the Woods' cottage was called, Gracie mused, as she turned on the lamp. It was much more than a shed, Dorothy had told her, with three bedrooms, steam heat, and a coal-burning stove. They could live there all winter, enabling Mr. Woods to keep track of the Crestmont while he taught at Westlawn Academy for Boys.

She opened the dictionary and found "acquiesce." After writing down the definitions for all of her vocabulary words, she closed the heavy book and shut off the lamp. The full moon shone through the curtain casting a delicate pattern of lace on the wall. It illuminated a plaque on the desk:

William Warner

1853-1911

Creator of the Crestmont Dream

Gracie remembered the wistful expression on Mrs. Woods face when she had shown her father's portrait after the interview. It seemed like Mrs. Woods missed her father a lot. Gracie hardly ever thought about her parents. What was wrong with her? The only people she missed from home were Lily, George and Rev. Herbst. Telling Mrs. Woods her parents were pleased she was in Eagles Mere was a lie, but on the other hand, she wasn't sure they really cared where she was. Lily would care, though. And George, well, she didn't permit herself to think about him. Oh, but she just had, hadn't she? Folding her arms in front of her on the desk, she lay her head down and let the tears come. She had to write the letter.

♋

Feeling restless after her shift the next day, Gracie decided to brave the laundry. She grabbed her soiled uniform, not bothering to change out of the one she wore, and headed down the back hill toward a small white-washed building. The fresh smell of soap, hissing of ironing machines, and chatting of female voices greeted her. A lovely whitewashed porch with rocking chairs, railings and delicate filigree invited her to sit down. Smoothing her skirt, she sank wearily into a rocker. Even though she was lonely, Gracie found peace in being alone. She peered up at the big house, standing brown and majestic on the hill. Laughter from guests strolling on the lawn drifted down to her. She watched them enviously between the branches of the huge blue spruce tree next to the porch, noticing how at ease they seemed to be with each other.

"I see you survived your interview." PT startled Gracie when he clambered into the other rocker. He lit a cigarette, then flapped out his match.

"Oh, that was the easy part, I guess," Gracie sighed. "It's the fitting in that I'm not so good at. Most of the girls are much younger than I am, except Dorothy, of course. So far, she's the only friend I've made."

"You met Magdalena yet?"

"Who?"

He tipped his head back toward the small building attached. "Heads up the laundry. Army sergeant type. Don't let her catch you in that uniform when you are off shift. You'll get a scolding for dirtying it up." Gracie's right eyebrow shot up as she checked the laundry door.

He gave the stem of his pocket watch a couple of twists and checked the time. "Bowling alley opens in ten minutes. Some guests can't figure out their own scores. Mr. Woods counts on me to help with the tallying without them knowing."

"Oh, well, thanks for the company. This is the first real conversation with a staffer near my age I've had since I arrived. Oh, and I liked your piano playing. It was different than anything I've heard."

"Yup."

Gracie scrambled up the hill to the big house, sure he must have thought her incredibly stupid to have said such a thing.

III

"HEY, JIMMY, GREAT DAY FOR MISCHIEF, EH?" ZEKE SAID, RUBBING HIS hands together. "The best part is tonight's my first Saturday night off this summer. Heck, I even had to work the 4th of July."

Guests, eager to begin their Crestmont vacations, streamed through the lobby past the two bellhops. Amidst the flutter of activity, Zeke kept one eye out to see who might need assistance with their luggage while he coached Jimmy on the finer points of his new job.

Jimmy's chunky fingers fiddled uneasily with the gold buttons on his maroon bellhop uniform. Pushing his brows together he said, "Thanks for showin' me the ropes about bellhoppin', Zeke, but I'm thinkin' bein' a lawn boy was easier. At least when you get done cuttin' and prunin' you can clean up and you're done. I don't like what you're tellin' me about the guests callin' us bellhops anytime of the evenin'. That's gonna seriously cut into my love life."

"Oh, you and Bessie had something cooking tonight? Guess you couldn't tell Mr. W about that." Zeke laughed. "Well, you won't work every Saturday night. Anyhow, you'll get tips as a bellhop so you can buy Bessie some little trinket to keep her happy, then love her up the next week."

"Yeah, I was supposed to meet her down on the dock after dark. I know we ain't supposed to be up in that part of the second sleepin' floor, but maybe we could slip a note under her door. I know her room number. She's had enough of that singin' in the staff lounge stuff and is gonna hit the roof if I don't show up tonight." Jimmy shifted uncomfortably from one foot to the other.

"You can go up there, if you want, but I'm not getting myself fired."

"Damn, you never saw Bessie really mad, have you, Zeke?" Jimmy asked. "Oh, yeah, and Mr. W said somethin' about after I do check in for the big house that he'd give me the cottages to bellhop. They've got call bells in those, too. Can those guests call me any time of the night, too?"

"If you're the bellboy on duty, yessiree."

"Geez, I gotta tramp all over Crestmont campus, and for what? I hear they give the worst tips."

"You're all wet, Jimmy. The cottage guests are much nicer than the ones in the big house. But don't even try to top me at pleasing any guest. Even those Rude Regals love me," Zeke boasted. "They ring my bell and I appear at their door, towel over my arm, ice and lemonade or Bromo Seltzer on my tray. Last year I had to carry a hot pan of water to Mrs. Pennington so she could soak her feet. She gave me fifty cents and asked me not to tell her husband. She's what they call a hy-po-con-driak and I heard she carries her husband around with a ball and chain. Come on, let's get a wiggle on and I'll show you how to get great tips." Zeke hurried over to a couple surrounded by assorted luggage and two unruly children.

"Allow me to show you to your room, sir," offered Zeke, taking a suitcase out of the man's hand. Winking at Jimmy, Zeke adeptly placed one suitcase under his left arm, put another in his left hand and picked up the largest with his right hand. He made chit chat with the family that trailed after him and Jimmy took up the rear, carrying two hat boxes and a large stuffed rabbit.

Once upstairs, Zeke threw open the guest room door, set down the bags importantly, and cracked the window. "Wonderful view. Have you stayed with us before?" Opening and closing each faucet, he said, "Here is your hot and cold running water. May I help you in any other way, sir?" he said with finesse, flashing a crooked smile.

"Thank you, sir, mighty generous of you." Zeke's head bobbed as he accepted his tip. "Welcome to the Crestmont and we hope you enjoy your stay."

"See, Jimmy? Be all nicey-nice and give 'em a twenty dollar smile for an extra nickel tip. You'll make out great," Zeke said when they were back in the hallway out of earshot. "Another thing. Always say your 'ing's' at the ends of your words. Don't say 'lookin' and draggin'. Highly educated guests stay here at the Crestmont. They'll respect you more if you clean up how you talk. Now, did you see how I carried those bags perfectly evenly? Mind you, one suitcase is usually much heavier than the others because that's where they keep their bootleg. You get a better tip if you pretend they're all light as a feather."

"Whadya mean, their bootleg? People bring their own hooch?"

"Sure! They've got their own personal speakeasy in a boodle bag. Okay, let's get a move on down to the lobby and you do the next guest."

Bessie was on her knees on the landing, wiping up spilled tea. Mr. Woods stood uncomfortably by, holding a tray of broken tea cups, nodding and smiling to guests as they passed. "Please report to Mrs. Woods when you are done here, Bessie."

Mr. Woods pulled Zeke and Jimmy to the side. "Boys, what was that all about?" He demanded, clasping his hands behind his back.

"Nothing, sir," Zeke said. "I'm just showing Jimmy the ropes, like you asked me."

Mr. Woods opened his mouth to say something, gave an authoritative nod and turned on his heel. After he had descended the staircase, Bessie demanded, "What the Sam Hill are ya doin' in that uniform, Jimmy? Shouldn't ya be cuttin' grass or somethin?"

He flushed proudly, straightening his maroon cap. "Mr. W made me a bellhop this morning, Bessie." He leaned in and whispered in her ear. "I was tryin' to find you to tell you I gotta work, so I can't meetcha tonight, snookie."

"Slammin Jack, Jimmy!" Bessie pushed herself to her feet and whacked him with the damp cloth. Why didn't ya tell Mr. W ya had personal matters to attend to?"

"Well, look at you, being all tetchy, Bessie." Jimmy whipped the rag out of her hand and waved it back and forth in front of her nose. "I noticed you weren't tellin' him you had somethin' else to do when he had you wipin' up somethin'."

"I'm off, lovers." Zeke chirped, trying to steer clear of their squabbling. "You know the ropes now, Jimmy. Got a hot date with my harmonica and a sweet blue-eyed waitress. Thanks, buddy. Because of you, now I'll get every other Saturday night off."

෨෧

"I say, Margaret, how do we survive Saturday registration each week? I was showing Celeste Woodford to her room and that damned black cat ran in front of Mae, causing her to spill her tea tray. I want to know who owns that cat and why it is always in here," William Woods demanded, meticulously straightening the chairs in her office.

"I don't know, dear, but it is very friendly. Actually, most of our guests love it. Mrs. Pennington sits on the porch for hours with it curled up on her lap. Just shoo it outdoors if it bothers you."

"Well, that's the least of our worries. I overheard Zeke just now telling Jimmy how to help our guests sneak in their alcohol. He said something about not letting on that one suitcase was heavy with bottles." He rapped his knuckles on her desk. "I will allow neither local moonshine nor Canadian contraband in this establishment. We will not be party to breaking the Prohibition Act."

"Remember, dear, national prohibition states that it is a crime to sell alcoholic beverages. There is no ban on personal consumption. What do you propose we do, William, inspect the guests' bags as they check in for their stay?"

"If that is what is needed to maintain our standards, yes." William reddened.

Margaret rose. Gently placing her hand on his shoulder, she said evenly, "William, perhaps you feel it is your moral obligation to police the guests, but to inspect their luggage is illegal. The best we can do is to set an example by remaining liquor-free in our establishment in accordance with the law. If the guests want to have a cocktail in their rooms before dinner, I think we had best turn a blind eye."

"Your mother would be appalled, Margaret."

"And Father would have approved. The guests have a right to conduct themselves as they see fit as long as they are circumspect and respectful of others. I think we can no more ask them to check their liquor at the door than we can demand they attend church services or participate in water activities on the lake."

William's eyes flitted from desk to ceiling, floor and window. The cleft in his chin twitched as he pondered her point. Margaret waited calmly.

Finally, he wagged a playful finger. "No one can quarrel with those dark, knowing eyes of yours, my dear. Time for me to scout out the gentlemen's activities on the lawn."

"Good, I'll see to Miss Woodford. She brought a new music box this summer and I know she will want to show it to me."

ം൭

Mr. Woods made his daily stroll around the grounds to ensure that things were running smoothly. He slipped quietly into the two lane bowling alley. PT was tactfully advising the bowlers on their form. He had quite a knack in dealing with bowlers who liked to brag about the quality of their technique. Tightening his lips in a slight grin, PT gave his boss an imperceptible nod as he erased the slate scoreboard in preparation for a new game.

PT was the kind of employee William Woods could trust with responsibility and discretion. He was mature, polite, and a man of carefully chosen words. "PT must be twenty-eight by now," Woods pondered. "I wonder how many more summers we will have him? Soon he will surely find something full-time instead of dividing himself between the Crestmont in summer and Philadelphia in winter. As a reward for his loyalty to us, I must remember to have him play piano for one of our functions."

Continuing down the back lawn, he noticed the wood pile was low. Fires in the lobby and parlors provided not only warmth on cool evenings, but more importantly, ambiance. Masculine cries of "Got it!" and "A slam dunk!" greeted him as he paused at the shuffleboard courts.

He cheered when a round of applause indicated that a game was over. "Mr. Swett, you are a winner again."

They invited him to join them, but he waved them away with, "Would love to, but must keep my boys running this place efficiently. I'll see you tomorrow on the baseball field for sure. Gents, bring your families to our water games on Saturday morning. In my humble opinion, the Crestmont hosts the most exciting sailing races on Eagles Mere Lake."

He headed down to the garage and was annoyed to see Otto, white shirt and tie under his dark blue mechanics overalls, sitting on the hood of the Crestmont touring car, smoking a cigarette. Otto jumped down the minute he saw his boss and guiltily squished the butt under his heel.

"Afternoon, sir." His eyes struggled to meet his boss's.

"Good afternoon, Otto. I noticed the wood pile is very low. Instead of dithering away your time down here awaiting a repair, I suggest you find one of the lawn boys and get to chopping."

"I'll get right on that, sir."

"That's the ticket, Otto. There are times when you can be downright responsible. Come to my office on Monday. I have an idea for keeping the garage open year round for the general public. I'd like to discuss your role in that."

"Yes, sir." Otto tightened the buckles on his overall straps envisioning a brighter future for his mechanic skills.

It was Gracie's Sunday morning to work, but bad dreams woke her up before daylight. She lit the kerosene lamp next to her bed, put on her pink shrug, and decided to get the letter over with.

Sunday, July 3, 1925

Dear Lily,

I sincerely hope you are well and that you and George have found marriage pleasing. I was so proud to stand up for you at the wedding. I think of you often and miss you.

It must have seemed unbecoming of me to leave home with no explanation. I've wanted to write to you, but just couldn't until now. There was nothing for me in Bethlehem. I felt there was no way to better myself there, to try anything new. I saw myself doing laundry for the rest of my life and couldn't bear it.

Lily, I want to sing. Mother and Father would never understand that I had to get out. I want to try to get to a big city and see if I can do vaudeville, to be somebody people would know about and respect. I had to slip away quietly and not tell anyone, so they wouldn't come looking for me. In doing it that way, I know I hurt you and I'm sorry. Please forgive me.

Anyway, I'm working this summer at a wonderful resort inn and feel fulfilled. The job is hard, but I have oodles of new friends. As soon as I make enough money, I'll continue on to a big city. I'll write again. Sending my love, I remain

Your sister,
Grace

Well, she was trying to make new friends, so that wasn't a total lie; anyway, she did feel more at home at the Crestmont than she had at home. She neglected to send love to George or her parents, she realized, and she hadn't left an address for Lily to write back. No matter, maybe she would feel up to that next time.

⚜

Gracie clattered down the hall with her mop and bucket of cleaning supplies on Monday morning. She stopped short when she saw Mrs. Woods walking deliberately toward her.

"A moment of your time, please, Gracie."

Sure she had missed something in one of her rooms, she said, "I'm sorry, ma'am."

"Have you done something to be sorry for?"

"I'm trying to be thorough, Mrs. Woods, but sometimes I'm a little slow."

"On the contrary, you are thorough, and your pace is more than acceptable. That is why I am assigning you three more rooms. You will do 57, 58 and 59 in addition to your regular rooms."

"Excuse me for saying it, ma'am, but aren't those Bessie's rooms?"

"Bessie has been reassigned elsewhere. Begin there tomorrow, please."

Gracie dipped her head in acknowledgement, her green eyes seeing a pointy nose and freckles swimming in the floor boards.

"Good day, Gracie."

"Thank you, Mrs. Woods."

⚜

William Woods closed his office door and opened the bottom drawer of his desk. He fingered through several ties and pulled out the yellow one with navy diamonds. Whistling into the mirror on the back of the door, he replaced this morning's blue and gold striped tie with the preferred selection. He admired how it complimented his light blue seersucker suit. The drearier the day, the more yellow he wanted in his tie. He checked his pocket handkerchief in the mirror and aligned his cufflinks. Did he remember what guest had given them to him? A mystification to tackle another day.

He rocked on his heels and said, "Time for work, Woods."

His wife slipped through the open door. Two inches taller than he, she peered down and brushed a few wisps of his plentiful sandy, silky hair into place. "Afraid the sun will not poke through that gray, dear?" Margaret said, gently fingering his new tie.

"Good morning, Margaret. I was just selecting the hymns for Sunday's hymn sing and am considering doing a solo on 'Rock of Ages.' Do you recall us singing that last week? Celeste Woodford, the Penningtons and the Swetts are here for a month and I don't want undue repetition."

"If you would write down the hymns you select, William, you surely could recall what you have sung."

"Hm, I shall have to remember to do that. Margaret, my dear, you would have been proud of me this morning." His words erupted in crisp, staccato phrases. "Agnes Swett hurled me an insult. I dodged." Margaret's brown eyes widened with interest. "She was fussing. Remember we could not put her in Room 1— you know—with the private balcony she had last year? I shot her an explanation—off the top of my head, of course. We had purposefully put her in 34 at the west end of the hall so she could enjoy a superb view of the lake—she perked up at that—and dispense her vast knowledge of the Crestmont with guests that share the public balcony."

"Well done, William. You always handle Mrs. Swett with great aplomb." She applauded softly. "We must move to another topic, however." Margaret explained that Gracie, in cleaning servants' quarters as the newest housemaid, was receiving low tips, although she was a good worker. Bessie, on the other hand, was slackening her effort on the preferred front second floor rooms.

"I refuse to abrogate her of responsibility, so I reassigned her to cleaning the staff dining room and gave Gracie three of her guest rooms. Perhaps if Bessie has less tip money to spend on eyeliner and chewing gum, she will take her job more seriously. In the short term, I suspect, she will be angry enough to cause trouble. I would let her go, but I feel it is part of my job to teach my girls responsibility."

"And how will this affect the guests, Margaret?"

"The ones staying in 57, 58, and 59 will be happy for cleaner rooms, I suspect."

৽৾

Gracie raced to her room after her shift, quickly changed into her skirt and blouse and grabbed her dirty clothes to take to the laundry. She stole down the back steps checking to make sure Bessie wasn't around, and ran down the back lawn. Relieved to see Olivia and Isaiah on the laundry porch, she headed toward them.

"Hey, Gracie," said Isaiah. "Bessie was in the kitchen looking for you before I came down here to take my break."

"Oh, no. Please don't tell her where I am!" Gracie shot a nervous glance back toward the big house.

"Gotta run, Olivia, my love. My break's over and I've got twenty chickens to season and truss before they go in the oven. Tough life keeping the Crestmont table famous." He kissed her gently murmuring, "Tonight, sweet."

She smiled and her blush made her copper skin glow. Gracie envied the tenderness in Olivia's eyes as they followed Isaiah up the hill. Her friend turned and examined her with kind concern.

"What's wrong, Gracie? You're upset, I can tell."

"Mrs. Woods gave me some of Bessie's rooms and Bessie is going to be red in the tooth and claw mad at me. Oh, honestly, Olivia, she is one of the meanest people I ever met. She'll blame it all on me, you wait."

"She probably will. I'll bet she feels threatened because Mrs. Woods likes you."

"Well, if she catches me down here, she's likely to put me through the wringer of Magdalena's biggest washing machine."

"Gracie, I'm sewing a burnished rose charmeuse gown for Miss. Woodford for the Saturday night dance. Would you like to see it?"

"Yes, hide me, please." Gracie said as they made for Olivia's dressmaking room at the rear of the building.

When she left Olivia's shop, Gracie snuck back around to the front of the laundry, hoping to avoid Bessie. She was relieved to see PT lounging in a white rocker, his gangly legs crossed and propped up on the railing. His thin fingers raked his hair out of his eyes, and then stroked his brown mustache. Some of the lightest hairs caught the afternoon sun.

"So what's the scuttlebutt, Gracie? Bessie livening up your life any?"

"How did you know?"

"Just figured, you being new and all. That's what Bessie does. The more people she can make feel small, the happier she is."

"Oh," she sighed, slinking into a rocker. "Have you seen her? She's trying to find me."

"Yup. Just went into the big house."

"Good. I'm safe for awhile."

"So why did you leave home?" he asked abruptly.

Her right eyebrow shot up. "How did you know...?"

"Oh, I know the look. Catches me in the mirror sometimes when I shave. Besides, I carried your suitcase inside on that first day. Too light to have much more in it than the two books you told me you packed."

Flustered, she felt like a small child caught in a trespass. She stuck out her chin and blurted, "I'm only here for the summer and then it's off to a big city to be on the stage."

"On stage doing what?"

"I'm going to do vaudeville. I can sing, you know."

"Oh yeah, up there on the boards with the acrobats and trained seals. Hard to believe you want to go on tour and live out of a suitcase for ten weeks."

"Oh, what do you know about it, PT?" She was angry because he made her dream sound sordid.

"Not much, I guess." He snapped his suspenders and got up.

As he made his way up toward the bowling alley, she shouted, "Why did *you* leave home?" Horrified at her outburst, she clamped her hands over her mouth, ducked her head, and ran for the big house.

ೲ

Safe in her room that night, Gracie placed her writing tablet on her lap and turned to her list of things to work on. Organizing it a little, she added "Make New Friends" and wrote "Dorothy" underneath. Thinking how kind it was of Olivia to take Gracie back to her workshop to protect her from Bessie, she wrote "Olivia." She started to write PT's name but then erased it, deciding that two conversations did not a friendship make, especially since today's was a fiasco in her opinion.

Lifting her jewelry box off the dresser, she emptied it and counted her tips. Turning to the next page in her tablet, she examined the tally of her savings.

Total upon arrival = $6.00
June salary = $15.00
Tips as of June 30, 1925 = $2.25

She added "Tips as of July 12 = $2.75," biting the pencil while she added the total. Twenty-six dollars. She was pretty sure a new dress would be at least half that amount. She wanted to buy sheet music so she could learn some new songs before she went on the road. A stylish hat and gloves would cost her dear as well. Sighing, she wrote these down under "Need to buy". She set the latest tips aside to put in the hotel safe with the rest of her money. She had not permitted herself to buy anything since she had arrived at the Crestmont, but she would soon need toothpaste and soap. Mrs.

Woods had mentioned better tips when she revised Gracie's room assignment. She wondered if Mrs. Woods had any inkling about her financial predicament.

IV

GRACIE'S NEW ROOMS WERE A WHOLE NEW WORLD FOR HER. NOW SHE got to see what the high-end guest accommodations were like. The rooms were graced with two twin bedsteads of fine white enamel instead of a lonely twin mattress on a frame. The hardwood floors gleamed. Two windows were topped with a gold fabric valance with tasseled fringe. Venetian blinds kept the sun out. In addition to a bureau and wardrobe, each room had a desk which she was to keep stocked with Crestmont stationery. Next to the beds were electric call bells for the bellhop and a potted plant. Gracie regularly checked the transoms over the doors to make sure they opened and closed easily, then left them just slightly open for some air circulation. She was proud of herself for thinking of one little extra to please the guests, just like the Woods would want.

Room 58 was her favorite. It had a tiny enameled corner sink, a real clothes closet and a water closet tucked in next to it with a large siphon tank and long pull for flushing.

Checking the room again to make sure she had not missed anything, she noticed cobwebs behind the dresser. When she eased it away from the wall, a paper bag dropped to the floor. Fearing she had come upon something personal the guests wanted to hide, she hastened to put it back. She picked up the stained, yellowed bag and read "From Johnny, 1909." Sixteen years ago! Fascinated by her find, she quickly cleared out a space in her cleaning bucket, and put the paper bag under the can of Solvo. Satisfied that the room was done, Gracie happily pocketed the two quarters from the tip envelope. That was far more than she had made in a week in her other rooms.

After her shift, she took her copy of *Time* from her dresser and went back to where she hid her bucket in the cleaning supply closet. Slipping the paper bag carefully inside the magazine, she carried it back to her room. She threw her tips into her yellow jewelry box for safekeeping until she could stash them in the hotel safe.

Gingerly opening the paper bag, she pulled out several oddly assorted pieces of paper and spread them out on her bed. The writing seemed to be from the same hand—small and with funny curlicues. She picked up a paper entitled *But then, again* and read:

> I've fallen in love, again.
> > It seems like we met only—yesterday?
> We've loved and shared...
> We've loved and cared...
> > a lifetime. But then...
> We only met the other day!
>
> How could I have fallen in love again?
> > Our love spans so much time.
> We've grown and prospered...
> We've grown and fostered...
> > a loving life. But then...
> We only met the other day!
>
> Will I ever fall in love again?
> > I know we'll meet again, some special day.
> We'll fly away...
> We'll always stay
> > In love, I'm sure, but then...
> We only met the other day!

Struck by the poem, Gracie closed her eyes and let it fall onto her lap. Wondering what the next one might be about, she sifted carefully through several and chose one with "Limerick" scribbled in the top right hand corner.

Ticklish Rock

I once wooed a beauty so fine,
Whose lips were the color of wine.
    We walked through the wood
      To where Ticklish Rock stood.
I was consumed by her beauty divine.

Once in the precarious rock's shadow,
I behaved like a young boy so callow.
    I kissed her on the neck;
      'Twas but a mere peck.
I was a nervous, timid fellow.

The next time at the rock, however,
I seized on a bolder endeavor.
    We kissed by the rock
      And were joined in wedlock.
To live joyously, happily forever!

Gracie chuckled. Johnny, the mystery poet, had a sense of humor. Did he write the poems or copy them off and put them in the bag? Where was Ticklish Rock? The name gave her shivers. Who was Johnny? A guest? A staffer? Who hid the bag? How long had they known each other? Had they fallen in love during a whirlwind week's vacation or had their romance bloomed and deepened over many summers here?

She ripped off a piece of paper from her tablet and wrote down "limerick." When she stuffed it into her uniform pocket, her fingers touched a wad of other such papers, filed away to be dealt with later.

Dying with curiosity over the identity of the poet, Gracie wondered if she should ask around. Mrs. Woods might know who Johnny was, but Gracie didn't want to bother her. This treasure was her secret. She decided to put the poems back in the bag and save the rest for another day. Drawing out the pleasure might keep her in a happy mood longer. Besides, she felt like she had her own secret lover.

She put the bag in her drawer under her sweater. Then she removed it, wrapped the sweater around it, and laid them both back together.

$\wp\sim\varrho$

Bessie sashayed down the hall the next evening with a smug smile on her face that disappeared the minute she spied Gracie. Deciding the confrontation could not be put off any longer, Gracie moved her weight back on her right leg, crossed her arms over her chest, and waited.

"Stole my rooms, didya?" Bessie snarled.

"I didn't steal anything. Mrs. Woods assigned them to me," Gracie said coolly, fighting the hot flush that crept up her neck.

Bessie banged through the bathroom door in a huff. "I'll getcha for this, girlie."

Dizzy with triumph, Gracie walked as calmly as she could back to her room. Once inside, she dropped to the floor, leaned against the door and hugged herself. "I stood up to her!" Rising, she squared her shoulders and rewarded herself with another read through the Ticklish Rock Limerick.

$\wp\sim\varrho$

"Oh, Otto, I was nearly out of my mind without my car the first two weeks this summer. Why, Magdalena and I had to walk all the way downtown to go to church and the Sweet Shoppe. Then I looked back on myself and said, 'Time to pull yourself together, Dorothy, and do without some conveniences.'"

"Dorothy, the way you talk gets me every time," chuckled Otto. "Let's hope the next time your car gives you trouble I'll be around to fix it for you." He grinned when Gracie walked in. "Hey there, blondie, how are you tonight?"

"Well, the staff is piling in," Dorothy said hurriedly, offering her seat to Gracie. "Isaiah and Samuel prepared a delicious stew and biscuits for tonight. I'll put a fire under them to bring us some."

Gracie sat down across from Otto, barely met his eyes, and asked, "So, um, how is the garage business?"

ം≥ഉ

It was Gracie's turn to wipe down the tables after the staff cleared their dishes. Dorothy stayed behind and asked, "Well, how did it go, dear?"

"How did what go?"

"You and Otto. I left on purpose so you could talk. I believe he likes you. He would make a nice man for you to go around with."

"Oh." Gracie's cheeks tingled. "I don't know if I am ready for that."

"Of course you're not ready. You haven't bought that dress you've been talking about yet. I'm motoring into Wilkes-Barre next Thursday to attend to some personal business. That's your day off, isn't it?" Gracie nodded. "I would be happy for your company and could show you some nice consignment shops where you could buy a pretty dress at an affordable price."

"Dorothy, it sounds wonderful. Thank you."

"You'll need something special to wear for the staff talent show anyway."

"Talent show?"

"Oh, me, it's the most popular concert of the season. All us staffers get together and strut our stuff for the guests. I'm beside myself at some of the antics. Maybe you could sing a song. I've heard you in the lounge. You have a nice voice."

Gracie beamed at the compliment. She hustled to her room, estimating the tips she could make in the next two weeks so she could add them to her current tally.

Later that night, her head was buried in the women's section of the Sears Catalogue doing research on fashionable dresses when Mrs. Woods walked into the library.

"Gracie, I am glad I found you. How are you enjoying your new rooms?"

"Oh, honestly, I love them, Mrs. Woods. I appreciate the new assignment. The tips are much better."

"Good, I was hoping that would be so. I have had good reports about your work. Tell me, has Bessie mentioned anything untoward about the reassignment?"

"Oh, she might have been a bit upset, but I handled it." Gracie shrugged nonchalantly. Mrs. Woods gave her a knowing smile and disappeared into the hallway.

৩৵৶

"I like a touch of rouge high up on my cheeks, then I dust powder all over my face to take away the shine. For special occasions, I put on a bit of lipstick," Dorothy explained as they motored toward Wilkes-Barre Thursday morning.

"I like your makeup, Dorothy," said Gracie, tightly clutching her purse with the dress money in it, "but Bessie puts so much on it seems fake."

"That's because she uses makeup to excess."

"That's for certain. I mean, about makeup and other things. She's been at me ever since I came to the Crestmont."

"Now you listen to me, Gracie. Don't let her bother you. Please forgive me, Lord, for saying it, but Bessie is an imperious little so-and-so. Pay her no mind and keep your distance, my dear."

Fishing around in her purse she said, "Dorothy, do you have a piece of paper?"

"Whatever for?"

"I need to write down 'imperious' so I can check the definition later."

"It means Bessie deems herself so high and mighty you are better off ignoring her. How are you doing with making friends?"

"Well, Olivia and I get along well, and this was so nice of you to ask me to come along on this trip."

"I mean men, Gracie. You're twenty-two, aren't you? It's time for you to find someone to go around with. What about Otto? He's only a couple of years older than you and very attractive if you ask this old lady."

"Well, he is nice to me."

"Then there's PT. Of course, you might think he is a bit old for you, but he is a man of quality. Certainly not a man of many words," she chuckled, "but he has a good heart. I've tried to get to know him, but he doesn't talk much about his home life. Did you know he studied piano seriously in Philadelphia?"

"No, he mostly asks me questions and doesn't tell me much about himself."

Dorothy dropped her off in front of a store called Minnie's. "Minnie is a little snippy, but you can get good quality at a bargain price in there. See that lunch shop next door? I'll go do my banking and meet you in there in about an hour, then we can catch up with ourselves and eat. Their toasted sandwiches are divine."

The dress Gracie spotted was of a navy rayon fabric that swished when she walked. It sported a narrow v-neck with green ties that could be knotted or left open, and a matching green braid enhancing the dropped waist. Styled in the new boyish tubular fashion, it was three inches shorter than what Mother would have approved of.

I'll have to make up a name for this beauty.

"You do have better shoes to go with that, I hope." Minnie said.

Gracie held in her reaction, fixed her eyes on Minnie, and countered, "Do you have some St. Louis heels in stock? I don't see anything interesting here in your display."

Pursing her lips, the woman raised her index finger, walked to the back of the store, and produced two styles of the precious heels that were all the rage. Gracie chose the taller of the two styles, the three-inchers that narrowed to the size of a dime at the bottom, with a smart strap and a gold buckle. Although used, they were in good condition and a perfect match to the navy of the dress. She envisioned the next performance dress she would buy—a flowing creamy-colored fabric with navy trim to match the lucky St. Louis heels. She would call it her buttercream swish and maybe throw in some navy fishnet stockings for pizzazz.

ço❧

"Oh, honestly, Dorothy, it was great!" Gracie gushed as the waitress brought them menus. "I talked her down on the price of the dress so I could buy snazzy shoes, too. You were brilliant to send me to a consignment shop. I could never have afforded to buy new."

Dorothy plopped her ample behind into the chair and fanned herself with the menu. "Many well-to-do women wear a dress to one or two functions and then toss it aside, simply because they don't want to be seen in it again. It allows those of us with a flair for fashion and frugality an opportunity to be stylish."

Gracie peeked inside her shopping bag and announced, "I'll name it the green braid slink."

"What are you talking about?"

"Oh, you'll think I'm silly, but I give my clothes names. Then they are like my friends."

"I see. Well, that certainly is a unique concept, dear."

After examining the menu, Gracie settled for a bowl of chicken soup because the toasted sandwiches cost dear.

When the waitress brought them their food, Dorothy said, "You've never said a word about your family. Tell me about them."

"Oh, there's not much to say. I have a sister, Lily." She hesitated and then changed the subject. "Dorothy, I found something written about Ticklish Rock. Do you know where it is?"

"All right, we'll talk about Ticklish Rock then. Gracie, I was married for twenty years and have been a widow for eight. Now, what would I know about a place like Ticklish Rock? I heard it's a funny shaped rock further west from Eagles Mere in the Allegheny Mountains where lovers like to go. Planning to go there with someone I don't know about?" Dorothy probed.

"There's no one to go there with."

"Well, you just wait. A pretty girl like you will certainly find opportunities to wear that—what did you call it—'green braid dress'?"

"*Slink*, green braid slink." Gracie bit her lower lip and gave Dorothy a sly smile. "Now, maybe you could show me where I can buy cosmetics."

Gracie was dying to see Eagles Mere Lake up close as long as she didn't have to go in the water. She remembered how beautiful the lake looked when Mrs. Woods had pointed it out on her first night here. Tonight seemed the perfect time. The guests were still lingering with the Woods after dinner, and the staff that wasn't cleaning up the kitchen congregated in their hangout above the garage. Some private time was a pretty safe bet, so Gracie escaped onto the front porch to cool off. Even the mountain breeze couldn't remove the late July stickiness from the air.

The water below swirled with pink, cobalt and green, enticing her down the porch steps toward the lake. Gracie stopped short when she saw Isaiah and Olivia on the dock. He lovingly removed his wife's shoes. Then Olivia removed her garters and pushed down her stockings, allowing him to pull them the rest of the way off. Daintily dipping her tiny feet into the water, she nestled into his chest, talking softly.

Gracie visualized herself with George, taking a respite at the water's edge, and then scolded herself for allowing him into her fantasies. She yearned for her own man and her own serene lake time. Not wanting to disturb Olivia and Isaiah's togetherness, she retreated quietly back up the steps and went to her room. Maybe if she came back at dawn she would have time alone.

Feeling lonely, she gently pulled out the collection of poems written by Johnny, the man she fondly called the "Paperbag Poet." This evening's poem read:

I long for the gentle caress of your hand;
In your touch, I find peace.

I await the soft touch of your lips;
In your smile, I find happiness.

I yearn for the music of your voice;
In your laughter, I find joy.

God blesses me with your love;
In your faith, I find strength.

I would hold your heart in my hands;
But I am not strong enough.

But in your hands, my Love,
my heart is secure.

It took her breath away. That's what Olivia and Isaiah had and what she desperately wanted. She was tired of feeling dead inside.

ॐ✦

In addition to Thursday, Gracie had every other Sunday morning off so she could go to church. She really missed church. Gracie didn't want to forget God, but more importantly, she didn't want God to forget her. Because the service at the Crestmont Inn was so well attended by the guests, the Woods encouraged staffers to find a church in the town of Eagles Mere. Dorothy and Magdalena attended the Episcopal Church. Dorothy had invited her to join them, but Gracie made it a point to steer clear of Magdalena's stern, domineering nature.

Curious to see how she would feel about the Presbyterian Church, she set out to go. Her apprehension over venturing into the town had kept her away up to now. She felt guilty about that. She headed down the hill to the entrance of the Crestmont drive and was delighted to see the black cat. Shadow seemed to be waiting for her. The cat led her through the big pillars and then guided her down the road toward the center of town.

Two sweethearts, fingers intertwined, stood on the side of the road, gazing in mutual admiration at the footbridge near the bottom of the lake. Gracie averted her eyes, fastening them on Shadow, who padded steadily along.

No sooner had they turned onto Eagles Mere Avenue, when a large black poodle bounded over, prancing in excited circles around Gracie.

"Annie, bad dog, get back here!" A young man with dark hair scrambled after the dog, shot Gracie an apologetic glance, and playfully patted the dog's rump until she went back across the street. His mother, father and younger brother waved to Gracie without missing a step in their brisk walk. The older boy attached a leash to the dog and hurried to catch up to his family.

Gracie approached three men striding abreast in front of her. They parted when Shadow slinked between them. One tapped his walking stick on the ground in annoyance at the cat. The other two tipped the brim of their hats in friendly greeting to Gracie as she passed them.

She came upon a huge white house with a widow's walk and a wrap-around porch on the lake side of the street. Gaping at it, she estimated it to be twice the size of her home in Bethlehem. Olivia had described these stately cottages, where people spent their summers up here on the mountain.

A family gathered on the porch. The children giggled in their Sunday finest and squirmed as their mother tried to smooth the wrinkles out of their clothing. Giving them a little push toward the street, she led them up toward the churches. Their father took up the rear admonishing them not to get their shoes dirty.

The bustle on the street began to subside when Gracie passed the tiny post office and general store on the left. The cat turned right onto Pennsylvania Avenue, so she followed. Organ music came from the tiny stone church and to her horror she realized she was late for the service. Shadow sat down in front of the white daisies that almost covered the front stained glass window, and then scampered off across the street, disappearing behind the Edgemere Hotel.

Putting on her aloof face, Gracie mounted the steps, and slid into a back pew as the congregation finished the opening hymn. She hoped she could slip out quickly after the service before she had to talk to anyone.

V

MY, HOW HER LIFE HAD IMPROVED. OTTO WAS GOING TO TAKE HER TO meet his brother and sister-in-law who were in town for a stay at the Raymond Hotel. He was handsome when he cleaned up, but Gracie wished he could get the grease out from under his nails. She knew Mother would disapprove of him. No matter. At least he was older than she was, and self-assured. He was proud of being a crackerjack mechanic and often dominated the conversation. That suited Gracie just fine because it took her a while to think up the right thing to say.

Otto had cornered her at an ice cream slurp two weeks ago. The staff met on the back porch Wednesday evenings after the guests had eaten all the ice cream they could manage. Staffers were permitted to polish off what was left in the ice cream makers. Because they were financially responsible for their silverware, the waitresses always carefully locked up their stations, making spoons scarce. The staff improvised by using the small vegetable bowls as both container and utensil. PT had whittled himself a wooden spoon and a few staff members brought cheap spoons they normally kept in their rooms. The method for most, however, was to dip your bowl and slurp, then tip the bowl to drink the melted cream from the bottom. Shadow happily cleaned up what was left. Gracie volunteered that night to do the washing and restacking of the bowls.

Otto sidled up to her with a grin, twirling his black moustache. "They should pay you extra for this, blondie. How about a canoe ride sometime?"

"No thanks, I don't really like the water," Gracie stammered.

Undeterred, he managed to take her for ice cream at the Sweet Shoppe, hold her hand on the Laurel Path, and kiss her goodnight before lights out. Gracie finally had a man of her own to impress.

She was going to wear the green braid slink she had bought at the consignment shop. It took three hours for her to bathe, iron the dress, and tame her curly hair. She applied her new rouge and powder just like Dorothy had taught her, and added a touch of lipstick to be daring. Finally, she threw her pink shrug on the bed and transformed herself into a lady of style. A cloud of confidence enfolded her when she slipped the soft dress over her head. Safely buckled into her St. Louis heels, she did a few practice walks around her room and declared herself family-meeting material.

Meticulously pulling on the white gloves she had borrowed from Olivia, Gracie proudly floated down the center staircase of the big house as graceful as any guest. She crossed the lobby and waited at the screen door, trying not to bite her lips. When she saw the Model T Ford pull up out front, she took a deep breath, pushed open the screen door, and passed quickly through the cloud of stogie smoke on the porch. Otto jumped out of the car to greet her. Just as he offered her his arm, one of her heels caught between the boards of the step. Gracie landed hard on the lawn flat on her stomach. Scrambling to get up, she lost her balance for the want of her lost heel and tumbled down again. Otto helped her up. While he retrieved the broken heel, she brushed off grass and shame. He chuckled to his brother, "I told you she was a knockout."

Mortified, she graciously declined his offer to wait while she changed. She had nothing else to wear anyway. More concerned about where the dry cleaning money would come from to redeem the green braid slink, she allowed Otto to fade into a distant memory.

VI

MARGARET WOODS STEPPED OFF THE FRONT STEPS OF THE CRESTMONT, savoring a few quiet moments as she watched the lake sport with the late afternoon sun. The guests were indulging in either afternoon tea on the porch or clandestine cocktails in their rooms. Smiling, answering questions, solving problems and making small talk—all these obligations vanished during her hour of respite. Precious time alone was hers to roam the gardens she and her father had so lovingly planted. Flower picking was the first job he had given her when he built the Crestmont Inn. Because they had shared this gathering time together, Margaret often felt his presence, as strong as it had been before his death fourteen years ago.

Shadow, the cat that so annoyed William, sniffed its way through the herb garden as Margaret followed. They entered the colorful terraced beds that spilled over the hillside, bordered by picnic tables down near the water. Purple Echinacea petals surrounding golden centers, creamy daisies and the scent of sweet lavender helped center her. A hummingbird hovered over the border of red lobelia.

Margaret saw a flutter out of the corner of her eye. A familiar dark gray butterfly with iridescent blue markings on its wings swooped and dove, making continuous circles around her. It darted playfully away. Instinct told her to wait patiently until it fluttered back to her.

"Hello, Daddy," she sighed. "I still miss you." The butterfly alighted momentarily on the watch pin on her blouse. She remembered the touch of her father's hand so many years ago as he tucked a flower behind her ear and smoothed her hair. Checking the time, she saw that it was 4:40 p.m.

Shadow rubbed against her leg and then scampered off, swatting at a teasing chickadee. Margaret put her basket down, got out her shears, and began cutting huge yellow rosebuds, just open and perfect for picking. Drinking in the fragrances that always lifted her spirits, she added daisies and pink larkspur to her basket for contrast. Reluctant to leave her time of replenishment, she searched for the butterfly. It returned to make one more circle around her, then vanished. "Time to get back to work, right, Daddy?" She fingered her watch pin lightly.

Rising, she straightened her skirt, tucked in her white lace blouse and prepared to return to the big house to arrange the bouquets. She would be done just in time to hostess dinner. A quick addition of a dress jacket and scarf would complete her evening attire. Tonight's concert would be played by the Dolce Violin Trio from New York City. Anticipating the unusually high attendance the concert would draw; Margaret wanted to instruct Zeke as to how to set up the chairs. Then there was the music box Celeste Woodford had placed in the West Parlor for all to enjoy during her stay. As a thank you, Margaret wanted to have it playing while the guests took their seats.

Monday's staff meeting went smoothly. William and Margaret Woods met with Sid Fox, the steward; Dorothy, head waitress; Magdalena, who ran the laundry; chefs Isaiah and Samuel; Zeke and PT. Mr. Woods commended Sam, the new assistant chef, for his well received Baked Alaska. Young Zeke, the new head bellhop, sat wide-eyed and uncharacteristically solemn. The need for an assistant for Mr. Woods for water activities was discussed and tabled. They reviewed the schedule for the upcoming week and hammered out details about Friday's concert. PT reported on the progress of the staff talent show scheduled for the end of August.

The last people to leave were Isaiah and Sid Fox, who reviewed the weekly acquisitions list, based on Margaret's menu revisions.

"We are fortunate to have such a dedicated group of people, Margaret," stated William, "but we definitely need to augment our staff for next year. Sid is up to his ears keeping the place supplied and manicured. I need more time to put into water activities and I just don't know what day to carve it out of."

"More staff means more paychecks," Margaret reminded him. "Dorothy has impressed upon me the need for more waitresses, but at least those positions are funded largely by tips. William, there is something else on my mind. I would like to discuss Gracie."

"She's a go-getter for sure. Hard working and respectful. I like that."

"As do I. She is responsible and determined to please. I have received a request from the daughter of an elderly Eagles Mere resident who needs a companion. In my opinion, Gracie would be perfect. She would be needed on Thursday, her day off. I'll ask her if she feels this is too much for her."

"She will probably want to discuss it with her family first."

"I doubt it, William," Margaret sighed. "I have watched closely and see no evidence of Gracie communicating with her family. She is evasive when I inquire and never otherwise mentions them. I don't know what the problem is, but I feel it is our responsibility to nurture her and give her opportunities to grow."

"Well, if I had a daughter like Gracie I would encourage her."

"My point exactly. The Crestmont is as close to family as Gracie has, so that makes it our responsibility. I will talk with her about this opportunity tonight."

Taking a deep breath for courage, Gracie knocked. Mrs. Woods ushered her into the office with an encouraging smile. A tall, severe-looking woman impatiently paced the floor. She turned suddenly as Gracie entered, dubiously flicking her eyes from

Gracie's uniform to her face. The woman's short hair was combed close about her face in the new boyish manner and a single curl lay starkly on her right cheek.

"Gracie, I'd like you to meet Miss Madeleine Cunningham. She would like to interview you concerning care for her mother," Mrs. Woods said.

"Pleased to meet you, ma'am." Gracie smiled as they sat down.

Smoothing the burgundy silk skirt of her dress gracefully under her, Madeleine Cunningham pressed her back into the chair with an authoritative air. Gracie admired the stylish low draped bodice and loose cap sleeves of her dress.

"My mother needs a companion one day a week. I can't possibly care for her needs every day as I need a day to attend to my own affairs. I understand you have Thursdays available."

"Yes, I do," Gracie offered, eager to supplement her income.

"She will require lunch, tea, and supper. You do cook, don't you?"

Gracie shot an anxious glance at Mrs. Woods who nodded and pressed her lips together in a reassuring smile.

"Yes, ma'am."

"Good. My mother is legally blind and will need you to guide her about. She enjoys being read to and will keep you occupied with her chatter. I'll fix her breakfast and will expect you by nine in the morning. The salary will be two dollars for the day. You appear to be responsible and come highly recommended by Mrs. Woods. Do you accept the position?"

"Yes, thank you, Miss Cunningham," Gracie said, extending her hand. Embarrassed, she dropped it. Madeleine Cunningham had already risen and turned to shake Mrs. Woods' hand.

"Thank you for your assistance. Please give her the details."

"Indeed. I am confident Gracie will be a responsible and caring companion for your mother."

"May I have a light?" Madeleine Cunningham asked as she pulled a cigarette and ladies' holder from her purse.

"I'm sorry, no. Perhaps one of the gentlemen outside can help you. Let me show you out. Gracie, please wait here for me." Sure she had fumbled something in the interview, she wiped her perspiring hands on her apron and anxiously waited for Mrs. Woods to return.

"Come with me," Mrs. Woods crooked a finger for Gracie to follow. "We're going to the kitchen. I'll have Isaiah get you started on something simple like a roast, and then perhaps you can practice some other dishes from a cookbook. Remember, if you can read, you can cook." Gracie had to quick step to keep up with Mrs. Woods' brisk walk down the hall.

Later that morning Peg told her mother about Old Tim. "Eleanor and I were just playing a little in the lobby after breakfast. I didn't let her run around. There weren't many guests nearby because they had gone down to the lake to watch the canoe races. Honest, Mama, I'm sure we never bothered anyone."

"Peg, darling, you are rambling. Get to the point."

"Well, it's Old Tim. He stopped."

"Stopped? That clock hasn't stopped since my father had it shipped from Germany twenty years ago."

"Come see, Mama. He's stopped for sure."

Margaret walked to the lobby with her arm around her elder daughter. They studied the pendulum on the grandfather clock, hanging silent and motionless.

"Indeed, it seems Old Tim did stop, Peg. At twenty till five. It must have been early this morning, because I am sure I would have noticed this before dinner last night. Thank you, dear. Now, find Eleanor, and the two of you tell Isaiah I said you deserve some of those oatmeal cookies he is baking."

"Thanks, Mama." Peg called over her shoulder as she bounded out the door to find her sister.

Margaret stared at the clock. For some reason, the position of the hour hand on the four and the minute hand on the eight mystified her. Was that the time the butterfly came to her? Margaret suddenly remembered her father's whispering just before he died.

She was so numb about that time; it was hard to recall what he said. She closed her eyes and strained to remember. She could see his top teeth struggling over his bottom lip. Yes, she supposed, it was possible he was saying 440. But, why?

Eleanor Woods skipped into the huge kitchen, knocking over three empty pots, which clattered from the prep table to the floor. "Mama says you have oatmeal cookies for Peg and me," she announced. Her eyes widened in anticipation, stretching the tiny strawberry beauty mark embedded in her right eyebrow.

"Whoa, there, girl!" Isaiah boomed, swooping her up into his arms. "No jump rope in my kitchen. You could've gotten a bad burn if there had been something in those pots."

"Oh, Eleanor, what have you done now?" Peg picked up the pots and returned them to the huge wooden table.

"Now, Isaiah, don't you be like Peg and spoil my fun." Eleanor frowned and poked his stomach through his stained apron. "Hi, Gracie. What are you doing in here? I heard Mama gave you a bunch of new rooms. Are you chef's assistant now too?" She watched as Gracie clumsily hacked a knife through some parsley.

Isaiah gently lifted Eleanor up to sit on the prep table and said, "If you're quiet, maybe I'll give you some bare naked bread."

"Bare naked bread? I'm going to tell Mama you are saying improper things, as Papa would say," Eleanor declared with as much authority in her voice as a nine-year-old could muster.

"It's not improper, silly," her older sister chided. "It just means Isaiah doesn't like any butter on his bread."

"You said it, Peg, my dear. You are wise beyond your fifteen years. Watch the magic, ladies." Isaiah kept an eye on his audience as he pulled four large loaves out of the oven with a flourish. "Bare naked bread. A superior alternative to cookies." He flipped one loaf out of the pan and started slicing. Aromas of oatmeal, yeast and salt hit their noses.

"Here, Peg, run this piece over to Gracie and let her have a taste of heaven." Peg shook her head no in a "don't do it" warning as Gracie reached for the butter. "I am offended you might even think to cover up the taste of my oatmeal bread with butter," Isaiah criticized. "None of that malarkey, girl."

Eleanor took one bite out of her slice and set it down on the table. "Well, if there are no cookies, I'm off to find Dora for a game of marbles. Tell Mama I'll be back in time for dinner, Peg." Eleanor said.

"Okay, but less noise, Eleanor," Peg warned. Turning to Gracie she said, "Getting cooking lessons? Isaiah's a great teacher. He taught me how to mix the ice cream for the Wednesday picnics."

"Gracie, you're holding that knife like it's your worst enemy. Courage, young woman; a utensil is your servant." Isaiah closed his huge hand over hers and worked the knife expertly up and down through the parsley until Gracie's head started to spin.

"Okay, now drain those potatoes and put them gently back into the pot."

"But you said they went into the serving bowl." Exasperated, Gracie pushed some wet curls off her face.

"Later. If we put them back in the pot now, we'll keep them hot and evaporate any excess water. Nothing should come between those pretty potatoes and this butter. Nope," he said, spreading her fingers so she dropped the stick of butter on a plate next to the potato pot. "Don't dump it in one piece. You have to cut it into pieces so it melts evenly. Now sprinkle the parsley all over. No, not in one place. All over. Good. Now take your spoon and stir the potatoes to coat them with the butter and parsley. When you're ready, turn them gently out into the serving bowl and behold! You have a feast for the eye as well has the palate."

"Uh, huh." Gracie wiped her forehead with her apron and lifted the pot.

"You have to sing your love into each dish, Gracie. Makes it taste better." Isaiah's voice boomed out "If You Were the Only Girl in the World" as he stirred an immense pot. "Know the words to this one? Come on, sing along."

Trying to comply, Gracie sang "and I were the only boy..."
She held out the last note and gingerly turned the parsley potatoes
out into the serving bowl. She stopped promptly when Olivia
pushed through the swinging doors.

"Pudding." announced Olivia. She stepped up to the stove,
reaching on tiptoe to kiss Isaiah.

"What?" Gracie asked.

"He always sings that song when he makes pudding. I keep
telling him to switch it to a girl's name, but he says that would be
violating the lyricist's wishes. When he makes soup it's "I'm Just
Wild About Harry.""

"And 'Annie Laurie' when he makes his fancy French
cassoulet," Peg finished. "Have fun, grownups. I'm off for a swim."
She disappeared through the staff dining room door.

"Gracie here has a new job cooking for some woman in Eagles
Mere, so she's taking lessons," Isaiah told Olivia proudly.

"He's been real patient with me, Olivia," Gracie noted. "How
did you learn to cook so well, anyway, Isaiah?"

"Ahem," he cleared his throat, "the question should be 'how
did you become a master chef?' please."

"Okay, tell me how you became a master chef and such a
good singer," said Gracie, propping herself up on a stool.

"The singing part came from my granddaddy who was a slave
in Virginia. After he got freed, he taught my daddy how to be a
sharecropper, singing the whole time he was working that soil.
While I was playing in the field, I'd learn every song and sing
along with him. After he died, I farmed some with my daddy, but
it just wasn't for me. He said fine with him if I didn't want to
enjoy the calling God gave us, so he put my stuff on the front
lawn and locked the door. Well, I left without being able to say
goodbye to my mama and wound up in Philadelphia. I was walking
the back alleys and heard someone singing inside a restaurant
kitchen, so I knocked on the back door and asked for a job. The
owner said well maybe I could wash dishes, which I did, but I
didn't sing because the chef wanted to hear his own singing. The

line cook—you know, the guy who prepares the food so the chef can cook it—got sick; so they promoted me. Well, I guess that chef got mad because I learned too fast for him and he went and told the owner to get rid of me. So the owner, Joe Swanson was his name, liked me a lot, but he didn't want to make his chef mad. So he called a friend of his who had a really swanky restaurant called 'The Franklin Stove' in the historic district. That chef was French, Louis Dressout was his name and not a bit intimidated by a Negro who knew food, so he made me his apprentice. I had no money, so the owner got me a job cooking lunches in the city schools until he assumed I knew enough to make a decent salary. I spent my mornings singing my love into the children's lunches and then spent the rest of the day learning under a master chef."

"Excuse me, husband. You omitted the part about me fitting into this busy life of yours," chided Olivia, enjoying the story he had so often told.

"Well, this beautiful lady," he said twirling her around in a dance step, "waltzed into the cafeteria one day for lunch because she was sewing costumes for the kids' school play and my heart got stolen. That whole summer we went to all these concerts they had in the park where I learned a kit and caboodle of new songs and found the courage to propose marriage."

"And I said yes to this big lovable man," Olivia chimed in. "Now get back to your cooking, you two. That bread smells heavenly, Isaiah."

"How did you come to the Crestmont, Isaiah?" asked Gracie, waiting for another good tale.

"I started in 1923. Answered an ad in the paper. Olivia's mother had died and I wanted her to have a change of scenery. Besides, we had spent the summer before that on Coney Island. They had just built this swanky recreation center right on the boardwalk and there was a restaurant hiring summer help. Olivia really liked being near the water. Well, I figured if the ocean made her happy, maybe a lake would too. So we came here. Now I cook for Temple University during the school year and we come here for the summer. I am happy to say people like my cooking so much they keep coming back and bring their friends. This year we have so many guests the Woods had to hire an assistant cook."

"I remember seeing that advertisement in the paper. So that's how Sam came to be a staffer," Gracie observed.

"Yup, Sam's good. But it's my kitchen and don't let anyone tell you any different."

❧

After hurrying to finish her rooms for incoming guests, Gracie lay exhausted on her bed. It was stifling with the window closed, and with it open the exhaust from the incessant line of cars parking out back made her sick. Saturday afternoons the guests were busy checking in, so it was a good time to take a swim. If she could afford a bathing suit, she might have dipped into the lake to cool off and get some fresh air. But then again, she didn't know how to swim.

All the things she needed to digest clunked about in her brain. Thursday would be her first day with Mrs. Cunningham. She suspected she had the roast and the potatoes down, but cutting the parsley really worried her. Mrs. Woods had assumed cooking would be easy for Gracie to master, but instead it nearly sapped her resolve to take the extra job.

Then there was her future. In three weeks she would have to leave the Crestmont unless she opted to stay for another two to help close up for the season. She had permitted too much time to elapse without firming up plans to get to a big city and start auditioning.

She needed to assess her money situation. The extra money for making it through the season plus a bonus for staying to close up would help, but it wouldn't be enough to relocate. Bus fare, clothes, meals, deposit on a room when she got to her destination, a cushion till she got a job...were all needed. Everything weighed so heavily on her that she couldn't focus on any one problem to solve.

Taking out her tablet in an attempt to center herself, she examined her "Friends" list. She gladly added Isaiah's name, but not Otto, because technically he was in a different category. She wanted to add Eleanor and Peg, but came to the conclusion that children shouldn't count. The more she studied her list, the more she wanted the summer to last forever.

Longing to lose herself in more poems by Johnny, the Paperbag Poet, she decided she should finish *Sister Carrie* instead. Carrie had found success, but was depressed and alone at the end of the book, just like Mrs. Woods had said. Angry with the book that failed to bring her the inspiration she sought, Gracie kicked it across the floor. The summer had eased her into a sense of belonging, and the big city seemed unreal and scary. Not knowing what to make of her own dream, Gracie mulled over singing for PT. She would do it. Maybe he would tell her if she was any good even though he disapproved of her going on the road. She had snuck up to the staff lounge early on a Sunday morning to learn the new song she had bought on her shopping trip to Wilkes-Barre. She was sure that singing a newly-published song was just the thing for an impressive audition.

ুৎ৶

"Come on. You're such a good friend, we wanted to show you our secret hideout," Peg said, tugging on Gracie's arm.

Nine-year-old Eleanor nearly toppled her sister, hankering to get Gracie's attention. "It's the best place to play. We can do what we want and not have to worry a bit about bothering the guests."

"Hold it. See this?" Gracie pushed a tray of dirty water glasses and half-used soaps in their faces. "You'll have to show me after my shift is over."

"Okay. Then you can come up and teach us those new songs you're learning," Eleanor said.

Finally, they dragged her up the back stairs to the third sleeping floor, normally used as overflow only when the inn was completely full. "Look!" Eleanor pointed to a trap door in the ceiling in the middle of the hall. Peg brought a ladder from the utility closet and set it in place with her strong, suntanned arms.

"Oh no, girls, this isn't safe," Gracie cautioned, but Peg was already halfway up the ladder.

"Look, when I get to the top, all I have to do is push." And without another word, Peg disappeared through the hole into the room above. Gracie followed reluctantly.

"Eleanor, you keep watch," Peg called down. "If you hear anyone, hide the ladder and then come back and tell us when it's safe."

"I always get the bad jobs just because I'm the youngest," muttered Eleanor.

Gracie knew Mr. and Mrs. Woods would not like this, but concluded it was better that she, as an adult, was there to supervise. She climbed up into the secret room with Peg. Nothing much was there except an old mattress, a couple of chairs and a pile of stuff covered with a sheet. A small window looked out toward the laundry and the mountains beyond.

"Eleanor thinks there is treasure hidden up here," Peg giggled, "like maybe Grandfather's plans for when he built the Crestmont. Mama said he always kept secrets about it."

"I should tell your mother about this," Gracie said.

"No," Peg wailed, "It's our secret hide out. We have oodles of fun here. My parents would never let us come up here if they knew about it."

"And if they find out and realize I didn't tell them, they'll be very upset with me. I'm concerned for your safety, Peg. One of you could fall and get hurt."

Peg and Eleanor pleaded, "Ple-e-ease, Gracie."

"Well, if you promise me you won't come up here without an adult, then I will keep your secret."

"We promise." they agreed in unison.

∽∾

They had agreed to miss Wednesday's ice cream slurp so they could meet privately. Gracie was slumped over the newspaper in the staff lounge perusing audition notices when she heard PT's heavy feet on the stairs. She had finally worked up her courage to ask him to play for her.

"So what do you want to sing?" he asked, sliding onto the piano bench.

"'Tea for Two.' Oh, how silly, I didn't bring the music."

"Don't need it," he said, plunking it out easily by ear.

She conjured up her courage and asked, "Can you play it, just like it is in the sheet music, without those extra things you do?"

"Yup," he chuckled. "Will I? Okay, but only for you, Gracie."

Working up her courage, she sang. At the end of the song she was thrilled when he gave her an encouraging grin. Quickly handing him the sheet music for "That Certain Feeling" with a bright blue cover and an image of a couple dancing, she said, "Let's try this one."

Gracie blew a blonde curl off her forehead, locked her knees and managed to get through it without a hitch. When she was done, she cut her eyes over to see his reaction.

"Nice. So, why do you like to sing?" he asked bluntly.

"Oh honestly, PT, I just do. I guess because my mind's on the song and not myself."

"Hm," he replied, as he dove into a wild version of "Tea for Two," pouring increasing pep into his rhythm.

"What do you call the way you play that?"

"Improvisation."

"Why do you play it that way instead of the way it's supposed to be played?" Gracie asked, worried she had unwittingly insulted him.

"Ha! It's called 'jazz,' Gracie. When I play in the clubs in the city, I get paid to bend the rules and be creative."

"What clubs?"

"Speakeasies. Tons of improv going on there for sure."

Her eyes widened in unbelief. "Speakeasies? I thought those places served alcohol. Why do you play there?"

"Man, you can really topple a guy with questions." Eager to change the subject, he pinched his pointy chin and added, "I think maybe you should sing for the staff talent show."

"Me, really?"

"Sure, I'm in charge. I'll put you in it. Even play for you if you want, but just what's on the page. You're not ready for jazzing it up yet." He returned to his piano, doodling at a new melody.

"Thanks." She turned to go, dreaming of how confident she would feel singing in her green braid slink and St. Louis heels.

"Oh, Gracie," PT stopped her. "Do me a favor, would you, and don't mention the speakeasy thing to anyone."

"Sure, PT." She left, delighted he had shared a confidence with her, worrying about not being ready to jazz it up, and certain she had insulted him about changing the music when he played by ear.

৩৽৻

Gracie trudged up the hill to the Crestmont, clutching her perspiration-soaked handkerchief and shielding her eyes from the sun. Relieved to see that no one was on the laundry porch, she sank into one of the rockers. She had survived her first day with Mrs. Cunningham, a very nice person who even complimented her parsley potatoes. Gracie rocked and let the breeze cool her damp temples. The lawn was so brown. It hadn't rained for a month, very unusual for the mountains. It made it feel so much hotter.

The silver spoon chime clanked loudly in the wind. Annoyed, Gracie reached up to silence it. Wasn't there anywhere she could go to think?

She watched a giggling little girl tumble out of a Model T Ford up on the driveway. Her mother caught her in a hug and they stood, watching the father. He reached into the back seat, picked a boy up into his arms and set him in the wheelchair which he had pulled out of the trunk.

"Well, that was a short ride," announced Eleanor. She climbed onto the porch swing and pumped her legs to make it go. The skin on her sunburned nose was peeling and her brown hair stuck out in wayward wisps giving her a carefree rather than unkempt appearance. Squinting up at the family on the driveway she said, "There's the Brandon family, Gracie. That girl with the pretty hair is only seven, but she's my friend, Dora. We were having a swim when her mother told her to get out of the lake because they were taking her older brother Phillip out for a drive. He can't walk anymore, you know, because he is sick or something, but when he gets better he's going to marry me," Eleanor said fanning her fingers breezily through her hair to dry it. "Bye." She took off like a shot up the hill toward her friend.

"You finish all sheets today, not tomorrow!" Magdalena slammed the laundry door, muttering in German.

"Ach, you, new girl," Magdalena said, noting Gracie's presence. She plunked herself down into a chair, emitting a strong smell of laundry soap. Her feet bulged out of sturdy shoes she had planted directly under her. "You sang that song in talent show, ja?" Gracie nodded. "Gut. Pretty dress, too. Dorothy says you go Presbyterian Church. We go Episcopal church with heilig stones," Magdalena proclaimed proudly, nodding her head.

The German woman seemed much nicer than the rest of the staff had implied. Gracie wanted to understand this church business, so she asked, "Heilig stones?"

"Ja. Your church built with stones from burnt down barn. My church with new holy stones. Better church. I be married in church with heilig stones."

Squirming in her rocker, Gracie ventured, "I didn't realize you were getting married."

"Ja, I have boyfriend. His name Julius. Allentown. Das ist vere he lives."

"Allentown is a long ways away. Do you worry about him?" Gracie bit her lip, worried how this might be taken.

"Ach, you mean other women? Nein, Julius is good man. I trust him, he trust me. It's about trust. You have boyfriend?"

"No."

"Das ist okay. You pretty girl. You find someone." Magdalena slapped Gracie on the back, set her jaw and tromped back into the laundry.

VII

Three characteristic quick raps on her office door signaled Margaret her husband would momentarily enter. She pulled the last of the checkout bills from her typewriter and turned to face him. "Margaret," he blurted between short puffs of breath, "we have a problem."

"Tell me, William."

"The Swetts are bringing four friends next year. The Penningtons—an extra driver and a personal nurse. Six more calls—large families who want to stay with us."

"William, how wonderful."

"No, certainly not. We don't have enough available rooms."

"Of course." She sat down heavily.

"We could do it if we build that addition we have been talking about."

"Yes, but there is the small matter of finding the necessary funds."

"It is not so very far-fetched, my dear. We'll find a way. This is what your father dreamed about. Speaking of your father and 'no room at the inn'—we must find another place to store your father's old ledgers." he stated flatly. "There is simply no more room in my office. Your mother won't know the difference, now that she has retired to Germantown."

"I will take care of Daddy's ledgers. Perhaps I'll peruse them for my evening reading. I might find an idea on how to fund adding more guest rooms."

"As you wish, my dear. I'm off to work out some ideas of my own on the baseball field."

Pecking her on the cheek, he danced into the hall.

"Hello, Mr. Pennington. PT tells me you topped last year's bowling score." William said. Then Margaret heard a request she couldn't quite make out to which William replied, "I am sure we can accommodate you."

William was brilliant at keeping the guests happy. Why, he could even boomerang Agnes Swett's complaints swiftly back to her with hospitable satisfaction. Matters of money, however, seemed to escape him.

Sighing, Margaret removed her shoes, rubbed her swollen feet, and opened this summer's ledger book. On Monday she would motor to Laporte to check on their bank balance and to take care of the surprise she had in mind for Gracie. Her spirits were lifted by peals of laughter drifting up from the lake. Margaret went to the window, enjoying the children delighting in their Saturday morning water games. Most parents encouraged their families to pull every ounce of fun out of their last hours here before checking out. Putting her shoes back on, she went next door to William's office.

Her father's ledgers were in a neat pile on the floor of the closet. She blew the dust off the top one, curled her fingers under one-half of the pile and carried it, school-girl style, to her office. The sound of Celeste Woodford reprimanding Jimmy for leaving some of her luggage upstairs distracted her. If only they could afford to employ more than two bellhops. She hurried to begin checkout, the ledgers still in her arm. When she opened her office door, her foot caught on the doorjamb, sending her and the books flying. Getting to her feet, she pulled her skirt over the hole the fall had made in her hose, dusted off her navy blue suit, and checked her chignon in the mirror. She'd have to deal with the ledgers later.

Then she spied an envelope addressed to her. After picking it up, she hastily tucked it into her suit pocket and closed the door. Not wanting to invoke any of Miss Woodford's wrath, she hurried into the lobby.

"Miss Woodford," Margaret said warmly, handkerchief pressed

discreetly against the abrasion on her knee, "I hope you have enjoyed your month with us. We are always so sorry to see you go. I hope everything has been to your liking."

The attendance at the Saturday night dance would be light this week because the Swetts, the Penningtons and Miss Woodford had checked out after their four-week stay. Margaret loved the last two weeks in August because the demands on her were not as great as they were at the high point of the summer. Each year she anticipated spending time with John and Laura Brandon, guests from West Caldwell, New Jersey, who came with their frail son, Phillip, and doll-faced Dora, age seven. The Brandons were kind, genuine people without the airs many of the wealthier guests seemed unable to part with. Imbued with a courage that fed Margaret's spirits, the Brandons had returned to the Crestmont for the second year since the sobering diagnosis of Phillip's leukemia. John Brandon's playfulness reminded her of her father. She overheard him reading to Dora earlier in the library. He balanced a big *Raggedy Ann* book on his knee.

Raising his voice up into a childlike sound, he read, "'I can't seem to think clearly today,' said Aggendy Ran, 'it feels as if my head were dripped.'"

"No, no, no, Daddy!" Dora squealed, "It's Raggedy Ann, and she thought her head was all ripped, not dripped." Her blue eyes scolded him and she tapped the page of the book as if to say "Do it right this time."

"All right, let me try again." Mr. Brandon sighed, looking at her shamefaced, his eyes dancing over her flaxen hair.

Margaret envied their time together. Her summer duties were a major impediment to the time she coveted with her own daughters.

Impatiently walking down to the Woodshed, she wondered when she would find time alone to read her father's letter. Vacillating between worry and anticipation, she patted the envelope in her suit pocket. She would not have time to read it before the dance because William would already be home and would require more time than she to dress. Perhaps the music and the women's beautiful gowns, dipping and swirling as they danced, would move the evening along swiftly.

Giving William a kiss of greeting when she reached the cottage, she feigned fatigue. He offered to supervise setting up the West Parlor after the dance for church the next morning. Happy to have a husband so willing to assist, she dressed, picked up the present and headed for the library.

∾৹

Gracie sheltered herself in the library, assuming the guests would be getting ready for the dance. It was August 22nd, the day after her twenty-third birthday. No birthday wishes had arrived from her family because they didn't know her address, and the only person here who even knew her birthday was Otto. Funny, she had forgotten about him after their fiasco date as quickly as she had fallen for him. She had spent most of her off-duty time yesterday reading the poems she had found in the paper bag and longing for a man to cherish her.

Feeling particularly blue, Gracie dismissed all thoughts of the dictionary and pulled out the Sears Catalogue instead. She put off practical matters, like finding warmer clothes and a winter coat, since there was no money for them anyway. Even though she didn't know where she would go in the fall, eventually she would have to place a real order, have it delivered a week before closing up the Crestmont, and use her bonus to pay for it Cash On Delivery.

Tonight, however, she itched to play the Sears Catalogue game that so often consoled her. She imagined an exorbitant amount to spend and then wild. Tonight's allotment was thirty-five dollars. Her fantasy was to find all she needed to be a full-time companion to Mrs. Cunningham. Pretending to choose day dresses for work, a Sunday dress with a pretty pin to match, coat, gloves, hat, books, toiletries and sheet music was a welcome respite from reality. She carefully wrote down the articles she wanted, with page numbers and prices. After tallying up the imaginary purchases, she would refer back to the catalogue to finalize her selections.

"I was hoping to see you here." Gracie quickly closed the catalogue with her list sticking out the top and turned toward the familiar voice. Mrs. Woods stood before her, looking fresh and elegant in an ankle-length burnt orange charmeuse gown. Soft gathers from the right hip billowed over her shoes and were repeated in long flowing sleeves, which lay loose at the wrists. Her hair was down and swept back over one ear, secured with a day lily. "I'm sorry I didn't find you yesterday, Gracie. I know this is a day late, but Happy Birthday." Mrs. Woods smiled, holding out a package wrapped in pink paper with a matching satin bow.

"How did you know...?" Gracie asked incredulously.

"Your birthday was on your application, dear. Go on, open it."

Carefully undoing the paper so she could reuse it, Gracie found *Age of Innocence* by Edith Wharton in her hands.

"Oh, Mrs. Woods, one of the Pulitzers we talked about. And a female author! I can't wait to read it."

"Look, there's an inscription inside."

Opening the book, Gracie read, "Happy Birthday to a fellow reader. Fondly, Margaret Woods, 1925."

Squeezing Gracie's shoulder, Mrs. Woods said, "I hope you enjoy it, dear. I must run. Mr. Woods and I always start the first dance."

"A fellow reader." Mrs. Woods was kind enough to remember Gracie's birthday. Gracie gulped, remembering her promise to keep the girl's hideout a secret from their mother.

"It's about trust." Magdalena's words came back to Gracie as she guiltily closed the book, swallowing the bile that crept up in her throat.

&

August 20, 1908

Dear Moppet,

How is my big girl doing today? I hope I remember to leave this letter where you will find it. My memory doesn't seem to be what it was. I don't mean to upset you, but if you are reading this, I am either incapacitated or up in heaven.

Margaret, now that you are married to William, I am confident the two of you can run the Crestmont with the high standard I attempted to put into place when I built it. To do that, however, you may need financial assistance for which I have made provision. Go to the back wing of the third sleeping floor. You will see a small trap door in the hall ceiling. It leads to my little private hideaway where I used to escape to catch a nap, or just to be alone. There's a small safe in the room. I systematically saved a great deal of cash since we opened in 1900. I kept it secret from your mother, or she would have frittered it away. To access the room, use the ladder in the utility closet at the end of the hall.

I don't want to dictate how the money might be used, as I trust your judgment, but I suspect the concept of a flush toilet in one's own guest room will become increasingly popular. I regret not juicing the entire house when I built it, so you might want to electrify the upper sleeping floors. I am hoping the inn will become too small for the number of guests wanting to share our retreat, and that an addition might be helpful.

I call my hideaway Room 440. God showed me the empty cyclone hill which was to become the site of the most imposing hotel in Eagles Mere at precisely 4:40 p.m.

Moppet, listen to your father. Find your own Room 440 where you can replenish yourself. Our profession is rewarding, but exhausting. Make time for yourself, or you will never be able to properly attend to your guests, not to mention your family.

Search my desk for the combination to the safe.

Love, Daddy

P.S. In case you are wondering how I did it, I put the mattress up there after the floor joists were up, but before the carpenters put the floor in. Your daddy always was a good planner.

Alone in The Woodshed, Margaret refolded the letter and returned it to her suit pocket. Awed by her father's vision and his faith in her, she cried, fondly remembering his endearing joviality. She wanted to locate the safe and surprise William. Undressing, she slipped into her bathrobe to await his return, wondering if she would sleep at all tonight.

Her spirits buoyed by this morning's church service, Gracie bounced past the offices after staff lunch, winking at Old Tim in the lobby. The library was her friend. When Gracie got there, Mrs. Woods' favorite chair was empty. Sundays were busy for the Woods and any time off would be spent resting in their cottage. Gracie worked up her courage to sink into her mentor's chair. Settled there, she pondered her two new homes—this inn that she loved and the Presbyterian Church.

Conversations with people at church had moved beyond casual greetings. People called her by name and seemed genuinely happy to see her. The choir director introduced himself this morning, inviting her to sing a solo before the choir started back in the fall.

Astonished at her good fortune, she nodded yes, but later wished she had actually accepted out loud.

She loved Rev. Sturdy's sermons. He preached like he was teaching himself. Sometimes his message seemed so personal and sensitive, Gracie wondered if he was putting on an act, but the more she heard him, the more she felt he was genuine. "Who Is My Family?" was the title of this morning's sermon. He had talked a lot about God and the church being family. Something he said really struck her. "Your family consists of the people who love you."

Who loved her?

Pondering that, she guessed she should write to Lily again, but had forgotten to bring her pencil. She moved over to William Warner's desk and opened some of the drawers. A child's spinning top was in one, and some eraser gum in another. She pulled out the smallest drawer all the way on the right and saw some scrawly writing on the side. It was a series of numbers with L and R interspersed. She closed it quickly, feeling she had seen something she shouldn't have. Pulling down a pencil stuck in an upper cubby, she wrote to her sister.

ഔ

"That's the room you called 'storage' when I was young, isn't it?" Margaret questioned the charcoal eyes in the portrait when she finally had time on Monday. "Daddy, I had to empty your desk years ago. How will I ever know where the combination went?"

Sid Fox passed her in the hall, pushing a cart stacked with canned goods ahead of him. "Sid, do you remember seeing a box with the things my father used to store in his desk?"

He stopped, caught his breath and pushed his glasses back up on his nose. "No, Mrs. Woods, can't say as I have, although after twenty-five years I have to admit one storage box begins to look like every other."

"Twenty-five years. Good gracious, Sid. I had forgotten you've been here from the beginning." He tipped his cap to her and headed down the hall toward the dining room.

Anticipation made the climb easy, and soon Margaret found herself on the third sleeping floor, pondering the trap door above her head.

Whistling, Peg turned the corner and stopped dead in her tracks. "She told you!" Peg wailed. "She promised she wouldn't."

"Who told me what?" Margaret stared inexplicably at her daughter.

"Gracie. She promised she wouldn't tell you when Eleanor and I showed her our hideout."

"This," she said, pointing to the trap door "is your hideout? What is up there? I cannot believe you kept this from me." Not waiting for a response, she commanded, "Bring me a ladder." Too afraid to argue, Peg brought it and laid it in place.

"I can show you if you want, Mama."

Her mother cut her off. "No. You have been secretly climbing up here and allowing Eleanor to do the same. Don't you move an inch." Margaret made her way carefully up into the room above.

The small window was insufficient to fully illuminate the room. She stopped to let her eyes adjust after nearly tripping over an old mattress. A crudely placed white sheet covered something in the corner. Margaret lifted the sheet, coughing as dust hit her throat. She crouched before a foot-high gray steel safe sitting balanced on two boards. The numbers 440 were crudely painted in yellow next to a combination lock on the front.

"Peg, go back to the Woodshed and wait for me. Do not say a word of this to anyone. I will deal with you subsequently," her mother said sternly and clambered down the ladder.

Meanwhile, after tidying Room 58, Gracie lingered there, musing over the Paperbag Poet and the woman he loved. Maybe if she spent time where she found the poems she could fill out their story. She jumped when an uncharacteristically stone-faced, dirty Mrs. Woods flung open the door.

"Come with me this minute." A hot flash crept up Gracie's neck as she climbed to the third floor and followed Mrs. Woods up the ladder.

"How dare you allow my daughters to do such a dangerous thing without telling me? I suppose the three of you knew about this also." Mrs. Woods pointed to the safe.

"No, honestly, Peg and Eleanor just wanted me to sit with them on the mattress, sing and talk. They made me promise not to tell you, Mrs. Woods, but after I did, I knew it was wrong. I knew that ladder wasn't safe, so I told them they couldn't come up alone. I wanted to tell you, really, I did. I've been miserable."

"*You've* been miserable. Your feelings don't count for much at this point, Miss Antes. You will tell no one about this. Mr. Woods and I will deal with you later. Right now, I have to find the combination to this safe." Regretting the desperation she heard in her own voice, she sent Gracie down the ladder with instructions to wait.

Standing dumb and scared in the hall below, Gracie realized her discovery of the numbers and letters on the desk drawer might be considered a further indiscretion. "Uh, Mrs. Woods," she ventured, when her employer reached the floor, "I'm pretty sure I know where the combination is."

∽∾

"Sid, fetch PT to bring the car immediately!" Mr. Woods crouched over his wife as she lay on the first floor landing. Flowers and shards of pottery lay scattered all over and water dripped over onto the top step.

"Oh, William, I was careless. I didn't want to go all the way back to the kitchen and bring back the water pitcher. I added the water to the vase downstairs to save myself a trip. It was too heavy to carry all the way up the staircase and I knew it. When I tried to place the bouquet on the table, my leg gave out and I lost my footing. My arm must have become wedged into the table somehow."

"Everything's going to be fine, Margaret. I don't want you to move. We'll secure that arm and then drive you to the clinic in Dushore."

Hours later, frustrated because she couldn't sleep, Margaret wiped tears from her eyes, realizing she could never find the contents of the safe without help now that her right arm was wrapped in a plaster cast.

ဆုတ္

"Yes, William, I am well enough to work. I can type with my left hand." Margaret distractedly flipped papers from one side of her desk to the other the next morning. "Please find Gracie and send her in."

"Yes. Gracie. Splendid idea. She's the ticket," her husband replied helplessly as he hurried out.

When Gracie arrived, she was relieved to find Mrs. Woods more anxious than angry.

"I'm sorry, ma'am."

"We have much to sort out between us, but now is not the time. You kept my daughters' secret and now I request you keep mine. I need to get that safe out of that dark room and into a secure place so I can see what is inside. May I have what you copied off the desk drawer?" Gracie hastily handed the piece of paper with the combination on it. "You are to tell no one, not even Mr. Woods about this. Do you understand?"

"Yes, ma'am."

"Go tell Sid Fox you need one of his carts to distribute some cleaning supplies. Tonight during the concert, carry it up the back stairs to the trap door, along with twenty feet of rope and a flashlight. I will meet you there at eight o'clock."

Gracie stole down to the boat house on the dock during dinner, grabbed the rope and a flashlight and hid them both in the third floor utility closet. Getting the cart up the stairs was a losing battle until she realized she could tie the rope around it and pull the cart behind her, lifting it from step to step. She had

everything in place just as Mrs. Woods turned the corner, obviously uncomfortable in her cast and sling.

"Loop it around the top, cross the rope on the bottom and bring it up around the other side. Now, knot it well on top. You'll have to lie down, push it to the edge and lower it onto the cart. I can at least guide it with one hand. No one is in 78 at the end of the hall, so we will wheel it in there."

The cart creaked and almost buckled when the weight of the safe hit it. Gracie climbed down, her arms aching. Mrs. Woods dismissed her the minute they reached Room 78.

જ્જ

Gracie was so upset about Mrs. Woods; she had lost all her joy from singing at the staff talent show. Realizing she had never thanked PT, she went to find him. He and Otto had their heads together at the bowling alley entrance.

She rushed up to him the minute Otto was gone. "I wanted to thank you for playing for me at the talent show."

"Sure. It was nothing."

"I hope we can do it again. Oh, and your jazz solo was amazing." Trying to draw out their time together, she continued, "PT, remember when we talked about me leaving home?"

"Yup."

"Well, you were going to tell me your story and you never did."

"Listen, Gracie, I have to hit the road," he said evasively. "A bowling alley in Philly needs me." He stepped away uncomfortably, pushing his hair back out of his eyes.

"But how can you leave? The season's not over. What about the bowling alley here? Oh, now I know why you were talking to Otto. He's going to run it while you're gone. You are coming back, aren't you?" she cried, willing him to stay.

"Yup," he replied, stubbed out his cigarette, and ambled away.

જ્જ

William Woods sat at his desk, chin cradled in his hand, tapping his pencil pensively.

"Come in," he said, after four soft raps sounded on the door.

"Oh, Mr. Woods, I was just beside myself when I heard about your wife breaking her arm." Dorothy bustled in, straw hat and suitcase in hand. "I have already asked Adelle to hostess meals because I must leave to start my fall term at school. Mae will assume my role as head waitress. Is there anything else I can do?"

"No, thank you, we'll be fine—I think. Dorothy, can a woman cook with one hand?" he asked innocently.

"I believe that would be difficult, sir."

"So I assumed. A piece of your advice, Dorothy. We'll need some help around the Woodshed until my wife recovers. I was contemplating hiring Gracie. Margaret told me Isaiah taught her some things about cooking. I know she can clean and has a good rapport with my daughters. What do you think?"

"Gracie's a good girl. I'm certain she would do a fine job. She did have some travel plans for the fall, but I don't think she has decided definitely."

"Then I will ask her. Please don't mention it, Dorothy. I'd like to make it a surprise for my wife. I know I can depend on your discretion. I am so worried about her. She seems so down since this happened."

"Don't you have any qualms about Mrs. Woods, sir. I have seen her get behind herself and push time and time again. She will weather this as well."

"Indeed, Dorothy," he said warmly, shaking her hand. "You don't know what it means to us to have loyal, superlative employees such as yourself. We will see you next summer, won't we?"

"Absolutely." She dropped her suitcase to the floor with a thud and gave him an impulsive hug. "I love my summer family."

Flabbergasted, Gracie stared Mr. Woods full in the face.

"You mean to live with your family all winter?"

"Yes. What's wrong, child? You look like you've seen a ghost. Ah, that's right," he said knowingly. "Dorothy told me you had some travel plans."

"No, sir, it's not that."

"It's Eleanor, then. I understand. She can be so rambunctious. Don't worry. It won't be too difficult. I'll be home in the evening. All you'll need to do is tend to the girls and do a little cooking and cleaning until Mrs. Woods' arm heals. We have a spare room and will pay you well. You can continue to work for Mrs. Cunningham. Please say yes, Gracie. My wife thinks the world of you and this will be a marvelous surprise for her."

Woodshed on Crestmont Hill
September 1925

I

Setting her red suitcase down on the bed, Gracie unpacked with one ear on the conversation she could almost hear in the living room. After eating an uncommonly quiet dinner with the five remaining staffers and packing her belongings, she followed Mr. Woods over to the Woodshed, where she was to help out for the winter. She felt guilty that Peg had so willingly given up her room for Gracie to sleep in, but she was cheered by the youthful red and white gingham curtains and shelves piled with puzzles, books and board games.

"Margaret, because you kept this discord from me, it was impossible for me to properly assess the situation before I asked her. I was trying to help you," William said, exasperated. "Have you two talked yet?"

"Hush, William, Gracie might hear you. I will sort this out with her when the time is right."

Checking his pocket watch, he said, "I must be off. Tonight is the first choir rehearsal of the season. I will be home around ten."

"Eleanor keeps asking me about riding down the driveway to the pillars. Have you talked with her yet about her bicycle rules?"

"No, I shall have to remember to do that tomorrow. Margaret, you know Wednesdays are difficult for me. I am only nine days into the new academic year at Westlawn, and then I go directly to church choir in Laporte and home to fall into bed. It takes me awhile to adjust to the commute. I only stopped home today to get Gracie settled and check on you."

"I will be fine, William. I will kiss the girls goodnight for you." He leaned in to peck her on the cheek, but Margaret turned away to stoke the fire with her good arm. William slipped his raincoat off the coat tree and left.

Weary of creating new ways to remind her husband of what he needed to do, Margaret sank listlessly into the caned rocker in front of the hearth. This September felt so different. Normally, after closing the inn for the summer, the family would enjoy a celebratory dinner in their cottage with a fire to take off the September chill and tumble into bed without a care.

It wasn't the broken arm. She had learned to compensate for that in the three weeks since her accident. It was that her spirit also felt broken.

Margaret gazed apathetically around their living room. She had decorated it with casual blue and tan plaid upholstered chairs, a necessary change from the green, cream and yellow hues with floral themes permeating the Crestmont lobby. An untapped goldmine stared at her from its place next to the hearth—her father's safe. William had placed it there as a jabbing reminder for them to execute a huge building project before next summer's season. The money her father had left them brought with it decisions about what renovations would best serve the future of the Crestmont. The jaunty tone of his letter, however, was miles away from her current state of mind and her energy was too sapped to do any planning.

Then there was the young woman in the front bedroom. William had invited Gracie into their home without consulting

her. Although she had come to regard Gracie with fondness and
respect over the summer, the trust between them had been
threatened since the hideout incident. Still, Gracie had kept her
promise to Peg and Eleanor to keep it a secret. There was character
in that, Margaret supposed.

"Mama," Peg called as she rushed in, banging the screen door,
"We finished season close-up. It was so much fun. Zeke and I
took down all the screens. Otto did the things PT usually does.
He is acting all important now that Papa made him boss of the
year-round garage. Oh, and Julius, Magdalena's boyfriend, came
from Allentown and worked as hard as the rest of us. Mr. Fox
seemed sad not to be able to say goodbye to you and Daddy.
Everyone else is gone and..."

"I have asked you countless times not to slam that door, Peg."

"Sorry, Mama." Peg hastened on with the optimism of an
adolescent. "Are you happy Gracie is here? I know you're mad
about our secret hideout, but she will be a big help now that you
broke your arm. I'll help too. I can cook on Thursdays when
Gracie is at Mrs. Cunningham's." Peg kept a wary eye on her
mother's face as she closed the blinds behind the blue and white
ruffled curtains on both living room windows.

Margaret beckoned her eldest daughter over to her. Cradling
Peg's waist with her good arm she said, "I'm sorry to be cross. Mr.
Fox understands after all these summers that sometimes we are
just too worn out for emotional goodbyes. You have wonderful
ideas and help in so many ways. One day, you will make an amazing
administrator for the Crestmont...if that is what you want."

"I do, but I have to find a husband that wants to help me.
Papa has been teaching me how to run the water sports and Mr.
Fox explained how he figures out what supplies to order. You and
Papa aren't going to stop running the Crestmont, are you? I know
you get so tired."

"Now, don't you worry, darling. I can't conceive of not running
the Crestmont. What would your grandfather Warner say about
that if he were alive? Why don't you go see if Gracie is settled in
and then go on to bed." Peg kissed her mother's forehead and

rapped on the bedroom door. Murmurs of easy conversation between the girls melted through the wall.

First, Margaret resolved, she would have to forgive William. The concern he had displayed for her by arranging household assistance was commendable. Next, she would make it right with Gracie. For now, she drooped into the chair. Tucking one pillow under the cast on her right arm and another under her head, she tried to draw strength from the warmth of the fire. She drifted off, enveloped not just by the stifling fog of fatigue that always plagued her in September but also with a pervasive sense of ennui, which she did not understand.

The next morning Margaret awoke, ragged and peevish, to the sound of Eleanor's snoring. Her favorite shawl was wrapped around her shoulders. William must have covered her up when he came home last night. Relieved to have a few quiet moments before the rest of the family bustled into the kitchen, she prayed for rejuvenation. That she would not feel used up inside. That she would have something to give to someone else. That they would know best how to use the money from the safe.

She got up stiffly, shrugging off the shawl and wishing she had moved into one of the easy chairs before she fell asleep. When she opened the blinds on the living room windows, she watched the shaft of morning sunlight make faint fireflies out of the dead ash suspended in the air. "Why don't you take what is dead in me too, God, and bring it to life?" she asked bitterly as she made her way into the bathroom. As she rinsed her face with warm water, it occurred to Margaret the accident with her arm may have been a blessed gift for replenishment.

"Mama, let's do the exercise where you walk your fingers up the wall." Eleanor tumbled out of her bedroom, trying to catch the ties of her yellow bathrobe.

Blessing her younger daughter's eagerness to help, Margaret squeezed her close, kissing her unruly locks of brown hair. "Get some milk for your cereal," she said, combing out some of the tangles with her fingers. "We'll walk the wall when you get home from school."

"Must you be happy so loudly first thing in the morning, Eleanor?" Peg emerged from her sister's bedroom stretching unseen kinks out of her tall, athletic body. "Mama, she's got so many dolls and teddy bears, there's barely room for me. I'm boxing some up until I get my room back when Gracie leaves."

Gracie, who had quietly closed the bedroom door behind her, stole into the kitchen where the hub of family life was already humming. "You don't mind me going today, Mrs. Woods?" she asked, eager to escape to her job at Mrs. Cunningham's.

Margaret stiffened a little and said over her shoulder, "No, we agreed you would continue your Thursday job. Peg will cook tonight."

"All right, but I can cook tomorrow." She was dismissed by Mrs. Woods' silent nod.

෨෧

Woodshed Cottage sat east of the Crestmont, tucked back and a bit down the hill from the bowling alley, on the big driveway that led down to the pillars and into Eagles Mere. The front door faced the lake rather than the drive, Peg had explained last night, to give the family some privacy. Relieved to get away from Mrs. Woods' uncharacteristic remoteness, Gracie went through the porch and down the front steps, which were flanked by blue hydrangeas reluctant to give up their summer color. An eerie pull drew her attention back up toward the Crestmont. The building stood against the foggy morning—a brown, silent sentinel, lonely in its immensity. Two adolescent fawns, sensing the newfound calm on the Crestmont side of the lake, took a morning drink. A trio of squawking crows sent them scampering back up the hill between the bowling alley and the Woodshed.

Gracie wanted a peek at Mrs. Woods' famous gardens. She checked over her shoulder to see if anyone was looking and hurried down toward the lake. Wondering why this was her first waterside visit all summer, Gracie realized that other than her trip to church and an occasional rest on the laundry porch, she felt more comfortable staying inside. Well she had a different life now. Maybe she should mark it by going outside more often.

The flower beds were set over on the Woodshed side of the hill. The picnic tables that normally graced the water's edge at the base of the gardens had been put away for the winter. Some late summer roses were still blooming as well as begonias perched atop brick red stems. A bush replete with flowers, whose deep rosy centers bled spidery veins out into six voluminous white petals, caught her eye. Surely Mrs. Woods wouldn't mind if she picked a flower for the dinner table on her way home. Surely she would agree that was a nice thing to do.

Peg helped her mother dress and replaced the sling on her arm after breakfast. "You are such a help. Are you sure you can cook dinner and do your homework, too?"

Peg pulled her sister's coat off the coat tree near the door and held it out for her to put on. "Absolutely, Mama. I finish a lot of my school work while the teacher gives extra help to other students. Come on, Eleanor, we're going to be late," she said fondly to her younger sister.

Margaret sighed with relief. She was finally alone. Opening her Bible to the eleventh chapter of Matthew, she read "Come unto me, all ye that labour and are heavy laden and I will give you rest."

Rest. Exactly what I need. I need not to have to think.

Knowing the Laurel Path she loved would be quiet this time of day, she wandered down to follow it around the lake. The spring blossoms were gone, a myriad of brown leaves padded the path, and the scarcity of leaves on the bushes gave her a clearer view of the lake. She paused to listen to the birds and begged the comforting, lapping water to rejuvenate her. She gave the tangled rhododendron branches a doleful tap with her toe, feeling a kinship with how they twisted on the ground. When the Woods said goodbye to the last guest at season's end, she felt like a rumpled mess on the floor.

William, on the other hand, seemed to draw energy from the guests. Normally, his happy-go-lucky, it-will-all-work-out air made her feel stronger. Today, she resented that he interacted on the baseball field and in the smoking room while she worked out problems alone in her office. She knew she was being unfair. William, with his keen business sense and charm with people, certainly bore his share of the responsibility during hotel season. Neither one of them alone could have continued what her father had started.

She was confounded by her father's advice to replenish herself. The Crestmont was a much larger operation now than it was when he climbed up to nap on a hidden mattress.

"Dinner smells delicious, Peg," her father exclaimed, rubbing his palms together in anticipation when he returned home from teaching. "Not only do you have your mother's huge limpid eyes, but also her knack in the kitchen."

"And her big feet, too." She clucked her tongue against her cheek playfully. "I'm making chicken croquettes, baked potatoes, and I opened a jar of Isaiah's pickled peaches."

"Margaret, you grow the most beautiful hibiscus in Sullivan County." William touched the huge blossom on the table, hugged his wife and whispered, "We'll talk later, my dear."

"Actually, Gracie picked it for us to enjoy while we have dinner," Margaret said blandly. Unsettled by the strange tone, Gracie paused from setting the table to examine Mrs. Woods' taut expression. She noticed Mr. Woods doing the same.

"Well, if you can put up with what I serve, ladies, I will cook on Saturday," he offered, breaking the tension. They sat down to a quiet meal accompanied by silverware clacking against dishes.

It riddled Gracie that since the hideout incident Mrs. Woods had moved from red-in-the-tooth-and-claw mad at her to detached politeness. She missed the Mrs. Woods she had come to love and wondered what she ought to do to make things right between them. Today she was grateful she could remove herself from that by going to church. In the big house when she had a problem with someone like Bessie, she retreated to the reassuring safety of her room after her shift. Granted, the Woods had given her Peg's room, but it wasn't as private. She feared for the light shining out from under the door late at night when she read, and she had to temper her habit of talking out loud to make herself do things.

Gracie strolled around town a bit after the service, humming the last hymn. She turned down Lake Street and descended the steep hill, which she had learned was part of the famous Eagles Mere toboggan slide. Her heels hit so hard on the pavement that the balls of her feet made slapping sounds as she walked down to the lake.

She found she liked being alone outdoors, and felt especially peaceful standing back a little bit from the water. Perhaps next week she would come back and find a place where she could sit awhile.

The walk back up was a challenge. Even though the chilly breeze swirled playfully in the skirt of her green braid slink, she had to rest periodically to stop the burning in her thighs. Relieved when she reached the Sweet Shoppe porch, she sat down amidst the hastily placed pumpkins to catch her breath. The smell of apple pie drove her crazy while she waited for the Woods' car.

෨ඏ

"Why was it necessary for everyone to make a fuss about my arm? Honestly, half the women of the Laporte Lutheran Fellowship offered to send dinner over to us."

"They were being gracious, Margaret," William said patiently. "You would have been the first to offer had you been in their place. I find it inconceivable that you resent their help."

"Well, we don't need it because you hired Gracie," she said irritably.

"Margaret, tell me what is wrong," he said softly so that the girls in the back seat couldn't hear. "It's more than your arm, and I am worried about you."

She dismissed him by turning back to Peg and Eleanor. "I want no nonsense from you. Lunching at the Sweet Shoppe on Sunday is a treat. Do you hear my words?"

"Yes, Mama." Ready to cut and run from the tension, they tumbled out of the car, blew kisses back to their parents, and ran up the steps of the Sweet Shoppe toward Gracie.

❧

"There is no need to worry about me, William. We need to go home and count the money."

"There is every reason to worry, Margaret. You seem very distressed. You have been cool towards Gracie, and frankly, very cranky with the rest of us. I am sure I have done something to upset you." He stopped the car, moved over, and placed his arm lightly around her shoulder. "I am very sorry I didn't ask you first before inviting her to live with us. I was trying to give you a nice surprise."

"I feel betrayed, William," she said dully as the car turned up the Crestmont driveway. "Gracie knew about the girls' hiding place, knew they might hurt themselves climbing up and down the ladder, and she never told me. I have done a great deal to help her, and I suppose I expected more in return."

"Margaret, my love, you are forty-one years old. Gracie is only in her early twenties and appears to lack much life experience. She has a lot of learning to do. You were the one who told me that we were her family. We need to accept her as she is and be grateful for her gifts to us. You'll see it will be good all around for her to be with us this winter. She needs to learn how a family trust is built."

"Asking her was very chivalrous of you, William. I know I

have been in a bad humor lately. I'm sorry. I am just so weary."

"Well, let me conjure up a way to pep you up. Ever since we peeked into that safe, I dream about one hundred dollar bills. So many ideas are bouncing around in my head I couldn't concentrate on my Macbeth lecture Friday." He started the car and edged it onto Eagles Mere Avenue. "I have been bursting with anticipation for a free day. Now, let's go count that money!"

❦

Jumping up from the table, William delightfully touched each pile of one hundred dollar bills, punctuating his count with excited little gasps. "My dear, Margaret, get your pencil out and let's go to work now that we know how much we have to work with."

"William, even though I taught myself to write with my good hand, please be mindful that I have been doing ledgers all week. Perhaps you can do the writing." She lifted her feet onto the footstool with effort.

"Of course, how silly of me." Rubbing his hands together, he said, "Now, not only do we need more space for guests, we want to make sure we are more and more progressive. First, we must electrify everything—sleeping floors, cottages—all of it." He pulled the chair out, grabbed a pencil and started scribbling.

"We will need more bathrooms if we put in new rooms," Margaret pointed out. "And we must put more private bathrooms in existing rooms. That would at least help us catch up to what the Lakeside Inn offers."

"Yes, yes." William's head bobbed up and down as he wrote. "I have been pondering this for awhile, knowing we would have to do something. There is room on the west end of the house for eight rooms—on all three sleeping floors. Then we could expand the dining room out toward the lake more. How do those ideas strike you?"

"I agree with them. Consider also revamping the layout of our public rooms. I see no need for three ladies parlors, but a card room might be nice."

"And turn the unpopular guest rooms near the checkout desk into an office for Sid, a coat room and public lavatories. Our offices stay where they are."

"...and the library, William. It's perfect where it is. So what we are saying," Margaret clarified, "is to move all public areas to the west side of the lobby except the library, and convert the former public rooms of the east wing into larger accommodations with en suite baths. That would create a nice private wing."

"Look at this, Margaret." William tore off a piece of paper. "Instead of repairing those rotting balconies on the front, let's tear them off, extend the three sleeping floors out over the porch like this," he sketched, "and create four spacious rooms with baths on all three sleeping floors."

"Excellent. Of course, additional bellhop and waitress staff is necessary. I estimate we will serve at least thirty more people in the dining room. Perhaps we could host more conventions pre-season to pay for the extra staff. Those are always profitable."

"Yes, but because May is so cool we must steam heat the main and first sleeping floor."

"I need to work on these figures, William, before we proceed any further. All these new rooms will need furnishings, and goodness knows what bathroom fixtures will cost."

"I'll get a contractor here before next week. We could put the foundation and superstructure up this fall, and finish the inside over the winter."

"William, I want the contractors to close that entrance to my father's old hideaway and put a new ceiling in so the girls have no more access."

"Good. Oh, my dear, isn't this invigorating?"

"Yes. I find it wonderful to plan and dream with you, William. So often during the summer it feels like we have separate lives."

William shot out of his chair. "Tennis courts. That's the ticket—tennis courts!"

"Tennis...no. We don't have extra money for recreation. Even with this addition, it will be a challenge to accommodate our new influx of guests. We had better focus on that, not tennis courts."

In an attempt to steer him in a more practical direction, Margaret suggested they walk over to the big house to see what walls needed to be knocked down and what rooms could be made larger into suites with bathrooms.

But William persisted. "Listen, Margaret. It's not so very far-fetched." He crouched down in front of her. The cleft in his chin quivered excitedly while he made his case. "Swett told me last summer that the French Tennis Championship opened itself to international competitors. What if the United States National Championship in Forest Hills does the same? U.S. pros will be edged out by the Europeans and will be seeking another venue. We could run our own competition, attracting visitors tired of the big city to watch tennis in the fresh mountain air. This is our chance put ourselves prominently on the map. Just imagine—The Annual Eagles Mere Tennis Tournaments."

The girls headed back to the Woodshed after a lunch of tomato soup and olive and cream cheese sandwiches. Eleanor skipped ahead, occasionally twirling around to see if Gracie and Peg had caught up. She cupped her hands around her mouth and shouted, "I like the way you walk, Gracie. You kind of push your hips forward like this. See?" she placed her hands on her hips and demonstrated. "It makes your hair bounce like you have an important place to be." Her own unruly hair blew every which way in the breeze without her noticing or caring. Peg walked carefully next to Gracie, balancing a box of the Sweet Shoppe's special chocolate marshmallows for her mother.

"Is that the *Age of Innocence?*" Peg asked, nodding toward the book in Gracie's hand.

"Yes, how did you know?"

"I was with Mama when she bought it for you. She thinks you have 'potential,' as she puts it. She's impressed that you read all the time and study vocabulary. My mother likes people with a strong work ethic, as she puts it."

Caught off guard, Gracie searched for the right response. "Well, I'm just trying to better myself. I never paid much attention to good books or the news before I came here. Your mother has been encouraging me."

"So I've noticed."

II

THE CAST FINALLY CAME OFF.

"William, if you had taken the whole day off, we could have deposited the money in the bank to start earning interest," Margaret groused as he helped her into the car after the doctor's visit.

"We need to get you home, and I have a faculty meeting that I cannot miss. I want you to rest. Gracie cooks tonight, doesn't she?"

"Yes," Margaret groaned, rubbing the leathery skin on her newly freed arm.

"And have her help you soak your arm. Dr. Webber said that would help loosen it up before you do your exercises."

"I can soak my own arm, William."

"How long are you going to let this go on without making up with her?"

"As long as I need to."

Mrs. Woods went directly into her room for a nap after the doctor's visit. She had slept for two hours and Gracie still hadn't heard a sound from her. The Alpine Eggs Gracie had cooked on Friday were so bad that she threw them out and made toasted cheese and ham sandwiches instead. She had forgotten to add water to Monday's pot roast, but the family pretended to rave about the tough meat anyway.

Gracie knew there was a chicken in the icebox that Mr. Woods had brought home yesterday, so she pulled out the cookbook and ran her finger down the index. Surely she could make "Herb Roasted Chicken." She only had to read the cookbook carefully, just like Mrs. Woods told her when she started working for Mrs. Cunningham. Maybe if she made a nice dish, Mrs. Woods might cheer up. She opened a cupboard in the kitchen, pulled out some canned vegetables, and slid the roasting pan out as quietly as she could. She worked diligently and was finally starting to feel she was making a significant contribution to the Wood's family when Mrs. Woods emerged from her nap sleepily patting her hair into place.

"Do I smell creamed peas? Mm, my favorite."

Gracie nearly dropped the spoon in her hand. "I'm sorry if I woke you, ma'am."

"Sorry, sorry, that is all you ever say, Gracie. It's not necessary, you know." Margaret said gently, sitting down at the kitchen table. "Your dinner smells delicious and I am the one who is sorry. I have been out of sorts lately. Put the kettle on, won't you? We'll have tea and talk this out."

After the air was cleared, Gracie relaxed.

"Dr. Webber said it will be several weeks before I have the full use of my arm." Margaret said. "The ladies from church are sending dinner home on Sundays. Perhaps you could continue to cook four nights out of the week."

Gracie gulped, but tried to nod enthusiastically.

"We could motor to Laporte on Monday's to buy groceries, and tomorrow, have a little adventure in the laundry house."

"I'd like that." Gracie was relieved at the chance to blend in with the family.

"Thank you, Gracie. Your help is a godsend. Why don't you do something special with the girls on Friday after school?"

❧

"Oh honestly," marveled Gracie, "I always wondered what it was like in here, but I was too scared to find out." The sharp smell of bleach hung in the air. She moved in between the mass of washing machines and the row of ironing boards, each one the home of an iron with its electric cord wound around like a cat's tail. Several huge sinks stood against one wall and she noticed her favorite rocker from the porch wedged in a corner with some other outdoor furniture.

"What are these?" Gracie pointed to four massive, coffin-like machines with hinged aluminum covers.

"Those are mangles, industrial-size pressing machines. You can imagine how many sheets we launder all summer. The machines are helpful time savers, but they make it very hot for Magdalena and her crew. I know this may all seem a bit much for a family of four to use, but it's our property, so we take advantage of it during the off-season. I hope you find doing the laundry today to be an adventure. Use this Allen washer. All the moving parts are ball bearings, so you don't have to worry about oiling anything. Because it's electric, there is much less work. Watch." Mrs. Woods wet a towel in the sink, took it to the washer positioning it close to the cylindrical rolls, and pushed the button.

"That's amazing. After the rinse cycle all I do is adjust the wringer to the right height and push a button." Gracie said, watching the rubber rolls suck the towel through, squeezing out the water. "At home I had to I hand-crank it. This will be fun, Mrs. Woods. Is there a clothesline outside?"

"Yes, but when the cold weather comes we hang the wet laundry over here." She led Gracie to an additional room in the back that was strung with clothes lines. "I've been reading that we will soon have what they are calling tumble dryers, powered by electricity. So many modern conveniences. Well, I'll leave you then and send the girls down to help you carry the laundry back."

"The girls are here so you don't have to." Peg banged open the door and jumped up on one of the pressing machines.

"We knew where you were, so we came to help." Eleanor was carrying a wicker laundry basket over her head like an overturned canoe. "Wow, Gracie's in the laundry house. I'm telling Magdalena," she joked.

"Peg, I just turned that mangle on. Get down before you burn yourself."

She hopped off obediently. "Mama, that washer has to run awhile. I'm going to show Gracie where Isaiah, Olivia and Samuel live all summer." She made for the stairs to the second floor, taking them two at a time. Mrs. Woods smiled at her daughter and nodded for Gracie to follow.

"I got an A+, Mama!" Eleanor eagerly pulled a paper out of her pocket, unfolded it and handed it to her mother.

"An A+ in Arithmetic. How wonderful, Eleanor. That extra time on your homework paid off. I am so proud of you. You must show it to your father tonight at dinner."

"No, he won't care. He only cares how his students do."

"Eleanor, darling, of course he cares."

"Come on, Mama. Let's go home and do your exercises."

As they climbed the hill together, Eleanor caught red and gold leaves drifting off the trees and handed them to her mother. Once inside the Woodshed, she ran for the yardstick.

"I suppose that means we are ready, coach," Margaret said, reluctantly moving her index and middle fingers in a walking motion on the wall.

Eleanor moved the yardstick farther up the wall. "Come on, Mama, two more inches. Now that your cast is off, we're going to get you all the way up to the ceiling so when Christmas comes you can decorate the top of the tree."

❧

Madeleine Cunningham normally sat in her car with the motor running waiting for Gracie to arrive. Each Thursday Gracie tried to get to work a little earlier, but she never managed to find Madeleine still in the house. She looked unusually stormy today. She unloaded a large bushel of apples from the trunk of her car and plopped it into Gracie's arms. "It's about time," she complained. "I have a hair appointment at nine and I don't want to be late." Her normally pomaded black hair had been mussed by the wind giving her a frazzled rather than disheveled air.

"What are we going to do with the apples?" Gracie asked.

"We are not doing anything. You will be making my mother's applesauce."

"I don't know how..."

"Mother will show you everything," Madeleine snapped, plunking another bushel on the ground. "Just get these apples in the kitchen."

"Goodbye, dear. Tell Zelda I said hello," a soothing voice called from the parlor as Gracie opened the door.

"It's just me." Gracie called out. "Your daughter's left for a hair appointment." She stored the bushels next to the back pantry and went to find Mrs. Cunningham.

"Oh, good morning Grace," the old woman said, patting her gray hair. "Come on, fix me some toast and we'll get to work," she said, rising from her chair and heading toward the kitchen, fingering the furniture to guide herself.

"Grace, dear, we are making my famous applesauce today. I'll show you exactly what to do."

Up popped the toast. Gracie buttered it, placed it on the table and poured prune juice from the icebox.

"Ooh, smell those apples. They came down from New York on the train yesterday." Mrs. Cunningham placed a finger demurely over her mouth while she chewed. "Pull out the big white enameled pot from the cabinet to the left of the sink, dear. That's it. Now get the Foley mill behind it."

"Shouldn't I start peeling, Mrs. Cunningham? There are an awful lot of apples here."

"I never peel them. Even when I could see, I didn't peel them. 'Tis my secret, you see." She made two quick "t" sounds with her tongue on the roof of her mouth. "Just wash them well, take out the core and quarter them; then into the pot with a little water they go."

"Oh, what a relief." Gracie chuckled. "At home, Mother used to make Lily and I do the peeling. I hated that job." They chatted as she dropped apple quarters into the pot. Striking a match, she lit the gas burner and transferred the pot to the stove. "How much sugar?"

"None."

"Oh, my mother always added a lot. And cinnamon too."

"No cinnamon. It spoils the pink. Grace, my dear, for someone who never talks about her mother, you certainly remember a lot about how she made applesauce."

Gracie flushed. "Oh, sorry...er...I mean, I have to ask you something. May I leave at early today so I can check my post office box? I might have a package."

"Excellent, you opened the post office box. I'm so proud of you. There'll be a letter from your sister any day now. Tell me more about your mother, Grace," Mrs. Cunningham coaxed.

Eager to change the subject, Gracie said, "I've never heard of pink applesauce."

"Well, cooking the apples with the peel turns the applesauce pink and those Cortland apples are so sweet I don't add sugar. An old diabetic lady like me can enjoy sweet applesauce with no stern warnings from my doctor. I hear it bubbling. Turn the burner down, dear, and let's enjoy a cup of Postum in the living room."

"'...refuse to tax citizens who would not use the bridge in order to pay for those who would motor across to Philadelphia,' said Camden's mayor in a statement yesterday. 'So until Philadelphia agrees to turn the new Delaware River Bridge into a toll bridge, neither Pennsylvania nor New Jersey will be able to use the largest suspension bridge in the world.'" Mrs. Cunningham's cloudy eyes brightened with interest as Gracie read aloud.

"I wonder how long they are going to continue this nonsense." She clicked her tongue twice in reproach. "That beautiful new bridge has stood there unused for six months." Mrs. Cunningham sipped Postum from the cup she had balanced perfectly on her lap for twenty minutes.

"Six months?" Gracie asked, refolding the *Sullivan County Review*.

"Don't you read the newspapers?"

"Well, I guess only on Thursday when I read to you, but I read a news magazine every week."

"Grace, it is important to be informed about what is going on in state and local news. A weekly news magazine limits you to national and international concerns. There, dear. I am done." When Gracie brought the tea tray to her, Mrs. Cunningham felt for an empty space with her left hand and placed her cup gently down at exactly the right spot.

"Now let's finish canning the applesauce so you can leave early."

❧

Gracie turned on her heel off Mary Avenue on her way back to the Woodshed, pressing the package close to her chest to shield her from the wind and also to hold the letter tight against her. She wanted to run, but Mrs. Cunningham had tucked a pint jar of applesauce in each of the pockets of the coat Mrs. Woods had loaned her, and she didn't want them to break.

The applesauce was going to be the surprise star of tomorrow night's dinner, so she stashed it in her closet. She set the letter on the dresser and the Sears package on the bed, trying to decide which to open first. Before she could make up her mind, Peg called everyone to dinner.

"So you got a package today, Gracie." Eleanor said, passing the rice. "We want to see it."

"Just a minute, young lady. We are not done," said her father sternly. "What did I say about bicycling on the driveway?"

"I have to pull over to the side if I see or hear a car coming."

"In either..."

"In either direction, Papa. Cars, horses or bicycles. I promise. Gracie, what's in your package?"

"Eleanor, Gracie's mail is her private business," her mother chastised.

Gracie smiled happily at all of them. "Actually, I'd love to show you if you have time."

"I made Isaiah's butterscotch pudding. Can't we eat that first?" Peg pushed her chair back abruptly.

Eleanor popped out of her chair whistling Isaiah's pudding song while she stacked empty dinner plates and brought the dessert from the icebox.

"Dessert is delicious, Peg," Gracie gushed amidst appreciative murmurs from the family.

"Thank you."

"Mama, please let me do the dishes after Gracie shows us." Her mother nodded. Eleanor giggled as she dove with anticipation into the caned rocker in front of the fire to wait.

Running into her room, Gracie tore off her skirt and blouse and ripped open the package. She spread the long sleeved maroon wool dress with the velvet Peter Pan collar on her bed. After smoothing out some wrinkles, she tried on the dress and strode proudly out into the living room.

"Ooh...all those buttons." Eleanor squealed, running one finger down the front from collar to hem.

"Black velvet to match the collar. That's not all." Gracie turned around to show them the back of the dress. See the pleat?" She playfully kicked one leg back. "I'm going to call it my maroon slash."

Mrs. Woods gave her an impulsive hug. "It does my heart good to see you take delight in something, Gracie."

Peg rolled her eyes and pulled her sister into the kitchen to help clean up.

Gracie excused herself to her room. How kind it was of her borrowed family to want to see her new dress.

Lily's letter called to her from the dresser. She sat on the bed, exhaled loudly, and opened it. Lily said she was happy in her new life with George. She was going to have a baby in April. There were some details about how she had decorated their home. She didn't understand why Gracie had left home, but now that she had, Lily hoped they could at least write. Gracie turned the short letter over twice, astounded at its brevity. There was no mention of her parents asking for her, and Lily hadn't inquired about Gracie's life.

With mixed emotions, she put the letter aside, intending to answer soon. At least the twinge she felt in her chest when George's face trespassed through her brain was gone, but it hurt that her real family didn't seem to care much about her.

After the Woods left to play bridge on Friday night, Gracie felt very depressed, even though her fried pork chops and Mrs. Cunningham's applesauce were an obvious hit at the dinner table. She moped in her room, listlessly checking in the mirror to see how much her blonde hair had grown. She ought to have kept up the smart bob she had treated herself to when she first came to the Crestmont. She promised herself to find out more information about Zelda, the hairdresser.

To console herself, she pulled her red suitcase out from under the bed. She removed her yellow jewelry box and placed it next to her. Her friend, the old paper bag of poems, tempted her. She opened the old bag and drew out the first poem her fingers touched. The end of the poem read:

"I would hold your heart in my hands,
But I am not strong enough.

But in your hands, my Love,
My heart is secure."

She ached for someone to trust her that much. She wondered fleetingly if PT ever thought about her, and then pitched the thought away. Grabbing her book and the Cashmere Bouquet soap she had treated herself to, she went into the bathroom.

Gracie enjoyed a luxurious bath on Friday night because only she and the girls were at home. Opening the Cashmere Bouquet, she drank in the flowery fragrance from the pink bar. Once she was in the bathtub, she relaxed in the hot water and the scent of her new soap made her feel womanly. It was a contrast to the stark smell of the Ivory soap her family always used.

Relieved that she and Mrs. Woods had worked out their differences, she hoped all of the craziness about the secret hideout was gone. It seemed that the Woods had their troubles too, but unlike her family, they talked them out.

She fell asleep, feeling a bit happier. At four in the morning, however, she awoke from an odd dream about PT. He was curled over the piano as usual, but he was playing some kind of classical music, not his usual jazz. She stood silently behind him and when he finished she asked him what he had played. Wordlessly, he turned toward her, his brown eyes tormented. His mouth was wired shut.

Philadelphia, Pennsylvania
September 1925

DIM STREET LIGHTS CAST SPIDERY FINGERS OF PURPLE, BLUE AND YELLOW in the oil spills on the rain-soaked street leading away from the river. The snap of windshield wipers on the cars was occasionally interrupted by orders barked in hushed voices from the approaching boats. Three men, huddled under umbrellas, leaned against the dripping black cars that were backed up close to the dock. The taller man, Morton, clicked his flashlight on and off, signaling the boats in.

Morton shoved a scrawny, agitated man who kept wiping his nose on his sleeve. "Wait in the car. Yer makin' me nervous. Besides, Pete and me got business to discuss. And shut that door nice and quiet like."

"I hope they squabble about this toll thing a long time," muttered Morton to his partner. "Imagine building a newfangled suspension bridge over the Delaware River and not usin' it for months. Perfect for us, huh? While they dicker on how to pay for it, we paddle our boats over from Camden. No one knows; no one cares."

Pete pushed his cap back and listened to the oars slapping the water. "Yeah, we sure are makin' good dough while it lasts."

Morton flicked a toothpick around in his mouth and changed the subject. "We made the right call quittin' the beer trade, Pete. More buzz per ounce in the hard stuff means we don't transport as much to make a buck. What's yer handle on the skinny guy with the two letters instead of a real name? I thought he loaded okay last year, just not sure I trust him yet."

"Name's PT. He'll do. Didn't want to unload tonight, though," Pete said. "Said he'd be better in the spotter car. I said okay, thinkin' you'd agree." He grabbed Morton's flashlight. "How 'bout you check on him and I'll signal these guys in."

PT's intestines swam uneasily when he saw Morton approach. He wound the window down and Morton stuck his head in out of the rain.

"You're kiddin', right? Settled so nice and dry in this spotter car. Pete tells me even after we gave you the summer off yer too chicken-ass high and mighty to unload. We got sixty-eight bucks worth in these boats and yer goin' to unwrap those arms off that steerin' wheel and move hooch into cars or yer not gettin' a dime. Chew that one over awhile."

"I can do more for you as a spotter. Right here, ready to lead the cars out quick as they get loaded. Besides, I'm your best bet to give the cops the slip. I know four different ways to get to the warehouse. Walked those streets for weeks trying to find speakeasies to play in."

"Yeah," Morton bit off his cigar tip and spat it onto PT's lap. "I can see you drivin' away the minute you see a scout car's headlights shinin' in yer eyes, leavin' the rest of us to get picked up by whatever cops we forgot to pay off. Seems like yer tryin' to work your way down the ladder, not the other way around, bud." He closed one eye halfway, considering, held up the cigar, and waited for PT to light it.

"Won't let you down," PT said firmly, flapping out his match.

Morton drew in a long drag and blew smoke into PT's face. "Okay, but you cross me and I'll blackball you in every speakeasy in the Delaware Valley. You won't be playin' piano anywhere. Now turn off those damn lights and get in place."

"Yes, sir." He switched off the headlights and carefully backed up until the back bumper was six feet in front of the lead loading car.

He despised calling a guy like Morton "sir." Morton didn't deserve respect anymore than PT's father had.

"Don't you give me any lip, kid," his drunken father had said once after PT responded "Yup" instead of "Yes, sir." It took five weeks for PT's broken rib to heal. He started leaving the house then when his parents fought, and he didn't grieve a bit when his father's liver gave out.

After his father died, his mother let her crude boyfriend move in. PT dropped out of school when he was fifteen, left home for good, and gave his mother a post office box number. He hadn't heard a word from her since he stopped sending her money ten years ago. After all that time, she finally wrote. Her boyfriend moved out and she needed money. Such gall. But he felt obligated to help her out. Guilt could tug at a guy a long time.

Although he had been able to support himself working in bowling alleys and an occasional speakeasy gig, now he needed a boost in income. Working with bootleggers Morton and Jack solved the problem. What he hadn't realized was how it would eat at his conscience. Playing at speakeasies was one thing. Working in the illegal hooch trade was a whole different deal.

The picture of a pretty eyebrow arching up under blonde curls cut through his history review. He couldn't believe how innocent she sounded when she sang. Would a girl who went to church every week have any interest in man stuck in the middle of a crime scene? Only a muddleheaded dolt would think such a thing.

He was jolted back to reality by a tap on the rear windshield from Morton, signaling it was time to head out.

Woodshed on Crestmont Hill
Autumn 1925

I

"Peg, where is your sister?" asked Margaret.

"How should I know? I can't watch her every minute, Mama."

"Peg, I know we ask you to look after her during the summer when we are busy, but you know I don't expect...." She was interrupted by an odd sound coming from outside the front door. Her eyes went to the window and she saw Shadow, pacing back and forth, meowing insistently. Eleanor limped along behind.

"William, come here!" Margaret reached her wet, shivering daughter first. William scooped Eleanor up in his arms and carried her into the cottage.

"Gracie, bring a chair," Margaret ordered as they gingerly sat Eleanor down next to the warm coal stove. "Sweetheart, what happened? Here, let's get these wet things off."

Before Margaret could ask, Gracie handed her a towel and crouched next to Eleanor. Then she ran into the child's bedroom for her yellow bathrobe as Margaret carefully removed her daughter's clothes, inspecting for injuries.

"I'm not hurt, Mama, just w-wet," she managed, her purplish lips quivering.

"What happened?" her mother asked, awkwardly wiping her dry with her good arm. "Come on, put this on."

Eleanor stretched her arms into her bathrobe. Her mother wrapped an afghan around her shoulders. "I was fishing and I accidentally fell in."

"Gracie, heat up some of that lemonade for her. Fishing where?"

"In the outlet pond."

"What?" Both of her parents froze.

"Miss Eleanor, we have repeatedly told you that you are never to fish alone in the lake," her father reprimanded.

"Papa, I wasn't fishing in the lake; I went to the outlet pond. And I wasn't alone, either. Shadow was with me the whole time."

"Oh, this is preposterous." William threw his arms up and walked away.

"Well, something went wrong," Margaret said gently. "How did you get soaking wet?"

Eleanor honked loudly into the handkerchief her mother held for her, and said, "I had a really good bite. I mean, I think I had a big one, so I gave a good yank on my pole, but I guess I slipped in the mud and fell in."

"Where did you get this fishing pole?" her father demanded.

"I made it. Zeke taught me and gave me a couple of hooks so I could make my own. I can swim, you know, Papa. I'm not five years old anymore."

"William, she did get herself home all right and she doesn't seem to be hurt. Let's just concentrate on getting her warm." Margaret gratefully accepted the hot lemon toddy from Gracie and put the cup to Eleanor's lips. Peg sat on the floor and started to rub warmth back into her sister's legs.

"You really did it this time, you little nincompoop," she whispered to her sister.

❧❧

"Mama never gets a headache," Eleanor cried.

"Well, she has one this morning, so let's be quiet and let her rest. She doesn't feel well enough to go to church today. You girls go get dressed." William, who normally came to breakfast perfectly groomed, sat slouched and unshaven, his hair in disarray.

Eleanor jumped up from the table. "I'm going to go read to her. She reads to me when I am sick and it always makes me feel better."

"Whoa." Peg pulled Eleanor back by the sleeve of her yellow bathrobe. "Be quiet and let her rest. Mama has what is called a 'melancholy' and she needs sleep, not pestering."

"What's a melancholy?" Eleanor asked fearfully.

"Hush" said William. "Your mother is just tired. Gracie, please clear the table." He dismissed his daughters to Eleanor's room.

William sank into the plaid sofa, deliberating over his plans for the Crestmont addition. How he wished his wife was well. Her illness was both disquieting and ill-timed. He needed to confer with her on some details before the contractor came tomorrow. He repeatedly pulled his handkerchief out of the chest pocket of his bathrobe to wipe his hands. It was a very bad time for these vicissitudes.

"Here's some paper and a pencil, Mr. Woods. It seemed like you wanted to write something down." Gracie, looking spiffy in her new dress, opened the blinds to let the morning light shine on his work.

"What? Oh, thank you." His voice was edgy.

"Sir, I don't need to go to church today. I can stay home in case Mrs. Woods needs me while you and the girls go to church."

"Nonsense. You told me you have a solo today. Everyone will be disappointed if you don't sing."

She sat firmly in the rocker across from him and leaned forward. "I could telephone Rev. Sturdy and explain. He would make them all understand. Besides, Mrs. Woods is more important to me."

❧

But Mr. Woods said no. He wanted to stay home with his wife. Gracie's solo went well. Rev. Sturdy praised her after the service and she received countless compliments from her church friends.

She wandered down to the Edgemere dock, enjoying the smell of wood smoke from a nearby chimney. She folded the afghan into a cushion on the wooden bench and settled in for some precious solitude. A cardinal ordered his missus around and scolded Gracie for sitting near their nest.

The late morning kissed the tops of the golden oaks on the mountainside. Blurry images swam in the lake, a mirror of the vermillion and orange leaves that glistened from last night's gentle autumn rain and pocketed themselves amidst the emerald of the tall white pine trees. Gracie had never before seen the beauty of autumn in the mountains.

The imposing Crestmont Inn sat majestically across the lake on the hill. Unlike the lonely sentinel she had seen ten days ago after she moved into the Woodshed, it now seemed like a silent parent, nurturing the lives of people who passed through its doors. How it had changed her life in the few months she had been there. She said a silent prayer that Mrs. Woods would soon be as carefree and refreshed as if she herself were a guest in the inn.

Gracie jumped when Shadow rubbed against her leg. Sniffing the water suspiciously from the edge of the dock, the cat returned and jumped up on the bench.

The cat purred when she stroked its coal-colored fur. "You act as if you own the whole town. Come on, you can share." Gracie spread the orange and brown afghan out so it covered the seat and back of the bench. The cat curled its tail around itself and nestled next to her.

"The Woods needed some privacy, so I've come to do some money figuring. If you want to stay, you'll have to be still."

Studying the money page in her writing tablet, Gracie was amazed to find that even after buying the maroon slash, she had $72 saved from season close-up and her two jobs. The winter coat, shoes, hat and gloves she needed cost more than she had ever spent at one time in her life. Sending the money order to Sears was scary, but she decided to be bold and add some sheet music. She would sneak up to the library in the big house tonight and write up the order.

Shadow stopped purring the minute Gracie started humming. "Oh, sorry." She scratched the cat's silky place behind its ears. "It's Mrs. Sturdy's favorite hymn and I'm going to sing it soon. Rev. Sturdy said I could practice on the church piano Saturday mornings. I don't think Mrs. Woods will mind, do you?" Shadow bolted after a squirrel, leaving Gracie feeling foolish for talking to a cat.

Turning to the page where she wrote down her friends, she added Rev. and Mrs. Sturdy and wondered if PT would ever make the list. She hoped so.

⚘

"Do you feel better today, Mrs. Woods?" Gracie asked anxiously from the passenger seat as they drove to Laporte Monday morning. "I can do more around the house, even help you with your bookwork."

Mrs. Woods dismissed her with a wave of her hand. "Today I feel good and I want to enjoy it. First we'll go to the bank. I am hoping you will open a savings account, Gracie." Mrs. Woods advised. "Then you make what is called 'interest,' you see. Keeping your money in the hotel safe does keep it secure, but doesn't help it grow, and when the snow starts, we can't guarantee you'll be able to get into the big house any time you want."

The Sullivan Bank of Laporte was a solid brick structure with a thick carved oak door. Gracie smelled lemon oil as they entered. Funny gray fingers wiggled on the glowing marble floor from the light coming through the bars on the windows. Desks in the rear where typewriters clacked were separated from the main teller area by heavy wooden railings.

A bank officer opened a gate in the railing and ushered Mrs. Woods into a green leather chair in front of his desk. Gracie stepped up to the teller booth and spoke to a bald man in a navy blue suit with glasses threatening to come off the tip of his nose. "I'd like to open a savings account, please."

"Oh, good. I am glad you did it." Mrs. Woods said later, eyeing the little gray book Gracie was examining.

"Please excuse me, Mrs. Woods. I have another little transaction to make."

When the teller handed her the money order, she tucked it in her purse, promising herself to save the next three weeks salary.

They motored in silence until Mrs. Woods stopped the car in front of the Penn Economy Self-Serve. "I can get the groceries." Gracie asked. "You can rest in the car if you're tired. I've got a list of everything I need for my dinners."

"Oh, no, my head is much better today. Besides, shopping for food relaxes me. These new stores are wonderful. We can browse the shelves and make our own selections without having to go to the counter and hand the clerk a list. Let's do it together, shall we?"

They stood, considering the canned vegetables. Mrs. Woods had Gracie pull cans of beets, green beans and corn off the shelves.

"I'll show you how to make the scalloped corn my husband loves." Mrs. Woods checked her watch pin and threw a box of Shredded Wheat in the cart. "Oh, my dear, how the time has flown. Gracie, go see if the butcher has our order ready, and don't forget the newspaper. We must get home. A contractor is coming to consult about the addition plans and my husband won't be home from school in time to meet him."

Gracie's eyes didn't focus well on the newspaper because the car was jostling so much as they rode back to Eagles Mere. "May I borrow this tomorrow, Mrs. Woods?"

"Of course, but tomorrow it will be old news."

"That's okay. I have a lot to catch up on."

෧ര

On Wednesday evening, William excused himself from the

dinner table to dress for choir practice. Margaret wiped her mouth on her napkin and followed him. "You're going to have to be a little late for choir tonight, William. I have something on my mind, which we need to discuss."

"Margaret, I can't be late. The tenor section..."

She closed their bedroom door and he reluctantly put down his comb.

"I'm concerned that Peg and Eleanor feel the guests are more important to us than they are."

He regarded her with incredulity. "Well, this certainly came out of the blue. We give our girls a lot of love. And so does the Crestmont. Why, the staff is like a second family to them. Goodness, when Peg isn't off playing with her summer friends, she's right there helping me with all kinds of things at the inn. She is genuinely interested in learning the business."

She cut him off. "That's not the point; we never have family time to spend with them away from work in the summer. And I have been so handicapped, first by my broken arm and now this fatigue; I haven't been caring for them as I should."

"But you are home with them from September to May, for all intensive purposes. You do most of your Crestmont work while they are at school—you are a wonderful mother—Margaret, where has all this come from?"

"It's not just me, William; it is you. You are busy entertaining the guests in the summer; mind you, I know that is necessary. During the school year you have your teaching, church choir, Eagles Mere Association meetings. My point, dear, is that they need more of you, especially Eleanor. I am convinced of it since that fishing incident. The child is just crying for attention. William, do you realize she will be ten this year? I think you should plan something special for her birthday, just you and Eleanor."

"What on earth would we do?"

"Ask Eleanor. I know she's been dying to explore all the covered bridges around here." She sat down on the blue chenille bedspread and buried her face in her hands, then dropped her weak arm into her lap. He sat down beside her.

"All right, I'll plan something for just Eleanor and me. Anything she wants."

"Good." Margaret patted his thigh, went to the dresser and concentrated on the mirror. "Let's plan a family surprise for her birthday next Saturday."

"But that's the third game of the World Series. The Pittsburgh Pirates against the Washington Senators. I promised Peg we'd listen together," he said desperately.

"Then we'll plan it for the evening. They can't play baseball in the dark, can they?" Determined eyes bore into him from her reflection.

ॐ

William sat on the edge of the bed on Saturday, tracing circles with his finger on his wife's forehead. "You'll feel much better if you get out, my love. The sun is shining and the morning air is crisp. Take a walk with me, Margaret."

"I'm tired of being tired, William. I have Eleanor's birthday to plan and we have so much work to do on the addition." She dragged herself out of bed and wrapped herself in the blue bathrobe he had bought her last year for Christmas.

"Come on, I've made you one of my egg sandwiches. Gracie is at church practicing and the girls are off on their bicycles already." He led her into the kitchen, ushered her into a chair and poured her some juice.

"William, I must be very ill, because this tastes delicious and your egg sandwiches are usually terrible. Or did you remember to add salt this time?" Margaret teased.

"It's the catsup, my dear. It makes all the difference."

Margaret left him polishing the pine table and wiping the dishes. She heard him singing from the other side of the wall while she dressed.

"You'll need your hat and gloves, too, now that your pretty hand is out of the cast," he said, holding her coat for her.

They strolled, arm in arm, admiring the inn they loved on their left.

"We won't believe how much larger it will look next season. I'm already working on a new brochure advertising our improvements. Peg and I are planning more water sports to appeal to the young people. Otto says he has plenty of customers now that we've opened the garage year round." He prattled on until Margaret unexpectantly stopped walking.

The rippled clouds in the early morning threatened to steal the sun's glow from the yellow oak in front of the laundry. The tree stood with its partner, a blue spruce, the only survivors of the 1882 cyclone.

Margaret admired the tenacity of the leaves, which clung to the branches longer than any of the younger trees. She felt if she could just hold on like that her spirit would rejuvenate. Grateful for a husband who tried to help her through this difficult time, she caught a lone golden leaf that drifted down and held it out for William to see.

"Daddy used to call it our official accent color. The awnings, the lettering on the car..."

"My ties," he winked, taking the leaf. "I always entertained the notion that your father used the yellow as a symbol of fun under the summer sun."

"No. Daddy loved autumn in Eagles Mere. He said if this oak could survive the cyclone then we should take the special strength of its fall color and put it into the Crestmont so it would survive too." He handed her the leaf and she secreted it into her pocket.

William took her elbow and turned her toward the hill. He swept his arm over the expanse of the big house. "I rather like how your father designed the west wing as a kind of embrace of the hill. In my estimation our addition will enhance that effect. Now, for my surprise."

He grasped her firmly by the shoulders and pivoted her so she faced the muddy slope to the left of the laundry building. "Tell me what you see," he said eagerly.

"Besides the mud?" Margaret was cautious, knowing that her husband, the ambitious dreamer, was full of creative ideas about what would improve the Crestmont. Even though she firmly believed it was only in the details that their dream could be kept alive, she had to admit that he always saw the larger picture. "William, tell me what *you* see."

"I see a three-story staff dormitory right here next to the laundry—a matching white Victorian porch—a way to hide the steam room and maintain the symmetry of the area." He strode onto the open ground, oblivious to his shoes sinking into the muck. "The women can have the top two floors, and we'll put the senior male staff on the ground floor. Think of the rooms that will free up in the big house. Part of the basement could be a staff lounge with a ping pong table, a piano, and a big fireplace."

"We could put a white picket fence here along the drive, keeping the staff buildings at the bottom of the hill set apart from the rest of the campus." Margaret traced the path, careful to stay off the mud. "And plant some trees for privacy. Then the staff would truly have their own space and perhaps relax a bit more off duty. Oh, William, it's a brilliant idea."

"The contractors assured me the shell of the addition on the big house would be completed before the snow comes. We can finish the inside over the winter. Then the dormitory will have to go up quickly in the spring."

"William, slow down. Father only left us so much money. First you were talking tennis courts, and now this dormitory..."

"My love," he said, dancing her around in a waltz step, "your father is not the only one who saved money."

"You?" she laughed incredulously.

"There. You are laughing. Now we both feel better."

"How did you hide it from me?"

"That, my dear, remains a mystery even to me."

II

"WITH VANILLA FROSTING?"

"Yes, Eleanor, chocolate cake with vanilla frosting."

"And ten candles, all lit up."

"Ten candles, most definitely."

"Can we eat it now?"

"After dinner, darling. I'm making roast lamb, your favorite. You can wait that long."

"No I can't. It smells like cake in here and it's driving me bananas. When did you bake it, Mama?"

"Gracie and I made it after you went to bed last night."

Three teddy bears and a book dropped to the floor as Eleanor threw aside her blankets and bounded out of bed. "Papa is taking me to Loyalsock Creek Park to find the covered bridges today. Then cake after dinner. That's a pretty good birthday."

Margaret pulled black woolen leggings and a heavy blue sweater out of Eleanor's dresser. "What a cold day today. I don't care what other clothes you wear, but put these on too. I have some errands to run. Have fun with Papa. And don't grow up too fast, darling. I love you."

Eleanor threw her arms around her mother's waist. "I love you too, Mama."

Margaret marched into their bedroom, annoyed with William for planning the trip the same day as the birthday surprise. She worried Eleanor would be overtired.

"William, time to get up," she said, opening the curtains. "Gracie and I are going food shopping at the Penn Economy. Make sure you have Eleanor home by four. I want her to take a nap before dinner."

William lifted his head off the pillow, shielding his eyes from the light. "Mm? Yes, home by four, dear."

୨⸰୧

Peg lounged shoeless, her legs propped up on the arm of the couch. William crouched in front of the radio, turning the dial back and forth to tune the station in clearly. They could barely hear the announcer say, "This is Westinghouse Radio Network," over the static. The radio, with its little legs and huge black dial on the front, had been returned to its prominent place next to the fireplace, now that the empty safe had been removed to Margaret's office closet.

"Papa, I smell your egg burning. You don't want to miss the game," Peg warned.

Running into the kitchen, William slapped the crusty egg onto the bread, elected to forego the catsup, and thrust the sizzling cast iron skillet into the sink. Eleanor sat stony-faced at the kitchen table. He gave her a distracted pat on the head and scurried back into the living room, balancing his plate.

"Graham McAfee, broadcasting to you from Forbes Field in Pittsburgh. Here we are, the third game in the best of seven series between the Pittsburgh Pirates and the Washington Senators. Over forty-three thousand people here in the stadium have their eyes peeled on Johnson, the star pitcher for the Senator's. He's grinding his heel on the mound. He's winding up."

"You promised." Eleanor scolded, snapping off the radio.

"Honey, Pittsburg is about to stomp out the Washington Senators—promised what?"

"You said we could go up to Loyalsock Creek for my birthday."

"Well, of course I did." He put his plate down on the coffee table and crouched down in front of her. "But I thought we said we'd go tomorrow. We'll see the waterfall, the covered bridge and stop at the Forksville General store for a hotdog afterwards. What do you think?"

Eleanor flopped down, cross-legged on the floor, and pushed her fists into her chin. "You said today. And you said all five covered bridges," she grumbled.

"What are you doing here? You don't even like baseball," Peg asked her sister.

"I've got nothing else to do."

"They should have let Aldridge pitch the whole thing." Peg shut off the radio after the game was over and flounced off the sofa.

"Well, it's only the third game," her father said "and they won the first two. Peg, you're going to have to listen to tomorrow's for me."

"Yes, because Papa and I are going to find covered bridges. Sunday!" Eleanor slammed her bedroom door behind her.

ᖇᖇᖇ

"Where is Eleanor?" Margaret asked later when she and Gracie bustled in loaded with groceries.

"In her room," William said sheepishly, taking their coats.

"Peg, here are some birthday decorations. Please hide them. I'll put them up quickly when she dresses for dinner."

"Well, you're home early." Margaret gave William a kiss. "Did you find all the covered bridges?"

"No, I was under the impression it was tomorrow and I had promised Peg we would listen to the ball game together."

"You didn't go? William, you promised her, and you promised me. I would think an intelligent man like you would stop trusting his memory and write things down."

"Margaret, we are going tomorrow."

"Well, that's something, I suppose." She whipped her apron off the hook. "I have a roast to put in the oven."

Gracie went into Eleanor's room to cheer her up and escape the tension. Within fifteen minutes the two of them were on the living room floor playing Hearts. Gracie's curiosity was perked about the birthday surprise. She had heard Mrs. Woods telling someone on the telephone, "not until five minutes after six."

At precisely six o'clock, Margaret pushed Eleanor gently toward her room. "Go look in your closet for a new birthday dress and get all gussied up. I want everything to be perfect, so do not come out until I call you."

"William, take this bow and put it on her new sled on the porch and then keep watch for a car on the driveway."

"What car, Margaret?"

"I have a nice surprise for all of us." Margaret said. "Peg, you have to keep Eleanor in her room for at least fifteen minutes."

"How am I supposed to do that when she never stops moving?"

"Make up some game or something. Gracie and I have taken care of everything else."

Fifteen minutes later, her mother, father, sister and Gracie were all lined up near the fireplace facing the kitchen when Eleanor frolicked into the living room, caught the black taffeta skirt of her new dress and twirled around, showing off the red ribbon tied at her hip on the dropped waist.

"My beautiful little girl," her father said.

"It smells like roses. Did you buy me roses?" She clapped with delight turning around to look. A plump lady beamed at her from the kitchen table.

"Dorothy!" Eleanor threw her arms around her and sneezed from the Ashes of Roses cologne. "What a perfect surprise."

Eagles Mere, Pennsylvania
December 1925

"MY MOTHER SAID I COULD PICK UP THE MAIL." ELEANOR SCRAPED THE snow off her boots on the woven straw mat in front of the post office door and scuffed up to Mr. Rose, who was peering down his nose, sorting several piles of mail.

"Whatever you say, young lady, but it's a heavy load. Evidently, the Woods get a lot of Christmas cards." He pushed a tall stack tied with butcher's cord across the counter.

"Oh, yes, our guests send them from all over the country." Eleanor helped herself to the pile.

"Here's one for you, too, Miss Antes," Mr. Rose said handing a single ivory-colored envelope to Gracie.

"Who's that from?" Eleanor asked later, chomping on Crackerjacks in the General Store.

"My sister, Lily."

"Well, where are the rest of your cards?"

Gracie gathered the caramel popcorn and nuts that Eleanor had spilled on the counter, put them back in the box and said, "You had better eat this on the way home. We have beds to change before your mother gets home from her meeting with the contractor."

"Papa said they finished the shell of the addition. Mama was picking out bathtubs today." The air was cold and still, but lazy snowflakes began to dot Eleanor's yellow knit hat as they walked home.

"And faucets, bedspreads and curtains," Gracie added, checking and rechecking the thickness of the envelope in her pocket when they passed the stone pillars at the base of Crestmont Hill. It had the hardness of a card and wasn't thick enough to have a very long letter in it. She hadn't heard from Lily in over two months.

❧

"You have to shake these sheets till they snap," Eleanor instructed Gracie when they got home, unfolding a sheet and flapping it in the air before putting it on her bed. "Gets the bugs off when you take them off the clothesline. Now you snap the top sheet."

"So you're saying I left bugs on them when I ironed them?" Gracie teased, smoothing the sheet onto the bed and tucking in the corners.

"Naw, it's just what Magdalena taught me last summer, but I like watching your curls bounce and settle right back when you do it. That Zelda lady did a nice job cutting your bob. My hair is always flying all over. Mama moans because I got hers instead of Papa's. Is your sister's hair like yours?"

"It's blonde like mine, but nice and straight."

"Like my friend, Dora." Eleanor observed knowingly. "So, are you going to spend Christmas with us, or are you going home to see your sister?"

"I think I'll stay right here. Now, let's get your parents' bed made before they get home. And then, I need to see to dinner."

"I saw a hunk of beef in the icebox. Are you going to make pot roast again? Because now that you learned to keep water in the bottom, your pot roast is pretty good."

"Well, since you gave me such a nice compliment, Eleanor, I'll let you peel the potatoes."

⌘

On Thursday afternoon, Gracie sat on Mrs. Cunningham's sofa stringing popcorn for the tiny tree Madeleine had hastily placed in the front bay window two days ago. The crystal-leaded decorative pane above it shone like illuminated stained glass in a dark church. Mrs. Cunningham pulled her brown shawl around her, soaking up the sun's warmth as it filtered through the three windows in the parlor's side alcove.

"I want to hear all about it." Her face lit up with childlike enthusiasm.

"Sunday was a lovely day. We put the tree up so we could enjoy it for a week before Christmas. They made me put the star on top, but that was only because Mrs. Woods always does it and she couldn't reach with her right hand. They asked if they could come tonight to hear my solo and wanted to drive me so I wouldn't have to walk alone."

She paused, sucking on a finger the needle had pricked. "Then we sat around and they opened all their Christmas cards. They got one from PT..."

"And you didn't," Mrs. Cunningham soothed. Frowning, Gracie jumped up, draping the tree with the popcorn strand.

"He doesn't know you are there, dear. Didn't you tell me he left early last summer before Mrs. Woods broke her arm? Grace, it is quite proper in this day and age for a woman to send a man a card."

"I'll have to mull that over." She gently picked up cranberry strands from a bowl and interlaced them with the popcorn. "Will Madeleine be home soon? I have to go at five to be ready for church, and I don't want to leave you in alone in the dark."

"I won't be in the dark because I will have my music. Tune in my radio, won't you? St. Olaf's choir from that Lutheran college in Minnesota always broadcasts on Christmas Eve and I don't want to miss it."

"It's really pretty, if I do say so myself." Gracie backed away from the tree and crooked her head, examining the cranberry and popcorn strands amongst the gold bows she had tied on the ends of the boughs. The voices of the choir filled the room.

Families were packed into the pews at the Presbyterian Church. Beeswax Candles on poles with glass globes lined the center aisle, casting a magical glow throughout the sanctuary. The scent of pine permeated the air. Mothers shushed their children as the organ started the prelude.

It was Gracie's first Christmas away from home. She proceeded toward the front of the church, singing the opening carol with the choir. In her Moravian Church, the Christmas star with its twenty-six conical points representing the Star of Bethlehem would have greeted her. It always mesmerized her. The presence of the Woods family sitting in a pew toward the back of the Presbyterian Church attenuated that void.

When she sang her solo, a welcome wash of confidence kept her voice remarkable steady and her knees even cooperated by not shaking. The hush that swept through the congregation told her that the people were moved.

After the service, Gracie carefully hung up her robe in the choir room, wished her fellow choir members a Merry Christmas, and hurried back into the sanctuary to find the Woods. A cacophony of holiday wishes, babies crying, and children running had replaced the peaceful stillness of the service.

Suddenly she felt a warm breath on her ear. A deep voice from behind her sent a rippling sensation through her chest. "I understood every word."

She turned toward the voice. "Thank you." A handsome stranger stood before her. He had intelligent, sharp features, chestnut hair, and was dressed impeccably in a three-piece brown tweed suit.

"And your voice is really pretty, too," he added, chuckling to himself at his omission. "I'm Eric," he said, offering his hand.

"Pleased to meet you. Gracie," she said, thankful for the gloves that separated her perspiring hand from his as she shook it.

"I know. My parents told me all about you."

"Your parents?" Eric nodded toward Rev. and Mrs. Sturdy. "Oh. But I've never seen you here before," she said dumbly.

"I've been away at college. Just came home for Christmas holiday."

"Gracie, Gracie, you sounded beautiful," squealed Eleanor, flinging her arms around her waist. Gracie returned the hug. When she looked up, he was gone.

Gracie waited until after she was back in her room to open the card. A manger scene with the baby Jesus surrounded by angels and shepherds was on the cover. An impersonal "Merry Christmas" was imprinted on the inside, and Lily had written, "Love, Lily and George." So that was it. The door was really closed on her old life. She was relieved in a way, but she still wiped tears away as she hid the card in a drawer. After all, she was the one who had left.

She climbed into bed, tried to read, but was too distracted to concentrate. Sighing, she turned out the light. Before she went to sleep she asked God to help her know what would come next for her. She loved living with the Woods family, but she knew it wouldn't last forever.

That night she dreamed she walked down a windy path surrounded by hemlocks and holly bushes to a dark stone house with a tiny green door set in with wrought iron hinges. Gracie knocked.

A faceless man in a flowing robe opened the door. "You would not have knocked unless you believe. You may enter." Gracie followed the mysterious escort into the house.

"I will show you our rooms. You may choose where to spend your time, but you must be quiet. This is a library after all."

He opened a door to a music room illuminated by several roaring fireplaces. Five men held hymnals and hummed quietly while Mr. Woods conducted them with a stick from a music stand, his face raised exultantly toward heaven. His hair fell to his shoulders and flew about as he moved his arms. A young girl played a silent violin with vigorous bow strokes. Gracie stepped back out of the doorway and was led down three stone steps.

Vintage clothes filled the next room. Straw hats with ribbons, felt hats adorned with elaborate veils and jeweled pins sat on hooks all around the walls. A vase held feathers of many colors and sizes. Gracie was delighted to see a dress she had always wanted on a seamstress frame. Dress gloves and jewelry lay neatly arranged on a chest of drawers. When she saw her yellow jewelry box amidst the gloves, she realized she had been in the room before.

When she was done in that room, her guide instructed her to find the other rooms on her own. She could use whatever she wanted to in the rooms, but she couldn't take any items out into the world.

Gracie found a reading room, laden with bookshelves. The deep window sills held various candles, which burned bright against the pitch black outside. Spilled wax had run over and hardened on the sills and floor. Mrs. Woods stood on a little footstool, delightedly pulling one book and then another off the shelves. Finding one that pleased her, she settled comfortably on a big golden couch with pearly white throw pillows. A huge pillar candle on a tiny round table shed light on her book and face, illuminating her contented smile. She opened the book and eagerly turned the first page.

In the game room, Raggedy Ann dolls pumped their feet in miniature rocking chairs and ate purple ice cream cones. Eleanor set up a Parcheesi game and said, "Remember, Dora, you can only win if you believe you can." Dora sat across from her in the white shift with the blue ribbon at the hip she had worn last summer. Three of Eleanor's favorite teddy bears played jump rope in the corner, winking at each other with alternating eyes.

The last room was the writing room. There was no one in it, but a huge Christmas tree lit with candles stood in the corner. A large center table held Gracie's writing tablets, the card from Lily, as well as some old journals and many kinds of stationery. The room gave her a chill.

Gracie chose to spend her remaining time in the reading room. She sat next to Mrs. Woods on the couch for a long time, each absorbed in their own book, not aware the other was there.

"Where's Peg?" Gracie asked the escort, who came for her at closing time.

"She stays outside. Peg likes to feel the sun on her skin and plays badminton or volleyball with her friends. You needn't be alarmed. There is a locked gate, so she is safe."

Gracie was led to a different door from which she entered. She worried that she would get lost, but her escort assured her that she had received in the library precisely what she needed and once on the outside, she would know exactly where she was.

Camden, New Jersey
1914

HE LICKED THE TIP OF HIS PENCIL, WRAPPED A BLANK PIECE OF PAPER around the dollar bills and addressed the envelope. It was a ritual he had gone though the last Monday of every month for the past two years. Maybe it would make up for all the times he had discovered his mother putting ice on a black eye or moving as if she were favoring her ribs. PT knew his father was hitting her, but he had never had found a way to make him stop. Maybe he should have dropped out of school earlier so he could stay home more. Maybe she would have paid PT more attention after his father died if she hadn't let her lazy boyfriend move in.

Maybe he would stop sending her money.

Maybe.

He lay back on the thin, squeaky mattress thinking he didn't have it so bad for a seventeen-year-old boy. A room in a boarding house suited him. He scraped by just fine on what money he kept for himself.

He had long ago shut the doors of the rooms his parents had occupied in his head. Being alone was safe, and he liked it. The wall he had drawn around himself was a like a comforting shield, and when he walked into a bar after hours and asked to play the piano, the music washed over him, healing any residual sadness.

Today, however, he was on a mission. He was sick of washing dishes all over Camden and the occasional car mechanic's job didn't challenge him.

Heading south down North Fifth Street from his boarding house, PT dropped the envelope in a mailbox, then decided to see what was happening on Federal Street. He passed a new bowling alley called "Sloan's" and then backed up. Forming a visor with his hands on the glass to shield his eyes, he peered inside. Curiosity made him go in. The smell of pretzels, a gnawing reminder that he hadn't eaten breakfast today, hit him before he heard the Victrola.

Twenty polished wooden bowling lanes lined up on the right side of the place and a soda bar stood on the left wall. In the central area sat impressive cherry shelves displaying bowling shoes, balls and framed awards. A huge Victrola with a brass horn atop sat on the counter. A girl tying a brimmed blue hat trimmed with flowers under her chin touted, "Drink Coca Cola" from a huge calendar on the wall.

A door slammed. PT jumped. "I'm sick of telling those pin boys to speed it up, Eddie. You handle it." Warren Sloan emerged from the rear of the bowling lanes in a dapper black pinstriped suit and red bow tie. He cranked up the Victrola with one hand and pulled out a new record from under the counter. He was about to put it on the phonograph when he noticed PT.

"Hey, kid, what's up? Sorry, we're not running any games right now. You'll have to come back around eleven."

PT dipped his head down in acknowledgement, tucked his hands in his pockets, and cut his eyes over toward the soda bar. "If you need some help, I'm a pretty fast learner."

"Oh, you're looking for work. Come on over here," Sloan said, motioning toward the soda fountain. "Warren Sloan's the name," he said, offering his hand from the other side of the counter. "Boy, you're a scraggy one. I need some glasses from out back. Give me a minute and I'll fix you a root beer float."

PT pulled up a stool and slumped over the counter as Sloan disappeared through a door behind the pretzel machine. Stacked glasses, a big coffee urn and ads for malted milk, floats and beer half obscured the mirror behind the counter. Through an unoccupied corner PT saw the reflection of a piano on the same wall as the front door.

Sloan reentered with a tray loaded with thick soda glasses. He pumped root beer syrup into one, added seltzer water from the machine on the counter and a dollop of vanilla ice cream. After popping in a straw, he pushed the drink over the counter to PT. "Here."

Sloan pulled up a stool and idly drummed his fingers on the counter while the kid downed the drink. "Know anything about bowling?"

"Learned to bowl a bit when I played piano at that alley up on State Street."

"Good. Show me what you've got." They both stood, PT a head taller than Sloan, who was sizing up PT's feet. "You wear an eleven shoe, right?"

"Not bad," Sloan said later after the kid had thrown a few balls.

"Thanks."

"You don't say much, do you? I like that. You might even listen to me, unlike the knucklehead I just fired. I could teach you a thing or two about bowling if you like. How are you with figures?"

"Pretty good. I need a job, Mr. Sloan."

"Right. Come here a second." He went to the shoe rental counter, pulled out a sheet with numbers on it and pushed it over in front of PT. "I've got a bunch of people who've run up tabs renting shoes. Take a crack at adding these totals."

"This first guy owes you a dollar and a half."

"You added that in your head?"

"Yup."

"Impressive. Stand up and let me take a gander." Sloan pursed his lips and snapped one of PT's dirty suspenders. "Not only are you skinny, but a little scruffy too, pardon me saying it. Okay, I'll start you tomorrow, but you're going to have to clean up. Do you have a suit?" PT shook his head.

Sloan pulled his wallet and stuck some bills into the kid's hand. "Buy a new shirt, wash your suspenders and put on a tie. I need a guy out front to rent shoes and help players with scores. My partner, Eddie, can't be here all the time and I want to bowl more tournaments. We'll see how it goes."

సోయ

Warren Sloan, PT discovered after working for three weeks, ran two successful bowling alleys in Camden, had made a name for himself in tournaments along the east coast, wasn't in the war because of a slight heart condition, and continually talked about replacing pin boys with something mechanical. He never asked PT where he came from or where his family was. He treated him with respect and paid him a fair wage.

When PT asked to learn the soda fountain, Sloan corrected him, "It's a bar, kid. Soda fountains are for kids in drugstores. We sell beer, pretzels and some ice cream sodas for the tea-totallers." PT smiled widely. "Oh, so you can smile? Crack a few more of those out and you might find you get good tips. Okay, kid, I'll teach you how to run the bar. I like it that you want more responsibility. Close it up when I'm running a tournament because I don't want a sticky mess on my lanes, get it? Then you put the Victrola on and open back up for beer and root beer floats to celebrate after the last game."

"Got it." PT said. "And if you let me jam on the piano instead of playing that Victrola during tournaments, you'll have more customers walking through your door."

Sloan gradually took PT under his wing. He let him play piano and taught him not just the business of running a bowling alley, but also the sport of bowling. His only gripe was that he had to tear the kid away from the piano to help with the scoring during tournaments.

Woodshed on Crestmont Hill
February 5, 1926

WILLIAM SWITCHED OFF THE RADIO, HIS SLIGHT FRAME SWIMMING IN his camel and cream-colored blanket bathrobe. "No school again today, Margaret. The International News Service just reported twenty-two inches of snowfall and that roads all over the area are closed. You are stuck with me for your birthday," he announced.

"Our school is closed too, so we have a long weekend. Eleanor, now we'll have time for Gracie to cut our hair into bobs like hers. We'll be just like modern women." Peg jokingly tugged on a stray tuft of her sister's hair.

"We will discuss bobs later." Margaret brushed a kiss on her daughter's cheek as she headed into her bedroom to dress.

"Peg, bundle up and bring in some wood, please. The coal stove works wonders, but today we need a fire in the fireplace to make it extra cozy," William said.

Eleanor, still in her yellow bathrobe, plunked herself in the middle of the couch. "Let's have Mama open her birthday presents now instead of waiting until after dinner."

"Whoa, slow down, Eleanor. I haven't wrapped mine yet."

He frantically grabbed a pencil and paper, sat at the kitchen table and began to write. "Peg, I need a box and some ribbon."

"Hurry up, Papa," Eleanor said, rapping on Gracie's door. "Of course you should join us, silly," she insisted a moment later, pulling Gracie into the living room. "You sit here while I get Mama."

"You're going to have a wicky-wacky birthday, Mama," Eleanor explained, ushering her mother into the living room.

"What does 'wicky-wacky' mean, sweetheart?"

"You get to open your gifts before breakfast. We decided."

"But you won't have a birthday cake, because I can't get out to buy eggs," Peg moaned.

"Oh, no bother," their father said. "We'll make a big cake as soon as the snow clears. Time to open your gifts, Margaret."

"Me first, Papa." Eleanor undid her bathrobe, pulled out a picture she had drawn and handed it to her mother.

"You drew my hibiscus. Eleanor, it's beautiful. Just the thing to brighten up a winter day."

Peg gave her mother a collar and cuff set made with dainty Oriental lace. "It's a new color called ecru, Mama, and it was imported. You can wear it with your navy blue suit all buttoned up and people will think you have a whole new blouse underneath."

"Wherever did you get the money, Peg?"

"Mr. Swett is a real good tipper when I pull his canoe out of the water."

Gracie's gift was a bud vase in an unusual design of Japanese lusterware. "I wonder what catalogue you ordered this from," Margaret teased, placing it on the mantel.

"My turn. Your real gift is stuck on my desk at school, my love, so this will have to suffice." Her husband placed the small box delicately in her hands. "Happy Birthday, Margaret."

She untied the pink ribbon and opened the box. Her lips moved slightly when she read the words on the paper. "Oh, William, just what I wanted!"

"What does it say?" the girls asked.

Taking a deep breath, Margaret held up the paper importantly and read, "You have nothing to do today except what you want to do."

"Huh?" Eleanor scrunched her eyebrows together and her strawberry beauty mark almost disappeared.

"It means your father is giving me a day of rest. What a lovely gift."

"So what did you really give Mama?" Peg asked her father later while she broke the only egg in the house into the pancake batter.

"I find it curious you feel what I gave her isn't a real gift." William neatly lined up bacon in the cast iron skillet.

"You know what I mean, Papa."

"Well, two topaz earrings with diamond chips set in gold in the long dangling style are sitting on my desk at Westlawn, but it will be Monday before I can get to them. Wait until you see what a marvelous compliment they will be to the color of her eyes."

"And the shoulder of lamb I was going to roast for Mama's birthday dinner is stuck at the butcher's."

৯৶৶

"We're going to need to shovel the big house attic, Papa. That was a big snowstorm." Icy air blew into the Woodshed as Peg came back in from the porch while Gracie rinsed breakfast dishes in the sink.

"I'll give Sid a jingle to help, but I'm just not sure how he's going to get here."

"Oh, let's do it ourselves, Papa," Peg pleaded.

"Do it ourselves?" Margaret groaned, pushing herself out of her caned rocker. "Oh William, it's too much for the children."

He eased her back down. "Today was the day you weren't going to do anything taxing, Margaret. Relax here by the fire and we'll do the work."

"I'll go instead. It sounds like fun." Gracie said. "I mean—any way to help the family—that's what you hired me for, right, Mr. Woods?"

"Oh, goodie. You rest, Mama, and Gracie can borrow your boots." Eleanor grabbed her own boots, sat on the floor, and pulled them on.

"Not so fast, Miss Eleanor. Gracie's going to need more than boots. With this much snow on the ground, we need to snowshoe on over there."

"Snowshoes, the bees knees! You're going to love it, Gracie." Eleanor started furiously buttoning her coat.

"Have you walked on snowshoes before?" William asked. Gracie shook her head. "It's hard work, especially for the novice. Your feet are probably going to sink eight inches in this snow because it's fluffy. Then, it's difficult to pick your other foot up to take the next step. Are you sure you're up for this?"

"Yes, I'll be fine."

The ladder snapped into place as William reached up and pulled the rope. He climbed up to the crawl space above the kitchen. Accustomed to this ritual, Peg stood at the bottom and reached for the snowshoes when he handed them down to her.

Eleanor pulled two kitchen chairs side by side and indicated Gracie should sit down. Slapping a three-foot-long wooden framed lattice snowshoe on the floor, she pointed to the leather binding. "Put the ball of your foot boot in there." She put the rawhide straps into Gracie's hands. "Come on, I'll show you how to buckle them. If you don't do it right, one might come off and you'll go head-over-tea-kettles into the snow."

William led, carrying a shovel, as they trudged over to the big house in single file. Behind him, Eleanor bent over double, pumping her legs deliberately up and down in her snowshoes. Gracie followed with her eyes squinted against the cold and her feet slipping inside Mrs. Woods' boots. Peg brought up the rear, keeping her balance with another shovel.

It was incredibly windy. Gracie and Eleanor turned their backs to the blowing snow while they waited for the other two to shovel the steps of the inn and a path through the porch to the door.

Once inside, they removed their snowshoes. "I'll get the other shovels and a broom from the store room," said Peg, handing her shovel to Gracie to hold.

"It's really dark in here." Gracie blew on her gloved hands, gawking at the cold, empty shell of the inn.

William opened some blinds. "We keep the blinds on the main floor closed in case any unwelcome strangers come poking around peeking in the windows off season. It's colder in here than outside because it doesn't get any sun."

"All right, troops, upstairs we go. Stay close." He accepted the flashlight Peg handed him. They all trudged up to the first landing and then climbed four more flights. William waved the flashlight back and forth across the attic. "That's using your noggin, Peg. There's a good foot here in some places."

"Why does the snow collect inside the building?" Gracie asked, flapping her arms around herself for warmth.

"Well, don't tell my wife I told you, but her father skimped a bit on the construction of this place. The snow blows in through eaves and cracks around the windows. Then it melts and leaks down, creating water damage on the ceiling and walls. When the temperature drops, ice forms, making the floorboards buckle. We want to keep this place going as long as we can, so we shovel it."

"Where do you put the snow after you shovel it?"

Peg trudged over to open the window on the east end of the house. "Out there, silly. Sometimes we have to shovel a path to the windows."

Eleanor was busy throwing little shovelfuls of snow out the window while the others talked. They followed her lead and in forty minutes the attic was clear.

"Aw, Papa, can't we roam around?" Eleanor asked as her father swept up the snow the shovels missed. "I want to see the new addition. Can I use one of the new toilets?"

"There's not much to see. It's just a bunch of empty rooms now, Eleanor, and the water is turned off. If you need to use the toilet, you'll have to go back home."

"Papa, Gracie and I are going down to the kitchen. Maybe we can at least find some canned food to serve for Mama's birthday dinner."

When they got to the third sleeping floor, Peg peered up at the boarded up entrance to their hideout. "Do you really expect me to believe that you didn't tell my mother about this?"

Gracie shrugged her shoulders helplessly. "Honestly, Peg, she figured it out on her own."

"Hm." Peg turned abruptly and clopped down the stairs. Gracie tripped over her boots and landed on all fours on the next landing.

"Maybe you should buy your own boots for next year. They'll be on sale soon and you can get them cheaper than if you wait and buy them in the fall."

A stiff icicle replaced Gracie's backbone when Peg mentioned next year, but she kept her mouth shut and followed her into the kitchen.

Peg switched on a flashlight and the girls made a quick reconnaissance. Without Isaiah and Sam bustling about, the kitchen seemed bare and forbidding. It was pretty well cleaned out, but Gracie found some tins of dried beef in the pantry.

"I guess its creamed dried beef on toast points for Mama's dinner. What a far cry from roast lamb. I'll take care of it." Peg pocketed the beef. "Let's go."

"Wait. I saw something." Gracie pulled an old piece of paper from behind a shelf and tucked it into her pocket.

಄

Margaret stood at the stove, stirring the milk, frustrated that she couldn't get to the post office until Monday. Mrs. Pennington's special needs came in the mail like clockwork the first of February and Margaret compulsively made note of all requests immediately upon receipt. Invoices from the purchase of furnishings for the new wing would also be arriving and would need to be paid. It never ended. William did as much as he could to help, but his responsibilities at Westlawn meant that attending to most of these details fell to her.

Sighing, she stared listlessly out the window at the drifting snow and pried the top off a tin of cocoa powder. She dropped a few spoonfuls and some sugar into the pot. After turning down the flame so the milk didn't catch, she went to check her file of letters. The name of the guest and any requests made were carefully marked on the envelope in her own handwriting. Her memory was correct, of course. Mrs. Pennington's letter had not yet arrived.

Boots scraped on the steps and Margaret quickly put the letters away. By the time the others entered, she stood at the stove, placidly stirring the cocoa.

"Margaret, you weren't supposed to work today," William said gently.

"No, William, your gift said I didn't have to do anything I didn't want to. And I wanted to surprise you snow shovellers with cocoa."

"Cocoa?" Peg faked a smile, wondering how she was going to make creamed chipped beef on toast points without the milk her mother had just used.

"Don't worry. We have canned," Gracie whispered, reading her mind.

Gracie's hands felt warm around the cup as she contemplated her adoptive family. In whose kitchen would she be sipping cocoa in six months? Surely fretting about the long term was fruitless— but planning—evidently she was stuck in neutral about that. Perhaps the Woods would let her help decorate the addition to the big house. The prospect sounded like fun, but she also felt it prudent to make herself indispensable to them.

෨෪

The back of Margaret's hand patted her mouth to stifle a yawn. "I guess I need a nap."

"Then the rest of us shall be quiet," William said as his wife headed for their bedroom.

Peg pulled out a tablet, licked her pencil, and chewed on her brown hair. "I'm going to work on the water sport schedule." Eleanor wandered into her room.

Gracie tried to immerse herself in Willa Cather's latest book, but she kept seeing pictures of PT and the mystery man from Christmas Eve, Eric Sturdy. When she envisioned herself tripping onto the stage to do a singing audition, she switched to working on crossword puzzles.

William sat in his blue and tan plaid chair, tapping his pencil lightly on his ledger as he examined little pieces of paper that he kept pulling out of his pocket. He let out a big sigh when the clock on the mantel chimed twice.

Peg draped her arms over his shoulders from behind the couch and put her cheek up to his. "What are you working on, Papa?"

"Shhh," her father whispered, pointing toward the bedroom where Margaret slept. "Tennis courts."

"Oh," Peg mouthed. "Your secret is safe with me. I'll go make dinner."

 formulae

After downing her creamed chipped beef on toast points, Eleanor asked to be excused. The others lingered a long time over coffee. Gracie talked about the additional revenue Pennsylvania had brought in by raising the gasoline tax. Peg described the Clydesdale horses Zeke's brothers were raising.

"They're using them to pull the ice out of the lake and roll the snow down on the roads."

"You've been at Zeke's a lot lately," her father observed. "He's too old for you, Peg."

Peg rolled her eyes. "Papa, he's only my pal. He's also five inches shorter than I am."

"Well, I understand he and his brothers have been fixing the foot bridge at the bottom of the lake again," Margaret said.

"Again!" the three Woods laughed. Confused, Gracie scanned each face.

"The ice cuts through the bridge pilings every year." William explained, clearing the cups and saucers off the table.

"William, I hope you remember your promise to organize your cufflink collection. I kept all the gift tags and wrote down the descriptions. All you have to do is write the giver's name on the little boxes. Then you could wear the cufflinks the same week that guest stays at the hotel without me reminding you who gave them to you."

"I can't do that by myself, Margaret." William swatted her playfully with the dishtowel. "I need your organizational expertise."

"I'll do it," Gracie offered.

"Good, because I want to teach Peg how to embroider these fingertip towels with the Crestmont insignia for the guest rooms," Margaret said, pulling her sewing box out of the inlaid cabinet under the radio.

"Oh, Mama, you should teach Eleanor. She enjoys those feminine things more than I do."

"I wonder what she is doing. She has been in her room for over an hour and I haven't heard a peep out of her."

"Gracie, my cufflink collection is on the shelf in our closet. Would you get it while I see what my youngest has gotten herself into now, please?" William asked.

❧

"Look at all of this." her mother exclaimed as the family gathered in Eleanor's room.

"Oh, I was just guessing what Grampa Warner would have done to help the guests if they had been here in the snowstorm," Eleanor explained, busily cutting something the shape of a tall isosceles triangle out of green construction paper.

Her dolls sat on a chair, protected by a roof draped over the chair back made from a game board. Canopies made from napkins held by thumbtacks draped down the sides to create walls.

"That's the fireplace, right there." Eleanor pointed to a carved area at the base of the chair back.

"And this?" her father asked, amused. The pieces from the chess set they had given her for Christmas were scattered all over her dresser, with folded brown construction paper covering them like tents.

"Those are the children on the playground in tents. And these," she said holding up the green triangles, "are trees to make it pretty."

"It must be terribly cold out there on the playground," her father teased.

"Well, goodness, Papa, it's just pretend, after all."

"Grampa Warner would have been proud of you." Her mother hugged her.

"Oh, yes, he told me so." Eleanor said matter-of-factly.

"That's impossible. He died before you were born. You didn't even know him," said Peg.

"I do too know him. He has funny dark eyes and a pointy beard. He sits on the bottom of my bed and tells me stories sometimes when I can't sleep. He reads out of a big book called *440 Lakeside Curiosities*.

"Sweetheart, let's allow your guests to warm up in front of their fire while we enjoy our own before we go to bed." Her mother steered her into the living room.

William stoked the fire and then joined Gracie at the kitchen table where they sorted gift tags and cufflink boxes. Margaret worked green thread through a white fingertip towel.

"Let's tell stories," Eleanor coaxed.

"All right, here is a story that really happened, but you are going to assume I made it up." Margaret put down her sewing and leaned forward, propping her elbows up on her lap. "Before I met your father, we had a thunderstorm here in October. Sandwiches fell from the sky for several minutes."

"Sandwiches?" asked Eleanor, scrunching her eyebrows together.

"Ham and chicken, to be exact. Also pickles and chocolates. A twister hit some town nearby and carried people's picnic lunches to Eagles Mere." Margaret playfully checked the expressions on their faces.

"Mama, it's not like you to make up tall tales," Peg said flatly.

"It is no tall tale. I remember it well. If you like, on Monday when the snow is packed down, you can go look it up in the town's historical records. It was recorded in the newspaper."

"Your mother tells the truth. I have heard this tale many times, girls." William said.

The five of them chatted and listened to the radio. At nine o'clock William got up, gave an exaggerated stretch, and winked at Eleanor. "It has been a wicky-wacky birthday and I'm going to bed."

Margaret accepted the kiss he planted on her cheek and pulled a big envelope out from under her sewing box. "Come here, girls. Gracie, you too." All three sat in their bathrobes on the floor making a little circle around her. "Thank you for making my birthday special. Before you go to bed, I have a surprise for you. I found these things in my father's safe."

They watched as she pulled old, yellowed papers out of the envelope. "Here are some things he saved from the early days."

"Ooh, look," they said as they fingered each one and passed it around. A birthday card she had made for him when she was a child. A copy of Captain Chase's bill for laying the plans for the foundation in 1899 along with the guest register from the first season in 1900. A 1904 breakfast menu. Train tickets from the old Sonestown cog rail line.

"No train stops here, Mama," Peg said.

"Not now, but when I was a girl the guests would ride the small gauge train up from Sonestown, disembark at the base of Crestmont Hill near the outlet pond, and be ferried up to the big house by horse and carriage. Eventually, there was so much flooding that the trestles were washed away. They stopped using the train about the time your father and I assumed ownership of the Crestmont. Now people simply motor up the hill in their automobiles."

"We should display some of these things for the guests, Mama," Peg said importantly.

"Here's something you might want to keep," Gracie said, pulling the brochure out of her pocket. "I mean, I'm sure you have these in your files, but I found this when we went over to shovel the attic. It must be very old."

"Oh, my, I had almost forgotten that cover. It's one of my father's designs, so that would make it at least fifteen years old."

After she kissed her girls goodnight, Mrs. Woods gave Gracie a hug. "I hope you decide to work at the Crestmont again this summer." Gracie reddened, gave a quick nod, and vanished into her bedroom.

Someday, maybe someone would find these artifacts interesting, Margaret pondered as she put them away. If one of the girls took over when they retired, who knew how long the Crestmont would continue to breathe life into weary city people.

஧௸

William was in bed reading Henry Wadsworth Longfellow when Margaret came in from a final goodnight with the girls. "It was nice of Gracie to help you organize your cufflinks today, William. Now you can say thank you when you run into the guest who gave them to you."

"I always say thank you when I receive a gift, Margaret."

He closed his book and slid down under the covers extending his arm as an invitation. She curled, facing him in the bed, and put her head on his chest. "Having Gracie with us this winter has been good for us, despite what I said in September. She has a gift for grasping at life, which I cannot fathom."

"And your gift is serving our family and our guests. That's a tall order for a forty-two-year- old woman." He chucked his thumb playfully under her chin. They lay there, quietly listening to the wind. "Frankly, Margaret, you seem much better than last fall when you were, shall I say, somewhat depressed."

"Your gift of taking responsibility away from me today truly helped. It has been the most wonderful birthday I can remember."

"I think you deserve much more than one day of respite. Have you thought any more about your father's suggestion to find a way to restore yourself? He gave some good advice in his letter and I agree with him." He leaned down and kissed her. "I can picture him stealing catnaps up there in his hideaway."

"I have had no time." She turned over and they curled, spoon fashion, in the bed. Margaret's breathing slowed and he was sure she was asleep when she said, "Maybe you could row me around the lake for a little break from it all."

"Margaret, it is twelve degrees outside."

"In the spring, silly."

He chuckled, kissed the back of her neck and settled under the covers.

"What do you think Eleanor meant about my father reading her stories?"

"Just a child's imagination, Margaret. Creativity is a child's playground." He yawned loudly. "I just wish she would actually play chess with the chess set we gave her."

The Crestmont Inn
May 1926

"AND WE WERE WORRIED ABOUT MONEY. FEAST YOUR EYES ON THIS stack of mail." William gleefully dropped a fat pile of letters into his wife's lap.

"Let us hope they are reservations, William." Margaret set aside a letter written in a tiny, fussy script she had been reading.

"They have to be. The brochure I produced this year features ten carefully captioned photographs describing our upgraded accommodations, expanded activities for our younger clientele, and the elevation of our cultural aesthetic by featuring internationally known performers in our concert series."

"Asth...what, Papa?" Eleanor asked, perplexed. "How do you spell it? Remember you promised me you would help me with my words for the spelling bee."

"That I will, little one." William whirled Eleanor around in a dance step. "And we will go see the waterfall in Forksville that we missed on your birthday."

"Before you do, please bring over my typewriter from the big house. It is still too cold to work in my office. After I go through all of this mail I will be typing all week. Last minute requests for special needs continue to pour in. Can you believe this one?" She waived the tiny scripted letter. "Mrs. Pennington has sent an additional letter requesting four bed pillows this year."

"I marvel at your attention to detail, my love. One typewriter to the Woodshed. I'll do it right now." He ducked out the door exhilarated with pre-season anticipation.

"After that, can we work on my spelling words?" Eleanor asked, trailing behind him.

Margaret propped her feet on the footstool and opened the first letter.

The season is going to open whether you are ready for it or not.

ॐ

The sweet smell of the new wood permeated the chilly room. After setting the new lamp on the nightstand and plugging it in, Gracie dragged a box of curtains in from the hallway. She pulled out her rag to wipe the remnants of construction dust off the Venetian blinds. Twin white chenille bedspreads, dresser scarves and fingertip towels would complete the décor.

An urge to run up to her old room on the second sleeping floor pestered her. Images from last summer pummeled her brain. The encouraging smiles of the Woods at her interview. Hiding the Paperbag poems in her dresser. Her indecision about going on the road to sing. The little zing she felt when PT accompanied her on the piano. She had pondered all these things in the tiny, private room she loved in the big house.

The calm the huge hotel offered was contagious. Just as it enfolded Crestmont Hill in an embrace, it comforted Gracie with an identity, a place where she felt accepted. She had found parts of herself here she never knew had existed. Even though the winter with the Woods was a one-time experience, she had an inkling there would be a permanency here she had yet to understand.

The notion of sharing a room with a stranger in the new dormitory terrified her.

"Who is it?" Gracie had inquired, knowing Mrs. Woods wouldn't show favoritism by telling her in advance of her roommate assignment.

"Don't worry." Mrs. Woods reassured her. "Our choice will please you."

Mrs. Woods sang softly to herself while she worked decorating the room next door. Gracie hoped that meant she was looking forward to the summer. The new addition and staff dormitory were a lot of changes to absorb.

The lonely wail of a loon searching for its mate startled her. Gracie parted the curtains to look for it, but saw only the still, serene surface of the water. Soon its calm would be disturbed by laughter-filled water games and canoes cutting through the lake. The chatter that always filtered up from the main floor when she cleaned was remarkably absent. The quiet was eerie.

The ring of the telephone jolted her from her daydreaming. Mrs. Woods' steps on the stairs echoed as she ran down to the lobby to answer it. Whoever was on the other end of the line sparked a vivacity Gracie had never before heard in her voice.

Within five minutes Mrs. Woods rushed back upstairs calling her name.

"Oh, here you are. My, the room looks beautiful. Cheerful and inviting. Exactly what any guest wants. Gracie, I need to go get dressed for tonight. Excuse me, I mean I think we can finish up tomorrow, don't you?"

"I don't mind working a little longer on my own. Decorating the new rooms is more fun than I imagined."

"No, you don't understand." Words bubbled out, solving the mystery about the telephone call. "The annual hotel owners' party is tonight. Our friends from the Lakeside just called. The Raymond Hotel is hosting a big convention on Sunday, so they moved the party up two days. Everyone comes—all of our hotel friends, the people who tumble into Eagles Mere to open their cottages for the summer—it's like a tapestry of the whole town, before the hotels are filled with people, that is. We share hints about running the hotels, funny stories and quirky things that happen with the guests. Oh, I laugh more at this party than I do all year!"

"I can stay home with the girls if you like."

"No, all of the children come too. Please join us, Gracie."

"Thank you, Mrs. Woods, but I'm not sure I would fit in." Gracie envisioned herself surrounded by people she didn't know. An evening home alone with a good read might even be refreshing. "I'm amazed you hotel owners have the time to socialize...but I'm glad you do."

"We have surprises galore here in Eagles Mere."

The next morning, Sid Fox squinted against the sun while he brushed white paint on the porch railing of the Evergreen Lodge.

"Almost done." he said in greeting as Peg and her father strolled down the driveway toward the dormitory to inspect his progress.

"You're a master painter, Sid. I didn't expect you to have so much finished. Evidently last night's party inspired you." Silky wisps of William's blond hair danced in the morning breeze.

"I can just hear the staffers moving in, all excited and laughing, Papa," Peg said. "I'm sure you've thought this through, but how are you going to keep the boys from getting into the girls' rooms?"

Her father crooked his finger for her to follow. They descended several steps made of railroad ties on the laundry side of the building, bordered by rhododendrons sporting purple blossoms. He opened a bright red door with four small windows and his daughter peered inside. "This entrance only goes to the men's section, with no access to the women's quarters."

"Well, what's to keep them from walking around to use the other entrance?"

"A locked door after 10 p.m., a housemother personally

recommended by Mr. Rose, and PT to keep the boys in line," he said, counting all three on his fingers.

"PT will live in the dorm with the young guys?"

"All men except the bellhops will be in the dorm."

"Good, then you'll have room over the kitchen for Zeke."

"Zeke lives in town, Peg. Why should we house him here?"

"Because it would be the kind thing to do, to get him away from his nasty family for the summer. And he takes his job seriously. You and mother usually reward that."

"How do you know about Zeke's family?"

Peg blew out an exasperated breath. "Papa, I am not a child any more. I see things."

"I am proud that you do."

Running up the steps separating the dorm from the laundry, she pointed to an area between the outside steps and the front porch of Evergreen Lodge. "You should make a little fish pond here and plant flowers around it. Staffers will be going back and forth between the dorm and laundry porches on their time off and it will give them something pretty to look at. You always tell me a happy staff means happy guests."

"Peg, you have a flair for this. It's a superb idea, but I am afraid we are already extended above our means."

"I'll build it. I'll get Zeke to help me. All I have to do is dig and bring rocks to border it. I have allowance saved and I can buy some gold fish to put in it."

Her father gave her a big hug. "You remind me of your grandfather Warner," he said proudly. "Can you have it done before they move in?"

"Sure, Papa," she added. "And remember, I am your official assistant on water sports this season, with my name right up there on the bulletin board."

"Surely we could wait until you are eighteen for that."

Peg pursed her lips and purposefully shook her head.

The Crestmont Inn
Summer 1926

I

GRACIE WASN'T SURE WHAT AWAKENED HER FIRST; THE UNFAMILIAR creaking of the floorboards as girls walked around on the second floor above, the whooshing of the plumbing after a morning bathroom run, or the orchestra of birds chirping outside. It certainly wasn't Dorothy's snoring. Gracie had finally become accustomed to it when she fell asleep about one in the morning.

Dorothy lay across their tiny room in a red and white calico nightdress, half-in, half-out of the covers. Her ash brown hair splayed in waves on the pillow and her face was soft in sleep, oblivious to the ruckus.

Gracie snuck out of bed and cracked open the window in between the beds to enjoy the birds before Dorothy woke. Eighteen other female staffers chattered in the hallway of the Evergreen Lodge, beginning their day. She was thrilled to have been assigned a room on the peaceful, wooded side of the building where white pine, maple and hemlock trees sheltered rhododendron and ferns.

The rooms across the hall merely looked out over the laundry and steam room.

ഇ൞

Finishing the cleaning of the new bathrooms on the second sleeping floor before the first crop of guests checked in was a challenge, but she did it. Elated that Dorothy had recommended a mystery book with a woman detective and a lot of suspense, Gracie made a quick stop in the Crestmont library before lunch.

Time got away from her, so she scribbled down a couple of words to look up and put them in her pocket. She'd have to check them out later. Besides, she had other business in the staff dining room.

It was fairly empty when she arrived. Hank was up on a ladder changing light bulbs in the wall fixtures. Three chattering girls pushed away empty soup bowls.

But PT wasn't there.

She was sure he was supposed to arrive this morning. She was dying to be near him. Her plan was to ask about his winter and find out when they could jam together with a new song. After that, she would see where the conversation led them.

"Hey, Gracie. Grabbing a bite?" Zeke poked Gracie in the back, and then danced around in front of her, fanning one dollar bills in front of her face. "First day back and get a load of these tips. My twenty dollar smile and this new addition are happy partners." He dove toward the buffet, wrinkled his nose at the soup made from last night's asparagus, and piled his plate with sandwiches.

"I'll take some of that soup. You'd be amazed at what Isaiah can do with leftovers," Gracie said. They added beverages and carried their trays to a table.

Zeke wolfed down his sandwich, wiping crumbs off his mouth. One landed on her book. He flicked it away with his fingers.

"You're always reading. You really need to get out more, kiddo. The piano man was looking for you." Zeke poked her teasingly. "I wish you two would get together so we could all relax. Did you hear I'm sleeping over the kitchen this year? Better to hear your call bell, sir, and all that. Mr. W hired a new bellhop, some college guy from town. I'll have to give him some of my special training. Isn't the new staff lounge in the basement of your dorm downright hip to the jive?"

"I haven't seen it yet," Gracie admitted, weary of his chatter.

"You're kidding. A ping pong table, comfy couches, a fireplace, radio, card tables. Get this—Peg convinced Mr. W to put in a popcorn machine and he said he would move the piano from the old staff lounge down there. The best part is a screened-in porch on the side next to the woods. Kind of private, you know, just right for a little hanky-panky. Got my eye on Mae this year, if that housemother, Slagle will let me near her."

"Mae? I'll ring your neck if you hurt her, Zeke. You behave yourself." Gracie pulled his ear until he winced and got up to return her empty bowl and spoon to the dish cart.

Outside, the guests milled around, chatting and admiring the new addition. An unmistakable figure with sloping shoulders loped up the back lawn. Gracie gasped. Instead of the shirt sleeves and suspenders she was accustomed to when he was off duty, PT was smartly dressed in his gray jacket, pinstriped pants and yellow tie. He nodded slightly in her direction through the bobbing parasols of the women. She wanted to tell him how handsome he looked, but instead her blonde curls crawled around on her head rewiring the circuitry in her brain.

"So you're back," PT said, looking thinner than last year.

"Well that's a fine welcome. As it turns out, I never left." She forced a smile, appalled at her own words.

"Expected you'd be off singing on the road."

"Another employment opportunity presented itself after you left last summer."

His Adam's apple bobbed as he swallowed, searching for words. "You might have told me yourself. Had to find out from Zeke you stayed with the Woods." One bony finger checked his moustache. "Maybe we could do another jam session. Do any singing over the winter?"

"Not the kind that would interest you," she retorted, flustered by her own hostility.

"Would have been interested if you were doing the singing." Without another word he disappeared.

Frustrated, Gracie squeezed her book close to her chest, elbowing her way through the mingling guests back down to Evergreen Lodge.

ভ্ৰত্ন

Dorothy peered in the dresser mirror that evening, methodically running her index finger down the part in her hair. Wincing, she pulled out a silver strand. "Now I'm presentable," she said after carefully brushing her hair into loose waves.

Setting her brush down next to a mother-of-pearl barrette, she lifted a photograph out of her suitcase and placed it lovingly on the dresser. A uniformed officer smiled confidently into the camera. "There you go, Lawrence. This is our home for the next ten weeks."

"It must be hard to be a widow, Dorothy," Gracie said.

"It's been eight years since he was killed in the war, and I still miss him. But I'm not alone. I have my school children during the year and my Crestmont family in the summer."

Gracie changed into her pink shrug and hung her green uniform in the closet.

Dorothy mopped perspiration off her face. "Whew, it's hot in here already and it's only June. The big house definitely had better air circulation. I'd love to cool off with a double-decker chocolate cone from the Sweet Shoppe. We could motor down there..."

"I'm not quite finished getting settled. I didn't want to take over just because I moved in first." Gracie reached under her bed and pulled the yellow jewelry box out of her suitcase. Setting it on the dresser, she said, "Maybe this will keep your husband company." Both sets of eyes grazed over the twin beds, dresser, tiny chair and writing table near the door.

Dorothy broke the silence. "Funny they put such a big closet in this tiny room. I saw a maroon dress in there that certainly is pretty."

"My maroon slash." Gracie mentally measured the two and a half feet between the beds as she pushed her notebooks farther under hers with her big toe. She pulled her sheet music out of the suitcase and put it on a shelf in the closet.

"Naming your dresses is one of your peculiar but endearing qualities, Gracie, Why you do it?"

"I don't know. They keep me company. You know, Dorothy," she said defensively, "I hardly had any clothes when I came here."

"Well, there's another piece of the puzzle. It is entirely your business and not mine, but people around here wonder why you are so secretive about where you came from." Her face softened and she patted Gracie's cheek. "Mrs. Woods told me you were a great help over the winter, dear."

"They were wonderful, Dorothy. They treated me like family. Mrs. Cunningham, too. She's teaching me to sew."

Humming off key, the older woman sat down heavily on her bed, pulled up her waitress apron and fanned her face. "Did you see PT yet?"

Gracie removed her earrings, holding her breath momentarily before dropping them into the jewelry box. "Dorothy, he looked so handsome coming up the lawn, and when he talked to me I was nasty. I don't know what came over me."

Waving her hand, Dorothy said, "You were probably just jittery. A lot of people are obnoxious when they're nervous."

"But I didn't mean to be, and he's so abrupt and then I get all flustered." She yanked on the transom pole in frustration to get more air.

"See what you're doing to that poor thing? That's what you two do to each other. A window of opportunity opens and one of you slams it shut before either one of you can say something nice. PT is abrupt because he's attracted to you, Gracie. You've got to act coy with him so he relaxes."

"Oh, honestly, Dorothy, even if I knew what coy meant, I wouldn't know how to act that way."

Sarcastic cackling erupted from the bathroom down the hall. "Oh, my word. Bessie must have moved in. That voice of hers sets my teeth on edge. Let's go see what trouble she's caused now."

The commotion intensified after they pushed open the bathroom door. "I don't care what bed I have." Clearly distressed, Mae had wedged herself between two of the sinks.

"Girlie, ya have to learn how to assert yerself," Bessie needled. "Right or left side of the window?"

"Do you mean as you walk in the room or as you're in the bed?"

"Just make up yer mind, stupid. I'm tryin' to be nice here."

"I don't care," wailed Mae, wringing out her washcloth. The other girls in the bathroom had turned off the faucets to listen. "Which bed do you want?"

Bessie poked her freckled nose into Mae's face." I want the one ya don't, and ya have to choose." Mae started to cry. "Watch it girlie, or I'll turn ya into a pickle."

Dorothy broke in, planting herself between them. "Put a buckle on it, Bessie. It seems you're feeling especially surly tonight." She coaxed Mae out and pulled a dime out of her uniform pocket. "Flip this coin," she said soothingly. "If it comes up heads you'll take the bed on the left. Here we go."

Bessie grabbed the dime defiantly out of Dorothy's hand and tossed it into the air. She held one hand over the flipped coin and imitated Mae's soft mewy voice. "As we walk in the room or..."

Dorothy grabbed her arm. "As you walk in the room, Bessie. Now let's see it."

She revealed the coin and Dorothy gently said, "Mae, you're going to take the bed on the right. I'd be happy to help you to get settled."

"No, thank you, Dorothy." Mae blinked back tears, opened the linen closet and numbly took out her sheets. She carried them in front of her as straight as she would a dining room tray. "I can manage now."

Chatter filled the long narrow hall that separated the dorm rooms on the first floor while they filed out of the center bathroom. Mrs. Ethel Slagle, the housemother, stuck her head out of the room by the front entrance. "Cut the ruckus, girls. You are going to have to get along."

"I'm going to have to get behind myself and push to get through this," Dorothy groaned and sank heavily on her bed.

"Get through what?" asked Gracie.

"How would you like to be a forty-six year-old woman living right next to the bathroom in a dormitory of adolescents, present company excepted?"

"I'm sure the Woods wanted you here to try to help everyone get along."

"Then why did they hire Mrs. Slagle, on whose breath I detected liquor earlier?" Dorothy yawned. "I'm going to bed. I know you housemaids work hard, but you have no idea how early waitresses have to get up to get through the drudgery of pre-breakfast duties."

Gracie fell asleep wondering why Mae didn't stick up for herself, how she would feel if she had to room with Bessie, and whether she would ever have any time alone to work in her notebooks.

৩৵৶

All housemaids were to assemble in the new Ladies Lounge immediately after breakfast. Gracie wolfed down her food and managed to arrive before any of the other girls. Part of the renovation done over the winter was to combine the old parlors into one spacious lounge. Even though Gracie had helped open up the inn for the season, she had not yet seen what Mr. Woods called "Margaret's Masterpiece."

The satin-finished French doors with floral patterns etched in the corners stood open. As the younger girls filtered in, Gracie moved to the rear to enjoy the atmosphere, undisturbed. Elegant oriental carpets sectioned off conversation areas of chairs upholstered in soft rose and blue. Frosty glass lamps in hourglass shapes were painted with mauve roses. Powder blue wallpaper with a pattern of tiny pink roses set inside ivory cameos repeated the theme, accented by an ivory painted chair rail. Card tables for games of euchre or mahjong were arranged between the windows overlooking the back lawn. Sweet perfume from the vase of peonies on the mantel scented the air.

Bessie slithered in. She glowered around the room, spied Gracie and sidled up next to her like they were best friends.

"What's goin' on? I got rooms to clean," she said, cracking her Tutti Frutti in Gracie's ear.

Gracie shrugged and moved a step away. The rest of the girls chattered so loudly about the purpose of the meeting, they didn't notice Mrs. Woods move calmly through the lounge and step up onto the hearth.

"Good morning." The girls quieted immediately and retreated in lines like sloppy soldiers.

"We are now a week into our summer season. Mr. Woods and I hope you are pleased with the Evergreen Lodge. You have more privacy in your living space and the guests have more room here in the big house. However, the increase in guest rooms means more work for us all."

She motioned for two girls to come forward. "Most of you have met our new girls, Eunice and Martha, but I would like to formally introduce them." Light applause greeted them as they moved back into the ranks of the other housemaids.

"Our guests expect a more pristine environment when staying in a vacation accommodation such as ours than they would in their own homes. We work very hard to maintain the ambiance of our public rooms. After all, one does not come to the Crestmont to sit in one's guest room."

"I have had numerous complaints about the dust in this lounge." Mrs. Woods stepped off the hearth, and turned on a tall floor lamp with an ebony base and a frosted pink bowl-shaped globe. She walked among the girls, dipping her head to make eye contact with each one. "Yesterday I dismissed the young woman who was assigned this room because of her indifference to my warnings."

"So," she continued, "I have cleaned the room myself, leaving one item untouched. The girl who can identify what has been ignored will be given the duty of cleaning all the public rooms in the west wing for two weeks, with a significant increase in salary. If her work is acceptable, she will continue this assignment for the remainder of the summer and the number of guest rooms she cleans will be reduced."

Bessie hissed, "Aw, that's easy. She was standin' right on it, hopin' we won't notice. Watch, girlie." Sauntering up to the fireplace, she smugly licked her finger and made a circle on the hearth.

"Incorrect, Bessie," Mrs. Woods said.

The younger girls whispered questions as they scattered, inspecting the room for dust. Gracie wanted the promotion, but backed up against the wall, uncomfortable with the competition. Folding her arms behind her, she leaned back against the chair rail. A fly tickled her arm. Shooing it away, she noticed a line of dirt where her arm hit the chair rail. She quickly brushed it off. Better to keep her mouth shut.

"Hush, now, girls. It seems no one has earned the assignment, so I shall have to determine myself who will be cleaning the common rooms. You are dismissed."

Two hours went by before Gracie finally summoned the courage to knock on Mrs. Woods' office door.

"Ah, Gracie. The Woodshed doesn't seem the same without you. I hope you are comfortable in the Evergreen Lodge."

"It's lovely, Mrs. Woods. Thank you for putting me with Dorothy."

"My husband and I worked hard on those roommate assignments. We couldn't envision either of you sharing a room with a younger girl. What brings you here this morning?"

"It was the chair rail, ma'am. In the Ladies Lounge. That's what you left dirty."

Mrs. Woods sank into her chair, her mouth widening into a sad smile. "So it was. I wish you had said so in the lounge."

"I didn't want the other girls to think...well, I lived with you all winter and some of them are finding out. I didn't want it to seem like I was teacher's pet."

"But I hope you can see that you've made it all the harder. Because you did not speak up, it will seem like I chose you over the others."

"I know. I was stupid. I'm sorry, Mrs. Woods."

"You are not stupid by any stretch of the imagination. We all do silly things and try to learn from them. So, congratulations, you have earned the assignment. Beginning tomorrow, some of your guest rooms will be reassigned and you will begin cleaning the public rooms. I will show you exactly what to do after lunch."

"Thank you, Mrs. Woods. I'm just worried about Bessie."

"Bessie didn't find the dirt. Are you telling me you are afraid of her? I've always supposed it is quite possibly the other way around." Astounded, Gracie stood speechless. "Well, if you don't want others to think I am giving you preferential treatment, I could assign you Mrs. Pennington's room in addition." Mrs. Woods tapped her pencil on the desk.

"Why, Mrs. Woods, no one wants that room. Mrs. Pennington is too particular."

Mrs. Woods sat back in her chair. "As you wish."

"I'll take it." Gracie said quickly, grateful for the way Mrs. Woods always snuck in a little guidance. After all, a little self-imposed pressure must be a good thing.

"Gracie, you have a good mind. Give yourself permission to trust it. And those public rooms need to be spotless. Do you hear my words?"

"I hear them."

"Da da da *da*, da *da!*" Sam jauntily clicked his heels as he tapped. He gritted his teeth and held his lips in a tight, determined grin as he moved from one foot to the other. Eleanor snapped her fingers and tried to memorize the dance moves.

"Okay, my turn." She sucked in her cheeks and mimicked his steps, ending with her left heel anchored and her toe smartly up in the air.

He slapped his thigh. "You're getting it, kid. Hey, I got one more to show you before I start these rice cakes on the griddle. For this one you have to pump your arms back and forth like when you run, but in time with the music, like this. Deedle, deedle dop, *do-o-o-wop*, dop, *yeah!* Hands in the air on the *yeah*, get it, kid?"

"Hands in the air on the *yeah*. Got it!" Eleanor smashed her tongue through her teeth to concentrate, swung her arms rhythmically, and spread her fingers high above her head on her last step.

"Hands in the air? Let's put some hands on the food to make lunch," Isaiah boomed, leaving the swinging kitchen doors slapping behind him.

"Sorry, boss." Sam grabbed his apron and tied it in the back. "I was just teaching Eleanor here how to tap dance."

"We're going to do a number in the staff talent show together," she bragged as she turned a mixing bowl upside down on her head, "with hats." She quickly removed the bowl when a handsome man in a bellhop uniform entered. "Do you work for us—I mean my parents?"

"I guess I do. I'm Eric."

"You must be new or I would have noticed you before." Eleanor extended her hand as a graceful lady. "Eleanor Woods, p-pleased to meet you."

Eric shook her hand. "The pleasure is all mine, Miss Woods." Holding herself two inches taller, Eleanor glided toward the kitchen door.

"Hey, kid, what about our dance lesson?" Sam did a twirl and clicked his heels.

"We shall have to finish it another time, Samuel. I have responsibilities of my own to attend to," she said in her grown-up voice. Discreetly cutting her eyes over to the side, she sized Eric up and down as she left.

"Sam, I have never heard that child sound so grown-up," Isaiah hooted. "Looks like you have an admirer, Eric. This is Sam, my assistant chef, and I'm Isaiah. Welcome to the Crestmont. You a town boy?"

"Well, my father's the minister at the Eagles Mere Presbyterian church, but I go to college during the year, so I guess I qualify. Oh, almost forgot, I need five birch beers for guests on the porch, please."

Sam crooked a finger for Eric to watch, filled one glass with ice, pumped in syrup, and sprayed in the seltzer. "You're on your own for the rest. We do the food, but you bellhops fix your own drinks, okay?"

"Got it. Thanks." Eric finished making the sodas and loaded them on a tray. "Nice to meet you fellows."

Isaiah stuffed four loaves under his arm and grabbed a knife. He skillfully sliced the bread. Adjusting the fire under the grill pan, he grabbed the mayonnaise from the icebox and tossed it to Sam. "I'll do the grilled cheese and you finish the egg salad."

Sam nodded as he stood on the other end of the huge work table, fine-dicing onion and celery into a bowl of chopped hard boiled eggs. "Yep, and the fire's on under the soup. I just have to finish the rice cakes. There's cut melon in the icebox all set to go. Dorothy already set up the pickle trays."

Zeke entered, lifted the lid of the soup pot, and sniffed. "Chicken noodle, now that's a man's dish. That asparagus stuff you guys make is disgusting."

"Oh, now you're a man, huh?"

"Got me a girl, Isaiah. Not just a fling, I've got me a real girl. You know Mae, that pretty waitress? I was kind of thinking I might hang around to watch her set up her tables."

"You'd better stick with this one. You haven't been exactly on the level with those other girls you dally with."

"She's sweet and easily persuaded, if you know what I mean."

Isaiah pinned him against the table and wagged a warning finger in his face. "You knock her up and I'll slap you upside the head. Hear, boy?"

〜〜

"Olivia!" Gracie jumped up from the rocker and embraced her friend.

"Hello, Gracie. My, you look fine." Olivia gracefully settled her petite body into the laundry porch swing and draped the shimmering powder blue skirt she was hemming over her lap. She had tucked a tiny white blossom with red markings into her tightly pinned-back hair. "I wanted Isaiah to have something pretty to look at on his break," she said. Her tiny chin indicated the next building. "I thought you'd be over there on the Evergreen Lodge porch. My, a new addition and a new dormitory, too. How exciting. Why, we're neighbors now."

"This laundry porch feels more like home. And it's more private. Besides, the younger staff monopolizes the dorm porch. How was your winter?"

"A little lonely," Olivia sighed. "Isaiah is in great demand now. He was away a lot on weekends, catering conferences in different cities."

"You must have really missed him."

"Let's just say that I love our Crestmont summers because we are together every evening after he's done cooking dinner. He's so playful. An apartment can be eerie without all of his singing and whistling. Mind you, I love my dressmaking business, and I am with people all the time, but life without my man, it's just not the same." Gracie focused on the porch floor.

"Oh, Gracie, I'm sorry. I didn't mean…"

"No matter," She flipped her hand airily. "I just haven't found the right one yet, although it seems like I'm pretty behind schedule."

"I was certain something would happen with PT. He's an odd one, though. Very friendly, but hard to get to know. Why, come to think of it, the little he said to me last summer was about you."

Gracie stopped rocking, squirmed in her chair, and changed the subject.

"It was really nice working for the Woods all winter. Now Bessie's on a rampage because I got a promotion. She's sure it's because Mrs. Woods favors me."

"Bessie always has to be the big cheese. I feel sorry for her. A person that nasty must have something hurtful in her life."

Gracie leaned over and ran her fingertips lightly over the blue fabric. "It's amazing they can make it so shiny."

"A silver thread is run through every second warp." Olivia held the blue material up to the sun. "See? Like little tiny stars." All of a sudden, she collapsed the material onto her lap and bit her lip. "I have exciting news. A famous opera singer is coming to the Crestmont to do a concert and she wants me to make her a gown. Can you imagine? Me designing for a celebrity."

Gracie could hear the sewing machine whirring as Olivia's tiny foot pumped away and her delicate hands guided vivid fabrics into elegant gowns the women fancied for the dances and concerts. Her beautiful friend would finally get some of the recognition she deserved.

"Absolutely."

❦

Mrs. Slagle was snoring loudly when Gracie tiptoed out the front door. The waitresses were already up in the big house setting up for breakfast, so she could easily slip unnoticed out of the Evergreen Lodge. A chorus of bird calls kept her company as she went past Peg's goldfish pond and the laundry around the steam room into the woods. An ideal place for hiking, she decided, if one was so inclined. She yearned for solitude. Thinking about the Paperbag poems she had tucked under her mattress, she moped about PT, sure she had squelched anything they might have had.

She found a private rock blushed by the morning sun, sat down and peeled the banana she had taken from the fruit display in the dining room. To perk herself up, she pored over her notebooks. She wrote "Learn to swim" on her list of things to do. Realizing she was still afraid of the water she crossed that out and scribbled, "Buy bathing suit anyway." She turned the page to where she listed her friends and rested her hand over their names, imagining each face smiling back at her from the shifting hues of green in the trees. When murky images of Lily and her parents threatened to ruin her reverie, she slammed the notebook shut. A crow squawked in protest, landing to add a piece of dead squirrel to its breakfast.

She checked her watch. 8:30. Walking around the back of the garage, she started down the hill toward Mrs. Cunningham's and tried to enjoy the little patches of sun, which played like haloes on the tall trees.

Late afternoon storm clouds threatened overhead and the sound of the piano music was obscured by the howling of the wind. Shadow, smelling rain in the air, dashed in front of her into the garage for shelter. Gracie risked the downpour to follow the song that sounded like what PT called "blues." It led her to the old staff lounge above the garage.

PT was so absorbed in his playing; he didn't hear her come in. He had every right to be angry after their meeting on the lawn, but she prayed she might have a chance with him if she apologized.

"I don't know what came over me, PT. I was nasty to you and I'm sorry."

She knew he heard her, but he ducked his head down and switched to a huffy, rhythmic piece designed, she was certain, to drown her out. Sometimes she wished she could reach into his brain and pull out words, but she knew he'd rather communicate through the piano. It was a pretty safe bet that right now he was saying he was mad.

She took another step toward the piano. "I should have apologized last week, but I was scared."

"Oh." PT's eyes never left the keyboard.

She stamped her foot. "Honestly, PT, how hard are you going to make this for me?"

He swung his lanky legs around the piano bench to face her. His chest was caved and he looked miserably past her. "I'm not good at this."

She choked. "At what?"

"This." He wagged his finger back and forth between them.

Before she knew it, his arms were wrapped around her and he was kissing her hair, and then her ear. Then his mouth found hers as the rain thrummed on the roof.

The oars sloshed through the water until they reached the foot of the lake, far from the inn. "Let's stop here." Margaret Woods buttoned her sweater, smiled at her husband and reached out to pick blueberries from the bushes growing at the water's edge. Cicadas and bullfrogs said goodbye to the day. Orange, pink and lavender clouds played tag with the setting sun. The water, clear to the bottom during the day, snaked in huge black and purple waves toward the shore.

"I love Thursdays." Margaret said dropping berries lazily into her basket. "You were brilliant to let Sid take care of game night. We are free to escape and enjoy the lake. I never realized how much I need time to myself, William."

"Mm." William hummed a hymn, happy that his wife had accepted this tiny recess in her work week. He leaned over the boat to pick a pink water lily and waived it teasingly around her jaw before tucking it in her hair.

"I need to pocket this moment so I can pull it out to center me in July."

"Mm."

"William, I think we are ready for the surge."

"What surge, Margaret?" he asked absentmindedly.

"The Swetts, the Penningtons, Celeste Woodford. The opera singer."

"Margaret, of course we are ready. You have taken care of everything. You always do. Now stop troubling yourself and enjoy our time off."

They ducked their heads as he rowed under the footbridge into the outlet pond. A thorn hanging precariously in a huge spider web under the bridge nearly grazed Margaret's head and a family of ducks that had been trailing them turned back to the main part of the lake.

"No talk of running the Crestmont while in the outlet pond, dear." He switched to another hymn.

"Yes, you are right. Sing it out loud, William. I never hear you sing except at the hymn sings."

"No, no, Margaret. Please don't remind me of hymn sings at the Crestmont because now we are in the outlet pond where we are supposed to be on vacation." Margaret gave him a chagrined smile, rested her arms behind her on the side of the boat and lifted her face to smell the evening air. William pulled the oars in and they drifted in temporal, peaceful silence. A white deer watched them from his hiding place behind some bull pines, then scampered away to find its mate.

Moving the piano was no small feat. Mr. Woods, Sid Fox, Otto and Zeke carried it down the stairs from the old staff lounge above the garage and loaded it onto Sid's truck. After driving over to the Evergreen Lounge, they took it down the railroad-tie steps, setting it down twice to catch their breath. They balanced it on a dolly and wheeled it into the basement lounge.

The snap of ping pong balls stopped as did the chatter around the fireplace. Dorothy and Magdalena looked up from their euchre game. A saxophone from Paul Whiteman's band blared from the radio. Gracie and Mae turned to watch silently.

"Right here on the wall opposite the fireplace." Mr. Woods took his breath in big gulps and rested his hands on his knees. Slapping Sid on the back as Otto and Zeke moved the piano against the wall he said, "Care to join me in the Woodshed for some chess?"

"PT is going to be beside himself," Dorothy noted. "He wanted to supervise that."

"Mr. W wanted to surprise him," Zeke said.

Bessie lay on the couch, throwing popcorn kernels in the air from a bowl on her stomach. She caught them in her mouth while Jimmy massaged her feet. "Yeah, he and Mr. W are like bosom buddies, both wearin' those stupid yellow ties."

"His name is Mr. Woods," PT said, slamming the door. Everyone froze. Gracie ducked her head into her newspaper. He had avoided her since that night when they kissed.

He diddled a bit on the piano and muttered, "Oh, baby, do you need to be tuned."

Jimmy made a feeble attempt to break the tension. "Didya see Agnes Swett cannonball into the lake? Peg was lifeguardin' and even though the woman is twice her size, she went in to make sure she was okay. Every towel on the dock chairs got soaked."

"Yeah, snookie, and Mrs. W sent me to wring 'em out and take 'em to the laundry. What the Sam Hill was that about? I ain't no dock maid, just a housemaid."

"Ach, Bessie, complaints, all the time, complaints." Magdalena said. "My girls had to dry out towels."

Bessie bolted upright and spat, "Yer precious laundry girls ain't the only ones workin' hard in this place." Seeing a moment to send a dart, she pelted popcorn at Gracie's newspaper." If I were you, Miss I-Get-to-Clean-the-Common-Rooms, I'd get my nose outa there and up where it can be seen." She thumbed at PT. "He's gonna make a pass at you." Gracie feigned shock, smiling smugly to herself because he already had.

"Oh, stop your bickering," Dorothy said. "You know, PT is right, if you call them Mr. or Mrs. Woods, it is actually fewer syllables than Mr. or Mrs. W. I wonder if any of you have tickled your brains with that one."

Zeke capered over to Mae. "Care to dance, milady?" They did a few turns and then she dropped her arms and turned away shyly. "Let's get some air." He guided her to the screened porch, winking at Otto as he closed the sliding door.

ৡৣ৶

The morning was cool and clear. The early morning sun hadn't quite found its way into the lobby. Instead of the overhead chandelier, a few of the table lamps had been turned on, creating a softer effect. They coaxed a gleam out of the cream stripe in the wallpaper. The carving in the wood of the staircase was more apparent. It was yet another reason why Gracie was amazed by the Crestmont public rooms. Their beauty was different at all times of the day.

Old Tim ticked away, competing with the clattering of dishes coming from the dining room. A fire had been lit in the main fireplace to take the chill off, but was dying fast. Finding no wood inside, Gracie went out to raid the wood pile next to the back porch. She put another log on, but the fire died down even more. Worried about the time, she was about to turn on the electric vacuum machine to do the carpets when a masculine voice behind her startled her.

"Want me to get that going for you?" Eric Sturdy waved his cap at the fire and smiled.

"Yes, please." With the tongs, he lifted the log Gracie had

added and stashed a smaller log under it. Then he pushed the whole thing back until it started to glow.

"It just needed a little more air. You're Gracie, aren't you, the one who sang the solo on Christmas Eve. I'm Eric, remember?"

"Yes. Thank you. I mean about fixing the fire. I'm sorry; I have to get back to work. Mrs. Woods will want this room to be done before the guests come out from breakfast."

"Sure. I need to fix a window upstairs anyway."

Gracie watched his strong back disappear up the stairs as she pushed the vacuum on the carpet. A loud squall from the machine rebuked her for sucking up part of the rug. She quickly switched it off and forced her mind back onto her work.

II

AFTER ENSURING THAT THE TOWN OF EAGLES MERE WAS SETTLED FOR the day, the cat padded west to the Crestmont Inn. Shadow clawed its way up the stone pillars at the entrance, folded its legs under and settled in. The evening sun warmed its silky black coat as the cat surveyed its domain. A large blue convertible with matching blue on the wheels and deep gleaming running boards stopped momentarily. The driver stuck his head out the window and squinted at the Crestmont sign. Two fashionably dressed women in the back seat turned around to smile at the animal as the car chugged up the driveway.

ॐ

The Woods had welcomed many musicians for their concerts before, but this particular interview was completely unexpected. Miss Libbie Miller, booking agent for opera singer, Rosa Ponselle, had insisted that her client be settled promptly in her room after their arrival at seven p.m. with dinner to be sent up shortly. William led Miss Miller to his office and dashed to Margaret's office, quickly telephoning Isaiah to get back up to the kitchen immediately. He straightened his tie, returned and made chit-chat until Margaret returned from escorting Miss Ponselle to her room.

Once they were reassembled in his office, Miss Miller slid a typewritten list of instructions across the desk. Miss Ponselle was happy to accept their offer of two weeks of vacation in exchange for a one-hour concert on Friday, July 30th. The owners would supply the following: Miss Ponselle was to be given a table for one at all meals. Her privacy was to be respected at all times. A maid to attend to tidying her room, her laundry, and other personal requirements would be furnished. An appointment with a hair dresser each Thursday would be arranged. The piano in the performance space was to be tuned immediately and once again the day of the concert. A rehearsal with Miss Ponselle's accompanist, who would arrive on the 29th, would be required. Miss Miller then handed them a sizable check to cover the cost of a formal gown to be designed by the Crestmont dressmaker, announced that she would be leaving in the morning, and asked to see the performance space.

Though surprised by these additional requests, the Woods agreed immediately, eager to heighten the image of the concert series. When they returned to the Woodshed for the night, Margaret made tea and they talked over the kitchen table.

"Olivia will do a beautiful job on the gown. We will arrange a fitting as soon as possible."

William took off his jacket and vest, removed his cufflinks, and rolled up his shirt sleeves. "I assumed an opera singer would travel with her own maid. We don't really have the personnel to furnish one ourselves. Thank goodness PT anticipated the piano tuning. He's already called our man in Dushore."

"Let's tackle the other things first, William. Gracie loves that hairdresser, Zelda. Perhaps we could send Miss Ponselle to her."

"And set up a single table in the dining room..."

"Done. Now the maid. Dorothy is the most mature person on the female staff, but there are no waitresses to spare right now. Bessie would be a disaster. Gracie is the only choice, but now that she is cleaning the common rooms she is quite overloaded. I will simply have to temporarily suspend that assignment and supervise Eunice and Martha on that cleaning. Mrs. Pennington, however, refuses any other housemaid than Gracie, so I cannot take her off that room."

When they went to bed, Margaret listened to William's snoring, saying a prayer of thanks that she had the foresight to give Miss Ponselle a quiet room at the end of the east wing away from the livelier guests.

The woman held herself erect and confident, but seemed lost in the empty lobby. Her eyeliner was applied in a heavy line and she wore her thick bangs parted in the middle like the rest of her long, dark hair. Deliberately making eye contact with Gracie as she walked by, she dipped her head with a slight smile. Gracie returned the greeting and continued past her toward the library.

"Excuse me," the woman said. Feeling especially unpresentable after cleaning the Penningtons' room, Gracie smoothed the wrinkles out of her apron and tried to fluff up her hair before she turned around. Out came the standard response to an inquiry from a guest. "Yes, may I help you?"

The woman extended her arm slowly. "My name is Rosa," she said deliberately. She swept her eyes over the room dramatically. "Where am I?"

Happy for an easy request, Gracie relaxed. "This is the main lobby. Do you recall your room number? I'd be happy to take you there if you're lost. There are a lot of rooms here and it can be confusing."

"And what is your name, dear?" Rosa studied Gracie's face.

The woman was about thirty years old and had a magnetic, sultry sounding voice. One lone gold bangle decorated her bare arms. She was immaculately dressed in a fashionably short emerald green dress held up by thin straps which made her seem vaguely out of place at the Crestmont.

"Gracie." She picked up the sides of her uniform to do a little curtsy, then, feeling dowdy, tried to brush off a streak of dirt on her skirt. Rosa watched, faintly amused.

"I do hope you can help me, Gracie. I have no idea where I am. And I do not mean my room. Where am I in Pennsylvania? The ride here from New York City was beautiful, but my driver gave me no details at all."

"Oh, sure, I can show you on a map. Would that help?"

Rosa clasped her hands down into a bow and said appreciatively, "Yes."

Gracie led her past Old Tim into the library. Showing Rosa a chair, she pulled the atlas off the shelf and set it on the roll top desk. She had just finished her shift and felt unusually grimy next to this impeccably dressed woman, but she reminded herself to be as helpful as possible. After locating the atlas, she carried the book over to the chair.

"See this tiny town with the lake?" Gracie pointed to a dot on the map. "You are right here in Eagles Mere, in the Allegheny Mountains of north central Pennsylvania."

"And that charming little footbridge that I saw on the way here, that goes across this lake?"

Gracie nodded.

"Thank you, gracious Gracie. I hope I will see you again soon."

"Yes, ma'am. You're welcome."

ও∽ৡ

Mae twirled her auburn hair around her index finger on Saturday night as she sat in the little chair by the door, wrapped in a pink seersucker bathrobe. They passed around a huge bowl of popcorn Gracie had brought up from the staff lounge.

Dorothy shook her head in disbelief. "Rosa Ponselle, the famous opera singer from the Metropolitan Opera. You met her in the lobby and didn't know who she was? I can't believe you haven't seen her picture, the way your nose is always stuck in the newspaper. Gracie, I don't understand how you can aspire to be a singer and not stay informed about internationally recognized..."

"She's here to do a concert? I've been so busy I didn't see her name on the bulletin board."

Mae snuck a peek out the door. There was no sign of Mrs. Slagle, who was supposedly signing in and out the male staffers using the staff lounge. "She's been known to let a boy slip by once or twice," she giggled.

"Well, she doesn't have to worry about any men slipping in here," Gracie moaned.

"I'd like to stay awhile if you don't mind. Zeke's home with the horses and Bessie won't be home till curfew. I try to go to bed before she comes in or stay out until she's asleep. When she comes back at night she's usually loaded and goes out like a light."

Dorothy fished an unpopped kernel of corn out of her mouth and tossed it into the trash can. "I wonder where she gets the hooch."

"She brings it back when she visits her father. I think Jimmy hides it for her."

Dorothy rested her arm around Mae's shoulder. "I am so sorry you have to room with her. I'd be beside myself if it were me."

There was a sharp rap on the door. Gracie jumped up, tightened her pink shrug around her, and opened the door to an oddly standoffish Mrs. Woods.

"I have a matter of importance to discuss with you. Dorothy, would you and Mae excuse us, please?" Mrs. Woods was obviously distressed. Gracie apologized for not being dressed and for the messiness of the room. She babbled on until Mrs. Woods put up her hand for silence. "Gracie, I have just checked in on our concert guest, Miss Rosa Ponselle. She asked for some help sorting her clothing in the morning. Actually, she needs a personal assistant and I wondered if you would help us out by taking that on."

"You want me to be a personal assistant for the opera singer?"

"She seems very down to earth. You might enjoy it. It will just be for two weeks and I'll reassign some of your other jobs for that period. That is, if you would consent to do it," she said wearily, tracing a zigzag along the back of the chair, anxious for a reply.

"Don't worry, Mrs. Woods. I'll do it."

Mrs. Woods undid the top button of her suit. Sinking into the chair, she pulled out her lace collar and used it to fan her face. Gracie brought her a glass of water from the bathroom. She drank gratefully. "Here, I just read this detective story and it took my mind right off all my worries." Gracie handed her *The Woman in White* and walked her out to the entrance of the Evergreen Lodge.

Gracie missed church that Sunday. Miss Ponselle unpacked a small suitcase of essentials, but had left untouched two hat boxes and a steamer trunk, embossed with a large P and small letters C and R intertwined. Mrs. Woods gave her a choice corner room with en suite bath and a large closet to accommodate her gowns. The three windows were crowned with valances of a royal blue and gold chevron fabric. Drapes fell to the sides, pulled back with gold tassels. In addition to a desk and chair, two chairs were placed to entertain guests. A small vanity for applying makeup sat in front of the window that overlooked North Mountain, and a tall dresser stood in between the other two. The final touch was a five-foot adjustable oval mirror set into a self-standing wooden frame. Mrs. Woods hadn't overlooked anything.

Gracie pulled out jewelry, vials of various colors and sizes, perfume atomizers, gloves and shoes, arranging them as Miss Ponselle instructed. The gowns were hung and several day dresses lay on top of one of the twin beds.

"Would you mind ironing my dresses while I will put my intimates away?"

"Of course not, Miss Ponselle. Is there anything else you need?"

"I need for you to call me Rosa as you did when we met on Friday."

"Of course. Rosa." Gracie closed the door softly behind her before rushing to do the ironing. She returned later with the dresses and a small vase of flowers.

"How thoughtful." The opera singer smiled and placed the flowers on her dresser. "Tell me, Gracie, what would you have done this morning if you had not helped me?"

"I would have been in church, but it's all right because I can sing any week and God would like it that I'm helping you settle in."

"Hospitality. You have shown me hospitality and I thank you. So you are a singer."

"Oh, honestly, no—I mean—not like you. I sing a little in church and I'm thinking about going on the road to do vaudeville. I'm interested in how you got started in your career, that is, if I'm not out of place in asking."

"I started out singing in a movie theater between the films. Then, when I was nineteen, my sister Carmella and I were booked as an act on a vaudeville circuit starting in the Bronx."

"The letters on the steamer trunk. The R and C intertwined."

"Yes, Carmella and I packed together in those days. We sang popular songs and some classical pieces. It was a hard life." She sat at the vanity, checked her makeup, and sprayed herself with lavender water. "We went on strike in 1918 because they presumed to pay us less than we were worth, so during the strike I auditioned for the Metropolitan Opera. I'd never had a voice lesson in my life. They signed me immediately and assigned five opera roles for me to learn in so many months. In 1918 I made my debut opposite Caruso in *La Forza del Destino*. My manager changed my name from Ponzillo to Ponselle and I have sung at the Metropolitan ever since. There's more out there than vaudeville, Gracie. The public is flocking instead now to films and floor shows. You do dance, don't you?"

Gracie's jaw dropped. She stopped asking questions, ascertained whether Rosa needed anything else, and flew down to the laundry porch.

❧

When Bessie entered the kitchen she heard funny tapping sounds coming from inside the pantry. She tiptoed over to the chest of tiny wooden drawers where the spices were kept. Running her finger over the little labels, she located the cloves, pulled out a handful and put them in her apron pocket. Riotous laughter told her Isaiah and Sam were headed right for her. She ducked into the pantry just as they came through the kitchen door. Isaiah was singing like a girl. Sam drummed the prep table in time.

"I don't know how I do it, but sometimes in the song the girlfriend speaks, so when I do her part, I make my voice go way up into falsetto like a woman. Pretty good imitation, huh?"

"Maybe with your singing and my tapping we should get an act together," Sam said.

"We'd be wiser to stick to cooking. Now, let's figure out what kind of fancy dinner we can create for this opera singer. The Woods want something special the night of her concert because a lot of the town people will be dining here. We could do the crown roast of lamb with roasted potatoes and radish roses. Get it? Rosa— roses. Or we could try some of that new Italian food. It's all the rage now. Don't opera singers sing in Italian?"

"You're supposed to be the singing expert, Isaiah. And I don't know a thing about cooking Italian. Maybe we'd better see to what hor d'oeuvres we're going to serve at the dance tonight," Sam said.

Once her eyes adjusted to the dark, Bessie saw Eleanor on the floor surrounded by brown and silver candy wrappers, her mouth covered with chocolate. Eleanor cocked her head to the side and studied Bessie curiously as she unpeeled another chocolate bar.

"Whadya doin' here?" Bessie asked angrily.

"Well, I was practicing my tap dancing and it was so good I treated myself to a snack," Eleanor answered proudly. She wrinkled her nose. "You smell funny. What is that, cinnamon or cloves?"

"Ain't none of your business, Eleanor."

"It is if my parents paid for the cloves."

"I have a toothache and if I chew on a clove the pain goes away."

"Uh huh." Eleanor picked up her mess, stood; brushed chocolate bits off her dress and burst through the pantry door. "Da, da, da, *da*, da *da!*" Isaiah and Sam gave her a round of applause. "Something smells funny in that pantry," she said coolly as she left.

܀܀

Miss Ponselle sat in the Adirondack chair, her head resting against the back. Her straw hat was decorated with white gossamer fabric tied under her chin. Inhaling deeply, she waved a single peach-colored rose back and forth under her nostrils. Snapdragons, daisies and wild roses surrounded her. "I never smell things like wild roses in the city. Thank you for this chair, this place."

Margaret smiled, set down her basket of flowers and said, "It was a simple request. I should put a chair out here for myself sometime. My private garden is not shown when we give the Crestmont tour because I cut so many of the flowers for arrangements. Most guests don't dare to venture in here. I guess they are happy with the flowers planted elsewhere on the grounds."

"As it should be, Mrs. Woods."

Margaret put her finger to her lips and pointed to a diminutive bird hovering over the languid red petals of a bee balm blossom. She whispered, "A ruby-throated hummingbird." The bird noticed the movement, gave a mouse-like squeak and fled.

"Its wings beat so fast it literally hums," Miss Ponselle commented. "This truly is your sacred retreat to be treated with reverence. Thank you for sharing it with me. You have been so accommodating to my needs, and that young woman, Gracie, is very sweet. I have just one other thing to ask of you."

"Yes?"

"When we pray, do we not do it in private? It is the same for singers. I have nowhere to discreetly warm up my voice and coax it forth. The scales I sing to prepare for the demands of my music are not for the public's ears. The concert is for them. Where might I go to do this alone, for my voice?"

Margaret was dumbstruck. People were everywhere at the Crestmont. She promised to find a suitable place and excused herself to return to the big house.

Clouds of distress that Mrs. Woods was overworked racked Gracie's brain, but she felt she could be most helpful by making Rosa Ponselle's stay as pleasant as possible. She was proud of herself for thinking of Mrs. Cunningham's and the church as private places for the singer to practice. Madeleine was relieved for a reason to leave the house on an additional day and her mother promised to stay upstairs in her room to afford the singer privacy. Miss Ponselle seemed eager to walk down to the "charming little town," so on Tuesday Gracie left her at Mrs. Cunningham's piano, promising to disappear for two hours. Sneaking back early, she sat quietly on the front step to listen to the singing. The voice was deep, rich and velvety. Even though the words were in a foreign language, Gracie was so moved she didn't feel the need to understand their meaning.

After lunching at the Sweet Shoppe, Miss Ponselle made a little joke about her agent being upset that she was walking all over Eagles Mere. Gracie telephoned PT immediately to fetch them in the car after the hair appointment. He was polite to Miss Ponselle as they motored back to the Crestmont, but he looked right through Gracie like she was glass. Too busy to fret about how he was ignoring her, she couldn't help notice that he was never around. Even though he surely missed playing the piano, he was noticeably absent from the staff lounge. Isaiah said he often took his meals on a tray back to the bowling alley. Putting her feelings about him aside, she decided she no longer felt hurt. He was hiding from her and she was fed up.

Gracie opened the door after hearing two polite little taps.

"Ah, the dressmaker." Miss Ponselle welcomed Olivia. "Let me see what you have created since our first meeting."

"Good morning, Miss Ponselle. Mrs. Woods said you had some free time for a fitting?" Olivia wore a linen shift with a pleated bodice and cap sleeves. In her right hand she carried her sewing basket and her left arm was draped with large pieces of light teal silk. "May we pin up your hair until I fit the dress and then we can let it down and see the whole effect?"

Gracie assisted in removing the singer's day dress and Olivia pieced the dress sections together, remarking though pins in her mouth, "This light teal you have chosen will be stunning with your dark hair. I kept the dress simple and close to the body as you desired."

"I like the three tiers on the skirt. I am tired of the shapeless effect of today's fashions. Show me what you have done about a waist."

"Yes, I remembered. Olivia wound a long cord of twisted silver and black threads tight around the waist in the front, crossed it in the back, and returned it to the front, knotting it three inches below where it began. The extra cord fell loosely.

"Let us see the dress with the cape, please." The dressmaker attached a floor-length cape to the shoulder straps, draped it over the back of the gown and pulled the hem around in front. She moved the mirror so the whole effect could be seen.

Miss Ponselle turned to view the dress several ways in the mirror. "It needs something."

"Yes, I agree. I suggest that I knot some rhinestones into the ends of the cord to move and sparkle as you walk, and embroider the edges of the cape with black and silver silk thread to complete the design."

Gracie unpinned Miss Ponselle's long, wavy hair and spread it out over one shoulder. She and Olivia stood behind the opera star, all three of them gazing in the oval mirror.

Miss Ponselle gave Olivia an impulsive hug. "Magnificent."

"May I bring it back on Saturday for the final fitting?"

"You are an artist. I look forward to it." Gracie helped her friend gather the dress pieces and her sewing supplies and walked her to the door as they exchanged excited smiles.

ৡৣ

After lunch, Miss Ponselle worked at the desk, humming while she ran her fingers over each page in her opera score. "I would prefer a tray brought up for my dinner tonight. Three women and two men sit at a table behind mine and discuss me constantly. Granted, sometimes their conversation is complimentary, but really, how rude to talk behind one's back."

Gracie sat at the vanity, polishing some brooches.

"Oh, them. I heard them say something negative about Mrs. Woods once. I wanted to give them a piece of my mind, but they wouldn't have heard it anyway. That's why the staff calls them the Rude Regals. They act like royalty and gossip about everybody." She clapped her hand over her mouth. "Oh honestly, I shouldn't have said that."

Miss Ponselle turned around in her chair, slapped her thighs and giggled like a schoolgirl. "Gracie, you are so funny. Don't ever be afraid to be human. You can't like everyone, you know."

"Me, funny?"

"Yes. The refreshing part is that your humor is genuine, not contrived. Now, concerning my dinnertime commentators, I may complain about those people, but their gossip is a harmless part of their vacation relaxation. Don't take anything they say to heart. You may want to read that new F. Scott Fitzgerald book if you want to understand why people like your Rude Regals resort to such charades to be accepted socially."

"Now the press, they are the ones who do damage. Gossip is child's play next to their shenanigans. Once they contrived that I was having an affair with a tenor to elevate box office sales for an opera we were to sing together. An executive from the Met told me about an advance tip that the tenor was going to divorce his wife the next week and marry me. The notice was rushed to New York City and posted immediately. Box office sales soared. It hurts to be used so."

"It sounds like you needed a vacation. I am glad you came here. Will you sing an opera on your concert here?"

Miss Ponselle closed her opera score. "Oh, no, not a complete opera. I would need more singers to do the roles of the other characters. I could never do that alone with just my pianist. I have planned a varied program, however. You like the popular songs, yes?" Gracie nodded. "Those composers write for the masses; songs to sing along with during everyday life. So when I plan a concert, such as the one I will perform here next week, I program something familiar like some Stephen Foster songs to make the people happy. Then I sing my favorite arias on the second half, to stretch the audience, to take them to a place they have never been. The great operatic composers explore the depth of the human voice, emotion, musical and orchestral complexity to paint pictures in sound. If sung well, opera can take you to a magical place, just as when you study a beautiful painting or read an absorbing book."

Gracie was afraid she was being too inquisitive, but it seemed that the opera star wanted to talk, so she asked, "Isn't it a lot of pressure?"

"It is hard work, but I love to sing." She stood up, closed her eyes and gave her head an imperceptible shake. "The rigors of performing, learning new roles and traveling are great, and they pay me well, but to do all of that and not lose my joy of singing—very challenging. I have to work at finding a balance."

"How?" Gracie sat very still as Miss Ponselle paced from one side of the room to the other, stopping from time to time, quietly talking to herself.

"By singing meaningfully, hoping to touch another soul. The voice is a powerfully communicative instrument. God has given me an amazing gift and if I use it correctly, someone in the audience, perhaps just one, may be lifted above their everyday struggle and refreshed for a few moments. And when I truly listen to the music and allow it to move me, I am taken to a magical, blessed place where I find that my own soul has been replenished. This is what feeds me and keeps me centered as an artist and as a person."

❧❧

William quick-stepped to open the door, cupped his hand around his mouth and called, "Okay, boys, bring it in. Careful." Giving his wife a snappy nod, he said, "You will love this, Margaret."

Otto and Sid hauled in a six-foot-tall cherry filing cabinet with fifteen narrow drawers and set it against the wall. Speechless, Margaret stared at her husband. He nearly burst with excitement. Perspiration trickled down his temples.

"Look," he said, pulling on several of the brass knobs. "I have taken the liberty of labeling each drawer alphabetically. I was so impressed by your attention to detail when you told me about the person that required four pillows, I bought you this. You can keep all of your notes concerning the guests' preferences organized in these drawers."

"Like these notes?" She testily pulled a paper from her desk and recited,

> Mrs. Pennington:
> Window to be shut at all times due to allergies.
> Needs electric fan.
> Prefers Room C with private bath and close proximity to dining room.
> Housemaid should eliminate spider webs on regular basis.
> Bellboy to be discreet concerning ice requests for foot baths.
> 4 bed pillows.
> Prone to sunstroke.
> 1925 – 3 requests for doctor.
> Dietary restrictions– made nauseous by milk.

So you feel I need further organization than my current system."

"I thought it might help you, Margaret."

"William, I know you meant well, but why should I replace one system I have perfected with another that you feel will work better?"

Gracie had heard every word through the open door as she ran toward the office. "Mrs. Woods, I went to check on Mrs. Pennington's ice water and found her on the bed. She says she feels faint."

Margaret sent her to the kitchen for ice and headed for Room C to tend to their guest, leaving William in her office scratching his head.

"I'm sorry I stayed so long with Miss Ponselle. I might have gotten to clean Mrs. Pennington's room earlier and prevented her spell. I've never seen anyone with so many ailments," Gracie said later as they left her propped up on pillows with the fan blowing around the room.

"You can't be everywhere at all times, Gracie, although I know you try. Mrs. Pennington can't help her problems. She prefers to swim in them because she doesn't have the wherewithal to rise above them. The least we can do is to shower her with the attention she craves."

੭੦ન૨

"Delicious," pronounced Miss Ponselle, wiping the corners of her mouth and dropping her napkin onto the dinner tray Gracie had brought. "Now, we talked about me all afternoon and it is time I heard you sing."

"Here?" Gracie whispered, panic-stricken.

"As you said, the other guests are probably still in the dining room, so this may be the most privacy we have. You mentioned a song you wanted to sing for the staff talent show?"

"'I'll Build a Stairway to Paradise.'"

"Yes, let me hear it."

Gracie ran her tongue around the inside of her bottom teeth, studied the floor and sucked a big breath through her nose. Then she fixed her eyes on a blank space on the wall and sang:

> I'll build a stairway to Paradise
> With a new step every day.
> I'm going to get there at any price.
> Stand aside, I'm on my way....

"Good, good. You have a pretty voice. Now continue."

She was sure she was a dismal failure, but Gracie desperately wanted to make a good impression and made herself keep singing. She actually started to relax until Miss Ponselle stopped her midstream.

"Tell me why you chose this song."

"Excuse me, ma'am?"

"You must like this song or you would not want to sing it. Why do you like it?"

"Well, it's peppy so it's fun to sing, and PT, the man who drove you, can play it really well...and I have these shoes..."

"Shoes. You mean when you sing about stepping you see yourself in these shoes?"

"Yes." Gracie's voice trailed off weakly.

"Excellent. Tomorrow you must wear the shoes and we will do this again. But now, I am tired. Would you bring me a fresh glass of water?" Miss Ponselle slipped into her dressing gown and added a dropper from a blue vial into the water. "Go, get some sleep. Tomorrow I will teach you more about singing."

The three of them smiled sweetly as they filed past Mrs. Slagle out of the Evergreen Lodge and over to the laundry porch. "Back by eleven, girls," she warned, scrutinizing them over her reading glasses while she wrote their names on her clipboard.

"I'm trying to remember the last time I was given a curfew...or called a girl." Dorothy laughed. The laundry was shut down for the evening and the porch was quiet with a lovely breeze tinkling the wind chimes. "Imagine what Celeste Woodford would say if she knew we were eating Rosa Ponselle's chocolates."

Gracie passed around the box, waving off the gnats. "Rosa says the chocolate clogs her throat and that she's too fat already."

"That tiny thing?" Dorothy said, biting into a chocolate caramel.

Mae pushed the box away. "You two take what you want and I'll eat what you don't."

"Oh, honestly, Mae, just take the one you want instead of always putting yourself last." Gracie stuck the box in her face, "Here, choose and enjoy."

"A funny thing happened though." Mae and Dorothy leaned in with curiosity.

"She has a little blue bottle on her nightstand. She added a few drops from it to her water. Said it helped her sleep."

"Probably laudanum." Dorothy ticked her tongue. "Poor thing, she must be beside herself with pressure." Mae gingerly lifted a chocolate out of the box and took a bite.

"What else did she say?"

"Well, she told me she had terrible stage fright, and then she asked me to sing."

"How does she remember all those Italian words when she doesn't speak the language?" Dorothy asked.

"I guess she's memorized so many foreign words, she practically does speak the language. She's really nice. She wants me to call her Rosa. And tomorrow, she wants me to wear my St. Louis heels when I sing." Dorothy narrowed her eyes and elbowed Mae. "Don't ask me," Gracie continued, "she's the famous singer. I'll take whatever help she'll give me. Maybe PT will finally jam with me if I take some voice lessons."

"Oh my word, Gracie, I am so tired of hearing you moan about that man. You two obviously had a little spat. If you want him, go after him," Dorothy said.

❧

Gracie followed the finger in the oval mirror while Miss Ponselle pointed from her blonde bob down to her St. Louis heels. "Look at how the back of your knees are pushed back. You must unlock them." Gracie snapped her knees forward. "How you stand is a reflection of how you feel about yourself. These hunched shoulders tell me a great deal." She gently, but firmly pulled Gracie's shoulders back.

"Excuse me, Miss Rosa, but I was hoping we could get to the singing part of the lesson soon."

"We will sing soon enough, but before that we must do something about your bearing. You are like a tightly wound ball of twine, afraid to let go. Now shake your arms out and pull your head up like this." Miss Ponselle loosely swung her arms back and forth and seemed to grow two inches taller.

"No, no, not like that. Don't tip your chin up, but rather pull up your carriage and your neck from the back of your head as if you were looking over an imaginary fence." Gracie straightened the crook in her neck and raised the crown of her head. The mirror now reflected a confident looking woman.

"Now, breathe deeply and sing me the song while you look over the fence."

The sound came out more naturally and it was easier to hit the high notes. Gracie let go and began to enjoy herself.

"Yes, much better. The sound is freer now." She pointed to Gracie's hands, which lay plastered to the front of her uniform skirt. "Tell me, what do those hands say?"

"They're not saying anything. They're just there."

"Nonsense, they are saying 'Here are my thighs.' Very unladylike."

Gracie nodded dumbly and acquiesced as her hands were moved around to the sides of her skirt. She walked around the room, singing, trying to keep her body positioned as her teacher instructed.

"Now it is time to envision your shoes. Does the little gold buckle glint in the light when you move? Listen to your heels clicking on the floor when you sing the line about a new step every day."

Gracie closed her eyes, stepping and singing with increasing confidence. Gone was any memory of her heel catching in the stairs in front of Otto's brother.

"Good. Now you are one with the song, not just singing the song. Practice this way when you work with the pianist you mentioned."

᭡ᨁᨁ᭡

On Thursday, PT drove them down into town. Miss Ponselle insisted on being let off at the Presbyterian Church first because she had much practicing to do for the concert. Gracie went in with her to make sure the lights were on and reminded Rev. Sturdy the opera singer would need privacy.

Once back in the car, she tried to make chit chat about her voice lesson, but PT was remote. He did agree to play for her at the talent show, but expressed no interest in being alone with her. When he dropped her at Mrs. Cunningham's, he said nothing more than "Be back at five."

Mrs. Cunningham chatted cheerfully during breakfast, but Gracie hardly heard a word. All morning she tried to work off her tension by cleaning out the refrigerator, washing down cupboards, and reorganizing the linen closet. When she broke a dish while washing up after lunch, Mrs. Cunningham called her into the living room, asking what was wrong. Relieved the old woman wanted to help, she confided in her about what had happened.

"Grace, it is wrongheaded of you to infer that he doesn't care for you just because he hides. There must be something in his life holding him back from being with you. If you really care for PT, then you must give him time to work out his problems—if you care for him, that is."

She did care for him, but the summer was short and she couldn't wait. She was going to go after him.

ת

Margaret seemed surprised when William offered to make the weekly deposit at the bank. "Let me lighten your load a bit. Peg can run the water activities for me this morning," he explained.

William savored his drive alone to Laporte. Even though he thrived on his relationships with the Crestmont guests, he still needed an hour or so of solitude on Monday to recharge. Their bi-weekly row on the lake helped as well. Relaxation was hard for his wife, even on the water, but William slipped easily into the rest time away from their duties.

He found the challenge of running the inn, teaching at Westlawn, balancing family and community activities exhilarating. His brain constantly percolated new ideas like tennis courts, the Evergreen Lodge and elevating the profile of the concert series. Margaret was the cautious, deliberate one, working out the details, determined to keep her father's dream alive. Together, they were the success of the Crestmont. The guests were content because Margaret attended so faithfully to their needs, but they relished William's flair for articulating his delight in their company.

Vision and implementation were the skills his father-in-law, William Warner, had preached when he built the Crestmont. Before his dementia, he talked about the day Margaret and William would inherit the inn, ecstatic that as a team they embodied both. But it was to William the visionary, that Warner had charged, "If you're not looking forward, you are moving backward."

William worried constantly that Margaret was overburdened. He regretted that she perceived him as forgetful, but he simply did not feel gifted in dealing with nuts and bolts. She was so adept at keeping the administrative bits and pieces together, he hadn't seen them drive her into the melancholy that frightened them so last autumn. He had never given up on his dream of the

Eagles Mere Tennis Tournaments, but he didn't want his idea to burden her. He did, however, need for her to agree. Surely she would if he presented her with a plan well-formulated from start to finish with appropriate funding. He would just have to manage the implementation himself.

Mr. Crittendon, a stooped man of about sixty with a ruddy face, ushered him into a green leather chair. The bank president coughed and folded his wrinkled hands on the desk.

"I am honored, sir," William Woods began. "I assume your family founded this bank."

"My grandfather moved here from Chicago in 1860 to establish The Crittendon Bank of Laporte. It has remained in our family ever since."

"Marvelous. I, too, come from a family business. My wife and I inherited the Crestmont Inn from her father."

Mr. Crittendon coughed again and William resisted the urge offer him his own handkerchief. "Yes, Mrs. Woods. Lovely woman. However, it is she who has always done business with us in the past. I don't recall meeting you before."

"A circumstance now rectified. Now, down to business. Shall we visit my account history? Let us examine my personal accounts as well as the Crestmont's."

Mr. Crittendon shuffled to the cabinets on the back wall. He returned, frowning as he thumbed through the file. "Yes, the Crestmont account lists you as co-owner with your wife. Please accept my apology, Mr. Woods. I'm listening."

William knew in advance what the bank president would say. He carefully outlined his request, intent on proving himself.

Mr. Crittendon ran his index finger down the entries in their file, shaking his head. "I see that the Crestmont has never before asked the bank for a loan."

"My good man, surely such a thing works in our favor. Do you mean that because we have never needed to borrow in the past that a loan for the Crestmont cannot be granted now?"

"Bank policy is that if credit is not established, credit may not be granted without a thorough review of the lendee's accounts."

"The lendee has been a valued customer of this bank for twenty-six years. The lendee is the owner of one of the most prestigious summer hotels in the northern Allegheny Mountains. The lendee's accounts are right here on your desk. What further review is necessary?" William rose and walked decisively back and forth in front of Crittendon's desk, his shoes clicking on the marble floor.

"I am not talking about tennis courts merely for recreational use at the Crestmont, Mr.Crittendon," he said passionately. "I intend to run tennis tournaments second only to those in Forest Hills, New York. We will attract the best players from all over the country. People will flock here. Do you have any idea how much revenue that will create, not just for Eagles Mere, but for all of Sullivan County? If you examine my figures, you will see that the entire loan will be paid off in two years."

"You would have to put the Crestmont up as collateral against the loan."

"The value of the Crestmont is out of the ballpark compared to the amount I am requesting. I have three guest cottages on the property. I offer them as collateral, with the understanding that we will continue to administer and maintain them, but all rental income be funneled directly to the bank if we default."

"I shall have to discuss this with my other officers."

"I find it incongruous that a man of your position would need to consult with his subordinates."

Fifteen minutes later the papers were signed. Motoring home, William sang one of his favorite Fanny Crosby hymns, as the wind whipped through the car. The Eagles Mere Tennis Tournaments would be in place by next summer.

PT chatted with Miss Ponselle all the way back in the car. Gracie didn't mind that he ignored her because she needed time to plan. When Rosa was settled back at the Crestmont, Gracie ran back to her dorm room and pulled out her notebook. At the top of the page she wrote:

Thursday, July 22
I get out now and don't get hurt anymore.
I go after him, he comes around, and we are happy together.
I go after him and he says no.
He comes around, we have some happy times, then he hurts me
again.
I do nothing, fret about what his problem is, and miss any love
we might share.

He was worth the risk. Feeling emboldened, she ran to the bathroom to wash up. She freshened her makeup, changed into her dress and heels, and headed for the bowling alley. PT was probably still at dinner and most of the guests would be with Sid on the front lawn for game night. Gracie went in, saw that no one was there, and sat on one of the little stools under the scoreboard. When he came back she would tell him how she felt.

Time ticked by and the bowling alley grew dark as the sun went down. She turned on a light so he would think a guest was there when he returned. Making herself small on the stool, she waited.

When he came through the door his expression was inscrutable. "Come for a bowling lesson?" he asked nonchalantly, lighting a cigarette.

"I was just in the neighborhood." She mentally smacked herself for not working out a better opening line.

PT went to the other side of the room and took a couple of long drags before tapping out his cigarette. Changing into his bowling shoes, he returned with a can of oil and some rags. He poured out some oil, polishing one of the lanes. Gracie sat quietly, waiting for a response. He worked another twenty minutes, wiping down the wood with a clean rag until it glowed. Then he cleaned out the gutters of the other lane and repeated the oiling process. The more he stalled, the angrier she got.

She drummed the sole of her right foot on the floor. "You were the one who kissed me, you know."

"Yup. Liked it, too."

She got up and sat down on the floor next to where he was working. "I'm glad you did." He kept his arm moving, just out of her reach. "PT, I care about you."

He wanted her, but he was wary. "I've been a loner for a long time, Gracie. I told you I wasn't good at this."

They stayed there a few more minutes in silence.

"Can we still jam together? Just share some music."

He nodded, looking back at her like a lost little boy.

"Well then, I should go."

He flashed into a storm cloud. "Why are you always telling yourself what you should do? Do what you want to do for a change."

"What I want is to stay here, but you don't want me to. I'll see you in the staff lounge sometime," she said, not looking back as she left.

ϖ∞

Rosa cheered her up. She told stories about opera and kept Gracie's mind off PT. At one time, she imagined them going on the road together, but now she knew that wouldn't happen. Having no idea what her future held, she wished she could play a role in an opera so she could become someone other than herself for a while. Instead, she listened to Rosa's experiences.

"Now Caruso, there was a tenor." The singer draped her hand dramatically across her heart. "His singing was virile. I could feel his whole body vibrate against mine when we were on stage singing a lovers' duet. He was the king of Italian opera. Oh, yes, sometimes he overworked his acting, but his sound—it was like gold coming from his throat. He encouraged me and calmed me when I was nervous or disheartened. I have a big voice and the critics sometimes say I sacrifice quality of sound for volume. Caruso taught me to use the voice with which I have been endowed and pay no attention to them."

"When will you sing with him again?" Gracie asked.

"Never. He died five years ago, in his late forties. What a loss." Rosa sat down at her vanity concentrating on the view out her window. "Now we must move into the future, not dwell on the past."

She went to her closet and pulled out two gowns. "For my concert next week I would like to wear one of these for the first part of the program when I sing the lighter songs." Rosa discussed the pros and cons of the dresses. "I have worn this cobalt organza for much of my tour this summer. The lightness is good in the heat, but I fear it is too tight, and will impede my breathing. No, I will wear the honey-colored one. It reminds me of sunshine, yes, like my days here at the Crestmont. Then in keeping with the new fashion on the recital stage in New York, I will change into Olivia's creation during the intermission. When I return for the second half of the concert, the audience will sense a transition in the flavor of the music because of my attire."

Laying the golden gown down on the bed, Gracie said, "I don't think it needs to be pressed."

"No, no, it is fine. My dear, I would appreciate it if you would assist me in dressing for Friday's concert. I never seem to be able to relax. Perhaps you could talk to me and help me not to dwell on my stage fright. But I want to see you in a real dress the night of the concert, not this 'thing'." Miss Ponselle tweaked the collar of Gracie's uniform.

"I have a dress. I'll wear my green braid slink." She blushed, embarrassed that naming a dress must seem immature to such a great performer.

"Do not be embarrassed. You must love your clothes if you name them. I put on a costume for a role. It helps me to become the character. We are alike. Clothes are part of our identity."

୨◦ଏ

"She doesn't eat?" Isaiah took off his chef's hat and wiped his forehead on the sleeve of his white uniform.

"Not before she sings a concert, no." William rocked on his heels and waited for the burly man's tirade to subside.

"Mr. Woods, we've got lobsters and prime rib ordered." He waved a large bowl under William's nose. "Just take a whiff of this apricot stuffing for the roast duck. I've got French artichoke canapés and medallions of *foie gras* on toast points with a fancy watermelon sherbet punch for appetizers; caramelized onions, sautéed mushrooms, tomato aspic, green beans with hollandaise and my special poppy seed bread sticks. Sam's making baked Alaska and steamed marmalade pudding with hard sauce for dessert." Frustrated, Isaiah counted off each menu item on his fingers. "The dinner is going to cost, boss. Sid okayed all the requisitions, but without Miss Ponselle there... Do you want me to tinker with the menu?"

"Your menu sounds brilliant. Don't alter a thing. We've advertized well and have many reservations from people in Eagles Mere and the surrounding area. We will treat everyone to an extravagant dinner and a fabulous concert afterward."

As Isaiah calmed down, his sense of humor returned. "Well, the woman has to work up an appetite after all that singing. Do you think she'd fancy a nice cold sliced duck sandwich after she's done?"

"I'd say, add the tomato aspic and *foie gras* with some fresh fruit and she should be very happy. And put doilies and flowers on the tray. Miss Ponselle has been a lovely guest. I want her to remember her stay with fondness."

৵৵

Gracie had never felt so important. Rosa insisted on her help with preparations for the Thursday rehearsal and on keeping her company in the evening. Arrangements had been made for Peg to be Mrs. Cunningham's companion that day.

The opera singer requested a green room where she could focus and dress before the concert and during intermission. Mrs. Woods unlocked an unused room arranged like a small parlor near the landing on the first sleeping floor and handed the key to Gracie. "My father's old office," she said proudly. I've never had the heart to make it over into a guest room. You see, it is just a few steps from the main staircase where Miss Ponselle will make her entrance."

Rosa and Gracie sat there Thursday evening, eagerly awaiting Olivia. She was to deliver the gown after the final hemming.

"Not every role is equally dear to a singer's heart," the singer chattered nervously. "One must modulate the voice to suit the composer's intent and the character's emotions. To sing Leonora in *Il Trovatore*, I must lighten to execute the trills, but never forget the depth of her character and convey that in the sound I produce. I try to both dwell in the character's mind and sing her through my heart. I love the opera—not so much the treacherous arias, but the lavish music and plot."

Gracie asked about the opera's story, sensing that the more Rosa talked, the more she would relax so she would sleep well the night before the concert.

"Leonora and Manrico are lovers. Manrico's enemy, Di Luna, threatens to kill him unless Leonora promises herself to him. Leonora is cunning and self-sacrificing. She loves Manrico and would do anything to save his life, but she respects herself too much to do this terrible thing. Before Di Luna can possess her, she drinks poison from a ring she has procured from an apothecary. The orchestration is very dramatic here. The music ascends as she lies dying in Marico's arms, and as my voice goes up and up, I feel I am no longer on stage but in some other world."

Olivia tapped on the green room door an hour before the concert. After the opera singer dressed, she sent Gracie and Olivia to wait below in the lobby so they could see the full effect. Rosa Ponselle stopped on the first landing in front of the mirror that stretched from floor to ceiling. She swished the silk fabric and practiced a low opera bow, then turned to them, extending the cape as far to the side as her arm could reach.

"It is more than I dreamed of. Shall we call it 'The Ponselle'?"

Because of the number of guest inquiries and flurry of telephone calls from Eagles Mere residents, the Woods moved the concert from the West Lounge into the largest space possible. Miss Ponselle had concurred, waiving the necessity of calling her agent for approval. Chairs were set up in the lobby, in the hallway near the Woods' offices, and outside on the front and back porches. Overflow seating was in the Ladies Lounge where the sound would carry well through the open French doors. The Woods had given no one preference, but rather announced seats could be obtained on a first-come, first-serve basis. The piano was moved close to the east wing hall.

The audience filtered in, raving about the elaborate dinner served at the Crestmont table. Men turned out in tuxedos. Women wore formal gowns and cloche hats decorated with feathers, or ribbons wound around their hair secured behind one ear with elaborate pins.

After helping to put the final touches on the singer's appearance, Gracie went from the green room down the back stairs and found a seat near the rear so she could easily slip out to help with the gown switch at intermission. No sooner had she sat down than she saw a strong hand grip the back of the chair next to her. "Would you mind if I sit here?" She barely had a moment to consider when Eric Sturdy sat down next to her.

On Friday, July 30th, William Woods, looking classy in formal wear, stood in the crook of the grand piano. He punctuated his eloquent welcome and introduction with a dramatic gesture toward the landing. A hush spread over the audience as Miss Ponselle's tiny feet descended the center staircase. Her honey-colored gown glowed from the light of the huge chandelier. She met her accompanist at the grand piano and they bowed deeply, accepting the welcoming applause.

The Stephen Foster songs were easy on Gracie's ears. Her cares and worries dropped away. In the Schubert section that followed, Gracie seemed to understand the words even though she didn't speak German, because of the ever changing expressions on Rosa's face.

After intermission, the experience was transformed. A woman in the front row shouted "Brava" when the singer returned in The Ponselle, prompting numerous other cries of acclamation. Miss Ponselle sang the opera arias she loved. Her sound was so powerful and resonant that a pulsation vibrated against Gracie's eardrums. The depth of the music communicated warmth that stroked her heart like soft velvet. Gracie searched the audience. When she saw Mrs. Woods, her eyes were closed and her face was peaceful as if she were lifted out of herself.

After the final vibrant high note of the encore subsided, the audience leapt to their feet in thunderous applause. Gracie pulled herself up from the back of her neck to better see her friend bowing next to the piano.

"You carry yourself differently," Eric noticed.

"Just a little trick Miss Ponselle taught me."

"May I walk you back to your dorm?"

"I have to help Miss Ponselle. I've been a kind of companion to her since she arrived."

"I'm sure you have been a kind companion to her. Another time, then?"

Gracie nodded. Out of the corner of her eye, she noticed PT. He scowled at her and stalked off down the back stairs.

III

GRACIE OVERSLEPT THE MORNING AFTER THE CONCERT. WHEN SHE woke, she scrambled to get dressed so she could say goodbye to Rosa. The sound of a vacuuming machine coming from the end of the east wing gave her a bad feeling.

"Yer bosom buddy checked out," Bessie said, leaving Rosa's room with her cleaning supplies in hand.

Crestfallen, Gracie found Mrs. Woods at the checkout desk, surrounded by guests. Awaiting her turn, she nervously shifted her weight from one foot to the other. Mrs. Woods gave her a pained look as the last guest lingered, recounting a story about her husband's croquette match. Finally, they were alone.

"Unfortunately for you, Gracie, Miss Ponselle's driver arrived early this morning. She has a concert in Pittsburgh tomorrow and wanted to get on the road early." Mrs. Woods pulled out a parcel wrapped in brown paper from under the desk. A letter was attached. "She left this for you."

Dearest Gracie,

You were most gracious to me during my stay at the Crestmont. I leave you this token of my appreciation. I enjoyed teaching you a bit about singing. Remember you will touch people the most when you sing what is meaningful to you.

Affectionately,
Rosa Ponselle

Gracie gave Mrs. Woods the note to read and carefully opened the package. Her hand flew to her throat when she saw light teal silk.

"Oh, Mrs. Woods, I can't accept this."

"Of course you can. She obviously wanted you to have it." Mrs. Woods rested her elbows on the desk gazing at the empty lobby. "Everyone's checked out. Try it on. Go ahead; you can use the green room." Mrs. Woods handed her the key.

"Will you stay here to see me in it?"

Mrs. Woods nodded eagerly.

Five minutes later Gracie appeared, dressed in The Ponselle. She held her head high as she had been taught and descended the staircase, trying to imitate Rosa's light step. She stopped halfway, sweeping the cape around to the front so Mrs. Woods would get the whole effect.

"You are beautiful, Gracie." Dabbing her eyes with her handkerchief, she excused herself to her office.

Gracie lifted up the three tiered skirt so she wouldn't trip and mounted the stairs to the first floor landing. Pausing in front of the floor-length mirror, she practiced a curtsy as she had seen the opera singer do. Something shifted inside of her. The old nervousness was less. It seemed the only person she needed to please was herself.

"Nothing like a cigar and baseball to clear the mind," William said as he and Mr. Swett sent relaxed puffs of smoke into the evening air. Some children had made a makeshift court on the back lawn and cheered on a skinny boy of about ten who flailed his arms as he ran the bases. Swett gave William the low-down on the Saratoga horse races, then switched topics to tennis. William welcomed the sizable donation Swett offered for the construction of the tennis courts. It was all taken care of, but a little cushion wouldn't hurt. "Well, old sport, if you will excuse me, I need to go find my man, PT, and discuss some business."

The Eagles Mere Hotel Association had discussed valet service at their last meeting. Most hotels in town were going for it. In addition, The Raymond and Edgemere Inns planned to revamp their entire tipping system, inflating the guests' fees to include all gratuities. Concluding that implementing such a thing at the Crestmont would discourage the staff from applying themselves to superior service, William decided against it.

When he found PT, he explained the new valet parking idea as they walked together down the drive toward the Evergreen Lodge. PT would be the boss, with Otto and Hank assisting. The parking lot would be extended farther away from the big house.

What William did not share was that this was part of his plan to make room for the tennis courts. Then he switched to other matters of importance. The Lakeside had won the baseball championship in the hotel league last year and had their trophy prominently on display at the Association meeting.

He was interrupted by Peg's call from the Crestmont porch. She waved and ran down the lawn to join them.

"Baseball's not my game, sir."

"I know you've got a good arm, PT, because I have seen all those strikes you throw in the alley. I'll coach you. You would just be a backup pitcher. You probably won't even have to play. Picture that gold trophy on the welcome desk!"

He opened his arms to hug his daughter. "PT, I'd like to introduce my new water activities assistant."

"PT and I have met probably 287 times over the years. Papa, we need more life jackets. Many of the ladies won't sit on the floating dock without them. May I ask Mr. Fox to requisition them?"

"Requisition. Did you hear her? She's talking administrative language already."

PT chuckled and said, "Anything else, Mr. Woods?"

"No, but give it some thought. The Crestmont Baseball Team needs you." William slapped him on the back and PT headed off.

"Papa, he doesn't want to play baseball. He's been waiting for you to ask him to play a concert."

"Well, yes, I did mention the possibility to him last year. I'll mull it over. But that jazz he plays, I don't know. I understand some people actually consider it to be real music."

"Papa, you were the one who said exploring new options around here was a high priority." She linked her arm playfully in his.

❧

Gracie couldn't wait to tell someone about The Ponselle. She found Dorothy in the kitchen, unlocking her silverware drawer.

"I was nearly out of my mind having to miss her concert to chop ice for that reception punch, but I still heard her through three doors. What a voice." Carefully placing the silverware in a basket, she crooked her arm under the handle and carried it into the dining room. "She left you her gown?"

"Yes, and I want to write her a thank you note but I don't know where to begin. I mean, she's a big opera star and I was just her maid."

"Just say what you feel. From what you told me, she considered you a friend. Everyone else was running around calling her 'Miss Ponselle,' but she wanted you to call her 'Rosa'." She handed Gracie a huge tray loaded with green and white plates, cups and saucers. "You carry, I'll set. Now tell me everything."

She babbled on about all the details as Dorothy arranged place settings. The moment she mentioned Eric Sturdy, Dorothy stopped her cold. "That handsome Princeton man sat with you? What about PT?"

Gracie's knees felt weak. She set the tray down on an empty table and sat down. The whole story tumbled out about how she camped out at the bowling alley.

"Gracie, you can't handle one man. I just don't know what you would do with two."

"I don't have two. I don't think I even have one."

Dorothy stuck her nose into a sideboard and returned with a tall pile of butter pat dishes. "Well, if it were me, I'd gather myself together and go get the one who's interested. I hope you're still going to be in the staff talent show. You were all excited about that song *Rosa* helped you with."

"After those lessons she gave me, I'm going to sing my song, with him or without him."

∽≈

Margaret agreed. William stood dumbfounded, waiting for questions about the details, but they never came. She said she was impressed with William's plan for funding, then bustled Peg and Eleanor into the car to shop for clothes in Williamsport. He lifted the receiver and asked the operator to connect him with the West Side Tennis Club in Forest Hills, New York. His tennis courts would be state-of-the-art red clay and would be laid in by experts.

Routine. Going to church, cleaning the lobby and figuring up her money situation helped Gracie come back down to earth after Rosa Ponselle left. She walked down after her shift on Wednesday to pick up her laundered uniforms. The clouds twirled like white feathers in the sky. Then the laundry door slammed. Magdalena stomped out and dumped a huge wicker basket of wet clothes on the porch. Sticky bits of white clung randomly to the garments in the basket.

"Dumkopf!" she said. Magdalena ripped a uniform with "Antes" written inside the neck out from under her arm and waved it in Gracie's nose. "Was ist das?" she screamed, pointing to the gummy white globs in the outturned pocket.

Flashes of heat prickled up Gracie's neck. Her vocabulary word papers. She hadn't taken them out of her pocket when she sent her uniform to be laundered.

Magdalena pried off a piece of paper with her fingernail and stuck it under Gracie's nose. "You. Clean. Then bring back." Gathering her skirts in a huff, she tromped back into the laundry.

Gracie ran next door and returned to the laundry porch with the wastebasket from her room. One by one she pried pasty bits of paper off the clothing and deposited them in the basket.

Olivia appeared from around the other side of the building. "What on earth?"

Gracie explained her predicament.

"Oh, my. I'm on a break, let me help."

"It's my mess, I should clean it up."

Perturbed, Olivia pulled the basket over and put some uniforms on her lap. They worked in silence as the breeze blew the spicy scent of orange and red nasturtiums their way.

"Lovely, aren't they?" Olivia nodded toward the pots. "Peg planted them. She's always finding some nice little thing to do. Enjoy them while you may because Isaiah is putting the flowers in tonight's salad." She rubbed her fingers together, trying to dislodge a sticky bit.

They picked in companionable monotony until Olivia leaned over toward Gracie. "Isaiah and I saw something odd last night. When we were out walking we saw Bessie and Hank duck into the steam room. She acted downright sloppy drunk."

"I guess Jimmy finally got tired of her bossing him around."

They both jumped when Eleanor climbed over the porch railing and upset the wastebasket. "Uh, oh," she said frowning at Gracie. "I knew those pieces of paper you kept stuffing in your pocket were going to get you in trouble." Eleanor licked two fingers and used them to pick up what had fallen out of the wastebasket. Dusting off her hands, she climbed into the porch swing. "So now we know why Bessie steals the cloves."

"What cloves?"

"The ones she steals from the kitchen. She said they were for her toothache, but they're probably to cover up the liquor on her breath."

"Oh, my, you overheard. Eleanor, you're just a child." Olivia said. "You shouldn't know about such things."

"Why does everyone treat me like such a baby? Bessie isn't so bad. Well, I'm mean right back to her when she's nasty, but I see her crying sometimes when she thinks no one is around."

Gracie's soft hello fell unanswered after she let herself in with her key. Mrs. Cunningham slept late more frequently now. Gracie fixed breakfast, but didn't see the note Madeleine had left until she was heading up the stairs with a tray. She went back to read it.

Mother felt feverish this morning. Call the doctor if she worsens. This letter must be posted by two. Madeleine.

Typically, there was no please or thank you included, although Madeleine had left a few coins for postage. The letter was addressed to Salisbury, England.

By afternoon Mrs. Cunningham felt much better and asked to sit on the front porch. Her chalky eyes stared straight ahead as she nudged each step with her right toe. She stabilized herself with her left hand on the banister and Gracie supported her right arm. They stopped before they reached the bottom for a rest.

Wouldn't it be better to convert the dining room into a bedroom for her? The drop leaves on the dining room table could easily be collapsed and the table pushed against the back wall to make room for a bed. Granted, the sun streaming in from the octagonal tower of the second-floor bedroom would be missed, but the bay windows in the dining room flooded it with light. The only problem was that the bath was on the second floor.

Pushing Gracie's arm away when they reached the bottom of the stairs, Mrs. Cunningham felt her way out to the front porch. Annie, the large black poodle who had evidently given her family the slip, sat at the foot of the steps, thumping her tail on the ground.

The old woman perked up. "Is that my little friend I hear?"

Annie answered with a friendly woof.

"Play with her, Grace," she urged. "I know there are crab apples on our lawn because I can't smell the blossoms from the tree anymore."

Annie bounded back from each throw with an apple in her mouth. She dropped every fetch at Gracie's feet and panted with her tongue hanging out of the side of her mouth waiting for more. When the delivery boy threw the newspaper onto the porch, the dog bolted toward the street.

"Annie, let's play some more," Mrs. Cunningham called, but the dog was gone.

Opening up the newspaper, Gracie read the headlines out loud, asking what article her charge wanted to hear. "The one about the Army Air Corps, I suppose," she said distractedly. After a few articles, she waived the paper away and Gracie read to herself.

People strolled by. Mrs. Cunningham greeted each person by name, recognizing the sound of their voices. She frowned at a young couple who stopped to let their dog lift its leg on the oak tree at the curb while they heatedly discussed the future of the railroad that had brought vacationers to Eagles Mere for three decades.

"You know I can hear you turn those pages, Grace," she said irritably when they left. "It is rude of you to read to yourself while I sit here."

"Sorry. I was reading the Cultural and Arts section. You usually only want me to read the news to you."

"Now don't you start acting high and mighty with me, young lady, just because you've met some famous opera singer."

"Do you want to hear about her?" Gracie asked eagerly.

"She's all you've talked about all week, so no; I've heard enough. You may recall that I heard her sing as well. Mrs. Woods kindly arranged for a car and Peg to escort me. Peg described both gowns to me and," her blank eyes bore into Gracie's, "told me you sat with Eric Sturdy."

"I didn't sit with him. He sat with me."

"Fine young man. He arranged for the young people from the church to keep our walk clear of snow all winter. Very considerate."

Feebly trying to turn her attention to something else, Gracie mentioned a squirrel with a red crab apple in its mouth, scampering across the lawn.

"Yes, I hear him." Mrs. Cunningham said. "You must need to be somewhere else because you keep checking your watch." Not understanding the unusual crankiness, Gracie explained that she needed to post Madeleine's letter before two p.m.

"I'd like for you to make us some tea and tell me more about that great-grandfather missionary of yours, the one who was in Egypt."

Promising tea as soon as she returned, she grabbed the letter and headed off toward the village green. "I'll be back in five minutes." She couldn't figure out why Mrs. Cunningham wanted to hear more about her great-grandfather Antes when she had politely stifled yawns the last two times Gracie had talked about him.

When she got back, the old woman was talking to herself, so she went inside to put the teakettle on to boil. Gracie placed two blueberry muffins onto the tray and took it out. They ate quietly, Mrs. Cunningham's finger pressed onto her mouth as she chewed as if to keep it closed.

"It was addressed to a man in England, wasn't it?" Not waiting for an answer, Mrs. Cunningham crumpled into her chair and turned her face away. She pulled her brown shawl tightly around her and spoke with a bitterness that broke Gracie's heart. Madeleine had met a rich man who asked her to accompany him to Europe. She was to sail to London to meet him. They would be gone for eight months, starting the end of September.

"She hasn't asked you yet, has she? I can't believe it. She's known for two weeks."

♀∞♀

"Mae's father just shook Zeke's hand, and now he's smiling, so it must be going okay," Peg said, peering with her cohorts out the back kitchen window. "I guess he doesn't know that Zeke put her step-in's up on the water tower," she giggled.

Dorothy arrived singing off-key, carrying a hatbox and a grained leather suitcase. "I can't believe the summer's over. I'll be teaching in a week." Oblivious, Peg, Olivia, Adelle, Gracie and Jimmy continued staring curiously out the window. "What are you all doing?"

"Mae's father just came to pick her up and she wanted Zeke to meet him." Jimmy said, quickly wiping the foggy window clear as the sound of the harmonica came closer. In two minutes Zeke passed the kitchen window, wiggling his fingers in a playful hello with Shadow draped around the back of his neck.

The show was over, so they turned away from the window and hugged each other goodbye. Isaiah held a blue and yellow can of lemon oil in one massive hand and lovingly buffed the prep table with the other. He capped the can and spread his fingertips, barely touching the table. "Goodbye, my friend, till next year."

"I hate to hurry off, but Adelle, if I am to drop you home on my way to Wilkes-Barre, we'd better get going." Dorothy plopped a squishy kiss on everyone's cheek and said, "Be good, my little chickens. I was just thinking ahead of myself that if you let me sing in the talent show next year, I just might come back."

"Isaiah, remember you promised to give me recipes," Gracie said. Everyone stayed put, awaiting some memorable entertainment.

"Ah, yes, Gracie, my dear. At the conventions I cater, my clients lift the silver chafing lids expecting something unique and different each morning on their buffet table." He loosened his tie, pulled a long wooden recipe file off the shelf above the spice cabinet and stepped up on an overturned box, relishing the snickers and whistles from his audience.

"The king of the egg will now share some of the ideas I have stored up for years to be served for breakfast, lunch or supper." Isaiah, well-turned-out in street clothes instead of his chef's apron, cradled the maple box lovingly against his chest and waxed rhapsodic. "What you need are some end-of-the-week-no-meat-left-in-the-icebox-and-all-I-can-do-is-get-to-the-general-store-to-buy-eggs-milk-and-bread recipes. Poached, scrambled, fried, baked, coddled, hard or soft boiled eggs and toast. Fresh baked tomatoes stuffed with scrambled eggs. A bounty of recipes to tickle the tongue. Alpine Eggs, Deviled Eggs, Shirred Eggs and Ham, Eggs a la Goldenrod, Egg and Cheese Soufflé, Creamed Eggs, French Toast and Bread Pudding. And we don't waste food, so take any leftover eggs, cook them till they are hard, chop them small and add to your soup for extra protein."

Jumping off the box, he placed the recipe file in Gracie's hands, drummed the fingers of his right hand on the lid and said, "Copy any recipe you want." He extended his arm chivalrously to his wife. "Come away, dear Olivia; our little love nest in Philly awaits."

"Isaiah, wait. You need this." Gracie held the recipe box out to him.

"Nope. It's all in here." He knocked his head with his fist.

A horn blared and Olivia said, "Oh my, that'll be PT with the car to the train station. Goodbye, everyone."

"Not PT," said Jimmy. "I saw him leavin' yesterday. Mr. W's got Otto drivin' today."

All heads silently turned toward Gracie, who stood frozen, holding the recipe box.

Eagles Mere, Pennsylvania
1926

THE ROBINS WERE LONG GONE WHEN GRACIE MOVED FROM THE
Evergreen Lodge to be Mrs. Cunningham's full-time companion.
Her old friend seemed to have come to grips with her daughter's
European trip.

Madeleine had freshened up the spare room before she left
in the middle of September. The room was right next to Mrs.
Cunningham's bedroom with one window over the front porch.
It didn't matter to Gracie that it was tiny, because it was private.

"Can you imagine a house with no closet in the front
bedroom?" Mrs. Cunningham railed the day Gracie moved in. "I
want you to put your good clothes like Miss Ponselle's gown in
Madeleine's closet to keep them safe and clean. You can play my
piano and sing anytime you want. Go visit the Woods. And I
want you to go to church. Just because I can't cook doesn't mean
I need to be babysat every minute. I am thrilled to have you here
while Madeleine is off scampering all over with her gentleman
friend, but I want you to have your own life too."

Gracie quickly learned that although Mrs. Cunningham was
blind, she could clearly see life. "My Madeleine is as she is," she

commented one evening over dinner. "I accept her and try not to expect more than she can give me. Funny how we trade losses for happiness. I know my daughter doesn't want to be around me, but then again, she found you, Grace."

The next morning, the smell of melted peanut butter from the breakfast toast lingered in the air as they sat at the kitchen table drinking coffee, talking through finances. Madeleine had arranged for all monthly payments to be made by the accountant who handled the trust fund from her father's estate. She had left the icebox full and would send her mother money monthly for food, clothing, Gracie's wages and other necessities. "Well, there is not going to be much left over, I can tell you that, Grace."

Boisterous laughter tumbled through the open window of the Eagles Mere Inn kitchen next door. Ignoring it, she laid out some of her plans. "I can get a better price for you on ice from Zeke," she told Mrs. Cunningham, pointing to the icebox with her pencil. "I've already asked Mrs. Woods if I can ride with her for groceries on Monday, but I'd like to give her a little for the gasoline, if it's okay with you. I have some new recipes Isaiah gave me. I know we can save on food if you don't mind me using leftovers. I've checked what's in the icebox. How about pot roast and boiled potatoes tonight?" Gracie asked, scribbling a few items on her grocery list.

"Doesn't your thinker ever get tired, child?"

Gracie said no, curled a lock of her hair behind her ear, and counted out the money Madeleine had left in the Fig Newton can.

The doorbell rang. Stuffing the money back into the can, she went to the front door to find Eric Sturdy holding a huge box. "Vegetables my mother canned," he was saying as she brought him back to the kitchen through the small reception hall.

"I know that voice. Hello, Eric," said Mrs. Cunningham as he set the box in front of her on the table.

"How are you doing?" Eric asked.

"Not bad for an old lady. How nice of your mother to send all of this. Please thank her for me." And with that, she excused herself to the parlor to listen to the radio.

Grinning, Eric carefully lifted out an apple cranberry pie and placed it on the table. Then he handed Gracie jars of tomatoes, green beans, pickled cauliflower, beets and carrots, which she stacked on the shelves of the back pantry.

Inviting him to sit down, she said, "I'm afraid Mrs. Cunningham can't eat that pie because of her diabetes."

"We could eat it." He winked. "My mother makes a great pie. It would be a shame to let it go to waste."

Her blouse rode up as she reached to get the plates from the cupboard. Embarrassed, she quickly pulled it down while Eric helped himself to the forks. He talked about leaving tomorrow for the fall semester at Princeton. "I especially enjoy the train ride," he said, "because I can read the whole way."

Happy for some common ground, Gracie told him what she had read over the summer, then dropped silent, embarrassed to be discussing such things with a college man.

"Don't stop. I haven't gotten around to *The Great Gatsby* yet. I'd be interested to hear your comments on it."

Words started to come, but Gracie wasn't sure from where. And they came easily. When he said he had to go, she was disappointed. Mrs. Cunningham was still engrossed in her radio program when they walked to the front door.

He pulled a plaid cap over his chestnut hair.

"You know," he hesitated, "After I started bellhopping, I was going to ask you if you wanted to take a ride down to the Sonestown Bridge, but you seemed so busy I didn't. Maybe we could do it when I come home for Christmas break?"

She felt her head nod yes and watched from the porch while his plaid cap disappeared down Mary Avenue.

Mrs. Sturdy kept tabs on them. She telephoned, asking if they needed anything and chatting about how Eric was doing at college. She stopped over one day with a casserole and package, shooing

Gracie upstairs. After she was given permission to come down, she realized the older women were in cahoots.

When she went into the kitchen, Mrs. Sturdy immediately stopped kneading and wiped bread dough off her fingers. She ushered Gracie into the dining room. Mrs. Cunningham's sewing machine was set up. A new pattern for a One Day Sack lay on top of some peach material.

"Open it up," the older woman commanded. The pattern was a simple step-in dress with a scoop neck and cap sleeves. The neck was finished with a white and peach diamond patterned band that was mirrored on the hem. "Mrs. Sturdy ordered it from Montgomery Ward for me. They even supply the trimmings."

"But why? Pardon me for saying it, Mrs. Cunningham, but we don't have money left over to treat me to a dress."

"Hush. Madeleine isn't the only one to whom my husband left a trust fund. Grace, it shouldn't surprise you that I know exactly what is due on the mortgage and how much we spend on heat and groceries per month by memory. Just get going. It's the newest thing and I want you to have it. You're supposed to be able to make it in one day."

Gracie spread the peach fabric out on the dining room table and started pinning on the pattern. Mrs. Cunningham warned her to cut it long enough to cover her knees and then talked her through how to operate the sewing machine.

Rev. Sturdy joined them for dinner, and afterward, Gracie modeled her dress.

"You need a matching white velvet headband that fastens at the back." Mrs. Sturdy said, combing her fingers through Gracie's curls. "I saw one with a pearl drop rhinestone that rests on the forehead for dress up. It would be exquisite with your hair."

The Woods had fired Mrs. Slagle, the housemother, two weeks before the end of the season for tippling on the job. Dorothy substituted, but stated firmly that she would not be available to continue in that capacity next summer. Hank had signed a contract a year in advance because William knew the upkeep on the tennis courts would require special attention.

"Needs for staff mushroom every year. New housemother, waitress, and housemaids. I am going to have to tinker with the room assignments at the Evergreen." Margaret poured coffee and sliced marbled pound cake during their private Saturday afternoon Crestmont evaluation. Stalling, she ate half of her cake before continuing. "William, I had to hear it from our baby, Eleanor, that Bessie has also been consuming alcohol, albeit after working hours. She is respectful to me and a good worker, but evidently her attitude toward the staff has deteriorated."

William shook his head. "Talking about Bessie is long overdue. We shouldn't stand for her behavior."

"I would like to give her another chance."

William dropped his fork. "Surely you're not serious, Margaret."

"I will write her a letter before next summer's season and spell it out. Define our standards. William, we know the girl has family problems. Let's keep her on staff, but put her on probation. One infraction and we will fire her."

She deftly moved the conversation to a Guest Services Room over which she had deliberated. "The unused room that used to be my father's old office, the one Miss Ponselle used as a green room. Professionals and service providers could rent it one day a week and provide special amenities for the guests. We can plant a few shade trees each year with the rental income. You got your tennis courts, William. I want this. You always say we must update a bit each season."

Cutting himself a second piece of cake, William bit the inside of his cheeks to keep from grinning. "Margaret, my love, you shall have your Guest Services Room and your trees and whatever else makes you happy. Do you realize this time last year..."

"Do not talk about last year, William. I am thankful to be past that malaise. Now, what else shall we go over?"

William pulled a letter out of his shirt pocket and spread it on the table. "This is from the Forest Hills expert who is coming to install the tennis courts. The courts have to go in now so that the weight of the snow and early play next summer will compact the clay on the courts. That way we'll have a smoother playing surface for next year's August tournaments. I can't wait for a photograph so I can design our new brochure."

Margaret cleared their coffee cups from the table. "I saw Otto and Hank digging down there in back of the garage. Your little scheme will provide a challenge for our more athletic guests as well as entertainment for the others, William."

"My plan," he said planting a kiss on her forehead as he ran the water and squeezed soap into the sink, "is to attract famous players from all over and turn the Crestmont into the tennis capital of Pennsylvania."

੭੦੶੭

A week later four dump trucks loaded with red shale made their way up Crestmont Hill. Emmett Thompson, the engineer from the Forest Hills Tennis Club, drove the lead truck with a huge rake attached behind. Otto directed them down the hill past the water tower behind the parking garage. He and Hank had earned double wages for the back-breaking hours they spent clearing the land, digging and filling the courts with layers of rock and gravel, and burying gasoline tanks in preparation for the delivery.

The trucks backed up, spread out along the clearing. Each driver cranked up the back of the truck bed, dumping shale onto the courts. Three drove back up and parked in front of the big house. The rake was reattached to the fourth truck and Thompson directed the driver back and forth, in order to spread the shale evenly over the courts.

"All they need now is to be fired several times."

"So that's what packs it into clay," William noted, giving Otto a nod.

Releasing the handle on the hose, Otto carefully sprayed a

thin layer of gasoline, which covered the crushed brick like a slick
blanket. Mr. Thompson tossed a lit match. The three men stood
like sentries, arms crossed over their chests, watching the flames
spread on the two courts like carpets being unrolled. One nodded
confidently. Another watched the process curiously. The third
held his breath until the fire was out. The process was repeated
twice.

"Wait a couple of days and then paint your lines. Make sure
any bleachers you build are collapsible so you can get them out of
the way. You're going to have to fire the courts after each rain.
Keep them brushed, and if you have a dry spell, water them
yourselves, then fire them."

"After each rain?" William handed him a check.

"If you don't, they're going to buckle and your lines will get
wiggly."

"That might be fun," Otto smirked, cracking his knuckles.

"Close the garage on Friday, Otto. I want you to paint those
lines and start on the bleachers. I need a photograph within the
week."

"Whatever you say, boss."

ॐ

"What did the Sturdys call it, an orphan's dinner?"

"Yes, they invite young single people who don't have families
over for dinner before Christmas Eve service."

Mrs. Cunningham stopped her knitting and frowned. "I feel
sad that you won't go. There's no need for you to stay home with
me. I could have listened to St. Olaf's and been perfectly happy.
The Sturdy's have been so kind to us. I know, let's invite them all
for the day after Christmas. No one wants to cook then."

Gracie's eyebrow shot up. "The whole family?"

"Well, if you prefer, we can just invite their son. Eric is a fine
young man and I enjoy his company."

Gracie grabbed the telephone receiver. "I'll telephone Mrs.
Sturdy right now."

Shadow chased the broom, frustrating the woman who tried to sweep snow off the porch of the Self Help Lodge. Mrs. Woods admitted she had never seen the woman before. "But that's unusual because I know everyone in town. She must be a visiting relative." She turned the car left onto Mary Avenue. Christmas was on Saturday, so she and Gracie had moved their shopping day to Thursday.

"Now do you know why it is called the Self Help Lodge? Anyone who visits pitches in to help." Mrs. Woods teased Gracie for living in Eagles Mere for over a year without noticing all the houses had names instead of numbers. "You lived in the Woodshed for a winter, and here we are at the Maytown," she laughed, stopping the car in front of Mrs. Cunningham's house. The chalkboard in front of the Eagles Mere Inn next door boasted "Special—Oyster Stew," and the smell of fresh bread made their mouths water.

Reverend Study was very apologetic when he telephoned on Christmas to say that he and his wife couldn't come to dinner. A family in the church needed pastoral care and Mrs. Sturdy wanted to go with him because she had been close to the woman who died. Gracie decided to cook the whole meal anyway, figuring she could do a lot with the leftover ham.

"I know it seems vain," Mrs. Cunningham said the next day while Gracie combed her white hair, "but I want other people to see me well-groomed, even though I can't see myself." Gracie was hesitant to use the electric curling iron because she didn't want to burn Mrs. Cunningham's scalp, so she coaxed her into the new curling combs that were left in the hair for four hours.

Gracie relented after being asked twice and rattled off the names of the people that sent her Christmas cards.

"PT? And he wrote a note too?"

Excusing herself to put the ham in the oven, Gracie went downstairs to avoid further probing then returned to get dressed. Her maroon slash was the best choice for dinner. She applied subtle makeup and wondered why she was more nervous about the cooking than about Eric coming for dinner.

Gracie left them chatting about the Moravians to check on dinner. Evidently Eric was already knowledgeable about her church background, or he had done some research. She wrestled the roasting pan out of the oven with huge quilted oven mitts. The ham was huge and she extended her arms out as far as she could to lift it out of the pan so she wouldn't get drippings on her dress. Finally she managed it onto the cutting board. She tried to get the knife right next to the bone to make a horizontal cut as Isaiah had taught her, but it slipped. The ham thwacked on its side, splattering all over her apron. Carving as best as she could, she piled the ham on the platter, surrounded by the roasted potatoes and pineapple rings.

"Everything okay in here?" Eric poked his head in the kitchen. "I'll get this." He picked up the platter and held his other hand out palm up, awaiting a serving bowl. "Anything else?" Gracie gave him the creamed peas and she brought up the rear with rolls and boiled onions.

"The vase Madeleine sent from Germany is right on the center of the table, Mrs. Cunningham," Gracie indicated after they said a blessing over the meal.

"Porcelain with gold plated ribbons. I ran my fingers all up and down the design. It's beautiful," the woman explained to Eric.

Gracie passed the food to Eric, then cut some ham on Mrs. Cunningham's plate and arranged portions of the rest neatly. "Ham at six o'clock," she told Mrs. Cunningham, who felt for her fork and dug in, complimenting Gracie on her cooking.

Mrs. Cunningham soon forgot her food when she got lost in

her stories. "When my husband was alive we lived in that huge yellow cottage with the two story wrap-around porch over where Lewis's glass factory used to be. This town was in its glory days then, when they built the great hotels and wooden sidewalks."

In a more confidential tone, she explained that after her husband's death, Madeleine wanted more money for travel and so forth. "She wanted something smaller and modern, not like the old Victorian cottages. We are sitting on what used to be the parking lot for the Eagles Mere Inn. They needed to finance some improvements back then and Madeleine offered to buy this lot. It was quite the thing then to order those modern homes Sears Roebuck would deliver, so we picked out this Maytown model. Madeleine enjoys the status of living next to the inn, you know." She coughed into her napkin. "I was able to take care of myself back then."

She grew quiet and started to eat. Eric told her about Gracie's singing in the staff talent show last August. "She was dressed to the nines in fishnet stockings, heels and a dress the color of butter, and high heels." He poked his fork in Gracie's direction.

"The one I told you Olivia made with the handkerchief hem," Gracie explained, discretely replacing a piece of dropped pineapple onto Mrs. Cunningham's plate.

"You should have seen her fancy stepping through her song," Eric continued. "A beautiful songstress having a ball. And that pianist, PT, wow, can he play! They did a turn-around, you know, where they repeat the last part of the song twice, and he followed her beautifully."

Gracie's mind wandered back to the talent show, remembering feeling unfulfilled and not understanding why. She was glad she had put on a good show for the audience. When she started listening again, Eric was commenting on PT's talent and asking whether or not he played classical music.

"Sonestown covered bridge?" He spread his hands out palm-side up when it was time to leave. "It would be a good way to start the New Year. Can you get away next Saturday? My mother said she'd take Mrs. Cunningham over to our house for the day."

"I don't see how I could say no."

સ્જ

The child had George's eyes and appeared to be about seven months old. Gracie stood facing the window, staring at the photograph that had come with Lily's Christmas card.

"One more to go," Mrs. Cunningham said as she ran her fingers over the maroon strip she was knitting for her afghan, counting the stitches. "You've been terribly quiet, Grace."

Gracie wondered why she so stubbornly kept it all to herself and felt it would help her to confide in her kind friend. She was tired of being ripped up inside.

"I did a terrible thing when I left home," she said to the window.

"Do you mean Bethlehem? I thought you left because you wanted a stage career." Her knitting needles clicked soothingly through the pause that followed.

"Well, it was my dream, but that's not why I really left. My sister, Lily, was to be married and I felt things for her fiancé that were not appropriate."

Mrs. Cunningham set her knitting down and patted the seat next to her. Turning at the sound, Gracie sat down on the edge of the sofa and interlaced her fingers. "No one else knows this. I've never told." The old woman sat quietly and listened to Gracie's story.

"Did you pursue George after that?"

"No, I left. I really wanted to put it behind me and start over, but it gnaws at me sometimes." Her left thumbnail dug grooves into her right palm.

"What you did was to remove the temptation from both of you so that they could have their happiness together. Am I correct, Grace?"

"I suppose."

"That was an act of grace. You set out on your own so they could have their family—your parents, Lily, George, this baby."

"But Lily had my address here. Why didn't my parents try to find me?"

"Grace, I don't understand why your parents would throw a wonderful woman like you away, but maybe they consider you a rebel and can't accept that. There is something in the Bible that says we should live life that really is life. Are you happy with your life here?"

"Yes."

"Then let go of your guilt. Don't go back home, and for heaven's sake, don't go singing on the road for people who don't know you. Sing if you want, but stay here with the people who love you." Mrs. Cunningham proudly stacked each knitted strip on her lap.

Gracie wiped her eyes. Searching in the knitting basket for the huge needle she said, "Would you like me to sew those strips together now?"

Camden, New Jersey
1917

"Got you something for our third anniversary, kid." Warren Sloan pushed a small box across the bar while PT refilled syrup bottles. "I remember you walking in here all scrawny when you were seventeen."

PT nodded, opened the box, and pulled out an expensive pocket watch. He thanked Sloan and asked how the tournament had gone.

"I got the most strikes out of three games, plus the silver cup in Atlantic City." Sloan smacked his palm on the bar in triumph.

"Then you should be the one getting the watch."

"Nope. Couldn't have concentrated on knocking down all those pins unless I knew you were back here holding down the fort."

That evening, people clapped and cheered as balls cracked on the lanes, but PT made his own rhythm, improvising on a peppy Irving Berlin tune. Pipe smoke blurred his vision when he started another variation. "Great rhythmic sense, but your technique's lousy." A short, pudgy man with smeary reading glasses clacked his pipe between his back teeth and sat down next to him on the piano bench.

"Try this." He brushed PT's hands off the piano and played a bit of Beethoven. Annoyed, PT easily played it back.

"And this..." PT reluctantly relinquished the bench and slouched over the piano as the man's dry, scaly hands sounded out a Russian piece with heavy dense chords in the middle of the piano, repeated in the bass. The man rose, gesturing toward the keyboard.

Marveling at what PT again reproduced he said, "What an ear. Like Hofmann." Anchoring his thumb on PT's first knuckle, he measured the finger span with his rough, reddened middle finger.

"Have you heard Jozef Hofmann, the Polish-American pianist?" PT shook his head blankly.

"He could play anything after hearing it once, but your hands are huge compared to his." PT pulled his fingers away from the man's grip.

While he cleaned his glasses on the lining of his open suit jacket, Thaddeus P. Fassbinder introduced himself as a professor of piano from Temple University, gave a stern lecture about playing by ear, and arranged a lesson in his Philadelphia studio. "Up in the northern part of the city near Girard, that boarding school for orphans. The lesson would be gratis, of course. I just want to see what you can do under pressure."

Intrigued, PT agreed to play for the teacher after work on Friday night. "I'll set you up with some shoes so you can get to your bowling, Professor Fassbinder."

"Don't tell me you entertained the notion that I came in here to bowl. I was merely taking in some air and your playing lured me into this ludicrous facility of folly." He pulled his business card out of the worn suit pocket, handed it to PT and shuffled out.

Three months. Crossing the Delaware River on ferries, sloshing through snow drifts, slush and ice on the streets of Camden and Philadelphia, back and forth between Temple

University and Sloan's bowling alley. Professor Thaddeus P. Fassbinder guiding him through scales, finger exercises by some Austrian pianist named Czerny, compositions by Brahms, Bach and Mozart. Leaving each lesson smelling of pipe smoke with the sound of the professor's pinched voice in his head saying this is what you were meant to do. Seeing the inside of a great concert hall for the first time when he went with Fassbinder to hear the great Jozef Hofmann at the Academy of Music. Staring at the music in front of him for hours, trying to master the technique. Sloan scratching his head with concern, asking PT if he was getting enough sleep. Listening to Fassbinder's exhortations—any fool can improvise. You need the basics, you're so musical, but your reading stinks. Fassbinder correcting PT's finger position with his own eczema-covered hands. Fassbinder pushing him to forget the bowling alley and get a high school equivalency diploma at Temple's night division. Fassbinder complaining—what a waste, you could play Liszt with those hands. Twenty years old. Practice, practice, practice. You're way behind already.

Enough. PT up and decided he couldn't take it anymore one Sunday while he sat in his apartment paging through the newspaper. He didn't have the heart to leave Sloan, but Fassbinder had him in a vise, so he answered an ad for a blowing alley attendant at some swanky summer place up in the northern Allegheny's. Hell, at least the guy's name was only one syllable: Woods.

Eagles Mere, Pennsylvania
1927

LEAVING THE COMFORTING SMELL OF BEAN AND HAM SOUP, GRACIE stood in the cold, pulling her navy wool coat tight around her. The newspaper boy had managed to get there, but not another soul had ventured out. Snow drifts covered the walk the boys from the Presbyterian Church had cleared just two hours ago. This was the fourth heavy snow in three weeks. Invigorated by the clean air, she wondered what Isaiah would have said about her idea to add onion to the soup. Onions, she had read, were good for colds, and she wanted Mrs. Cunningham's to go away quickly. The wind died down and she heard an unfamiliar creaking sound. She moved over to the other side of the porch and listened. The noise was coming from above her head.

Mrs. Cunningham was napping on the sofa so Gracie tiptoed up the stairs, careful to skip the one that squeaked. Her bedroom was unusually dark because the snow had piled up against the bottom pane of her window. She went back down to the pantry and returned with the push broom. When she opened her bedroom window, the wet snow settled down into a crusty frozen wall. She pushed hard against it with the broom, but nothing happened. Turning the broom end around, she poked holes in the snow with the end. The wall collapsed a bit. She worked like this for a while until she was able to push the snow away from the window. Sweating from the effort, she unbuttoned her coat and let it drop to the floor.

Worried that the weight of the snow was putting a strain on the porch roof, she kept working until she could push some off onto the ground. Random thoughts came as she worked. How much she missed Dorothy. Eleanor's leaf scrapbook. Wishing she could get over her fear of the water. How unappetizing the creamed hard-boiled eggs on toast she had made Monday looked until she put the paprika and parsley on the top. PT's Christmas card apologizing for not saying goodbye and how angry she was for caring. Feeling cozy under the covers as she read Robert Frost poems in her tiny bedroom at night. Mrs. Cunningham talking about trading loss for happiness.

Before she knew it, she was kneeling on the porch roof on a path she had cleared. She climbed back down into her room and grabbed a blanket so her knees wouldn't freeze. She worried about her added weight on the roof. Kneeling on the blanket, she worked until she pushed some snow over the edge onto the ground.

"Whoa, there, girl. Just stay put. I'll get my roof rake," Mr. Glaubner from the Eagles Mere Inn next door shouted to her. He had on fishing boots and a fur-stuffed leather hat with ear flaps. Gracie kept pushing while she waited.

"I saw you up there on the roof from my kitchen window. Go back inside. I'll pull it down from out here," he said, hoisting the rake up from the side of the house.

Gracie went back down and kicked snow drifts aside so she could watch from the front walk. Big hunks of wet snow thudded on the ground as Mr. Glaubner pulled with the rake. "Seems like every year we get a doozy like this. It was February last year, as I recall." He stopped working, huffing hard. "Smart girl. The weight on that flat roof. Who knows how long it would have held."

She asked him to come in for some soup, but he said his wife needed help cleaning out the cellar. "Just being neighborly," he said, grinning, and headed back to his inn.

The second week in January, Peg and Zeke showed up at the front door. Raving about the bracing cold, they begged Gracie to go tobogganing with them. Zeke and his brothers had cut ice from the lake for a week and then used their horses to haul the ice blocks up Lake Street. Twelve other men from town worked with them, grooving and fitting the blocks, to make a solid ice slide down the steep hill.

"The ice has to be a at least foot thick and we cleared so much snow the toboggan might even make it all the way over to the far side of the lake. Skaters beware!" Zeke said, urging Gracie to get her coat.

A nasty purple egg with a line of dried blood bulged out of his cap. "How'd you get that gash on your forehead?" Gracie asked, lifting up his hat. "Let me put something on it."

"Aw, one of our Clydesdales kicked me. It's nothing." Pulling down his cap, he checked his reflection in the hall mirror. "It'd better heal up before my pretty Mae comes in March."

"Yakkety-yak, Zeke," Peg said. "I've heard about her visit three times already. Let's get to the snowball fight. Remember, whoever wins gets the first seat on the toboggan."

"Oh, you kids go have fun." Mrs. Cunningham, who had evidently been standing there listening, held onto the mahogany arch that separated the parlor from the reception hall.

"Thanks, Mrs. Cunningham. My mother said she'll be down later this week for a visit." Peg was out the door before the woman could reply.

"Are you sure you don't mind? I have a pork loin in the oven, but it should be fine until I get back." Gracie wound the long green scarf her elderly companion had knitted for a Christmas present around her neck.

"I won't mind if you wear your red knitted hat that covers

your ears, Madeleine. You know, the one I made for your seventeenth birthday."

Peg and Zeke hooted and threw snowballs on the front lawn while Gracie stood there, dumbstruck.

"Listen to your mother, Madeleine. The cold will make you ill if you don't bundle up."

Not wanting to add to Mrs. Cunningham's confusion, Gracie merely patted her coat and said, "The hat's right here in my pocket."

"That's a good girl. Now go play. Your friends are waiting." Gracie hurried out into the snow.

Peg and Zeke were too busy with their fun to notice the pained expression on Gracie's face. Zeke bragged about how well he and his brothers had rolled the roads, while they all walked over packed snow toward the toboggan slide. The screams and laughter of those already enjoying a ride ameliorated the cold. Peg and Zeke ran ahead, impatient to get on the next toboggan.

Mr. Rose huddled over a card table set up on the side of the slide near the warm up shed. He sipped from his thermos cup and scratched a name off his clipboard. "What'd you say?" he asked, pulling an earmuff away from his left ear when Gracie approached. "Signing up for a ride, Miss Antes? Fastest ice slide in the country, right here in Eagles Mere." Stamping her feet to stay warm, Gracie waited her turn.

"Hey, blondie, wouldn't a nice hot restaurant meal taste good after this?" Otto asked, appearing out of nowhere. "Geez, Gracie, we had it good that first summer you were here. Let's give it another go." When he moved in for a kiss, Gracie turned aside and fell into a snow drift. Otto twirled his moustache mischievously before deciding to help her up.

When Gracie scanned the crowd for rescue, Peg and Zeke were already on the next toboggan with Shadow perched between them, eagerly awaiting their slide onto the lake. Gracie made excuses that she had to cook dinner for someone. She hurried back home trying to understand what had happened with Mrs. Cunningham.

❧

Mrs. Cunningham's cough worsened three weeks after Gracie's aborted toboggan ride. She lay listlessly in bed, complaining that her ears were blocked. Gracie's suggestion to move her bed to the dining room so she could look out at the snow prompted a caustic response.

"It's my bedroom and I'll keep it where I want. Maybe you are just tired of running up and down stairs to wait on me, Madeleine."

Dr. Webber was on his way to deliver a baby when Gracie telephoned, but said to keep Mrs. Cunningham warm in bed and give her fluids until he could get there. Mrs. Sturdy sounded alarmed over the telephone and promised to be over right after church. By the end of Sunday service she had all the church women organized to send food.

"Stay with her," Mrs. Woods said, trying to calm her down when Gracie phoned her on Monday. "Tell me what you need and I'll bring the shopping to you at noon." She was putting away groceries and heating up a casserole that had been sent over when Dr. Webber arrived.

"Ah, Mrs. Woods," he said, setting down his doctor bag, then handing her his coat, hat and gloves at the front door. "I see you have full use of your arm now. How long has it been, over a year now?"

"My arm is fine, thank you." She handed him his black doctor's bag. "Mrs. Cunningham is upstairs."

"I'd like to examine the patient alone, please," he said. Mrs. Sturdy and Gracie went downstairs to join Mrs. Woods.

"She had a little cold at Christmas, that's all." Gracie rubbed the heel of her hand back and forth over her forehead, her head bent over a teacup.

"Eric said she seemed fine when he came here for dinner. It's just a catarrh. Older folks need a little more time to recuperate." Mrs. Sturdy said.

"How wonderful of you to arrange for people to send over dinners, Mrs. Sturdy," said Margaret. "I'd like to help too. How ironic that I was resentful when the people from my church did this for me. Pride is so silly."

The doctor came into the kitchen, sighed, and set his doctor bag on the table. "Well, she certainly is cranky."

"Never mind about that. How is she?" Gracie insisted.

Dr. Webber said she had a slight fever. The catarrh had progressed into Mrs. Cunningham's ears and chest. He prescribed aspirin, fluids, and said he would send over a vaporizer to help her breathe. "Check her temperature regularly and if it goes up, telephone me."

She started refusing solid food. Within a week her temperature was up and her cough relentless. Dr. Webber let Gracie stay in the room when he examined Mrs. Cunningham this time. Shaking his head, he eased the stethoscope out of his ears. "We can keep her comfortable, but I hear a lot of crackling in her lungs and she's very weak. There's a vaccine I could give her, but it might make her worse. I don't want to chance it. Broth and barley water, as much as she'll take. Keep her warm. Call me if there is any change." He packed up his doctor bag and left.

By the end of February Gracie, Mrs. Sturdy, and Mrs. Woods alternated shifts. One cared for Mrs. Cunningham; one did household chores while the third slept. They left the front door unlocked so the doorbell would not disturb. Anonymous angels left chicken soup, beef broth, and Mr. Glaubner's famous healing ginger soup. Peg telephoned every day, held the Woods' household together and sent a pineapple upside down cake for the caretakers. Rev. Sturdy came over often to read the Bible and pray at the woman's bedside. Eleanor braved the relentless cold to walk down every day after school with her reading books.

One afternoon Mrs. Sturdy sang hymns to their patient in her soft alto voice. Some of the words trickled down to the kitchen where Gracie strained the barley water into a cup. How there could be any nutrition left in three quarts of water after boiling one cup of barley for three hours was mystifying to her, but she did what Dr. Webber said. When it was cool, she took it upstairs to relieve Mrs. Sturdy.

When she saw Mrs. Cunningham's ashen face, Gracie crumbled. "I should have done more when she first got sick."

Mrs. Sturdy put her arms around her and said into her ear, "People get sick, Gracie. There's nothing else you could have done." Then she went home to sleep.

"Grace, is that you?" Mrs. Cunningham whispered after she sipped barley water from the spoon Gracie touched to her lips. She sat on the bed and held a cool cloth on the old woman's forehead.

"Yes."

"Thank you, dear." She shifted in bed, winced, and fell asleep.

ৡৣ

"I'm not sure she can hear you when you read, Eleanor, but go ahead and try." Her mother kissed the top of her head.

"I'm going to read you some of the Bobbsey Twins stories today, Mrs. Cunningham. They are a funny, mischievous pair. This will cheer you right up."

Margaret sat listening, proud of her daughter for being so attentive and nurturing. Eleanor's voice eventually lulled her to sleep. The child crept over to sit on Mrs. Cunningham's bed so she could read without disturbing her mother. The old woman's eyes were closed, but Eleanor read anyway.

Eleanor shook her mother awake from a dream. "Mama, wake up. She looks funny."

Margaret got up and put her ear to the old woman's chest as she had done with her father so many years ago. "Go wake Gracie, Eleanor, and then do your homework in the living room."

Gracie asked Mrs. Woods to pull the sheet over Mrs. Cunningham's face. They stood at the foot of the bed with their arms intertwined for a long time. Then Gracie broke the silence. "I'll wire Madeleine in the morning."

The response came quickly. "Postpone funeral until I return in May. STOP. May stay in house until then. STOP."

Mrs. Woods was uncomfortable with Gracie staying alone in Mrs. Cunningham's house and insisted that Peg move down with her or that she move back into the Woodshed. Gracie declined, saying she needed time to sort things out. She walked the house idly for days, watching the last snowfall of the season and listening to the radio without hearing the broadcasts. One day, she went upstairs to Madeleine's room. Removing her clothes from the closet, she carried them to Mrs. Cunningham's, made a small pocket between her dear friend's clothes and hung her own in the middle so they would touch.

Woodshed on Crestmont Hill
May 1927

Margaret Woods sat at the kitchen table with four pairs of shoes, polish and brush laid out before her on yesterday's newspaper.

"It's my turn, my dear." William said, pushing the shoe-shining paraphernalia to the other side of the table.

"But you did it last time."

"Why keep track? It makes me happy to do little labors of love for you when I can. Besides," William dramatically unfolded the brochure he had toiled over for a month. "I've been dying to show this to you. Here is our first aerial photo, Margaret."

His finger sprang off the page after pointing to the caption. "See how the inn embraces Crestmont Hill from its commanding location 2200 feet above sea level with a view of twelve counties. A vast and inspiring panorama spreads before you from our cool guest rooms and breezy porches, rivaling the scenery found elsewhere in our country."

He tapped the photo of the new tennis courts. "I took this shot as soon as they painted the lines in." He placed the brochure in her hands as if it were an old document of inestimable worth. Attempting to entertain her, he flung out his arms ostentatiously and quoted, "State-of-the-art red clay tennis courts invite not only each guest, but also professional players from all over the country. Spectators can enjoy the game from conveniently placed bleachers. Join us for the 1st Annual Crestmont Tennis Tournament in August 1927."

Margaret gave the brochure a perfunctory look and set it down, stopping him flat.

Here it was again. She was always in another world on the anniversary of her father's death despite any attempts he made to alleviate her yearly brooding. Boat rides, motoring to the Sonestown Hotel for dinner, taking the family for a picnic at World's End State Park—nothing helped. He felt incapable of consoling her, but he never stopped trying. Frustrated, William continued with the brochure, hoping to cheer her up.

"Peg wants to add canoe tilting and underwater rope races to the Water Carnival activities. I predict it will reach a new level this year." He tried to show Margaret the caption Peg had written in contribution.

"Both of our girls amaze me, William." Margaret laced her fingers together as a signal for quiet. William waited. Finally she spoke. "It's been sixteen years since Daddy died. Every May...it feels like...an ambush."

William hesitated, wondering if he should say aloud what he had believed for years. "Margaret, do you think it is possible that you hold onto your grief so you can feel closer to your father?"

She answered with cold silence.

"I do not mean you do it intentionally, Margaret," he said gently. "People react to loss in odd ways."

Cutting him off, she got up and restacked a jumbled pile of papers, smacking them hard on the pine kitchen table. "I will be myself by the time the season starts."

"You always are, my love," he said, resigned.

Eleanor and Peg came home from school and their mother

sent them abruptly to their rooms to do homework. William dipped his rag into the black shoe polish, assuming the conversation was over.

Margaret filled a pot with water and set it on the table along with the potato peeler. Pushing a potato down onto the prongs, she turned the crank. "Gracie, on the other hand, certainly seems to have gotten over Mrs. Cunningham's death easily," she said bitterly. "I will never understand how she was able to sing at that funeral. I could hardly breathe. She seems to have an inexhaustible supply of resilience."

Thankful for a different topic, he said offhandedly, "Gracie has the energy of youth and replenishes herself with her music, her clothes, her books..."

"And her hair! Remember when she insisted I try that hairdresser, Zelda, one week after the funeral? 'Research for my guest services room,' she called it." Irritated, Margaret plopped a potato in the pot, sending water splashing.

William was appalled at the derision in his wife's tone. Mopping the table before her papers got wet he said, "Gracie leads a simpler life than you do. She does not spend her summers concerning herself with the needs and desires of umpteen guests and she is not a middle-aged mother caring for two daughters." He laid his other hand on her shoulder. "Gracie did not lose a parent, Margaret."

Ignoring him, Margaret announced that she had altered the roommate assignments because of the bunk beds they had added in some rooms to accommodate additional staff in the Evergreen Lodge. "Gracie will have to waitress this year because we are down one in the dining room. Mae won't be staying in the dorm anymore, so I have moved Bessie into Dorothy and Gracie's room."

William said nothing, but cocked his head to the side, waiting.

"As we have said, she is resilient, so she will be fine," Margaret said with finality.

The Crestmont Inn
Summer 1927

I

Y ELLOW FINCHES, BLUEBIRDS AND CHICKADEES SANG ALONG WHILE Z EKE played a wistful ballad on his harmonica. At the conclusion, he dropped the harmonica from his mouth and sought approval in his bride's eyes. "I now pronounce you man and wife," the minister said after Zeke finished. A few guests staying at the big house leaned forward on their chairs, quietly watching from the front porch, as the birds twittered their blessing over the union. One woman rocked a perambulator back and forth to keep her baby quiet.

"Thank you for such a beautiful song," Mae whispered in her new husband's ear after he lifted her veil to kiss her. Plump bride and curly black-haired groom stood under an arbor decorated with ribbons and flowers, both sets of blue eyes beaming into the camera. The morning sun wove strands of gold and red into Mae's auburn hair and she held a bouquet of white and purple lilacs. William sang "Amazing Grace" while the newlyweds, best man Isaiah and Mae's sister as maid-of-honor, processed between the rows of folding chairs. Mae's parents followed. Zeke was too dizzy with happiness to care that his brothers had stayed home, unloading their huge ice house to make their pre-season delivery to all the hotels in town.

"Whew, glad that's over," Isaiah said, pumping Zeke's hand after the wedding. "Never had to keep track of a wedding ring before. Thanks for asking me to be best man. Now that you've found a woman to make you settle down, you take care of her, boy. She needs a special kind of love, what with the little one on the way and all." Zeke shushed him.

"You might want to hang onto this. It might come in handy after those inevitable lovers' spats." Isaiah handed him the harmonica he had dropped. "Glad Olivia and I could make it. Temple finished their spring semester just in time. That the suit Mr. Woods loaned you?" He pinched some loose material in the back of the jacket. "A little big, but not bad. Nice of him, though. I told Sam he was going to have to handle the reception food because I couldn't possibly be best man and cook too. Man, smell that chicken. I'm starved." He slapped Zeke on the back and headed toward the food table where Olivia was ladling punch.

Much of the staff had not yet arrived for the season, but the Woods, Magdalena and her new husband Julius, Sid Fox and his wife, Hank, Otto, Rev. and Mrs. Sturdy, Gracie and some of Zeke's Eagles Mere friends milled around the newlyweds, extending congratulations. Fried chicken, potato salad, baked beans, biscuits, pickles, salted peanuts, peppermints and punch bowl were laid out. The star of the table, however, was a thirty-inch wooden salad bowl Sam had found in the garage, cleaned up and loaded with chunks of cantaloupe, green grapes and strawberries, topped with marshmallows. Eleanor hovered near the table, stole a strawberry, popped it into her mouth and held it there whole while she wiped her fingers on the back of her dress.

It was June 5th, a week before the official opening of the Crestmont. As a wedding present, the Woods gave Zeke and Mae a two-week stay in the Grandchildren Cottage, so named due to its size rather than the age of the occupants. A quarter of a mile down the hill from the big house, the tiny cottage was accessible only by a short walk on a footpath. After the honeymoon, Zeke would resume his duties as head bellhop and Mae would help with setting up the dining room, but would not actually waitress due to her delicate condition.

When Zeke told his brothers that Mae was pregnant they had shown their true colors, hooting and hollering it was about time their shrimpy little brother finally got it together to make a girl preggers. He paid Mr. and Mrs. Woods a visit then, in the middle of May, sitting solemn and red-faced in the Woodshed. Could he and Mae get married at the Crestmont?

"I hope you enjoyed your breakfast, sir." William Woods sounded especially chipper Monday morning as he greeted a participant in The Shorthand Reporters Convention. "Yes, I agree. Two of the best chefs in the state. Your meeting is in the smoking room this morning? That's way down here at the end of the east wing. I'll show you myself."

Chatting with the guest as they strolled through the lobby, he found Gracie dusting Old Tim. He pointed a finger in her direction and then at his chest and mouthed, "Five minutes." The old uncertainty burned like acid in her throat, but Gracie swallowed it down, telling herself that Mr. Woods probably wanted something other than to complain about her cleaning schedule.

The Woods had insisted she stay in one of the steam-heated rooms on the first sleeping floor after Madeleine returned home to Eagles Mere. "Someone might as well enjoy looking at the lake," they said. For the two weeks before some early bird guests arrived for the wedding, Gracie was the only person sleeping in the hotel. Finally able to cry about Mrs. Cunningham's death, she didn't care if her sobs echoed through the empty halls. Just being in the big house made her feel sheltered and comforted.

Mr. Woods returned, rubbing his hands together with satisfaction. "These conventions are great money makers, Gracie.

Granted, we go through a lot of wood to keep the fireplaces going, but other than that it's too cold for water activities; there are no concerts or dances because of round-the-clock meetings, and we run on a shoestring staff." He tipped his head slightly in her direction. "A superlative shoestring staff."

Taking the dust cloth from her hand, he led her to the front porch. The whack of axes splitting wood came from down near the garage where Otto and Hank worked cracking jokes. Zeke and Mae, arms around each other's waists, strolled down the driveway oblivious to anyone else's presence.

"I hope they will be happy. They are so young. And Zeke even younger than Mae." Mr. Woods said.

"I know people wonder about Zeke, given the circumstances and all, but he really loves her."

Mr. Woods rocked on his heels, watching the newlyweds disappear past the west wing. "Gracie, why don't you move into the Evergreen before the staff from out of town arrives on Saturday? First one in gets the best bed and all," he chuckled, fiddling nervously with his onyx cufflinks. "Given to me by Mrs. Swett. I know that now, because you helped me sort them out last winter." He let out a big sigh, peering up at the yellow awnings on the west wing. "Just replaced the ones out back. Next year, the ones on the west wing."

Finally, taking in a big whiff of the wood smoke lacing the morning air, he said, "Sit down, Gracie, I have a matter of some delicacy to discuss with you." He explained that a great influx of additional staff necessitated the addition of bunk beds in the Evergreen Lodge. Regretfully, the Woods were forced to house three women in some rooms. Dorothy and Gracie, being the eldest staff in the dorm, seemed the right choice to share a room with Bessie, now that Mae was married.

"Confidentially, Gracie, we need to know if you see anything amiss with Bessie."

"She's always churlish, sir. Is that what you mean?"

"No, we are concerned primarily about alcohol consumption.

Do you have any idea why she might seek out alcohol?" Gracie said no, but that she would let them know.

"I will have this same conversation with Dorothy when she arrives," He slapped his thighs as he rose, leaving his rocking chair clattering back and forth.

"How are your tennis courts, Mr. Woods?" Gracie asked, trying to lighten the conversation.

"All set to go for guest players when our season opens, and we have several reservations from professionals who want to play in the August tournament. It will be an exciting year for the Crestmont." Meekly handing back the dust cloth, he said, "Tell my wife it was my fault if she is upset that you haven't finished the lobby."

⚬⚬

"Whooee, it's cold!" Isaiah yelled after his crooked cannonball into the lake sent water splashing all over the dock.

"Oh my, Isaiah, I would have said so if I wanted to go swimming," Olivia said, brushing the water off her arms.

The morning sun reflecting off the water looked like tinsel on the trees near the shore. He treaded water, admiring his wife. "We've got to see if Mr. Woods will let us come a week early every year. Being in a wedding at the Crestmont has its benefits. We got us a week's vacation." After he climbed out, he hopped from one big foot to the other, banging his head with his hands to get the water out of his ears.

Eleanor crouched nearby, her toes dug into the sand, preoccupied with her tin boat. Ten inches long, the wind-up boat was very narrow with a red hull, cabin, smokestack and wood-grained painted deck. They watched her move it along the sand, then down into the three inches of water that lapped up against the shore. Guiding it as it floated in the water, she switched hands to move it around the dock post. Finally, she pulled it out and wound the metal spring as if ready to launch.

"Hey, Eleanor, that's some nifty boat, but I'm not going back in after it. Those fancy underwater artesian springs were freezing my keister off," Isaiah called.

"Don't worry. Papa's going to be here any minute. He promised he'd measure how far my boat will go in the water." She sat down on the sand to wait.

Olivia nudged Isaiah and he jumped off the dock and squatted beside the little girl. "How's your tap dancing coming?"

She shrugged. "Sam said I'm good enough for us to do a showier number in the talent show this year with piano, harmonica and drums. Is Eric bell hopping this year? I'm looking for him."

"Haven't seen him. Why do you ask?" Isaiah said.

"Well, I figured maybe he could be our drummer. We need to practice with our band." Screwing her eyes up toward the big house, she tossed the boat from one hand to the other.

"I don't want to be a flat tire or anything, kid, but I told Sam I'd relieve him for lunch, so Olivia and I have to go."

"It's okay. Papa will be along soon."

∾

But William was on the porch of the big house. A severe-looking man with a pock-marked face, dressed in a gabardine suit with worn cuffs on his trousers, had cornered him.

"I'm trying to find this man." He pulled a photograph out of his briefcase and held it under William's nose, watching his face for a response. Julius, Magdalena's new husband with the coke bottle glasses and paunchy stomach, stared back at William from the picture.

"Yes, I know him."

"When did you see him last?"

"Early this morning. He was up on a ladder out back installing awnings."

"On a ladder, you say?"

"Yes. Why, is there a problem?"

"Just some state business. Where is he now? I need to speak with him."

"I'm not sure, but he has to be somewhere on the grounds. That's his car right out there in the driveway." William pointed to a dilapidated looking wood-framed Franklin with spongy looking tires.

"His car, you say. May I have your name, sir?"

"William Woods. I own this inn."

The man flashed him a business card from the Division of Social Services. "When you see this person, please tell him it is imperative that he telephone me immediately. It seems Pennsylvania has been paying disability benefits for his alleged blindness for several months now."

Pocketing the card, William hurried down to the dock to find Eleanor.

$\wp\!\prec\!\wp$

Gracie's favorite common room was Margaret's Masterpiece, decorated in soft blue and rose tones. After she finished that, she would tackle the Woods' offices while they hosted the convention guests at lunch. Mr. Woods always placed great importance on convention guests, saying that if treated right, they would usually come back for a summer vacation.

Hemlock logs snapped as the heat of the fire released their trapped moisture, sending sparks out onto the rug. Gracie whisked them quickly into her dustpan and threw them back into the fire when a familiar voice startled her.

"Going to rain today."

She jumped at the sound of PT's voice. "The sky was pretty clear when I got up," she said.

He crouched down, pointing to the tiny glowing coals on the rear wall of the firebox. "See those geese on the fireplace? They're little patches of soot that burn only when bad weather is coming."

"Whatever are you doing in the Ladies Lounge, PT?" She leaned on the vacuum, relieved they weren't jumping down each other's throats.

He turned to sit down on the hearth, extending his long legs out across the Oriental rug. "Came to find you. Get my Christmas card?"

Gracie nodded, swishing her feather duster over mauve roses on the frosty glass lamp globes.

"Am I forgiven?"

"For what, leaving without saying goodbye? It's a habit of yours I've grown accustomed to." Her tongue nearly bled when she bit it.

"I'm not good at goodbyes."

"According to what you told me last year, there's a lot you're not good at. You know, it wasn't easy for me to get up the courage to camp out at your bowling alley."

"Yup. You've got spunk." PT fiddled with his pocket watch. "Heard that lady you took care of died. My condolences."

"Thanks. I didn't know if you knew." They were quiet for awhile. "Isn't this the day you go to the train station to pick up out-of-town staffers?"

"Nope. That's Tuesday. Just got here today myself."

"Oh."

"Remember when I picked you up at the Wilkes-Barre station two years ago? You were a scared rabbit. You couldn't wait to get out of here to go on the road singing. Now you can't seem to leave."

Gracie switched to another lamp, enjoying his attention.

Wiping his palms on his thighs, he got up and pulled some folded wrinkled paper from his breast pocket. "Wrote this for you." When he handed it to her, his long fingers ran fleetingly over hers, lingering on the tip of her middle finger.

She hesitated and then opened up three pages of hand-written musical notation. He had written "Gracie's Refrain" at the top of the first. "I didn't realize you composed."

"Studied a little classical music." Brushing the song sheepishly he said, "Sorry, didn't come up with any lyrics, but something'll come to you. You're good with words."

Clambering up from the hearth, he grazed her cheek with a kiss, ducked his head, and disappeared through the French doors.

᯽

"I'm sorry, Mrs. Woods, I wanted to be done in here before you finished hostessing lunch." She shined the last brass knob on the immense filing cabinet.

Smiling, Margaret Woods nonchalantly opened the file drawer labeled "P" and pulled out a piece of paper. Gracie asked what new demands Mrs. Pennington had for cleaning her room this year, but Mrs. Woods said no, it wasn't that at all. Rosa Ponselle had directed her agent to write to the Crestmont Inn. She enjoyed her stay so much last year that she would be receptive to returning for another concert in the summer of 1928. "Look at the postscript, Gracie. Miss Ponselle sends her regards to you. See how you helped us in taking such good care of her."

Gracie smiled. She had often recalled Miss Ponselle and her desire to touch people with her singing. "I remember when you put that chair in your garden for her. She called it a sacred retreat. You should sit out there yourself, ma'am, if you don't mind me saying so. Just seeing this filing cabinet makes me wonder how you keep so many things in your head to make people happy."

Laughing, Mrs. Woods said, "You must be prophetic, Gracie. Some of my jobs are more troublesome than others. Like what I am about to ask you. Would you be willing to waitress this year?"

"Yes, ma'am, whatever you need me to do."

"And I need to tell you about the roommate assignments."

"Your husband explained it to me. It's all fine."

"You are always so kindhearted, Gracie. Do you have some time to help me in the library? I need to shelve some new books." Pausing in the hall, Mrs. Woods smiled wistfully at her father's portrait.

In the library, she pulled books out of a newly opened box. They passed them back and forth with mutual appreciation. Working together to rearrange the shelves, they stocked the new acquisitions at eye level.

"Remember when we used to chat in here at night after the

guests were settled in their rooms? I miss those times now that you are down in the dorm."

"Mrs. Woods, we haven't talked much since Mrs. Cunningham died. We got so close, caring for her together at the end. Sometimes I feel like we're family and then other times..."

Margaret leaned disconcertedly against the roll top desk. "We certainly have had our ups and downs. Gracie, it is difficult because we have two different relationships. One is a professional relationship because you are on staff here, and we have also developed a close personal relationship, like family, as you said. Sometimes the lines between the two get blurred. Since her funeral, it has been difficult for me because it brought back my father's death. I fear I have not acted as kindly toward you as you deserve. Please forgive me."

"Oh honestly, it's all right. I think a lot about what Rev. Sturdy said at her funeral." Mrs. Woods' limpid brown eyes widened.

"'Our grief in loss is a measure of a love that supersedes death.'"

"I remember that now." Pushing herself up off the desk, a transformed Margaret Woods twirled around, smoothing her hair. "And I never thanked you for sending me to Zelda. Now that my hair is shorter, I have so many more waves." Gracie was about to compliment her on her hair, but the telephone rang in the lobby and Mrs. Woods ran to answer it.

Sam cooked a new dish Monday night he had learned from a new Italian restaurant back home in Harrisburg. The Woods family joined the shoestring staff for a dinner of spaghetti, meatballs and cooked tomato sauce. Everyone talked about the stables the Chautauqua Inn had built to house their new horses. Eleanor speared a meatball and held it up, trying to guess the ingredients. The meatball plopped off her fork, splattering tomato sauce all over her blue dress. A stern William probed Julius while handing over the business card he had received earlier that day. Magdalena left in a huff. PT and Gracie kicked around song ideas for the talent show. Peg huddled with Otto and Hank, picking their brains about the techniques they used to plug leaks in canoes.

Needing to take stock, Gracie excused herself early. So much to absorb in one day. The song PT wrote for her was a complete surprise. She couldn't wait to take it to the staff lounge tomorrow to play it. Maybe rooming with Bessie wouldn't be so bad since Dorothy would be there too. Waitressing really worried her. Training was scheduled for Friday when the new girls arrived. Thursday seemed the logical day to move into the Evergreen Lodge.

Captivated by the moon dancing on the gentle evening waves, Gracie watched the lake from her choice big house window, enjoying this treat the Woods had given her. She complimented herself for being good with words, just like PT had said. Hadn't she used "churlish" correctly in describing Bessie's behavior to Mr. Woods?

She and PT hadn't bitten each other's heads off today and he had talked more than ever before. What an enigma. He could whip her around from being infuriated for his inability to handle romance to feeling all softhearted because he wrote her a song. Once in a while he let her in, like telling her about the speakeasies. Other than that, he was very secretive about his life apart from the Crestmont. Aware there was much more to him than he allowed anyone to see, Gracie decided to tread on that uneven ground. But carefully.

She got in bed, congratulating herself on how she had moved forward since coming here. Her first summer at the Crestmont, she had kept a list of friends to convince herself that she wasn't alone. Today, she no longer felt empty inside. God turned her coming here to the good, just as she had prayed that first day in the touring car on the way from the train station.

Eric's last letter lay in her left hand. PT's song was on her lap. She put both aside and pulled out the Paperbag poems from her nightstand. She fell asleep reading them.

❧

"Hot, hot, hot," Gracie grumbled when she saw the room. Two bunk beds replaced the twin she had slept in last summer. Olivia stayed behind to prop the front door open. Setting her hanging clothes on the twin bed, Gracie threw open the window and pushed the door wide, not caring if the flies came in. She was arranging her clothes in the closet when Olivia interrupted her. "Oh, no you don't."

Olivia put down Gracie's red suitcase and a satchel full of sheet music. "You're not going to hang my beautiful gown in that closet," she said, taking The Ponselle out of Gracie's hand. "I can just picture Bessie stepping accidentally on purpose all over my embroidery."

Her index finger punctured a dimple in her cheek while she considered the dilemma. "Wait just a minute. Magdalena won't miss one little sheet." She bustled back five minutes later with a sheet folded over her arm. We'll fold it and wrap it; then put it up there." Olivia said pointing to the top shelf. "Bessie's too short to even see it." Gracie dragged the chair over so she could reach the shelf and Olivia handed her the teal silk gown Miss Ponselle had worn for her concert.

"I have to go and hem Mrs. Woods' gown for Saturday's dance. Season opening and all."

"Thanks for your help, Olivia."

Gracie flounced down on the bottom bunk, angry to have to share a room with Bessie, and sorted it out. Dorothy would need the twin bed, so she'd take the bottom bunk. Once Bessie was up on top, maybe she would stop blathering on and just go to sleep. Gracie placed her intimates in the top drawer of the dresser, piled her sheet music on the bottom shelf of the closet and her books on the little shelf under the table near the door. Next, she hid her most personal items—her jewelry box, the Paperbag poems and her notebooks—in the red suitcase which she tucked under her bunk.

While in the bathtub, she worried that Dorothy and Bessie would say she had taken over the room. Sure, she had a lot of stuff, but it was part of her and she wasn't willing to part with a thing. Well, they would just have to work it out. She wrapped herself in a towel. Once back in her room, she opened the transom all the way, changed her mind about the jewelry box, and put it on the dresser. At least her money was in the hotel safe. No worries there.

ço∞

"You want me to what?" Isaiah asked, scratching his head when Gracie carried a big round tray into the kitchen.

"Wait till I pick it up, then put two cake pans full of water on the top. If I'm going to waitress on Saturday I need to practice carrying a lot of weight."

"I thought Mrs. Woods trained you waitresses."

"She does, but I'm nervous about this part. Dorothy talked me through how to do it on the telephone." Gracie balanced the tray on two fingers and her thumb, careful to keep her fingers straight.

Isaiah muttered something to himself as he filled the pans at the faucet. "Ready?"

She nodded. He placed the pans on the tray, crossed his arms across his stout chest and said, "This ought to be good."

"Now tell me if I'm tipping it." Gracie stepped tentatively around the kitchen.

"No tipping so far. But if you do tip, you're going to get soaked."

Eleanor barged through the swinging doors. "Whatcha doing, Gracie?" Startled, Gracie wobbled, trying to keep her balance. The tray slipped off her fingers and the cake pans clattered to the floor. The three of them grabbed rags and knelt down to mop.

"Mama asked you to waitress, didn't she?" Eleanor asked. "Maybe you should try one cake pan next time."

ço∞

The butter smell from the twice-baked bread Sam had made for breakfast made Gracie's mouth water. She wondered how she would survive the long stretch between eating breakfast at 6 a.m. and waiting until after she had served lunch to eat her own. "Make sure you eat eggs to tide you over," Dorothy had warned.

"Follow me to the kitchen." Mrs. Woods pushed briskly through the swinging doors, leaving each girl to hold them open for the next. Sam tipped his chef's hat in greeting and finished wiping down the egg grill.

"Your silverware is stored in individual chests here according to your assigned tables. You are responsible to count it every evening after dinner and lock it up overnight. Do you understand?" Flicking a finger authoritatively toward the doors, she led them back to the dining room. Isaiah and Sam followed their trail, throwing sawdust on the floor to absorb cooking grease before they swept up.

Five silent waitresses-in-training followed Mrs. Wood single file into the dining room.

"Proper setup is as important as excellent service. Bring clean tablecloths and napkins from the laundry prior to each meal. Isaiah will show you where to chop your ice. Glasses and china are here." She opened a door with three huge glass panes against the kitchen wall. Taking a white plate with a border of green vines and berries out of the immense china cabinet, she rotated it, pointing to a spot where the vine hung down. "This is the top of the plate and should be placed exactly at twelve o'clock."

Pointing out water pitchers and silver coffee pots on the lower tier of tables that hugged six wooden columns scattered throughout the room, she walked to a huge maple sideboard on the same wall as her greeting station. "Creamers, sugar bowls, salt and pepper shakers and small service dishes are here. Close these doors once you have your supplies." Dainty tiny crystal bowls for jelly or lemon slices were stacked neatly in the sideboard, along with butter pats in the china pattern.

"You should be able to set a table for six in five minutes. The silverware must be set in the order in which it will be used. Place water glasses one inch above the tip of the knife." She beckoned them over to a table where Mae was placing teaspoons.

"This is an example of what I expect. Well done, Mae." Gracie and Mae exchanged lip-bitten smiles.

Mrs. Woods continued. "You will be assigned six tables, each of them numbered. Take orders one table at a time without writing them down. You will soon train yourself to be able to memorize each guest's selections. Sam and Isaiah call out table numbers when your orders are ready. Fill your tray and call 'Orders out' to alert any incoming waitresses when you walk through the right swinging door from kitchen to the dining room. To reenter the kitchen, use the opposite door." Doors swung as she illustrated by walking through one, then the other. "Serve meals from the left and collect dirty dishes from the right. Before I teach you how to hold a tray, are there any questions?"

Their eyes were like glass, but each one shook her head no. Eleanor was evidently standing on a chair in the kitchen. She made faces at them through one of the round windows on the doors.

"I prefer that you converse minimally with the people at your tables. Many of them want to be left alone while on vacation and do not indulge in idle conversation with the staff. Some may want to chat with you. Listen to them, but do not offer information about yourself unless asked. When asked, keep your answers to a minimum. Do not offer suggestions on the menu, but be quick to respond to any criticisms you receive about the food. Guests are generally very good about leaving tips, but if someone does not, speak to me about it and I will make sure you are taken care of."

Then Mrs. Woods illustrated carrying the tray with the same technique Dorothy had described to Gracie over the telephone.

When she was done, she walked to the French doors that led to the hall and then turned back toward them as if to make a point. In a managerial tone, she said, "Your job as waitresses is to enhance the Crestmont table with impeccable service. Ten minutes before mealtime you must be lined up in front of the windows in clean, starched uniforms, indicating you are ready to serve. Do you hear my words?"

Overlapping voices responded, "Yes, ma'am."

"Good. Mae will stay to help you practice. Come to my office when you are done to receive your assignments."

"I was so sorry I couldn't get here for Mrs. Cunningham's funeral. They put the screws to us teachers with mandatory meetings." Gracie said she understood and was feeling much better now.

Dorothy unpacked while she talked. "We have one night of peace. Bessie isn't coming in until tomorrow—something about her father couldn't get her here on time."

Gracie lay on her side on the bottom bunk, head propped up on one elbow.

"She's not going to be happy about taking a top bunk, you know. It'll be hot as blazes up there," Dorothy said as she put Lawrence's picture on the dresser and got ready for bed. "Mr. Woods spoke to me, too. I'm not crazy about being her policeman. You can't talk to her about a thing. Bessie doesn't exactly take incoming calls."

Gracie told Dorothy about Mrs. Woods firing off instructions for the new waitresses.

"Oh, I got that speech when I started too. Really had to buckle myself up to absorb it all. Look at me now. Head waitress!" She made a billowy curtsy in her navy and red calico nightgown. "Go ahead and talk to the people at your tables. I love to. Most of them know me well. Mrs. Pennington loves to go on and on about her ailments and Miss Woodford gives me reviews of the latest New York City plays. It doesn't hurt your tips to show a little interest, you know, as long as it is genuine. People can spot a fake immediately. Most of them are very nice and will make your day brighter. Who is at your tables?"

"I don't know yet."

"You'll do fine, now that you're not afraid of people anymore."

Dorothy shielded herself from the pillow Gracie threw at her. The conversation meandered around to the subject of men.

"I want to hear everything," Dorothy encouraged. "He wrote you a song? He's a mystery man for sure. Holds his cards close to his vest. He told me once about a piano teacher who tried to take over his life."

"Now my Lawrence, he was the silent type like PT. He wrote more words to me in his letters when he was in the war in Europe than he ever said aloud in person. He taught me that what people say to you isn't nearly as important as how they treat you."

Gracie fell asleep listening to Dorothy talking about how it irked her that Lawrence used his pocket knife to pick his teeth.

II

MODERN TENNIS COURTS AND IMPROVED SERVICES FOR GUESTS MARKED the opening of the 1927 summer season at the Crestmont. People always delighted in new amenities the Woods provided, but there was overwhelming enthusiasm about the opening of the William Warner Memorial Guest Services Room.

On Saturday, as guests checked in, Margaret Woods proudly handed out cards detailing the experts they had lined up to render professional services each weekday. Dr. Webber rented the room on Tuesday and the eccentric herbalist on Wednesday. Ladies raved vociferously about Zelda, the hairdresser, who came in by train on Thursday to work wonders so they would look their finest for the formal concert. Happy to trade convenience for cost, guests eagerly visited the specialists that each rented the room one day a week. The Crestmont received dual benefits of happy guests and rental income from the service providers.

Steady streams of people climbed up and down the chestnut staircase, colliding with bellhops on their way to the room on the first landing. Women lined up on the chairs set in the hallway, but men also took advantage of the medical and alternative services offered since there was no hospital within forty miles of Eagles

Mere. Dr. Webber treated lumbago, headaches, spider bites, infected cuts, water in the ear and sunstroke, along with chronic conditions normally monitored by the guest's regular doctors. The herbalist offered more natural options. Flower essences and herbal tinctures from medicinal plants were his specialty.

Usage of the room soared as word got out that Olivia was available for fittings and alterations on Monday and Friday before the dances. Women appreciated the ease of working with the dressmaker right in the big house where they stayed, rather than trekking down the back lawn to her small shop behind the laundry.

Relieved to be off her feet after five days of waitressing, Gracie sat in the bleachers down at the new courts on her day off. Eric had invited her to watch him play. Although he was clearly the better player, William Woods rooted for Eric's opponent, Mr. Swett. Peg challenged the daughter of another guest in the second court. Gracie's first exposure to tennis gave her great appreciation for the athletic ability and precision needed.

"Saw that he-man play tennis, didya? I could go for that one." Bessie entered their room after her bath wrapped in a dingy terry cloth robe. Her red hair dripped under a small white towel she wore like a hood. She was pale. "Heard Mr. W whistled and cheered his head off for Sweaty's husband instead. Gotta keep those guests thinkin' they're the best and all."

Dorothy and Gracie had hardly recognized her when she moved in on Sunday. Bessie still had a fresh mouth on her, but the chewing gum and ankle bracelet were gone. She wore no makeup at all. Her large freckles made her nose seem even smaller and she seemed prettier, in a coarse kind of way. She pressed her shoulders down protectively when she walked, making her seem shorter than usual.

"Saw that bathin' suit ya bought. Ever goin' in the water in it?" Bessie asked snidely. Dorothy avoided the confrontation by singing while she brushed her hair.

Gracie raised an eyebrow. "I resent you looting around in my drawer." she said, thankful her spare money was secured in the hotel safe.

"*Drawers.* Ya took half the bottom one too, plus most of the closet with those fancy clothes of yers. Slammin' Jack, Dorothy, yer drivin' me crazy with that off-key singin', and couldya take it easy with that perfume yer always sprayin' all over. It makes me sick to my stomach."

"You should go see the herbalist in the guest services room. I'm sure he has something good for nausea," Dorothy said sweetly.

Bessie climbed up into her bed in a huff. "Ya know Mae was a much nicer roommate than you two," she said to the ceiling.

The next morning, Dorothy and Gracie rolled their eyes when she whined about getting dizzy when she got down from her bunk.

What a quandary. Gracie was meeting one man for church, but couldn't get the one she had spent last evening with out of her head.

PT seemed more at ease around her now. He had even come in when the waitresses were having their late supper to invite her to the staff lounge. When she arrived, he got up from the piano and ushered her over to a corner table for a private game of cards. Two years after she originally asked him, he told her under his breath why he had left home.

It must have been terrible for him to deal with an abusive father.

Eric offered to pick her up in his car this morning. How silly, she had said. After all, he would have to drive all the way over town from his house right next to the church. Besides, she enjoyed walking alone. Truth be told, she planned to get there long before the morning service to play undisturbed through some sheet music and the song PT had written for her.

"I see you've got your glad rags on," Eric said when they stepped off the church steps, holding his arms out as if inviting her to dance.

"I sewed it in one day. Your mother helped. I call it my peach sack." Gracie mentally smacked herself. Surely he would find her habit of naming her clothes childish.

"That's great. I love it," Eric hooted with delight, "but it hardly looks like a sack. May I escort you home?"

"Sure." Gracie started to turn right past the Sweet Shoppe.

"Walking isn't exactly what I have in mind." Eric said, cupping his hand around her left elbow. He led her down to the Edgemere dock. Some people from church sat on little red bench seats in a huge green rowboat with a tan canvas roof tied on with rope. "Each week," he explained, "a group from church makes reservations for Sunday dinner at a different hotel in town. This week we are going to the Crestmont and the boat is the easiest way to get to there."

Gracie hung back, paralyzed by visions of the boat tipping, dresses swirling in the water and her going under unless someone pulled her to shore. When she came back to reality, Eric was apologizing that he would have to pass on dinner. They could still have fun on the boat on their way over the lake, but one of the bellhops got sick. He had to fill in.

Gracie didn't mind. She couldn't wait to start her new book before waitressing supper. Eric got in the boat, turned and extended his hand to her. Handing him her satchel of music, she grabbed his other hand and stepped in.

Two men in their sixties each grabbed an oar and rowed side by side. Their wives fussed over their grandchildren, trying to keep them in their seats. Eric guided her up to the bow of the boat so they would have a good view.

The morning sun reflected off the water onto the pine boughs that hung over the edge. The gleam crept up the branches like water flowing upstream and glistened on the needles. Gracie peered up at the imposing water tower, the highest point in town behind the Crestmont Inn. From this perspective, the big house looked like it was safeguarding the lake.

A mother duck protectively herded a trail of ducklings up onto the land when the boat approached. Little waves lapped against the shore. Eric pointed out a dark brown bird with a white head, beating his wings while clutching a chipmunk in his talons.

He stood and pointed. "Bald eagle with dinner for the family," he grinned. "Do you know how the lake got its name?"

Gracie shook her head, gingerly standing up so she could hear him over the grandchildren's chatter.

"The legend is that there is a Native American burial ground under the lake. It was defiled by an Indian chief from another tribe. While the tribe slept, the Great Spirit cried tears of forgiveness for the chief's stupidity. The eagles cried with him. Supposedly all those tears created rain that filled the lake and washed away the evil that had been done. So they named the lake Eagles Tears, or Eagles Mere." He shrugged. "Could be true. God works in mysterious ways."

A large steamer with a life preserver painted next to the words "Hardly Able" overtook them, leaving large waves in its wake. The people on the steamer waved. The men stopped rowing, allowing the boat to roll with the waves. Gracie fearfully grabbed the ropes that secured the canvas on the top of the boat and sat down.

"The only powerboat allowed on the lake. It's a ferry that drops people off from one hotel dock to another."

"How do you know all this?" Gracie asked.

"I grew up here. I'll bet you've never been down on the lake at six in the morning with the sun burning away the mist. Find a nice rock near the shore and do it, but go by yourself. You won't ever forget it."

The rowers secured the boat to the Crestmont dock. "That wasn't so bad, was it?" he asked after they were out of the boat.

She dropped her satchel and sheet music scattered on the back lawn. Laughing, they collected it. "How did you know I was afraid of the water?" she asked when they reached the back porch.

"Male intuition." Over Eric's shoulder Gracie saw PT turn on his heel to go inside.

છ—જ

Phyllis Rice from Bennington, Vermont, sat at table seven with her husband Wilmer and their daughters Edna, eight, and Louise, ten. Her ample bosom was stuffed into a lace covered blouse, draped with several long strings of pearls. Her blonde hair was tied with a matching lace ribbon and lay in a fat braid over one shoulder. Peering over her reading spectacles to scrutinize the dining room occupants, she quickly surmised that her family was the most educated at the Crestmont.

Gracie set glasses of ice water on the table and was told that ice gave little Louise a headache and that Mrs. Rice preferred lemon in her water.

Principal of the Bennington Price Secondary School, Mrs. Rice spent her after-school hours teaching her daughters elocution and monitoring their private music and ballet classes.

After substituting the waters to suit, Gracie said "May I take your orders? Our special tonight is pork cassoulet."

Mrs. Rice removed her glasses and dangled them over the menu. "Is the cassoulet a French recipe?" she inquired, indicating that her daughters studied the language.

"I'm not certain, but I would be happy to ask the chef." Mrs. Rice handed a fork back to Gracie tine side down, complaining that it was dirty. She ordered the broiled chicken for her daughters, the cassoulet for herself, and suggested the roast beef to her husband, Wilmer. Examining Gracie's left hand, she asked her age.

"I'm twenty-three."

"And unmarried," Mrs. Rice whispered to her husband from behind her napkin, adding that Gracie didn't appear to be the college type either.

"No, I'm not in college. I'll put those orders right in for you."

Edna, who had had tiny eyes and worry lines between her eyebrows, was reciting a poem to her mother when Gracie returned with their dinners. Mrs. Rice lectured her daughter on the importance of emphasizing key words and twisted her torso away stiffly when Gracie set her cassoulet at her place, warning her that the dish was hot.

"I know that poem. It's Robert Frost." Gracie said to little Edna, who promptly sought a response from her mother. Gracie was told that Edna and Louise memorized Yeats and Tennyson and warned not to speak of things about which she had no knowledge. She returned to the kitchen for their side dishes, remembering what Dorothy had said about the people at her tables making her day brighter.

Carrying the tray expertly on two fingers and her thumb, Gracie set it down and placed buttered beets and potatoes au gratin on the table. When she served the asparagus tips, Mrs. Rice pulled on Gracie's sleeve, indicating she would like to see the chef.

A hush came over the dining room when Isaiah entered. People watched as he strode calmly across to table seven and planted his big legs firmly next to Mrs. Rice. His black cheeks mottled in shades of purple and red as she spoke, waving her fork contemptuously back and forth over his cassoulet.

"I served you last night's dinner, you say. Let's see," his voice rose as he held up the cassoulet dish on his fingertips. "We have here fresh sweet peas, Swiss chard, thyme and sage, all grown on Crestmont grounds. White beans, homemade sausage, new potatoes and morsels of savory pork in an aromatic sauce are all topped with a crust flakier than any other in Sullivan County."

Dorothy intervened, steering him back toward the kitchen. "Tell Gracie to recommend the broiled salmon tomorrow night," he muttered "It's boring, but maybe it'll be pure enough for her."

Mrs. Rice accepted the roast beef Gracie offered as an appropriate substitute, sent the rice pudding back when dessert was served indicating that her daughters did not like cooked raisins, and left Gracie no tip for that evening.

The teenage staff was down on the tennis courts for a young adult tournament. Taking advantage of the quiet, empty Evergreen Lodge porch, Dorothy sat alone. She no longer felt it necessary to keep track of the girls in the dorm because the new housemother was very effective. Free to concentrate on the dining room, she made an effort to keep one eye on Gracie because it seemed she had some difficult people at her tables. She stood when she saw Mae walking down the drive.

"Oh, my word, I'm so happy you've come for a visit." Dorothy gave her a big hug. "You look happy. How do you feel?"

"I am well. I just started my fourth month so I'm not queasy every morning now." They talked about the challenges of being an expectant mother. The conversation slipped into subdued comments about Mrs. Woods. "She works so hard making sure things are done properly that she has no energy left to enjoy the guests," Dorothy said.

Mae listened, but seemed to be elsewhere.

"Tell me all about being married, Mae. How do you like living at the Self Help Lodge?"

"It's good. We have two rooms on the second floor. They're really nice people, and at least we don't have to live with Zeke's brothers." A lone tear streaked down her cheek.

"What is it, Mae?" Dorothy leaned forward and took her hands in her own.

"It's Zeke."

"I see Zeke every day. He seems happy and he talks about you all the time. I know he loves you."

"No, we're fine. It's his brothers. He comes home from working with them and the horses and he's exhausted. And he has bruises."

"Bruises? The horses kick him?"

"That's what he tells everybody if his clothes don't hide them, but it's just a cover. His brothers are mean. He's the youngest and the smallest and they beat him up for not working hard enough. You know him, Dorothy. He works harder than anyone I've ever seen."

"I'm so sorry."

Gracie came out of the laundry, carrying clean uniforms on hangers, and broke into a trot as soon as she saw Mae.

"Oh, honestly, we miss you." She leaned against the railing, wanting to get caught up. Mae and Dorothy were so quiet; she realized she had interrupted something.

Finally, Dorothy broke the silence. "Well, that Mrs. Rice certainly holds herself in high esteem."

"Thanks for getting Isaiah out of there, Dorothy," Gracie said. "I was sure he was going to blow his top."

"Please tell me all about it." Mae urged. "I miss the excitement of waiting tables."

Gracie babbled on about Mrs. Rice, Isaiah, and how she didn't get a tip last night.

"You should tell Mrs. Woods. That's not right," said Mae.

"Atta girl, Mae. Look who's telling her to be assertive," encouraged Dorothy.

Mae let Gracie feel her bulging abdomen. "Married life seems to agree with you. Twenty years old, married, and a baby on the way. I'm twenty-three and I still haven't decided what to do with my life."

"Oh my word, Gracie, you'll figure it out. I was thirty-seven before I passed the teacher's exam. Lawrence was a career man in the army, you know. I followed him around for eighteen years before he was shipped overseas. After he died I had to find a way to make a living."

Mae asked how rooming with Bessie was going. She was still a spitfire, they said, but more sullen and cranky.

"You and Zeke should come to the ice cream slurp. You need a diversion from being down in town every evening. It's very entertaining," Dorothy said. "This week Isaiah told the whole staff the Mrs. Rice story. He went on and on about his cassoulet, how he sang over it and everything."

"Does Bessie come? The only way I got along with her last summer was to stay away from her."

"Bessie stays clear of most of us," Dorothy said.

Dorothy wagged a finger at Gracie. "You haven't been at the slurp for two weeks. What's going on?"

"It's a little uncomfortable with both PT and Eric there."

"Oh?" Mae and Dorothy asked wide-eyed. "Who's winning?"

"There's no winning. PT and I are friends, that's all."

"Well, what about Eric?"

"He invited me for dinner with his parents. I think I should go."

"You have such a bad case of the 'shoulds' Gracie. I know you're attracted to him. And you love his parents. Go, if you want to. You don't have to marry him. Have some fun, for Pete's sake, and get off this hill for a while."

❧

"Ya hoard all this stuff and we ain't even got room for our uniforms," Bessie hissed and stormed out, slamming the door.

Her revenge was to be as messy as possible. Gracie was tempted to take all of Bessie's clothes and pile them on her top bunk, but she warned herself not to do it. The dirty clothes Bessie hadn't thrown in the bottom of the closet were strewn under Dorothy's bed. Her nightgown, half stuffed under her mattress during the day, usually hung down over Gracie's bunk. Her pillow often fell down and lay on the floor between the beds all day, with dirty intimates sticking out of the pillowcase. After washing the rayon stockings she was so proud of she hung them over the chair at the door, leaving them long after they were dry.

Gracie chided herself for taking over most of the storage. She should have known people would take offense. Even Dorothy was mad last week when she had brought an Operaradio back from home and there was no place to put it because Gracie's sheet music was scattered all over the table. Their room was small and it would only be right for her to make more space for the others. But her stuff made her life feel more complete.

Well, then, it was time to do some creative magic. She snapped on the radio for inspiration. The harmony of a barbershop quartet filled the room.

The closet was a dual purpose affair, with a hanging bar about two feet wide filled with their uniforms and dresses, and three deep shelves on the right. She had taken over the bottom shelf when she moved in, leaving Dorothy and Bessie to share the middle one. The top one was too high for anyone to reach without a chair.

She wailed "Hard Hearted Hannah" with the vocalist on the radio and removed all of her things from the bottom shelf, temporarily storing them on her bunk. She dragged the chair over, carefully lifted The Ponselle, and wiped the top shelf clean. Making several trips, she stacked her records up there and topped her sheet music with her hat in front of The Ponselle. To show good faith, she'd let Bessie know the bottom shelf was hers if she wanted it. Maybe that would cheer her up.

Removing her pile of books from the table near the door, she put some of them in the red suitcase along with her St. Louis heels, and piled the books she was reading under her bunk. She sweated from the effort. She shut off the radio when she moved it to the shelf under the table because the Irving Berlin tune being broadcast bored her. Now someone could actually play cards on the tabletop.

Time to start on the dresser. Bessie would feel like the cat's pajamas if given the top drawer, so Gracie switched her things to the bottom. A hymn she loved played itself over and over through her mind:

> Since Christ is Lord of heaven and earth,
> how can I keep from singing?

Singing it aloud lifted her out of the drudgery of rearranging the room. Stacking up garters on her arm like bracelets, she suddenly remembered Rosa Ponselle talking about raising people above their everyday struggles. She set down the garters and pulled out the letter the singer had written when she left. She reread Rosa's words: "You will touch people the most when you sing what is meaningful to you."

She stopped fussing about the room and lay down to rest on her bunk. Hopefully, Bessie and Dorothy would appreciate her efforts. Even with the window and the transom open, the lace curtains barely riffled with the faint breeze. As she dozed, Gracie dreamed of Mrs. Cunningham stacking her afghan strips, begging her to stay in Eagles Mere.

That was it.

The reason she never could fulfill her pipe dream of singing on the road was because something greater than herself stopped her. God never intended for her to sing popular songs on the road, but hymns. Right here. She fell asleep, realizing she was home.

Gracie paused on the porch of Evergreen Lodge before the evening bull session in the lounge. The air was sticky with humidity but a half moon managed to penetrate the hazy sky. She realized she was happy. The carefully crafted plan she had designed to keep her in Eagles Mere after her Crestmont summer gave her confidence.

The boisterous laughter tumbling down from the guests on the big house porch almost drowned out the cicadas and crickets. Excitement was keen before the August water festival. Guests banded together to make a float representing the inn and the competition with the other hotels in town was fierce.

The staff entered their own every year. This summer's was called the SS Sundae. Eight of them had gone straight to the Sweet Shoppe to request sponsorship. The float would be decorated with huge painted ice cream cones and root beer fizzes. A lantern placed behind translucent paper would make the froth on top of the root beer float look fizzy. The crowning event would be to dock the float after the parade around the lake, and serve ice cream provided in coolers by the Sweet Shoppe to the children. Surely the Crestmont staff would win first prize for their ingenuity.

"Broadcasting to you on this beautiful Saturday evening from Saratoga, New York. They're waving the flag...the shot...and they're off. Razzmatazz taking the rail. Diamond Gypper one length behind. Jazzy Runner's a bit sluggish, taking up the rear. Up comes Swanky Sue on Diamond Gypper's left flank. They're tight today, but the red silks of Razzmatazz's jockey are clearly ahead of the other silks. Razzmatazz definitely pulling ahead. But wait, folks, no collecting your bets yet. Here she comes. Diamond Gypper is streaking by. Can she do it?"

PT, Otto, Hank, Isaiah and Jimmy crouched, heads together, around the radio. Hank's hat was on the floor, stuffed with dollar bills.

"Diamond Gypper wins it...and takes the blue ribbon!"

"Knew I shoulda bet on that Gypper filly. Damn, there goes last week's tips," Jimmy slapped his cap on his thigh as Hank and Zeke dove into the money in the hat, dividing their winnings.

"Thanks for the spoils, boys. Hey, Mae, now we can buy baby stuff."

"Yer too young to be a father," Jimmy touted.

"Not too young if he made the baby, boys," Isaiah laughed.

"Hey, Isaiah, do us all a favor and cut out that singing on the way to make breakfast tomorrow," Otto warned. "I'm not bright and cheery like you at 5 a.m. I enjoy a good snore with my eyes closed until at least six. You've got no business singing that song about a roving gambler anyway. You lost bad today, too."

Bessie was flopped on the couch, trying to nap. Dorothy, Adelle, Mae and Olivia played whist at the card table. They stopped when Gracie came in, followed by Peg and Eleanor. Everyone piled into the screened porch to get some air, safely away from the mosquitoes.

PT led the meeting. "Okay, we've got an idea and a name. Now who's going to do what?"

Zeke blew on his fist and rubbed his chest proudly "I brainstormed the name. SS for the ship and Sundae for the ice cream."

"I'll help with the frame. I'm pretty hep with a hammer," Isaiah offered.

They tossed ideas around. Hank piped up during a lull. "Did you hear Swett caught two huge trout right down near the foot bridge?"

"Isaiah's going to put them on the menu as tonight's dinner special." Olivia proudly kissed her husband's cheek.

"Mm, mm, mm. Butter and lemon sauce to mop up with bare naked bread." Isaiah licked his lips.

"Ha! Swett." Bessie finally got off the couch and flopped onto Hank's lap. Jimmy scowled. "Bet his wife melts extra butter on top. Wonder if he has to lace her corset. One uh these days it's gonna burst. Can ya picture it? What a sight. Hey, girlie, where's Eric?" she teased Gracie. "Too holy to help with our float?"

"His church is making their own. He told me all about it like a secret," Eleanor said, sitting on her hands to make herself taller.

"Cotton candy," Peg announced. A room full of blank faces stared at her.

"We can't paint the ice cream on; it won't look real. The Sweet Shoppe has a cotton candy machine that makes different colors. Pink for strawberry. Green for pistachio. We could mound it up like dipped cones. And make a big banner saying 'End your evening sweetly at the Sweet Shoppe.' They'll pull in even more business that way so they won't mind the added expense." Heads nodded in approval.

"I want a job on the float," Eleanor pouted.

"I don't mean to put the kibosh on it or anything, nincompoop, but everything is pretty much done." Peg tugged on her sister's ear. "You're going to have to come up with something on your own."

"Well, make that float strong, whatever ya do, or it'll break yer heart. Listen to this," Bessie jeered, waving a piece of paper. "I would hold your heart in my hands, but I am not strong enough, But in your hands, my love..."

The Paperbag poems. Gracie's skin crawled as she pictured Bessie nosing around the room after she had rearranged it. "Shut up, Bessie," she growled, clenching her fingers around her wrist until she released the poem.

"That's it. This meeting's over," PT said.

❧

A week had passed and Gracie sat in shock on her familiar rock in the woods behind the steam room.

A flicker behind a maple tree roused her. Eleanor wound her arms around the tree and peered around from behind it. "Are you okay, Gracie?" she asked in a shaky voice.

"How did you know where I was?" Gracie wiped her wet cheeks hastily with the back of her hand. Eleanor came out from behind the tree, taking tiny steps as if she was afraid to break a twig on the ground.

"I follow you sometimes but I know you like your privacy, so I never let you know...but today I heard you crying and I wanted to help." Moving shyly closer, Eleanor asked about the letter in Gracie's hand.

"It's from my sister."

"Lily, with the pretty long blonde hair."

Gracie nodded and looked vacantly off into the woods. Eleanor sat on the ground next to her. Finally, she asked, "What did she say?"

"My father died. The funeral was last month. If they had told me, I could have gone."

"I love you Gracie." Eleanor put her head on Gracie's lap and listened to her cry for a long time.

Then she got up and dusted off her dress. "I guess you want to be alone now."

She meandered back to the hotel campus, wondering if she should get her mother. Shadow meowed up at her and padded up the hill. Eleanor followed the cat all the way to the bowling alley, so she told PT instead. Excusing himself from the bowlers, he hurried down to find Gracie.

He cupped his hands around his mouth calling out her name through the woods until she answered. Sitting down on the moss in front of her, he wrapped his long arms around his knees.

"Eleanor told me. I'm so sorry."

"I thought I could block them out, PT. I abandoned them when I left home. I feel so guilty."

"Sounds like they're the ones who abandoned you. I mean, somebody could have told you earlier so you could get to the funeral."

She hunched over, her arms draped down in front of her, and nodded.

In an attempt to comfort her, PT filled in more details about his home life. Both parents ignored him. His mother was so busy protecting herself from his father; she had no energy left to pay any attention to PT, and when his father did notice him, he was drunk and dangerous.

"Remember you told me how your parents made fun of you wanting to sing and all? They smacked you around by keeping you from figuring out your life. My old man used his belt. Same difference. Don't feel guilty. It'll kill you."

"I was starting to be really happy here."

"Then be happy. Gracie. You lost your parents a long time ago."

They smelled the dampness of a front coming in and walked together back to the Crestmont, stopping to watch a white deer feed in the bushes. After saying goodbye, PT turned up the drive to the bowling alley.

III

"ANYTHING AMISS," MR. WOODS HAD SAID. BROADCASTING THE Paperbag poems to the whole staff rankled Gracie, but Bessie had not consumed any alcohol as far as they could tell, so there was nothing to report to the Woods. Thursday was still Gracie's day off. Grateful that Dorothy busied herself in the dining room late in the afternoon and Bessie was off doing goodness knows what, Gracie sat alone in their room, composing a letter to her mother and sister.

The front door of the Evergreen Lodge was propped open to allow some ventilation and the housemother's door was closed.

Shadow brushed by Gracie's leg. "Get out of here, silly." Setting aside her letter, she picked up the cat and set it outside the front door, but it shot back inside the dorm. Gracie followed it down the hall into the bathroom. She heard water running.

Bessie leaned over a sink, one hand massaging her abdomen. The other laboriously turned something over and over in the water.

"These sheets. Can't let Mrs. Woods know," she whimpered. Drops of perspiration from her pale face dripped into the pink water.

Stunned, Gracie stood there awkwardly until she realized what had happened. "I'll get the bleach."

She started down the hall, stopped short, and returned to the bathroom.

"Bessie, go lie down. Don't try to climb up to your bunk. Use mine. I'll take your sheets to the laundry."

"No. That old battle-ax'll turn me in."

"Here, give them to me. Don't worry; I know how to use the machines. I'll go tonight when no one is there." Gracie helped her walk back to their room and settled her in the bottom bunk.

"Thanks," Bessie said weakly. "I'm sorry about your father."

"Thanks." Gracie said.

"I'm even sorrier about mine."

❦

"Go. Go!" William Woods waved his arms, shooing away the black clouds that rolled in from the west. He laced his hands on top of his blond head in frustration when thunder rumbled in the distance. Sid Fox stood next to him on the tennis court.

"It'll blow over, sir. If we get the nickel-size hail the radio predicted, we'll just sweep it off the courts. Maybe we'll be lucky and it'll just rain a bit. I told Otto to get the mats ready to put on the bleachers if they get wet."

"Good, Sid." William checked his watch. "We've got doubles on one court and singles on the other in an hour. I suppose we could start late, but they can't play in the dark. Next year I'm putting up electric lights out here and a huge Windsor clock right there in full view." He framed a circle with his hands against the clubhouse wall.

The lightening and hail never came. The pros suited up to practice at 3:30 were so busy compensating for the wind that they were oblivious to the storm clouds it blew away.

"Celeste Woodford said we have lost all gentility." Margaret chuckled as they sat in bed that night, their books abandoned on their laps. "You should have seen her face when she saw the ladies out on the courts in their cotton frocks with their white stockings rolled to their knees. Of course, she didn't actually go watch them play; she merely strolled down the driveway with her parasol, pretending not to notice. I doubt if she has ever seen a tennis court before in her life."

"Margaret, I scheduled those tournaments to coincide with our country's most famous in Forest Hills, New York. We would have lost all clout if we had to cancel because of weather. I can't believe the storm blew over."

"But it did, thank God. You were right, William. The tournaments were a huge success. I admit I was dubious at first, but you certainly pulled it off. And the clock will be a perfect addition." She poked him in the ribs. "You asked me to remind you to call Sterling and Windsor to place the order."

"Yes, dear, I shall have to remember to do that tomorrow." Wordlessly, his wife handed him a pencil and a piece of paper from her nightstand.

William removed his arm from around her shoulders, wrote himself a note, then fiddled with the top of the sheet, folding and unfolding it over the blankets so it was perfectly even. "I had to fire Julius today. He was dithering away his time. When I asked him to mow the front lawn he told me that wasn't his job. Worst thing you can say to your employer."

"I am glad you let him go. I doubt if he ever called the state about those disability payments he was collecting, but I wish you had talked it over with me first, William. If Magdalena quits over this, we will lose a valued and trusted employee."

"Don't fret, Margaret. I will talk with her." He knocked playfully on the side of her head. "I need to recalibrate your worry meter." Trying to steer her off course, he said, "You look mighty fine in a canoe, Margaret. What a good move to ask Dorothy to hostess on Thursday so you can have a quiet paddle around the lake."

"You are so right, William. One can abide the banality of chatting with guests about mealtimes, amenities in rooms and the evening activities for only so long. Do you remember that letter Daddy wrote about the money in the safe? I'm trying to take his advice about finding myself some kind of respite."

"Your father found a gold mine when he saw Cyclone Hill. He told me he wouldn't have had the money to both take down the trees and build the inn. God stripped the hill for him and look at where we are now. Next year we'll have to put up a fourth sleeping floor for the tennis pros. By Jove, if Charles Lindberg can fly 'The Spirit of St. Louis' across the Atlantic, we can be the Tennis Tournament King of Pennsylvania. A harbinger of things to come, Margaret, my love."

৩৵৶

Isaiah stuck his lower lip out blowing bugs off his face away as he drove the last nail into the wooden ice cream cone to be featured on the staff float. "What'd you say, Eleanor?"

"Colored sprinkles on the ice cream cones. That's my job." Eleanor sat watching him the day before the Water Carnival, with her legs crossed on the dock, her little toy boat cradled in her lap.

"You mean those huge colored cotton candy balls Peg wants to put on top of these fake wooden cones?"

"Yep. But you need to paint little brown intersecting lines on the cones so they look more like the ones you actually eat."

Isaiah lifted her up and set her on the float. "Now you are a detail-oriented woman, Miss Eleanor Woods, if I ever saw one. And just how are you going to make these sprinkles?"

"You've never seen me with scissors and construction paper. I can make anything. They'll be ready for sprinkling before lunch."

Chuckling, Isaiah, put his tools back in the tool box. "I'll bet they will. I will inform the rest of the staff that Eleanor has colored sprinkles under control."

The Annual Water Carnival was one of the most anticipated events in Eagles Mere. A spirit of friendly competition pervaded the town the second week of August because many civic organizations and hotels participated in the float contest. People came in droves to feast at cookouts open to the public, admire fireworks on the lake, and watch the famous flotilla.

Individual hotels held their own festivities. Hammer in hand, William stood back to admire the poster Peg had designed for the Crestmont's water games. Under the usual listing of swimming, diving and boating activities, she had added "Canoe Tilting, Tug of War, Swimming Races, Illuminated Floating Parade." Her multicolored drawings of shooting fireworks added pizzazz to the poster.

Her father had reluctantly agreed to stretch a rope underwater from the shore to the floating dock fifty feet out. The contest was to see who could pull themselves farthest on the rope while keeping their head underwater. She wanted to name it the Underwater Pull.

"The Underwater Pull is an experiment whose future is yet undetermined," he told her.

Eleanor sat, telephone to her ear, lazily swinging her legs over the side of her father's desk.

"Miss Eleanor, you get off that telephone right now. I have business calls to make," her father said, slamming the door.

"Bye. Call you later." She clicked off the connection and held the receiver calmly in her lap.

"Who were you talking to?"

"Just Dora, Papa."

"You put a call in to New Jersey? How did you convince the operator to do that?"

"I pretended I was Peg ordering supplies for the carnival."

William recognized it had been a hard summer for Eleanor. He was preoccupied with the tennis courts, and Peg, Eleanor's primary summer companion, was absorbed in water activities. Eleanor had her friends on staff—Gracie, Isaiah, and Sam—but no child her age was around for more than a week or two on vacation. Foregoing a punishment, he removed the receiver from her hand, set it in the cradle and said, "No more."

"Papa, Dora's family is all sad now that Philip is so sick. That's why they're not here this year. Can we all pose on the float this afternoon so I can send her a photograph? I want to be taking a big bite out of the pistachio cone."

"Eleanor, that cone is going to be six feet tall. Very well, I could hold you on the step ladder and place staffers in front so no one knows how you got up there. You may be on the float for the ice cream photograph, but you may not be in the flotilla. It is much too dangerous out there after the sun goes down."

She jumped off his desk chair, flung her arms around his waist and bolted out the door.

❦

Preparations were underway all over the Crestmont campus for the evening's celebration. Hank and Otto carried picnic tables down near the water and strung electric lights around the eating area. The Woods family made oversized blue, red and yellow ribbons with pins attached. Three extra trips to Williamsport were needed for all the food. Waitresses secured tablecloths on the picnic tables and laid out china buffet-style, covered with sheets secured with rocks, until serving time. Magdalena and her crew ironed dresses for the ladies and Olivia attached matching bows to straw hats.

William Woods announced each event through a big megaphone. People cheered through cupped hands for their favorite contestants, their shouts amplified by the water. Echoes from similar events at other hotels along the lake mixed with the splashing and applause on the Crestmont waterfront.

When each event was won, Sid clanged a big brass bell. Mr. Swett strutted around the beach, proudly displaying the Canoe Race winner's plaque with his named etched in first place for the fourth year in a row. Buddies of the Underwater Pull winner carried him around on their shoulders, hooting and hollering while dumping him off the end of the dock.

After the water games, the staff docked the SS Sundae in full view of the big house, but the guests had covered their own float with canvas and moored it down the shore. They wanted it to be a surprise for Mr. Woods.

A ham turned on a spit over an open fire. Sam and Isaiah lay huge pork ribs lathered with barbeque sauce on the outdoor brick grill. Aromas of cooking meat and roasted corn coaxed people away from their bathing suits, horseshoes and croquet mallets. Soon men in linen suits and women in pastel dresses and straw hats leaned over the porch railing, hungrily awaiting the dinner bell.

Dusk settled. People waved away mosquitoes while they ooh'd and aah'd at the town fireworks set off from the north beach, signaling the beginning of the flotilla. Built with wood, paper maché, and other concoctions, the floats were lit by Japanese lanterns. The Volunteer Fire Department had done a tribute to the Pittsburgh Pirates. The Eagles Mere Inn featured a bald eagle in flight with Lindberg's plane in tandem. Women's Suffrage came from the Ladies Auxiliary. A fake raccoon with a fish stuck in his mouth represented the Chamber of Commerce. Zeke played his harmonica on the SS Sundae. A paper maché Palomino sporting a black baseball cap and a sash that read "The Forest Inn" stood in a fake canoe. The guests of the Crestmont had fashioned a huge golden trophy with two men standing on either side, arms linked through the trophy handles, swinging tennis rackets in their free hands. The flotilla ended at the Edgemere dock for judging.

The raccoon got first place, but the SS Sundae returned to the Crestmont with a big red ribbon while the town band played. Crowding around their float, the staff congratulated themselves as they served ice cream to the children. Gracie saw someone peek out from behind one of the huge fake cones on the float and realized it was Eleanor.

No one heard the golf balls hit the lake because there was too much noise. Then the band stopped.

"Crack!" The ominous sound was duller than a residual firecracker.

"It's Eleanor!" Gracie cried, watching a golf ball hit Eleanor on the side of the head. Eleanor's arms were wrapped around one of the huge cotton candy cones. Both fell backwards with a splash into the dark water.

Her mother dropped a tray of desserts and ran for the dock. "William!" He ripped off his jacket and dove in, not knowing where to search for his daughter. Men removed their shoes, ready to go in the water. All flashlights and lanterns turned toward the spot.

Someone close to Gracie plunged into the water, but by the time she looked, no one was there.

"Here, take her," Bessie said a few minutes later, hoisting Eleanor's body up onto the dock toward waiting hands.

৵৶

"Everything fell out of me." Margaret said the next day to the reporter.

"This idiot will be located and prosecuted." William's voice was sharp and shrill. "We have every policeman in Sullivan County searching for him. What kind of a fool hits golf balls toward a crowded waterfront after dark?"

"Yes, I saw it hit her. I'm sure it was a golf ball," Gracie told another reporter from the *Sullivan Review*. "No, I'm not the one who went in after her," she said, ashamed. "I can't swim. It was Bessie...I'm sorry...I don't know her last name. She's been on staff here for five years. No, I don't know where she is now."

෨෯

The late afternoon sun cast gold and silver gemstones on the water as William and Margaret Woods stood on the Crestmont dock, looking at the spot where Eleanor had gone under.

"I wonder how many other golf balls that lunatic drove into this lake. I blame myself. I should have seen him on the lawn. Surely it wasn't one of our guests," William said.

"We should go back."

"She wanted Gracie to sit with her. Try to breathe, Margaret."

"I never even saw her on the float."

William comforted her. "Dr. Webber said she'll be fine. Just a day in bed and she'll have a full recovery."

"Thank God for Bessie."

"Yes, thank God for Bessie."

Margaret pressed her face into her husband's shoulder and sobbed.

෨෯

William breathed in the sweet smell of newly mowed grass the next Saturday evening as he made his way from the garage up to the big house. Hank waved to his boss from behind the lawnmower on the top of the back lawn. "Do it while they are eating," William always said to his lawn boys, "so as not to interfere with the guests' time on the grounds." He was pleased to see Hank taking the initiative without a reminder.

The valet parking William had instituted the year before was a boon to their business. Dinner reservations doubled from people living in the surrounding area because parking was not a concern. Otto had waved his boss away when William went to check on the overflow of cars in the parking lot. "I've got it covered, boss," was the most comforting thing William had heard all week.

The police had searched since last Saturday and never found a suspect for the golf ball incident. They let the matter drop, since no one had been badly hurt.

After Eleanor's accident, the staff had really pulled together. Apparently they sensed that the Woods needed to funnel their energy into recovering from the shock. William wondered if some of them felt responsible. Eleanor, after all, was not supposed to have been on the float. Knowing his daughter, he assumed she had finagled a way to go aboard without anyone else knowing until they had joined the flotilla. At that point, the staffers had probably turned a blind eye. He blamed none of them and was grateful that Eleanor was back to her sweet, rambunctious self, seemingly unaffected by the bizarre incident.

There was a gracious outpouring of concern from the town and the guests. The Woods received cards and telephone calls aplenty. Eleanor was given so many gifts of candy that Margaret had begun hiding it so her daughter wouldn't get sick.

William stuck his nose in the dining room. The waitresses were really hopping to keep the food service moving. He basked in pride watching his wife. She expertly flowed from escorting incoming people to their tables to inquiring of those eating dessert about their dinners.

Margaret chatted with two older couples who were finishing apple crisp and coffee at a choice table near the fireplace. They had driven two hours to come to the Crestmont for an anniversary dinner. When she inquired about how they had enjoyed their meal, they responded with murmurs of satisfaction. The younger of the two women abruptly pushed her chair back, knocking over her cup and saucer. Coffee splattered all over the tablecloth. The other three diners jumped up, startled.

"Liar! Liar! Liar!"

She berated her companions one by one, flinging reproachful fingers in their faces. Shamefaced, they averted their eyes while their accuser informed Margaret that they had grumbled about the food from appetizer through dessert. Graciously offering to refund the cost of their dinners, Margaret calmly escorted them out of the dining room.

When she returned, Dorothy had already cleaned up the broken china and stained cloth and was wiping the table clean. Margaret pulled a newly starched tablecloth from the shelf next to the china cabinet and shook it out before she lay in on the table. It flew out of her hands and landed in the fire. Instinctively, she reached into the fireplace to pull out the burning cloth. Dropping it onto the hearth before she burned herself, she stamped on it until the flames were gone.

The remaining diners burst into applause shouting "Bravo, Mrs. Woods!" A blush crept over her face. She sank into a deep bow.

৩৵৵

"Is this what they call a date?" Eleanor sat with her ankles crossed in the blue lace dress her mother had worked so hard to get the tomato stains out of. Gracie and Peg sat on either side of her on the front porch swing of the Crestmont, waiting for Eric to pick them up in his family's car.

"It's only a date when there are two people, nincompoop," Peg said.

"Well, where is he?"

"Eleanor, Eric was nice enough to ask us to come along, so don't fuss about the time when he gets here."

"Well, we shouldn't be dilly-dallying. You know those summer people all march their kids down to the Sweet Shoppe right at six-thirty after supper. If we don't get there before them we're going to have to wait in line."

Gracie opened her purse, checked herself in the mirror and dabbed her nose with powder. "Well, I'm glad he asked you both to come along." Gracie tickled the tip of Eleanor's nose playfully with the velour powder puff. "It makes it a special birthday for me."

"So you turn twenty-four today, Gracie? Wow, that's more than twice my age." Eleanor said, proud of her arithmetic skills. "How old is Eric?"

"Well, he just graduated from college, so I guess he's probably twenty-two."

"Is that allowed?"

"What are you talking about?" Peg said, annoyed.

"For Gracie to...go on a date. Can a girl go around with a boy that's younger?"

"Yes, it's allowed, Eleanor." Gracie laughed. "But Eric and I are not 'going around.' We're just friends."

"But you went over to his house for dinner. And I know you like him."

"Yes, I do."

"Why?"

Gracie saw the sincerity on the girl's face and decided she been asked a very grown-up question. "Well, I guess it's because I feel like he sees all of me, not just the part I think he would like, and he likes me anyway."

Eleanor nodded her head knowingly. "That's a very good reason." His car wound up the driveway.

Peg rolled her eyes and said, "Hush. Here he is."

Several people had gotten there ahead of them, so Eric dropped Gracie and Peg off to save a spot in line at the ice cream shop.

"Peg, would you give me some swimming lessons?" Gracie asked as they stood waiting. "But don't expect me to be a very good student. I'm really afraid of the water. I was paralyzed when I saw Eleanor go in after she got hit with that golf ball. If Bessie hadn't gone in after her..."

"It's okay, Gracie. We'll take it slow. You'll do fine. I'll have you swimming races by next year's water carnival."

"Thanks. I did buy a bathing suit at least."

Meanwhile, Eleanor had wanted to stay in the car with Eric and felt it was her job to come up with something to talk about.

"Did you hear that my mama put out a fire in the dining room last night? All the guests clapped for her."

"You must be very proud of your mother."

"Yes, I am."

Eric turned into the driveway of the parsonage next to the church.

"Do you remember that lady, Mrs. Cunningham, who died in March? Gracie said she was like a grandmother to her. I miss her, too, but I know she will always stay in our hearts. I'll bet she's talking to my Grampa Warner right now in heaven."

"You have very mature thoughts for a girl your age, Eleanor."

"Really?" She chewed on her lip, studying the side window awkwardly so he couldn't see her glow. Then Eric came around to open the car door and the two of them walked the half block down to meet Peg and Gracie.

"I'm sorry, we're out of pistachio," the girl at the Sweet Shoppe said when Eleanor placed her order at the window.

"That's okay. I'm sick of ice cream anyway. I'll try one of those new Reese's peanut butter cups."

Pots of pink and purple petunias dotted the tiny patio behind the ice cream shop. Gracie saved seats at a round glass-topped table surrounded by four wrought iron chairs. Eleanor swooped up a straw hat with a yellow ribbon that had been left on the ground and placed it lovingly on Gracie's blonde head. "For the birthday girl."

Eric handed Gracie a double strawberry cone. "For the birthday girl." Peg lifted her chocolate cone toward Gracie as in a toast. Eleanor's eyes never left Eric's face while she ate her candy.

"My degree is in Civil Engineering," Eric explained when Peg asked him what his plans were now that he was done at Princeton, "but I am really interested in a new field where people work to improve the environment."

"Huh?" Eleanor asked, licking the last of the chocolate off the orange and brown paper.

"I'm sure you know how the people of Eagles Mere bought the lake and the land around it to protect it from people just coming in and throwing their garbage or whatever into it. What I'd like to do is something similar. I'll be helping cities and towns keep their water supplies pure. Find ways to get the water into the towns so people can use it."

"Like the water tower in back of the Crestmont supplies the town," Gracie noted.

"Precisely."

"If you get a job like that, can you stay in Eagles Mere?" Eleanor asked.

"Well, I'm sure I could live here, but I'll probably have to travel around a lot."

He checked Gracie's reaction, but she was distracted by a child crying when the top of her triple cone plopped on the flagstones. Shadow appeared and calmly licked up the vanilla ice cream. After cleaning its face, the cat jumped up into Eric's lap. Gracie smiled longingly at it.

"Oh." Eric laughed. "You wanted the cat on your lap. I thought you knew it was ours. Shadow is very independent and my mother says she likes it that way."

An entire year had gone by since Rosa Ponselle had relaxed in the Adirondack chair, complimenting Margaret's flowers. Margaret finally asked William to move the chair into their private garden so she could indulge herself a bit. This afternoon, after gathering flowers for the lobby arrangement, she sat enjoying the fragrance the breeze brought her way. Adelle was hostessing dinner and Margaret was free of responsibilities.

Had it really been a week since Eleanor's accident? She thanked God that her daughter was safe. Then she said a prayer for Bessie.

The young woman had packed up her belongings and left mysteriously the next day without telling anyone where she was going. The Woods deeply regretted missing the opportunity to thank her for her heroic act.

Taking off her shoes, Margaret dug her toes into the moist grass. The late afternoon sun cast a shadow just before the five on the sundial.

She reviewed what had happened at dinner last night. She was astounded the guests had applauded so enthusiastically for her when she pulled the tablecloth out of the fire. They were too kind to point out that it would have been better to simply let the silly thing burn up. She realized they loved her.

Why had she never noticed? She supposed she put so much effort into ensuring their happiness that she was never open to receiving any of the blessings they sent her way. She was thankful they had finally punctured her armor.

The familiar butterfly with iridescent blue markings on its wings hovered above her big toe, then alighted on the sundial. Margaret gazed at it for a long time. Her face melted into a comforting softness.

"I suppose I have found the 440 you encouraged me to find, Daddy. Now I have to cultivate it. For me, it is not about an afternoon nap, but rather learning to enjoy the people who love this place as much as we do."

ക്ക

"We've never done this before," Gracie said on Labor Day weekend.

"Done what?" PT asked, his long legs propped up as usual on the laundry porch railing, with his ankles crossed.

"Said goodbye at the end of the summer."

"You razzing me, woman?"

"Well, you deserve it."

"Suppose I do."

They sat side by side on the rockers they had repositioned so they could look straight up toward the big house, sipping root beers they had carried down from the kitchen after Gracie said tearful goodbyes to Isaiah, Olivia and Sam.

PT squinted up at the filigree that hung from the rafters. "Always liked that curlicue woodworking on this porch."

"Me too," Gracie said.

"Sure are good people." He flicked his finger toward the big brown inn on the hill. "Mr. Woods is a man I truly respect. He's trusted me with a lot of responsibility through the years. "Hate to leave him," he said, fiddling with his pocket watch, "but there's somebody from way back I might want to track down."

"Who?"

"A guy named Warren Sloan. He hired me to work in his bowling alley when I was a green kid." PT opened the watch and wound it slowly. "Gave me this as a sign of good faith. Took me under his wing and let me be my own man."

Gracie leaned forward, hoping to find out more.

"I always wondered if he replaced those pin boys."

"What pin boys?"

"He was going to invent a machine to reset the pins in a bowling alley. I wonder if he ever did. He kept talking about kissing the pin boys goodbye," he chuckled.

"You should go find out."

"Just might. It's complicated, though. Some other guy had me in a vise. A piano teacher in Philly was trying to turn me into a concert pianist. I was a trapped kid, so I skipped town without telling Sloan. Never said thank you for all he did for me. That was a long time ago. Who knows what he thinks of me now."

"You could go find him. It would be good for you."

"Not used to doing what's good for me." He grinned at her. "Except coming here."

"PT, you can always come back here. The Woods love you."

"Can't come back if I'm working full time. I mean to stick with Sloan if I find him and he lets me work for him again. Do something solid. I'm too old for speakeasies and part time jobs. What about you?"

"The Woods said I could stay in the Evergreen until I get a job. I'd like to be a home companion, like I was for Mrs. Cunningham. I placed an advertisement in the newspaper and I have the money she left me as a cushion. Besides, Eagles Mere is my home. I don't want to leave."

"No singing on the road, huh?" He set his root beer down on the porch floor. "I know why. You want to stay and see what happens with Eric Sturdy. I know you threw me over for him."

"You threw yourself over by locking yourself up in there," she playfully poked his caved chest with her index finger, "with your Do Not Disturb sign." She lowered her voice. "Maybe after you find Warren Sloan, you'll find a woman to settle down with."

"Oh, I found the woman." He studied the blue spruce in front of the porch. "Just got stupid and pushed her away."

"I hope someday you let yourself out of prison."

He got up, turned around and leaned on the railing to face her. "So what about the Crestmont?"

"I'll miss it, but I'm sure it will survive without us. There's another waitress out there dying to work here. Besides, I'll be in the area. I'll see the Woods all year and come back to visit my friends here in the summer. They're all my family."

"Will you come to my concert?"

"Oh, good. Mr. Woods finally asked you."

"Yup. Put me on next year's concert series. Apologized for taking so long." PT gave her a funny look. "Wondering if someone might have reminded him. Mr. Woods said I could come up on the train for a weekend even if I'm not on staff. Wants me to play jazz, even though I'm sure he doesn't consider it acceptable music."

"I'll be there."

"Good. See you then, Gracie."

"I hope you find Warren Sloan."

He nodded, climbed over the rail and headed up the driveway.

Epilogue
Crestmont Hill
1977

"I HAVEN'T BEEN HERE SINCE MRS. WOODS'S FUNERAL IN 1941. ONCE she was gone, it just wasn't the same." Gracie Sturdy blinked back tears. "She was always so kind to me. Oh, Christiana, you should have seen me. I was naive and completely unsure of myself. Mrs. Woods helped build my self confidence. We bonded in some way right from the start." Gracie stopped her tan and white Buick at the little booth set up just before the pillars that marked the entrance to the hill.

She rolled down the window and poked her head out. "We're here for the auction."

"That'll be $5.00, please," said the woman in the booth.

"Does the money go to the Crestmont Inn?" Gracie asked.

"I don't know. Mr. Simpson just said to charge each car $5.00. Here, take this ticket. You can present it up there to get free hotdogs and soda." The woman waved them on. "Go ahead. You can drive on up."

"Who is Mr. Simpson, Grandma?" Gracie's granddaughter,

Cristiana, a sophomore at Penn State, sat in the passenger seat, cradling the old yellow jewelry box in her hands.

"He bought the place from the Dickerson's. I read in *The Crestmont News* that Mr. Dickerson is sick and can't run the inn anymore, so they sold it. Rumor has it the new owners are going to demolish the big house and put up condos. Peg Woods Dickerson is supposed to be here today. That's why I wanted to come. I lived with the Woods family over one winter and was close to Peg and her sister, Eleanor. Let's see, Peg would be in her late sixties now. I can't believe it. She was fifteen when I came in 1925 as a scared little housemaid."

"What about the other sister?"

"Eleanor has written to me all these years. She lives in Allentown, close to where I grew up. She's a grandmother herself now, but her arthritis is so bad she couldn't come today."

"It's beautiful here." Cristiana admired the white pine and hemlock when they rounded the driveway up the hill.

"Right there," Gracie noted, pointing left out her window to a small cedar shake cottage with blue shutters, "is the Woodshed, where I stayed with the Woods after my first summer here. I'm so happy it's still here."

The big house, however, carried so many memories; she wanted to stall before she saw it. Turning right at the water tower, she drove down to the two clay tennis courts. She nudged her granddaughter. "Back then people didn't wear little tennis shorts like they do today. Even so, I had a gander at your grandfather playing in trousers and a long sleeve shirt on that court and knew he was my man." She giggled. "I never told him until we had been married for two years."

She turned the car around and headed up toward the big house. At the top of the hill, she stopped the car.

"Is that it, Grandma?" asked Christiana, gazing at the huge brown structure.

"That's it, Christiana. The Crestmont Inn. I can't believe it. Those famous yellow awnings are gone, the porch has collapsed..." Her voice trailed off.

"It looks like it's ready to fall over, Grandma. What are those men with the axes doing?"

"I don't know, but I'm sure going to find out." Gracie got out of the car, stopped an important-looking man, and demanded, "Who are those men?"

"Those are the Mennonites. They bought the wood." He walked on, stuffing a hotdog in his mouth.

Two white open-sided tents, filled with lamps, mirrors, knickknacks and books were set up on the back lawn. Furniture from the big house was lined up in rows on the grass.

"Good," said Gracie, "they haven't started the auction yet. I'll show you the Evergreen Lodge, where I lived for two summers." She parked the car and led her granddaughter past the garage down to the laundry porch. The white filigree and railing welcomed her back. "I spent many a late afternoon after work cooling off on this porch."

A woman of about sixty sat stoically on the porch swing. Gracie recognized her immediately. Touching her granddaughter's arm, she said, "Give me a moment, Christiana. Wait over on that porch for me," she said, pointing to the Evergreen Lodge.

"Peg? It's me, Gracie, the one who promised not to tell your mother about Room 440, your secret hiding place."

"Gracie. Oh, my goodness, I don't believe it!" Peg Dickerson jumped up and gave her a big hug. "How many years has it been? You've been a stranger for too long. Where do you live now?" Curling her arm through Gracie's, she led her along the little path to the Evergreen Lodge past the fish pond she and Zeke had built in 1926.

"Eric and I moved to Harrisburg in 1958, soon after the grandchildren started coming. We didn't want to miss seeing them grow up. Peg, I'd like you to meet my granddaughter, Christiana. Christiana, this is Mrs. Dickerson."

"Nice to meet you. My grandmother has told me a lot of stories about you when you were young."

"Did she tell you I taught her to swim?" Peg Dickerson laughed and nodded toward the dorm. "Go on in and check it out. Your grandmother lived in the fourth room on the left for two summers."

"Oh, Gracie, how time has flown," she continued after Christiana ducked into the Evergreen Lodge. "Why haven't you come back for a visit?"

"I couldn't, not after your mother died. I know you and your husband breathed life into the Crestmont, but I couldn't bear to come back after she was gone."

Peg sat down heavily. "Look at what we've come to, Gracie. There's nothing classier here than a hot dog stand. Simpson and his auction have made a mockery of what my parents and grandfather spent their lives building. They're going to level the big house within the week."

The Mennonites worked steadily, tossing away crumbling cedar shakes and tearing down the hotel board by board, loading the wood into their trucks.

"They're taking it away?"

Peg nodded sadly. "They paid for it. I guess they can do what they want with it. They'll probably build barns or something."

"So the big house will live on in some twisted sense."

Peg shrugged. "They were kind enough to give me the family portraits."

Gracie put her arm around Peg's shoulders. "This is so sad."

"They're going to convert your old dormitory into a new Crestmont Inn. And this," she said, pointing to the laundry house, "will be the new reception area and dining room."

"Convert the Evergreen Lodge? But those rooms were so small. Oh, and so hot. I was always so thankful for those transoms to give us a little breeze."

"The plan is to rip out the wall between two rooms and convert them into one big suite. King size beds, air conditioners and Jacuzzis."

"What do you have there?" Peg asked, pointing to the yellow jewelry box.

"I bought this silly jewelry box on my way to the Crestmont that first summer and have kept it all this time for sentimental reasons. *The Crestmont News* said they might be interested in some antiques to decorate the new rooms."

"Yes, go to the second tent, just up from where the bowling alley used to be. Take it up there and tell the Simpson's your history here. I'm sure they'll pay you for it."

"I noticed the bowling alley was gone when I drove up. My good friend, PT, used to run that."

"The guests lost interest in bowling and we needed more guest cottages, so my husband and I had it cut in half, placed side by side, so to speak, to create what we call North South Cottage. It's up there near the Woodshed."

A message blared out over the loudspeaker.

"Oh dear," said Peg. "They're going to start the bidding. I'm not sure why I came today, except it didn't seem right not see this through to the very end."

"Will you be here for awhile, Peg? There is something I need to do, but I'd like to see you before I go."

"Yes, I am going to sit here and watch the sun go down over those trees one more time." She took Gracie's hand. "I can't tell you how much it means to me to see you again."

Gracie pulled Christiana away from exploring the second floor of the old dorm and steered her up to the furniture on the back lawn. They wound in and out of the rows of tables, bedsteads and chairs until she found what she was looking for. Settling into the folding chairs, they awaited the bidding. The auctioneer banged his gavel. The small pieces went first. Then Old Tim, the grandfather clock that had graced the lobby for seventy-eight years, went after only two bids.

The auctioneer flashed his gavel over to a roll top desk. Gracie patted her granddaughter's hand.

"Watch this." She calmly topped each bid on the desk.

"$700, do I hear 750?" The auctioneer's finger was in the air ready to point to the highest bidder.

"Grandma," Christiana whispered in her ear, "that's so much money!"

Gracie raised her hand to accept the bid. "It's okay," she said
to her granddaughter. "I have plenty. I was always a good saver."

Silence followed his plea for more. "Sold to the lady in the
rear for $750."

"I'll take this old plaque off if you want," Mr. Simpson asked
later when Gracie went to claim her ticket. "You can hardly read
the engraving."

"Don't you dare."

"Okay, lady, I didn't mean any disrespect. I must not have the
history here that you do. Here's your ticket. You can pick up the
desk when you leave. If you can't transport it today, you'll have to
make other arrangements. If it's not gone by Friday, we burn it
with the rest."

"Why did you want the desk, Grandma?" Christiana asked.

"You remember me telling you about Mrs. Woods, Peg
Dickerson's mother?" Christiana nodded.

"Well, this desk was in the library of the big house when I
worked here. Mrs. Woods cherished it because it belonged to her
father, the one who built the Crestmont. I spent a lot of time
sitting at it after my shifts, reading and trying to improve my
vocabulary. Quite often, I'd run into Mrs. Woods hiding out there
in the evening, trying to recoup from her day. We had some good
talks. She seemed to understand me, to know where I was weak,
and she tried to help me figure myself out."

"How?"

"Oh, she told me about good books to read, taught me to
cook, to trust my own mind."

Christiana squeezed her grandmother's hand. "So you're going
to give the desk to her daughter."

"That's why we came, Christiana. It's a way of giving back.
And I've changed my mind about the jewelry box. Would you
like to keep it?"

Christiana nodded enthusiastically.

"Take it back to the car and I'll meet you there in a few
minutes."

Gracie strolled back to the laundry porch, enjoying the mountain air one last time. She pressed the ticket into Peg's hand.

"What's this?" Peg asked.

"Your grandfather's desk. I want you to have it. It needs to stay in the family, don't you think? He was the one who started it."

"William Warner, Creator of the Crestmont dream," Peg smiled.

"He helped us all."

Something caught Peg's eye. "Gracie, look."

An eagle soared above the big house and graciously dipped one wing.

THE END

Afterword

Current day Crestmont Inn owners Fred and Elna Mulford uniquely defined their mission as innkeepers on their wedding day. The Crestmont Inn is normally closed on Christmas day, but in 2004, its rooms were packed. Twenty relatives of Bill Pass, a resident in the condos where the original Crestmont Inn stood, had come to be with him in his final days. The family expected Rev. Pass to end his suffering within a day or so, but he surprised them all by living until January 2nd. Because the relatives stayed so much longer than expected, the Pass and Mulford families had time to develop an unusually strong bond. Little did the Mulfords know that their wedding day would take an unexpected turn because of this man.

Bill Pass, a minister and resident of Eagles Mere, Pennsylvania, had battled his cancer a long time. His family poured into town from all over the country, needing a refuge while they cried, reminisced and laughed with him until the end. Fred and Elna opened the doors of the Crestmont, sensitively caring for the Pass family—providing beds they could sink into for comfort at night and delicious meals to sustain them. Days before his death, Bill, who shared a love of waterfowl with Fred, asked his family to prop him up and hand him his favorite photograph of a redhead duck. Laboriously, he inscribed the back:

Dear Fred and Elna,

You have become very special to the Pass family recently. You've opened your house and rooms to my clan guys—a brave thing to do. Mostly, you've opened your heart of love. There is very little in Eagles Mere of this kind of kindness, especially to take in my gang so we could all be here for this particular occasion. The Lord bless your Christian ministry, full of consideration and thoughtfulness! You made our day, our night and the happiness of our friends. The Lord bless you and your business—You are a wonderful asset to Eagles Mere,

Bill

P.S. I'll train your dog any time. 12/26/2004

Notes of thank you from many of his family members were added underneath.

On January 2nd, Fred and Elna stood before a minister in front of the fireplace in their beloved Crestmont pub. It was a simple ceremony, attended only by close family and friends.

Afterwards, arm in arm, they strode happily out into the Fouquet dining room, expecting to break open champagne and celebrate their marriage. The winter chill ushered in the Pass family when they poured through the front door of the Crestmont, oblivious to the "Closed" sign on the door. Having no idea that the Mulford's had just been married, the relatives crowded around them, needing and giving hugs, because Bill had just died. Fred and Elna said nothing about their wedding, but instead, shared moments comforting them. To this day, they believe the family didn't know they had been married that afternoon.

Although this was an unusual and poignant occurrence, the tone was set for the graciousness with which the Mulfords have treated their guests ever since. It is a reflection of the legacy of William Warner, who built The Crestmont Inn in 1899, as well as Margaret and William Woods and those who followed.

Endnotes:

Author's Note:

◆See Distinguished Inns of North America on www.selectregistry.com and the Crestmont Inn's own website, www.crestmont-inn.com .

◆James, Barbara and Bush. *Mere Reflections*. Montoursville, PA: Paulhamus Litho, Inc., 1988, preface. Used by permission.

Quotes Page:

◆*Non fatuum huc persecutes ignem.*

◆*The Holy Bible*, The Living Bible Translation. Wheaton, IL: Tyndale House Publishers, Inc., 2002.

Prologue:

◆Yeats, William Butler. "The Lake Isle of Innisfree." Untermeyer, Louis. *Modern British Poetry*. New York: Harcourt, Brace and Company, 1922, p. 257.

◆The author chose to deviate from the actual Native American legend as stated in *Eagles Mere and the Sullivan Highlands*. J. Horace and Robert B. McFarland, J. Horace McFarland Company, Harrisburg, PA, 1944, p. 1, which reads: "... the site of the lake was then a deep valley with many springs on its floor. The east side of the valley consisted of ledges of rock, and under the present Lover's Rock was a vast cavern. By enticing a beautiful Indian maiden into this cavern, an Indian chief, Stormy Torrent, angered the Great Spirit, who caused a great storm to come, with torrents of rain which blocked the former outlet of the stream flowing from the springs and thus filled the valley to the present lake level."

The Haudenosaunee Confederacy, or People of the Long House, is made up of the Mohawks, Oneidas, Ononodagas, Cayugas and

Senecas. These tribes originally lived along the Genesee and Mohawk Rivers and in the Finger Lakes region near Lake Ontario. Founded by the *Peacemaker* with the help of Hiawatha, it is one of the longest enduring democracies in the world. The French term assigned the derogatory term "Iroquois" to the Haudenosaunee, probably as an insult.

The Crestmont Inn
1910 – 1911:

♦Isaiah 41:13, King James Bible.

Bethlehem, Pennsylvania
1925:

♦Cather, Willa. *Song of the Lark*, 1915. New York: Houghton Mifflin Company, forwarded copyright, 1988.

♦The Crestmont Inn consistently hired only African-American male chefs because they were considered to be the most qualified.

♦This jewelry box sits on the dresser in the French Country Cottage room of today's Crestmont Inn.

En route to Eagles Mere
1925:

♦Dreiser, Theodore. *Sister Carrie*. New York: Barnes and Noble Classics, 1900.

The Crestmont Inn
Summer 1925
IV

♦Paperbag poems "I've fallen in love, again," "Ticklish Rock," "I long for the gentle caress of your hand," written by Ernest L. Whitehouse, husband of the author.

V

◆A revised version of "Homemade Ice Cream" from *Mere Tales* by Barbara and Bush James, Paulhamus Litho, 2005. Used by permission.

VI

◆Gruelle, Johnny. *Raggedy Ann Stories.* NY, NY: 1918.

VII

◆Wharton, Edith. *Age of Innocence*, 1920 D. Appleton and Company. New York: Collier Books, 1968.

Woodshed on Crestmont Hill
September 1925
II

◆The Delaware River Bridge, linking Camden and Philadelphia is now known as the Ben Franklin Bridge. It was constructed jointly by the Commonwealth of Pennsylvania, state of New Jersey and the city of Philadelphia between 1919-1926. For purposes of the flow of the novel, I have moved the date of its completion from 1926 to 1925. The opening of the bridge was delayed because neither side could agree on how to cover construction costs. New Jersey wanted to use a toll system, while Pennsylvania wanted the use of the bridge to be free, using tax money to cover costs. Eventually, the toll system prevailed. www.aviewoncities.com/philadelphia/benjaminfranklinbridge.htm

Camden, New Jersey
1914

◆Warren W. Sloan, maternal grandfather of the author, invented a version of the automatic pinsetter, along with his partner, Joseph Clark, in Clark's basement in Camden, New Jersey. They later sold the patent to AMF. An article, "Bowlers Soon May Kiss the Pin Boys Goodbye" by Mike Devitt, sportswriter for the *Courier Post* of Camden, NJ, dated Wednesday, April 9, 1941 states that Devitt attended the first demonstration of the automatic pinsetter, "the brainchild of Warren Sloan." The machine, which was distributed by the Automatic Pinsetting Machine Company of New Jersey, was constructed to conform to American Bowling Congress regulations. The article states, "It sets the pins accurately and can set as many as nine games per hour, per alley. It returns the ball to the bowler; it clears the alley of dead wood after the first ball in each frame and returns the remainder of the pins to exactly where they stood after the first ball had been delivered."

Sloan was an officer of the New Jersey Bowling Association for many years and served as representative of the American Bowling Congress. His untiring devotion to the sport was evidenced not only by his excellence as a bowler (averaging close to 200 for numerous years), but also by his dedication to instructing and forming leagues for area young people. Sloan, nominated by his son-in-law, N. John Weiss, (father of the author) is a member of the South Jersey Bowling Association's Hall of Fame. Sloan also invented the electric scissors in 1939.

Woodshed on Crestmont Hill
February 5, 1926

♦A fascinating detail about Eagles Mere history found in *Looking Back at Eagles Mere*, a history by Joe Mosbrook, published by the Eagles Mere Museum, 2008, p. 145.

♦Mosbrook, p. 144.

♦Captain Chase was a civil engineer in Eagles Mere in the early 20th century.

The Crestmont Inn
Summer 1926
II

♦Collins, Wilkie. *The Woman In White*, 1860.

◆*La Forza del Destino,* opera composed by Giuseppe Verdi, 1861.

◆Rosa Ponselle reigned as queen of the dramatic sopranos at the Metropolitan Opera in New York City for nineteen years. In 1927, at the age of forty, she retired from singing on the opera stage at the height of her career. She never lost her love for singing, but the ever-present stage fright, worry over the condition of her voice, coupled with the pressures and rigors of performing wore her down. After her retirement she married, moved to Baltimore and actively promoted the Baltimore Opera. She concertized and recorded for several years. Maria Callas called her "the greatest singer of us all." Ever supportive of young singers, Ponselle spent forty-four years nurturing aspiring opera singers from her beloved home, Villa Pace, in Maryland. Rosa Ponselle died in 1981. To my knowledge, she never actually visited The Crestmont Inn, although she sang concerts in cities and small towns all over the United States during this time period.

◆Fitzgerald, F. Scott. *The Great Gatsby.* New York: Scribner, 1925.

◆"I'll Build a Stairway to Paradise," George Gershwin/B.G. DeSylva and Arthur Francis, (pseudonym for the young Ira Gershwin) composed in 1922.

◆Tennis tournaments actually began at the Crestmont in 1907.

The Crestmont Inn
Summer 1926
II

◆*Il Trovatore,* opera composed by Giuseppe Verdi, 1857.

Eagles Mere, Pennsylvania
1926

◆Two original tennis courts were built by the Crestmont Inn. Five lower courts were added in 1926. The August tournaments coincided with those in Forest Hills, located in Queens, New York City, which ultimately moved to Flushing Meadows to become the U.S. Open. The Eagles Mere Tennis Tournaments, designed to attract the better players in the country who did not qualify for Forest Hills, ran for 63 years, from 1907 to 1970. Deer charging up and down the courts provided further challenges for maintenance.

◆The Holy Bible. Deuteronomy 30:19.

Eagles Mere, Pennsylvania
1927

◆Tobogganing has been the main winter sport in Eagles Mere for over one hundred years. The toboggan run is said to be the fastest in the nation, complete with warm up shack and refreshment stand. In 1904, Captain E.S. Chase, working with other residents, fit large ice blocks together to create a solid ice slide down steep Lake Street. He built a wooden toboggan with metals runners. The Eagles Mere Ice Toboggan Slide is an attraction for winter sports enthusiasts to this day. Mosbrook, p. 123-128.

The Crestmont Inn
Summer 1927
I

◆A salad bowl, thirty inches in diameter, hewn from one solid hemlock tree, belonged to the Crestmont in its early days. It is now on display at The Eagles Mere Museum, Eagles Mere, PA.

◆A revised version of "Blind Man Working" from *Mere Tales* by Barbara and Bush James, Paulhamus Litho, 2005. Used by permission.

II

◆The Operadio was a brand of radio invented in 1925. Public broadcasting had begun in 1921.

◆"How Can I Keep from Singing?" Words and music by Robert Lowry 1826-1899.
   1. My life flows on in endless song,
      above earth's lamentation.

I hear the clear, though faroff hymn
that hails a new creation.

Refrain:

No storm can shake my inmost calm
while to that Rock I'm clinging.
Since Christ is Lord of heaven and earth,
how can I keep from singing?

2. Through all the tumult and the strife,
   I hear that music ringing.
   It finds an echo in my soul.
   How can I keep from singing?
   (Refrain)
3. What though my joys and comforts die?
   I know my Savior liveth.
   What though the darkness gather round?
   Songs in the night he giveth.
   (Refrain)
4. The peace of Christ makes fresh my heart,
   a fountain ever springing!
   All things are mine since I am his!
   How can I keep from singing?
   (Refrain)

III

◆Now known as the US Open in Flushing Meadows.

◆*Courier Post Newspaper*, Camden, New Jersey, April 9, 1941.

Epilogue
Crestmont Hill
1977

◆Peg Woods Dickerson and her husband, Tingle, administered The
Crestmont Inn from 1947 (with William Woods as chairman and Tingle

Dickerson as president) until it closed in 1970. Peg was an avid golfer and frequently competed as a finalist in the July Women's Singles' Tennis Tournaments. The hotel contents were auctioned off over a four-day period in 1977, with Peg in attendance. Her husband, Tingle Dickerson, passed away in 1980 after a long illness. Peg Woods Dickerson died in 1983.

Sources

Books

Cather, Willa. *A Lost Lady*. New York: Alfred A. Knoff, 1923.

Cather, Willa. *Song of the Lark*. 1915. New York: Houghton Mifflin Company, forwarded copyright, 1988.

Dreiser, Theodore. *Sister Carrie*. New York: Barnes and Noble Classics, 1900.

Fitzgerald, F. Scott. *The Great Gatsby*. New York: Scribner, 1925.

Gruelle, Johnny. *Raggedy Ann Stories*. New York: The Bobbs-Merrill Co. Inc., 1918.

James, Bush and Barbara. *Mere Reflections: A Unique Journey Through Historic Eagles Mere*. Montoursville, PA: Paulhamus Litho, Inc.,1988. Third Printing.

James, Bush and Barbara. *Mere Tales: A Collection of Entertaining Stories About Eagles Mere*. Montoursville, PA: Paulhamus Litho, Inc., 2005.

James, Bush and Barbara. *The Crestmont Inn, A History*. (Out of print)

Kyvig, David E. *Daily Life in the United States 1920-1940 (How Americans Lived Through the "Roaring Twenties" and the Great Depression)*. Chicago, IL: Ivan R. Dee, 2004.

McFarland, L.H.D. and Robert B. McFarland. *Eagles Mere and the Sullivan Highlands*. Harrisburg, PA: J. Horace McFarland Company, 1944.

Meade, Marion. *Bobbed Hair and Bathtub Gin: Writers Running Wild in the Twenties*. New York: Doubleday & Co., 2004.

Mosbrook, Joseph. *Looking Back at Eagles Mere, A History*. Eagles Mere, PA: Eagles Mere Museum, 2008.

Ponselle, Rosa and James A. Drake. *Ponselle, A Singer's Life*. New York: Doubleday & Co., 1982.

The Holy Bible, King James Edition.

The Holy Bible, New Living Translation. Wheaton, IL: Tyndale House Publishers, Inc., 2002.

Remoff, Heather Trexler. *February Light*. New York: St. Martin's Press, 1997.

Sears, Roebuck Catalogue, 1923 Edition. Edited by Joseph J. Shroeder, Jr. Northfield, IL: DBI Books, 1973.

Sears, Roebuck Catalogue, 1927 Edition. Edited by Alan Mirke. Bounty Books, A Division of Crown Publishers, Inc., 1970.

Wharton, Edith. *Age of Innocence*. 1920. D. Appleton and Company. New York: Collier Books, 1968.

Yeats, William Butler. "The Lake Isle of Innisfree." Untermeyer, Louis. *Modern British Poetry*. New York: Harcourt, Brace and Company, 1920.

Websites

The Crestmont Inn: www.crestmont-inn.com.

Eagles Mere Online: www.eaglesmere.org.

The Life and Legacy of Rosa Ponselle: www.RosaPonselle.com.

1920s: Prohibition-era foods and speakeasy dining. Edited by Lynn Oliver. www.foodtimeline.org.

Select Registry: Distinguished Inns of North America: www.selectregistry.com.

The White Deer Named Virginia Dare. www.usscouts.org/stories/s_deer.asp.

www.foresthillstennis.com.

www.aviewoncities.com/philadelphia/benjaminfranklinbridge.htm.

www.haudenosauneeconfederacy.ca.

www.moravian.org.

Other Resources

Courier Post Newspaper, Camden, NJ, April 9, 1941.

Eagles Mere Museum, Eagles Mere, PA 17731.

Eagles Mere – A Short Guide to a Special Place. Eagles Mere, PA: Mere Trifles.

Hammarskjöld, Dag. *Markings.* Translated by Leif Sjöberg and W.H. Auden. London: Faber and Faber, 1964. New York: Knopf, 1964. Originally published in Swedish as Vägmärken: Stockholm, Bonniers, 1963.

Lowry, Robert. "How Can I Keep from Singing." 1860.

Rosa Ponselle: In Opera and Song, Prima Voce, Nimbus Records. CD set. 1996.

Whitehouse, Ernest L. *I long for the gentle caress of your hand,* 1995.
Whitehouse, Ernest L. *I've fallen in love, again,* 2002.
Whitehouse, Ernest L. *Ticklish Rock,* 2007.

Breinigsville, PA USA
13 June 2010
239782BV00001B/3/P